BLAME IT ON THE CHAMPAGNE

Blame it on the Alcohol: Book One

FIONA COLE

To everyone who helped me through this year.

Especially the wonderful women at the author retreat. You reminded me of everything I'd forgotten.

And to my husband. I couldn't do this without you.

Playlist

Kings and Queens - Ava Max
My Oh My (Remix) Camila Cabello (feat DaBaby & Gunna)
Light Me Up - Ingrid Michaelson
Kiss Me - Ed Sheeran
Everyone's Waiting - Missy Higgins
Secret - Missy Higgins
Over You - Ingrid Michaelson (feat. A Great Big World)
Glitter In the Air - P!nk

1

ONE

Vera

———

"Hey, Mom," I whispered to the picture on the wall.

Every time I came home, her memories wrapped around me like the warm hugs she gave me every chance she got.

"Can I take your purse?" Irene, my father's maid, asked.

"Of course, thank you."

I passed off the small bag but held on to the leather folder I'd brought with me, looking around the black and white tiled foyer that had been my only home outside of college. Despite my mother having passed away ten years ago, the bright sunset of peonies she always loved decorated the round table in the foyer.

"They always were your mother's favorite," my father's deep voice greeted me from the stairs.

"Papa." I watched the man who acted as my own personal playground descend the stairs. As always, he wore a dark suit, but since it was Saturday, no tie. *A man has to relax a little.*

"She always claimed this room needed a burst of color to liven it up a bit."

"Even though she picked out the color scheme in the first place," I said, laughing.

He laughed with me, closing the distance to pull me into a hug. "It's good to have you home, Verana. I wished you'd stay."

I bit back my initial retort and forced a smile. "I like being on my own."

"So independent, just like your mother."

At that, a real smile stretched my lips. "Thank you."

"Although, I'm not sure what she would say about your attire," he grumbled.

And just like that, the smile faded. "There's nothing wrong with what I'm wearing."

He scrunched his nose in distaste, taking in my cream cardigan, striped blouse, and pearls—and cut off jean shorts.

"College away has made you forget your appearances. Everyone is always watching, Verana."

It'd been nice to be away in Pennsylvania. To just be me and not worried about being on my best behavior in New York.

"Businesses are always waiting for the Marianos to slip up, and a family's reputation is just as important as the company's in the shipping industry. We must lead by example."

"Yes, sir," I responded dutifully. They were the same words that had been drilled into my head since I was little. As one of the top shipping companies from an overly traditional Italian family, I was always reminded of my place—of my role in this world.

"Now, come. Let's eat. I had Antonio make your favorite."

"Mama's stuffed meatballs?" I asked like a little kid.

His smile was the only confirmation I needed, and I almost ran to the dining room. We sat at our long wooden table, and Irene poured his glass of wine before looking to him for approval to fill mine.

Sometimes the traditions and etiquette hung around my neck like a noose, but it had been my life for so long, I'd grown used to it.

"I missed you at graduation," I said after he'd taken his first sip.

He winced, focusing his attention on the food being brought out rather than me. "I explained that. Work has been hectic, and I had an opportunity for a meeting I couldn't pass up."

Not having him there had been hard but expected.

He allowed me to go to college as a way to check a box—to keep me busy and brag to his colleagues about his daughter. Not because he ever intended on me working at Mariano Shipping. As his daughter, my role would be a figurehead—a socialite who sat on charity boards and planned events. My role as a woman would be to marry a man who would benefit our company— one chosen by my parents.

"Is everything okay?" I asked.

I loved our company. I loved the shipping industry. Add in that it was one of my last ties to my mother, and it was no wonder I went to school for business marketing.

"Nothing you need to worry about, Verana." The response never changed, and I never pushed the boundaries—until now.

With a deep breath, I opened the black file, extracting a thick, cream paper. "Actually, I wanted to talk to you about that."

I slid the paper across the slick wood and held his questioning stare, my chin high. He looked down, and his curiosity shifted to a scowl.

"What is this?"

"My resume. I wanted to give it to you personally, although I submitted one to HR also."

"You turned in a resume to Dane?" he asked.

"Yes." His scowl weighed down my confidence, but I pulled my shoulders back and pushed on. "As you can see, I graduated with Magna Cum Laude. I partook in multiple business societies, even starting a new one that has been very succ—"

"Verana," he interrupted, waving his hand like he would shoo a fly. "Why are you doing this?"

"Because I want to work at our company. I'm smart—an asset."

"You're an asset because you will marry a man who will carry this company into the future."

"Someday, you will have a husband to woo—someone to take care of. It's important to have proper table manners to impress your husband."

"But, Mama, shouldn't he woo me before we're married?"

She softly laughed. No woman would ever dare to open her mouth and let out a loud laugh. "Maybe. But you must prepare yourself that you won't have time for romance. If a marriage must happen, then it will, and it is your job to be a good wife and represent this family."

"What if I don't like him?"

"I didn't care for your father either. But we learned to love each other. Aren't we happy?"

I thought about the way they danced in the kitchen, and Papa always shared his food with her.

"Yeah. I guess."

"You will be happy too. Even if the way you get there isn't how you planned it."

I wondered if Mama was alive if she'd have shown up to my graduation. I wondered if she'd have stroked my father's tie and told him to give me a chance. She'd always reminded me of what my future held, but she also pushed me to achieve more.

"I can still do that, but maybe I can do more too," I argued gently. "I have time, and I can help with the business until the time comes for me to marry."

My father dug his hands into his eyes, a clear sign his stress was increasing as his patience decreased. Not that he ever lost his temper with Mama and me, but I knew it happened, and after Mama passed, he rubbed at his eyes more than he didn't.

"Verana," he half sighed-half warned. "I've hired a new CFO."

The seemingly random announcement had alarms whispering in the back of my head. But my father rarely spoke business, so I grasped on, absorbing every word. "Already? Roman passed away less than a month ago. What about the board?"

"The board approved."

"Who?"

"Camden Conti."

"Mr. Conti's son?"

"Yes, you've met him before. You were young though."

Mr. Conti had been my father's closest friend for years. I vaguely remembered his son with white-blonde hair and hunter green eyes. I remembered him not smiling much, and when he did, it never met his eyes, but he seemed polite. We all did in this world.

"Where did he work before? Does he have much experience?" I bombarded him with questions, trying to squeeze my way through the crack he opened.

"Of course, he does," he scoffed.

"Sorry, I'd just never heard your interest in him before. Where did he work before here?"

He sighed, a hint to his patience slipping even more. "Somewhere abroad. He left, and we took the opportunity to snatch him up."

"Why did he leave?"

"Not the right fit for them. But he's right for Mariano Shipping." His eyes narrowed for a moment before lowering to the wine he swirled in his glass. "He will be a good fit for you."

The alarms grew louder, and the opening he'd given to talk about the company grew—only it didn't reveal an in-depth conversation where I proved my value as an employee. No, something else waited for me.

"Me?"

"Yes, we went golfing last month and discussed everything."

"Everything being…"

"Your marriage together," he said, but it lacked his usual confidence.

The dark wood paneling closed in on me. "My what?"

"You've known you'd marry whoever suited this family since you were little. *That* is the job you have. Attending college was never meant to change that."

I knew that. I just thought I had more time. More life to experience before it was given away to someone I didn't want to have it.

"Papa…"

"It's done." His hand slashed through the air, and I jerked back. My father rode the line of patience with me, but he never crossed it, and the sharp movement shocked me. When he watched me swallow and pull back, he softened, regret pulling his shoulders down. He looked away, the lines around his pinched mouth hinting at more frowns than smiles. Before Mama passed, it had been all smiles. Now he shook his head, the silver in his dark hair standing out more than ever before under the lights.

I'd obviously visited home over my four years away, but I'd never taken note of how much he'd aged. When did the man who hung my moon and stars get so tired? When did the man who snuck me an extra cookie lose control of his emotions?

He swiped his hand down his face as if trying to wipe away the short-tempered man who snapped, but all that was left was exhaustion. "We're training him now, and once he settles in, we'll focus more on your wedding."

"He's almost forty," I said softly. I held tight to the emotions threatening to snap free, too nervous when he obviously sat so close to the edge.

"I was older than your mother," he said without any of the concern rioting through me.

"By five years." Panic slipped past my resolve to remain calm, and my voice rose. Camden was almost twice my age, and my father didn't seem to care at all. "This is completely different. You and Mama had—"

"An arranged marriage just like you will. She did what was best for her family, and she'd be ashamed to see you shirking your duties now." His words hit me like a slap to the face. "Now, stop arguing, Verana. It's pointless."

7

The finality in the sharp tone I'd never heard used with me urged me to plead harder than I'd ever done with him.

I was supposed to have more time to convince him I was more than a socialite. If I could just make him hear me. If I could just buy some time. I scooted to the edge of my seat, my hands out. "Papa, I'm smart. I can be useful to Mariano Shipping," I said, going back to how the night all started.

"It's not your job to be smart, Verana. You knew this," he almost pleaded. Like he knew he was close to the edge, and he was begging me not to push him.

But I was too far entrenched in panic over marrying Camden.

"But I am. If you'd just let me work a little b——"

"No," he interrupted with finality.

His harsh rebuttal snapped me back against my seat, my spine straight and tall. My desperation pleading for my father to hear me didn't break through, so I shut down, leaving the professional socialite to mix with the iota of defiance I'd gained in my freedom at college.

"Fine. I'll apply elsewhere."

He barked a laugh. "I don't think so, Verana."

I clenched my sweaty palms into frustrated fists, desperate to hold onto my composure—to not crumble under the discomfort of going against him. Usually, I sat back, but this was my life, and a tiny voice inside urged me to *fight*.

"If you won't hire me, then you can't stop me from applying to a company that will," I stated as I stood.

The man I only heard about from his coworkers made an appearance for the first time in my life.

His eyes narrowed to dark slits. "I'll shut you down at every turn. I know every shipping company in New York. You're a Mariano, act like it." He stood too, mirroring my position. "Since God didn't bless me with any male heirs, your job is to marry a man who will take care of our company. You'll make a good wife, period. Like your mother taught you."

Like a splinter in glass, I fractured—my father's cruel words dumping water on my fiery anger and I sat down, hard. Tears burned up the back of my throat and pooled on my lids, and I barely managed to keep them from falling.

But he saw the hurt, and it—like his anger—doused his fight too. His lids slid closed, and he shook his head, sagging back in his seat.

"It's getting late," I whispered.

He nodded, his eyes sliding open, not bothering to hide his regret. I swallowed the last bit of my tears down and stood. He stood with me and walked me out.

"You know I love you, Verana," he said at the door.

"I love you too."

He squeezed my hand. "And I love this company. It's what we have left of your mama. We must do what we have to, to keep it alive."

Unable to think of anything to respond with that would be productive to the night, I squeezed his hand back, and with a forced smile, left.

I made it to the end of the driveway before I pulled out my phone to message my friends.

Bitches: Arranged marriage is on…Kill me.

TWO

Vera

Raelynn: I thought you were joking…

Me: Nope. Welcome home to me. *eyeroll*

Raelynn: How about a girls' night?

Nova: Boo to arranged marriages.

Nova: And I can't do a girls' night. I'm out of town.

Raelynn: Clubbing it is.

Me: How about just a dinner instead.

Raelynn: At a strip club?

Nova: Ew.

Me: Hard pass on the strip club.

Raelynn: Such a good girl. Live a little.

Me: …

Raelynn: Fine. Dinner.

Raelynn: Party pooper.

Nova: Have a drink for me and be safe.

JUST KNOWING I'd be able to relax and talk the last twenty-four hours out with Raelynn tonight helped ease some of the stress that weighed on me since I left my father's last night.

10

I hated that Nova couldn't be there. She completed our love triangle, as Raelynn called it. She was the calm devil's advocate, always challenging us to think of the other person's point of view, while Raelynn plotted the murder of whatever hurt her or her friends.

We'd all met in our Freshman year of college when we stood by and watched in horror as someone performed all four parts of Bohemian Rhapsody by themselves for a talent show that didn't really exist. We'd caught each other's eyes and started laughing in unison, and the rest was history. We'd held each other through each crazy, emotional struggle and adventure over the last four years.

I was ready to laugh and have a little too much wine and pretend duty didn't pull me down with each step.

"Hey, bitch," Raelynn called as soon as I stepped through the door of the glitzy restaurant.

The host waiting to greet us, merely raised a brow at her loud greeting. Not that Raelynn cared. It didn't matter that we stood in one of the top restaurants filled with soft jazz and light conversations. She came barreling through like she had when we first met in college.

Loud and uncaring of what others thought, she was every-thing I never knew I needed in a friend. She took my proper slacks and had me switch them out for holey jeans. Needless to say, my father wasn't her biggest fan, but tolerated the friendship.

"Hey, bitch," I said much quieter once she was in my arms.

She smacked loud air kisses next to my cheek and declared, "Let the drinking commence."

People stared as she walked by in her fitted nude dress, barely staying up with thin spaghetti straps. Once we reached the table, we both waited for the host to help us into our seats and hand us our napkins.

Raelynn grew up in the same kind of world I had. The one of etiquette schools and charity galas and an extra house in the Hamptons. The only difference was that she was born with her freedom. She had zero expectations of who she needed to be as long as she didn't shame the family beyond repair.

"Can I get you ladies anything to drink other than water?"

"We'll take a bottle of Dom Perignon." She winked. "To start."

"I may not be up for the night you have planned," I said once the waiter walked away.

"You never are. Although you look like it in that jumper. All white looks good on you. And look at those shoulders. You pull off strapless well."

"And it has pockets," I joked.

"Even better."

The waiter came back with our champagne, filling the slim glasses until the bubbles almost overflowed.

"You know…" Raelynn started, the devious glint in her eyes. I tried to brace myself for what would come next, but I could rarely prepare for whatever came out of her mouth. "You should just start boinking everyone you can. Be the ho you want to be."

I almost choked on the drink I was taking.

"Oh, my god. I do not want to be a ho."

She sighed with disappointment. "I know. You're miss goody-goody. Missing the cardigan you love so much, but rocking the pearls still."

I wanted to argue with her. I wanted to adamantly deny and list off all the ways I challenged the rules, but I couldn't.

I was the rule follower of our group. Even Nova, the quietest of our tripod, broke more rules than I did.

"You know, you could still let loose even if you don't go full ho."

"I don't know," I said, fingering the pearls she'd mentioned. "You know I'm not great at one-night stands."

"Yeah, you tried it once and ended up dating him for almost

a year. And when that ended, you slapped your chastity belt on and threw away the key."

"Oh, my god. Keep your voice down," I said, glaring but still smiling.

She topped of her champagne and leaned back in her seat, looking around the restaurant.

"What about him?" she suggested, nodding her head to the back corner. "The one in the blue suit and no tie. Talking to the man in tweed. Who wears tweed in summer? Ew."

I covertly lifted my glass to my lips and slowly looked right before turning left to see who she pointed out.

The champagne I'd been drinking almost slipped from my dropped jaw.

Holy. Shit.

Holy, sex on a stick.

"Jesus..."

"Right? God, what I wouldn't do to feel that scruff between my thighs."

I couldn't even look away long enough to reprimand Raelynn.

"You should go talk to him."

"Absolutely not." I shook my head and faced her again. But adjusted my hips in my seat, so I could still sneak a few looks without being too obvious.

"Why not?"

"Because he looks...busy. I don't know. I can't just go up to someone in the middle of the restaurant and...and...what?"

"Please, sir," she said in a British accent. "Can I have some more?"

I laughed, watching his hand drag through his black hair. His long fingers driving through the thick strands. When he turned enough for me to get a more direct look, I melted a little more at his full lips. They were lush and even more pronounced from the surrounding scruff. How could a man look so unbeliev-ably masculine with lips like that?

"I can't." I shook off any ideas Raelynn tried to convince me to follow through on, coming back to reality. "Besides, he's probably taken. He's not exactly putting off welcoming vibes."

She rolled her eyes. "You and your vibes."

"You can tell a lot about a person based on the energy they put off. And not in an aura kind of way, but just the personality they portray. He hasn't even smiled."

He briefly glanced in our direction but was too far away for me to see his eye color; they'd looked like dark pools you'd get lost in. And not in the dreamy, good way. In the, fall into a dark pit of nothingness, hoping to find any light, only to find more darkness, kind of way. His dinner partner laughed, but the delicious stranger remained just as stoic.

"I'm getting the vibe that he'd put his all into fucking me until I forgot my name. With that scowl he's working, he probably angry fucks and makes you question how you liked something so rough."

"Uhhh…"

"God, he's hot. Go up to him and just fall into his lap. You're hot enough with all your lush dark hair and perky tits. You can blink those doe eyes up at him. He'll be forced to find out if you're as innocent as you look or if it's all a scam to cover the true freak you are."

I choked on an uncomfortable laugh, looking away to hide my blush. "I—I'm not a freak."

At least I didn't think so.

"That's because a man like him hasn't shown you that you'd do anything—even the freakiest shit—just to please him."

I watched him a little longer. Taking in the elegant movement of his fingers gripping the glass, bringing it to rest on the lushest lips I'd ever seen. I watched the thick column on his throat move up and down when he swallowed, and I may have even moaned when he pulled the glass away only to be followed by the quick swipe of his tongue.

For a moment, I imagined being the bold woman Raelynn

wanted me to be. I imagined strutting over there and falling into his lap, letting his strong arms catch me. I imagined his deep voice asking me if I was okay—asking me if I wanted to go home with him. I imagined saying yes.

"I can't," I said softly, forcing myself to look back at her.

"Ugh, fine. Help me finish this bottle, and I'll make sure you get home with your chastity belt still in place."

"So sweet of you," I deadpanned.

Our food arrived, and I explained the argument I had with my father. I'd vaguely explained my family dynamics when we met, but I never brought it up in detail. I was away from home and wanted to pretend my life didn't require me to live like we were ancient royals who used their daughters to barter with.

"I just wanted to work. I'd always known I'd eventually get married. I just thought I'd have more time. Maybe find someone on my own."

"Then work," she suggested, like it was the easiest solution in the world. "Maybe Camden is a slow learner and takes years to get to a place where he can focus on you."

"I wish. My dad promised to blacklist me. If I try anywhere, they'll recognize my last name and go to him for a reference, only to be told not to hire me."

Her lips curled in disgust. "I'll have to be extra careful around your dad now. I have words for him."

"I bet," I laughed

"Hmmm..." She narrowed her eyes and pursed her lips, looking around the restaurant, like an idea was hiding behind one of the plants.

"Why don't you apply with a different last name?"

"Because most businesses require identification of some sort, and all of those have my name on them. I wouldn't get far."

"You remember Jeb from college?"

"The computer guy who rarely left his dorm?"

"Yup. He makes legit fake IDs. What if he made one for you with a different last name?"

"I don't know. That sounds illegal."

She shrugged like legality was a minor detail. "You could use your mother's name. It's hard to blacklist someone when he doesn't know what's coming."

"My mother's last name is Mariano."

"What? Doesn't the woman usually take the man's last name?"

"Not when your family lives by midcentury rules and wants their company to stay with the family name. They agreed to let my father run the company as long as he took their last name. I guess he wanted the company more than his own legacy."

Not that I blamed him. He was a foster kid with no history who worked his way up at Mariano Shipping, making a name for himself.

"Okay … what about your grandmother's last name?"

"Hmm…Barrone?"

"Love it. Let's do it. Come on," she cajoled.

"What if they recognize me? I grew up in this world and around all the big names."

"Well, old money isn't the only place to work. Besides, you don't want to work with those old men set in their old ways. Remember all the bold, brash ideas you came up with? You'd get so excited, clutching your pearls."

"Shut up," I laughed.

"Come on, good girl. Take your brilliant ideas elsewhere and get to work."

Maybe it was the champagne. Maybe it was the flush still lingering on my cheeks from the sexy stranger in the corner. Maybe it was desperation to live a little longer before my life was given to someone else.

Right then, it didn't matter.

Right then, Raelynn's plan sounded damn good.

Finishing off my glass, I leaned forward.

Her lips tipped in a slow smile, knowing she'd won me over.

A thrill of excitement shot down my spine, washing away any fear that this would have drastic consequences.

I didn't care.

I'd blame it on the champagne.

"Okay. Let's make a plan."

THREE

Nico

"How many interviews do we have today?" I asked, already tired despite not having even started.

My assistant, Ryan, flipped through his stack of papers until he found what he was looking for. "Five."

My body sank into the plush leather of my chair. "Jesus," I muttered, dragging a hand over my face. "Remind me why I'm doing these again?"

Ryan cocked a brow and gave me his signature deadpanned stare he reserved just for me. We'd worked together almost longer than anyone, making him the only employee to be able to get away with it.

"Because you're a control freak who likes to micromanage even though you always regret how much it adds to your plate."

"I guess you're right."

"I know I am."

"Well, then, just keep the coffee coming all day."

"Will do." He made it to the door before stopping with one last thing. "Also, a Joseph Andrews called while you were away. I left a note with the papers, but it seemed important."

"Thank you, Ryan."

If possible, I sank even lower in my seat, tired down to my

bones. Digging through the papers, I pulled out the sticky note that had the number I was all too familiar with scrawled across it.

Joseph was one of the attendees at the assisted living center my grandfather lived at. I hated having him there, but he was beyond living on his own. Old age had crept up on him faster than it should have because of stress—unnecessary stress. I stuck the post-it to the edge of my computer, so I remembered to call at lunch. If it had been urgent, he would have reached out to me on my cell phone.

Either way, I needed to get back to Charleston. I'd been in New York for an entire week, and already the cramped city bore down on me. It was too loud, too busy, too…people-y. However, each year, my time in New York increased. What started as a third of the year was now turning into two-thirds of the year in New York. It was bittersweet, to say the least.

But work needed to be done. The New York office was growing faster than I'd anticipated, pulling in larger projects each week, and I needed more assistance to cover the workload. It wasn't a terrible problem to have. It was exactly what I'd been working for since I graduated over ten years ago. I'd worked tirelessly even through college to dig this company—my family's company—out of the rubble it'd been left in.

My grandfather and father had done their best, but outside sources played dirty when my family didn't, and it left us falling behind.

I wouldn't let it happen to me. I played fair—for the most part—but I also played smarter, harder. I had patience and a plan, and with that, I'd outwit the competition who'd cheated to the top.

Which was why I micromanaged as Ryan accused. This company—this plan—meant more to me than anything, and I'd do whatever it took to succeed. Even if it meant tirelessly interviewing each candidate myself.

I'd needed five new employees. Three were already filled,

leaving two to go. Maybe today would be the day a competent candidate would come in and blow my mind, allowing me to leave this city and go back to the warm, open air of Charleston.

My cell phone vibrated, and Xander's name crossed the screen.

"Hey, asshole," I greeted my friend from college.

"I saw I missed your call earlier. What's up? Need another shell company?"

Xander worked in computer technology and could create an entire world to look real on the internet from nothing. He was a genius, and I utilized every talent to my cause—my revenge.

"Maybe I just missed your voice."

"Oh, yeah. You like that," he said in his deep baritone like Barry White.

"Tell Nicholas I said hi," his wife shouted from the background.

"Maggie says, hi."

"Shouldn't she be worried to find you talking like that on the phone?"

"Nah, I only talk to you like that. I use a different voice with her."

"I don't want to hear it."

We both laughed before he sobered and asked again what I had called for earlier.

"I just wanted to check up on any new information you gathered. More stocks are coming up on the market, and I want to make sure I'm prepared for all possibilities."

"You know I would call you if I had anything. So far, all is quiet."

"Yeah, it's just been a while since I could acquire new stocks. I'm antsy."

"Have you tried calling up one of your black-book-ladies?"

My mind flashed to the stunning brunette at the restaurant I'd been unable to get off my mind. Shaking my head, I shoved it aside, annoyed that I'd only looked at her and still thought of her a week later. "Not since I've been in this damn city," I grumbled.

"Oh, yeah. New York always makes you pissy. Go get laid and know I'll call you if anything comes up."

"Thanks, man."

"Anything else? You sound more irritable than usual, which is saying something."

"Very funny. I've got a day full of interviews ahead of me."

"Still trying to replace that one chick?" he asked, laughing.

"Beth," I grumbled.

"You could always call her," he joked. "Or...who was the other one?"

"Shut up, asshole."

He laughed at my luck of hiring women who had applied to the job just to get close to me in hopes of bagging the boss. Beth was the most recent culprit and had started by offering to blow one of the supervisors to get placed on a project I headed.

Being desired for my money wasn't anything new, but I hated it even more because it fucked with my business...which fucked with my plans, and that crossed a line. My life centered around making this company successful enough to take what I wanted.

Add in my disgust for anyone cheating their way to the top, and I fired her instantly.

"I don't fuck employees."

"Hey, don't knock it. I fucked Maggie all over the office and now look at us."

I choked out a sound of disgust. "Married."

"Yeah, happily married. Nothing wrong with it."

"Maybe not. But I'm good without it. Women are a distraction, and I've got plenty who are perfectly fine with the occasional meet."

"Such a playboy," he joked. "Doesn't Grandpa Charlie want to see you happily married?"

My lip curled at the thought. I'd do anything for my

grandpa to make him happy, but that request was too much. "On that note, I have to go."

"Mr. Rush. Your first appointment has arrived," Ryan called through the intercom.

"That's my first interview," I said to a laughing Xander. "Say a prayer for me, and I'll call someone tonight."

"You better, or I'm sending you a hooker. And not a top-shelf one."

"Thanks, man."

"Anytime."

With that, I got off my phone and shoved it away, clicking the intercom to talk to Ryan. "Send them in, please."

A tall blonde walked in, confidence pouring off every inch of her. When she spotted me standing from my desk, she stumbled over her feet a bit.

"Okay?" I asked, rounding my desk.

"More than okay," she said with a slow smile.

Alarm bells rang when her eyes heated, and she bit at her lip. I held out my hand cautiously, hoping she wasn't anything like Beth, but not holding my breath. "I'm Nicholas Rush, nice to meet you."

"Cassie," she said, sliding her hand in mine. She held on longer than necessary and scanned my body head to toe.

Tugging my hand back, I rounded the desk, eager to put space between us. I watched her sit down and barely held back my cringe when she tugged her black skirt further up her legs than necessary and stroked her finger along the v of her blouse.

This was going to be a long fucking day.

THE FIRST THREE INTERVIEWS SUCKED. The first one flirted the entire interview until I began to feel so uncomfortable, I had to cut it short. The second was completely unqualified, and the third was a little racist.

The fourth sat across from my desk, barely hanging on by a thread. He had no actual work experience but expressed an eagerness to learn. It wasn't great, but at least it was something I could work with.

"Thank you, Kyle," I said, walking around the desk.

He stood from his chair and shook my hand. "Thank you for your time, Mr. Rush. I hope to hear from you."

Not making any promises, I merely nodded and walked him out. "Have a nice day."

As soon as he rounded the corner, I fell back into one of the seats across from Ryan's desk.

"Another dud?" he asked.

"Actually, not completely. Which is why I'll probably offer him the job. God, I just want this to be over."

"Should have let HR handle it."

"Thank you, Ryan, for your insightful, useless comments."

"It's what you pay me for."

I didn't even bother glaring. My eyes slid closed, and I grumbled.

"By the way, Joseph called again."

At that, I jerked upright, tugging my phone out of my pocket. Four missed calls. Fuck. Fucking fuck.

"Did he say what it was?"

"No, but he did ask me to let you know to call him back sooner rather than later."

I stood from the chair and checked the time. A little after one.

"I'm taking a lunch today. I need to call him back, and I need space from these damn interviews."

"But you have one last interview in thirty minutes."

"Reschedule," I said, running into my office to grab my wallet.

"It's a little late for that," Ryan reprimanded when I came back out.

"Fine. Then have HR do it."

23

"I don't know if I can find anyone on such short notice."

"Then you do it," I growled. He opened his mouth again, but my phone burned a hole in my jacket, and the need to escape these four walls thumped like a pulse inside me. I held up my hand. "Just handle it, Ryan. It's why I pay you as much as I do."

With that, I headed out, deciding a bar sounded like a nice place for lunch. Whatever Joseph called about, I was sure a bourbon would make it easier to handle.

For a moment, a tinge of guilt tried to flood my system, but I shoved it down, reasoning that the last interview would most likely be a dud like the rest of them.

FOUR

Vera

"Welcome, Miss Barrone. I'll be conducting your interview today."

I shook his hand and couldn't help my eyes narrowing at how young he looked. The last person I spoke with let me know the owner was conducting the interviews. The man, who didn't look much older than me, with his bow tie and thick-rimmed glasses, didn't scream owner of a burgeoning business.

"Mr. Rush?" I asked.

His soft laugh lacked humor as he dropped his gaze and readjusted his glasses before looking up with a forced smile. "No. I'm Ryan Saunders, Mr. Rush's personal assistant."

"Oh," I answered slowly, trying to process the change. I knew the ins and outs of a shipping company, and it was already odd enough that the owner would conduct the interview instead of HR, but I was told he liked to vet his employees himself. But to have an assistant interview me threw me off. "Not to be rude, but do assistants usually perform interviews at Rush Shipping Industries?"

"No, we sure don't."

I took note of his irritation, and my mind raced with what was going on. Was this a joke? Had they figured out who I was, and now my father was humoring me by letting me interview, but wasting my time with an assistant?

"Unfortunately, Mr. Rush had to run out, and we had hoped HR would take over. However, no one was available on such short notice," he explained, all irritation mostly gone.

"I understand."

"I assure you I know the position you're applying for and know each role as well as Mr. Rush himself."

"Of course."

It still pricked at my irritation that a company would be so aloof with their hires that they couldn't find someone to properly vet their employees, but I let it go. It wasn't like I was searching for my future career, just something to put at least an ounce of my degree to use.

Taking a deep breath, I sat up straight and smiled.

I wanted this job.

More to prove I could have one than any other reason, but I still wanted it.

"I see you graduated Magna Cum Laude at The Wharton School of Business." His brows rose high above the edge of his black glasses. "Wow. That's impressive."

"Thank you. I definitely enjoyed learning at Wharton. It offered me a plethora of experiences."

He looked up from the papers and tipped his head to the side. "Did you plan on continuing your MBA elsewhere?"

Why bother? The degree I have now would be useless in a year.

Covering my almost snort at his question with a soft laugh, I answered, "No. Not that I don't want to. It's just that now isn't the time."

"I see." He nodded and closed the folder holding my resume. "What makes you interested in the assistant project manager position? Your experience in college is impressive enough for a higher position. Unfortunately, we're not hiring for that now. So, what is it about Rush?"

It was small enough to not be on my father's radar and seemed to have minimal connections that my father could use to shut me out, which would prevent me from delivering the big fuck you to him and Camden.

"Rush Shipping is growing, and I want to grow with them."

He smiled and flipped open the folder again, making notes off to the side. But that small smile was all I needed to know. This job was mine.

The rest of the interview flew by, and by the end, I was determined to recruit Ryan into becoming my friend, no matter what I had to do. He had a sarcastic whit that reminded me of Raelynn.

"Well, Verana, I'll need to pass all this information along to my superiors, but you should be hearing from us soon."

Beaming, I stood and shook his offered hand, feeling lighter since I arrived home from college. Ryan walked me to the elevator and offered another smile. It took all I had not to break out into a full victory dance as soon as the door closed. Instead, I managed to keep it to a small bounce from one foot to the other, getting it together by the time the doors opened.

I couldn't wait to call the girls and let them know how the interview went. Before I could reach the front doors, I stopped and opened my bag to dig my phone out, but it wasn't in the pocket I usually kept it in. I flipped through each section, wondering if I'd misplaced it. Being so nervous before my interview would be the only explanation for it not being exactly where it always was, considering everything always had a place, and I didn't deviate from it.

I'd just unzipped the middle section when a wall clipped my shoulder and sent my bag flying off my arm onto the floor, all my belongings scattering out like water from a tipped-over glass.

"Shit," a deep voice said at the same time I did.

I jerked my head up, ready to lay into this asshole when my eyes locked with the most beautiful hazel eyes I'd ever seen. The light streamed in through the lobby and hit them just right to illuminate all the shades of brown and green mixing together.

"I'm so sorry. Are you all right?"

My gaze dropped from his eyes, down the strong bridge of his nose to settle on his full lips.

"Jesus," I said on an exhale. Dark stubble coated his jaw, and I clenched my hands to keep from reaching out and thumbing his plush bottom lip. I may have almost moaned when his tongue slicked out across the bottom before they began moving again.

"What was that?" he asked.

His hand gently rested on my shoulder, giving a soft squeeze. It swallowed my smaller frame, sending a heat that burned through my chest.

"Miss?" He spoke again and finally pulled me out of my trance.

Blinking and shaking my head, I reprimanded myself for becoming a woman who damn near melted into a pile of goo over some facial features.

"I'm sorry. Yes. You...you..." I looked down at the papers, pens, wallet, and other essentials scattered across the tile floor and collected myself. "Dammit," I muttered, dropping to my knees to collect everything.

"Here, let me help," he offered, dropping down next to me. I watched as he grabbed one of my small pouches, grateful I kept all my feminine products and condoms in there. Otherwise, they'd be scattered right next to everything else.

He held the black pouch between his long fingers and offered it back to me. Taking a few discreet deep breaths, I finally found the courage to really look up and see the man who sent me from angry to a puddle in point two seconds.

His large body crouched next to mine, and as soon as my eyes met his again, familiarity hit me, forcing my heart to flutter a little harder in my chest.

The man from the restaurant. The one Raelynn said I should offer a night to.

What were the odds?

Was it a sign?

"It's you," he said, his eyes scanning my features.

Like a record scratching, his words stopped my fantasies of fate with confusion. "What?"

"Sorry," he said with a laugh. He shook his head and looked down, running his hand through his hair. When he looked up again, his lips tipped, stretching his cheeks over sharp cheek-bones, resting underneath glassy eyes. "I saw you at the restaurant the other night."

Biting my lip, I tried to hold back my smile from growing too big. This man oozed sophistication, and I didn't want to come off as a giddy little girl. "You did?"

"You and your friend were hard to miss."

Did he mean Raelynn? Or me? Did he mean we were hard to miss because Raelynn owned a room and could get loud? Or did he really notice *me?* "We may have noticed you, too," I admitted, feeling bold.

He studied me a moment longer before grabbing the last of my papers and passing them over. We both stood, and he shoved his hands into his pockets. His shoulders pulled wide, and I guessed I was lucky he only clipped my shoulder. He could have taken me down completely with his size if he really bumped into me.

"I'm sorry I knocked into you," he apologized again. "I was looking at my phone."

His smile faded to a firm pout, but his eyes still twinkled. Usually, that would've been my moment to smile and walk away.

But I didn't want to.

Maybe it was the confidence of crushing the interview. Maybe it was Raelynn's voice in my head, reminding me to have some before I was sold off. Maybe it was something about this alluring man and the power he exuded that called to me—challenged me—to handle him.

I didn't know what the reason was, but it pushed me to throw caution to the wind and flirt with him—to see where it went.

"Responding to a girlfriend?" I asked, relaxing my posture, letting him see some of the desire brewing.

His head tipped to the side, his eyes narrowing, and I feared I went too far. Despite the embarrassed flush fighting its way into my cheeks, I held it back and stood strong. He flirted with me first.

Right?

Oh, god. Did I make it up? Had he just been friendly, and I assumed it was more because I was lost in gaga land?

Just as I was about to abandon ship and slink away, his lips soften again to a smirk, his tongue slicking across his bottom lip again.

"No. No girlfriend to talk to. What about you? A boyfriend?"

A boyfriend? No. An arranged fiancé? Well, he didn't ask about that.

"No."

"Well, then there is no one to protest me asking you out."

"I guess not."

His smirk grew at my evasive answers as he took a step closer. I craned my neck back to meet his eyes that now looked like pools of warm chocolate without the sun bringing out all the hidden depths. "How about drinks this Friday?"

"How about dinner on Friday, and we'll see about drinks?"

God, who was I? I wasn't this dominant woman who demanded what she wanted. I wasn't meek by any means, but usually, Raelynn filled the role of seductress who didn't hesitate to ask for what she wanted.

Either way, his smile grew, and a soft laugh escaped as if impressed.

Lifting my chin higher, I waited for his answer. If he shot me down, then at least I'd walk away with one hell of a story.

He stepped closer, almost closing the gap. "Deal."

I tipped my head back more and slowly dragged my teeth across my lips. He did the same, and the sexiest rumble escaped his lips that had my knees shaking. Fuck, this was crazy. We were in the middle of a lobby after literally colliding, and everything around us ceased to exist. My body throbbed with a need for him to wrap me in his arms and lift me high enough, so I could discover for myself how much his soft, pillowy lip would give under my teeth.

As if I willed him to do it, he leaned down.

Two things happened in the moment of only inches between us.

One, the strong scent of alcohol hit me before his lips could. And two, someone was calling my name.

"Miss Barrone."

Flustered, I stepped back and blinked, bringing myself back to the reality of where we were, and turned to find Ryan coming out of the elevator, his hand clutched around a small rectangle.

Had he seen me about to make out with a stranger in the lobby? Oh, my god, if he did, would he think less of me? Years of training to always be aware of how I looked and acted in public vanished in the presence of the man behind me. Not only would my dad be ashamed, but my mother would too. I'd been taught better.

"Miss Barrone," he said again, a little out of breath. He smiled when he saw me, and nothing on his face showed that he saw me about commit a PDA. "I thought I'd have missed you. You forgot your phone."

"Oh, thank you so much. I can't believe I did that." I turned back to my sexy stranger with an embarrassed smile to find him completely different than a moment before. His eyes no longer held any warmth. His lips no longer soft and inches from mine. His smile was nowhere to be seen. Left in its place was a man who looked like he was built from stone—his face cast in shadow. He made the cold man I saw in the restaurant look like a sunny oasis compared to who stood before me now.

"Mr. Rush, back just in time," Ryan said behind me.

Mr. Rush? Rush, Rush, Rush? As in the *Mr. Rush.*

"Miss Barrone was the last interview of the day, and I have to admit, she's a perfect fit for Rush Shipping."

The owner of the company? The man who was supposed to interview me? The man who bailed last minute? The man who smelled of alcohol before three in the afternoon?

The man who I almost begged to maul me in the middle of an office lobby?

Heat flooded my cheeks, and I struggled to pull myself together.

His eyes flashed to mine, and I rued the day I ever had the confidence to pursue a man so boldly. I should have just run.

Clearing my throat, I stood tall and offered my hand with an uncomfortable smile I hoped alleviated the awkwardness of the moment. "Mr. Rush, it's a pleasure to meet you."

Any hope of softening the statue before me vanished when he looked at my extended hand, and his lip curled in disgust. "Did you know I owned the company?"

"What?" I asked, slowly dropping my hand.

"Did. You. Know. I owned. The company?" he asked slower as if that would make it make more sense.

"Ummm...No. I mean, I knew Nicholas Rush owned the company, but I didn't know that was you."

His jaw ticked, and he took a step closer, but this time it wasn't in passion, but to intimidate.

Confused by the complete one-eighty, I stood tall, refusing to cower before any man.

"Are you sure? Maybe you saw me and bumped into me so you could flirt and increase your chances of being hired?"

"Excuse me?" I asked in a dangerously low tone.

"You came on pretty strong, Miss Barrone."

Fire burned in my chest, and it took everything I had to not slap the arrogant look off his face. Shoving it down into a little ball of rage, I harnessed my anger for confidence and took my own intimidating step forward. "For your information, *Mr.* Rush, *you* bumped into *me*. Maybe if you hadn't been out drinking before three and instead showed up to interview the employees you seem to need, you'd have seen that I am more than competent for this job and don't need to reduce myself to flirting with someone so unprofessional to get hired. Rush Shipping would be lucky to have me."

And with that, I stormed off, now needing to call the girls to let them know that I rocked an interview but most likely wouldn't get hired after almost kissing the boss and then basically telling him to fuck off.

I guessed it was back to the drawing board.

FIVE

Nico

"Good morning, everyone. First things first, I'd like to introduce our two newest assistant project managers, Kyle Rend and Verana Barrone." My eyes glossed over Verana and focused on Kyle instead. "They will be working with Domenic and me on the incoming project. Which I will let Domenic explain from here to get us started."

I sat back in my chair and let Domenic take the lead on discussing the ins and outs of the massive client he brought in. We'd already covered all our bases over our dinner meeting, so my attention easily shifted from him to Verana.

Shocked that she actually accepted the job didn't quite cover the way my body came to a complete halt watching her walk in today. She'd stormed out of the lobby, and I was sure I'd never see her again. Frankly, I wasn't sure I wanted to. She'd caught me in a rare moment of having an extra drink after lunch and considering skipping a number from my phone, and instead, using her. Xander's reminder to get laid was the only excuse for why I came on so strong in my own office building.

I wasn't sure how much I trusted that the whole thing was an accident. Yes, I'd bumped into her, but maybe she saw me coming and orchestrated it all after she'd missed me in the interview.

She wouldn't be the first woman to use her body to get her way. Hell, the first woman I'd interviewed that same day had called twice to check on her interview in as many days. And when I informed her we'd decided to pass on hiring her, she inquired if there were any other *services* I was looking for.

But after talking to Ryan and hearing him gush about Verana like she was the second coming of Christ, I gave in on offering her the job. Bottom line was that we needed help, and it was getting to the point of beggars can't be choosers. If I dismissed the whole possibility of her wanting more from me than just a job, I had to admit her credentials on her resume impressed me. She deserved more than a simple APM position, but Ryan assured me she was interested in growth.

Thankfully, I wouldn't be in New York City much longer to be part of that. All the interviews had been conducted, and I needed to get back to Charleston to take care of my grandfather and the office there.

She was a distraction I didn't need right now. My goals were inching closer, and I needed to focus on my company. Not on the woman who sat forward, taking notes on every word out of Dom's mouth. Not on the way, she rolled the pencil between her slim fingers. Not on the way, she slicked her tongue across her lips.

Fuck, she oozed sex in such an innocent way. Her slim pants and button-up blouse with pearls begged me to rip it all away to find what laid beneath. Her dimples and the way the left was a little deeper than the right urged me to dip my tongue into the crease and find if she tasted as good as she looked.

And I almost had. I'd been moments away from inhaling her right then in the lobby.

I'd lost my damn mind.

I'd had more to drink than I'd meant to, and we'd collided. My walls had been paper-thin at best, but when she'd turned to me with heated eyes and faded freckles, recognition brushed all barriers aside.

I'd seen her and her bold friend at the restaurant. I hadn't lied, she was hard to miss. Her friend had been dominating, but Vera's sly smiles and demure manners pulled my attention her way, making me want to uncover everything underneath.

I'd passed on approaching her then, but seeing her standing there in the lobby, I'd decided to flirt.

Why not? What would it hurt? It'd been too long since I'd gotten laid, and her smile promised sin wrapped in heaven.

Now, despite my doubts about her, my body remembered how ready it'd been to take, take, take, and I struggled to shut it off. I struggled to focus. She consumed my thoughts. The night after the restaurant, she'd come to me in my dreams, leaving me to wake up with an aching hard-on I'd been forced to relieve.

I'd thought about her more than I wanted to and hadn't even spoken to her.

And it pissed me off. If her goal was to sway me with her body, it was fucking working, and the more it worked, the more I wanted to break it.

"Mr. Rush?" Dom called like he'd said it more than once.

Her eyes clashed with mine just before I gave my attention to Dom. "Yes?"

"Do you have anything to add?"

All eyes turned to me, and I clenched my jaw, frustration bubbling up. Clearing my throat, I took a second to aimlessly flip through my papers, buying time. "No. I think we covered it all."

"Great." Dom smiled but narrowed his eyes. He knew me well enough to notice my distraction. "We're all up to date and have our assignments. Let's get to work, people."

With that, everyone gathered their belongings and piled out. I lingered behind, watching Verana, tensing when Domenic rested his hand on her shoulder, receiving her smile I couldn't stop thinking about.

I knew it meant nothing. Domenic was happily married. But did she know that? Did she care? Was she hoping to get further with him now that I was off the table?

Irritation bubbled up at their easy laughter until I heard myself call his name before I knew what I was doing. "Domenic," I barked.

He blinked, turning to me with wide eyes. "Yes?"

"Grab those extra files from your desk before heading to my office."

"But, they're on the computer file I sent."

"A hard copy will be good, too," I answered lamely.

His head tipped to the side, but after only a moment, he shrugged. "Sure. I'll meet you there in fifteen. Verana, I'm excited to have you on the team."

I clenched my fists at her easy smile. "Thank you. And please. Call me Vera."

"Vera. Will do."

And then it was only Vera and me in the empty meeting room.

I stood there waiting for her to collect her papers, studying the way her dark hair fell to her shoulders, no matter how many times she tucked it behind her ears.

"Can I help you with something?" she asked, standing upright, shoulders back and chin high. She looked like she should be running her own company.

"You know he's married."

"Excuse me?"

"Domenic. Happily so." Her eyes widened. "Just in case you were hoping to flirt with another man in charge to get ahead."

"I wasn't…"

"Maybe don't flirt with anyone here. We don't have any particular rules for fraternization, but it's best to not mix business and pleasure."

Her nostrils flared over pressed lips. "I wasn't freaking flirting with anyone."

"Just like you didn't run into me."

"That was an accident, and again, you ran into me. And if you think I'm such a threat to all the men at your company, why did you hire me?"

"Because Ryan was determined to."

"Did you even look over my resume?" she sneered, looking at me like a bug on the bottom of her shoe.

I didn't want to admit how impressed I was with her resume, so I directed the subject back to my point.

Stepping into her personal space, I looked down my nose at her. Maybe if I intimidated her enough, she'd give me a wide berth. "Did you stage the lobby because you saw me that night at the restaurant and wanted a second chance?"

"Hardly. You are unbelievably arrogant," she almost growled.

My muscles tensed, fighting the need to step closer and feel the heat radiating off her directly against me. Maybe if I did, she'd cave and admit what she really wanted.

"Trust me, I have a right to be arrogant," I taunted.

Instead of continuing our fight, she rolled her eyes and turned, going the long way around the table to avoid me.

"Make sure to grab two black coffees for Dom and me," I called before she could walk out.

"Yes, sir," she muttered over her shoulder.

Whatever it was between us—whatever hold she had on me and my attention—I needed to break it.

Nothing made that clearer than how much I loved hearing those words tumble from her supple mouth.

I needed to end it, and I needed to do it soon.

SIX

Vera

Nova: How's the boss?

PULLING MY WORK SHIRT OFF, I rolled my eyes. How was Nicholas Rush? A pain in my ass. A man on a mission to drive me insane. A man making me question how much I wanted to stick it to my father and work on my own.

A man that stole too much of my attention with how freaking alluring, dark, and cold he was when I remembered him as anything but for those few moments in the lobby.

But he'd made an assumption and seemed as determined to stick to it as I did to continue working for him. Despite not being able to decide if I liked looking at him more because I fantasized about slapping that perpetual scowl off his face or kissing it.

"Ugh." I fell back on the bed and grabbed my phone to reply, keeping my response simple.

Me: An asshole.
Raelynn: A fun one? *wink wink*
Nova: What's a fun asshole?
Raelynn: One that would spank you.

Nova: Gross.
Raelynn: Don't knock it 'til you've tried it.
Raelynn: So, does he talk down to you only to bend you over his desk later.
Nova: Jesus.
Me: Nope.
Raelynn: That's a shame. He was hot. It's been a few weeks, and I can still remember that rugged square jaw. YUM!
Me: He's more of a make me do demeaning jobs and just talk down to me. Everything I do is treated as if I'm trying to sleep my way to the top.
Raelynn: Ew. What a dick.
Me: Last week, we did a video conference call, and he asked to talk to me afterward and reprimanded me for what I wore.

He'd traveled back to the main office in Charleston for a week but still managed to be a pain in my ass. I'd thought it'd be a reprieve from the last month, but even through a little screen, he'd been able to pull my attention into fantasies that leaned more toward kissing over slapping. Maybe more so. I didn't know if it was just me, but he looked more relaxed there than he did here. His top buttons had been undone, his jaw a little less tight, covered in more scruff than usual.

Once, his mouth had even tipped into a smile, stretching his full lips I still dreamed about.

Again, I decided to keep that from the girls.

Nova: Men are assholes.
Raelynn: Except for the dreamy lead singer of the band you love so much. *heart eyes*
Nova: Shut up.
Me: How was the concert you went to last week?
Raelynn: Did you stalk him after?
Nova: OMG! Stop!

Raelynn: Did you sneak into his trailer and make him notice you.

Raelynn: With your mouth.

Raelynn: On his cock?

Raelynn: Please say yes!

Nova: *eye roll*

Me: As much as I'm enjoying this, I have to get going.

Me: Before I go, though, I have pics of two tops. Tell me your favorite.

Nova: What are you getting all dressed up for?

Me: I have a date.

Raelynn: A DATE? And you didn't tell us until now. With who? Are you going to bang them before being sold to the highest bidder? Please say yes. Make me the happiest woman ever and tell me you took my advice.

Me: Unfortunately, it's with Camden.

Nova: Ew.

Raelynn: So gross.

Nova: Do you have a parka to wear instead of either of those tops?

Raelynn: Maybe a habit from a nunnery.

Me: Unfortunately, no.

Raelynn: Damn.

Raelynn: Don't wear either of those. Go with the black fitted dress. It covers a lot but makes you look like a boss bitch while being sexy. Also, black like you're going to your own funeral. Perfect for Camden.

Nova: It says, "look at what you can't have, and I'd rather die than give it to you."

Raelynn: Exactly. *high five*

Nova: *high five back*

Me: Done. I'll let you know how it goes. Love you.

Nova: Love you too.

Raelynn: Love you, bitches.

I peeled myself off the bed and shoved the two tops back into the closet, opting instead for the black dress Raelynn suggested.

I *did* love the dress. It hugged my modest curves, covering me from my neck to my knees. Slipping on a pair of black pumps had me feeling strong and confident like I was channeling my inner Raelynn, daring some man to challenge me—to own me.

Yeah right.

With a Mona Lisa smile on my lips, I ordered a car and headed to meet Camden. I refused to let him drive me because I didn't want to be on his time, and I knew I'd need a drink or two to get through this meal.

I hoped it wouldn't always be like this.

Raelynn and Nova had scoffed and laughed when I'd told them about how I'd always known I'd most likely have an arranged marriage. Unless, by some miracle, I found a man on my own they approved of.

But it had always been my life. I'd always known. They'd asked why I would let that happen, and I guessed I could always turn my back on my father, but I didn't want to. I loved him. I trusted him. Yes, he had old-fashioned views, but it'd been how I'd been raised.

I remembered all the times my mother had tucked me in, and I'd asked her why this path was my future. She'd laughed softly and told me about how her marriage had been chosen by her parents and how she'd hated my father. He'd been arrogant and closed off. She'd rolled her eyes and shook her head.

"Then why did you marry him? Couldn't you have told your parents, no?"

"Mia bambina." She brushed my hair back softly and smiled down at me like she usually did when I asked silly questions. *"At that time, no. Grandpapa needed me to marry your father for the company, and so I did. It was my duty. An honor to do something for our family. Family means everything."*

My little brow scrunched in confusion. "What if I hate who Papa chooses for me to marry?"

"He will choose a good man for you to marry. I didn't love your father —he didn't love me much either." She laughed. "But it took time. It took work. Any marriage does. And your father is a good man who worked for my love."

She closed her eyes with a dreamy smile, and I remembered earlier in the night, hearing her giggles before coming into the kitchen to find Papa twirling her in his arms to the music playing on the stereo.

"I hope I fall in love with a boy like Aladdin, and Papa will be happy. I want a Prince Charming like all the princesses," I said with a giddy excitement only a girl could have.

"Mia bambina." She laughed again, stroking my cheek again. "If you wait for the perfect fairy tale, you will never find happiness. Sometimes Prince Charming is everything you need when you didn't know you needed it."

I'd had so many reminders over the years that an arranged marriage could work. My parents had been happy and in love, just like my grandparents.

I may not love Camden now, but my father wouldn't pick a bad man for me to marry. I had to have confidence in my mother's conviction behind those words.

I *really* had to have conviction behind those words when thirty minutes into dinner already had me wanting to run toward the door.

"Maybe you can wear a fitted wedding dress, too. Looks good on you," he said, his eyes glued to my chest. "You don't have many curves, but that tight dress really shows off what you do have. Maybe something a little more revealing up top."

My fists clenched under the table as he gestured toward my boobs with his hand holding his scotch, the amber liquid sloshing dangerously close to the edge.

With a clenched jaw, I forced a smile and the words, "I'll take it into consideration." I cleared my throat and opened and closed my fingers, trying to relax, and moved on to a safer topic.

"How's work going? Are you fitting in at Mariano Shipping okay? I know father runs a tight ship."

Camden barked an embarrassingly loud laugh that had me flicking my eyes left and right to take in how much attention he drew. A familiar face had every muscle in my body tightening in dread. Heat flooded my cheeks, and I quickly looked away, letting my hair fall like a curtain to hide behind. Maybe he wouldn't know it was me.

But when I brushed my hair aside and snuck a glance back in his direction, the dark eyes of Nicholas Rush met mine. They flicked toward Camden and quickly back to me before narrowing to judgmental slits. His tight lips curled in a disgusted snarl. But even beyond his obvious distaste of me and the situation—even beyond the space between us—I could feel the heat in his eyes stroke across my skin as if I sat completely bare.

I focused back on Camden and tried to shove down the heat flooding my veins.

"So, I take it work is going well?" I asked after clearing my throat.

Camden's blond hair fell from its perfect swoop when he tipped his head to the side and smiled like he saw a puppy he thought was adorable. "Of course, it is. But don't you worry your pretty little head about work. I'm good at everything I do, and your father and Mariano Shipping are no match for my talent." By some miracle, I held back my eye roll when he winked. "And Verana, I do mean I'm good at everything."

Ew.

His smile grew, and I realized he took my shocked silence as awe rather than speechless disgust. As if in slow motion, his hand moved across the table, and I jerked my own into my lap, knocking my fork off my plate. The chime of it hitting the china sounded like the warning bell clanging in my head to get the fuck away from that table.

I pulled my lips back into a smile I was sure looked more like a grimace, but it wasn't getting any better than that. "Excuse me," I said, scooting my chair back. "I need to use the restroom."

It took everything I had to continue to the back and not bolt for the doors and the freedom I desperately wanted from this night. Hiding away in the stall, I took several deep breaths, wondering how long it was acceptable to hide in the restroom before it started to look like I had stomach issues.

Knowing I'd reached my limit, I begrudgingly left the stall and ran cold water over my wrists, looking for any reason to not return to the table.

Mama always said it took time to fall in love, and that father was arrogant too, but tonight I'd reached my limit. And Camden wasn't even the only issue waiting for me. Freaking Nicholas Rush.

God, what if he came over and introduced himself?

What if he pieced together who I was in my connection to Camden? If he thought I was a trashy woman before, seeing me on a date with a man when I'd almost mounted him in the lobby, I could only imagine what he would think.

"Fuck."

I needed to get out of there. At that moment, I didn't care if Camden thought I had diarrhea; if it meant escaping, then so be it.

Two giggling women walked in, breaking me from the staring match I was having with myself in the mirror.

With one last deep breath, I pushed open the bathroom door and headed back.

Like Deja vu, I looked down to close the latch on my purse and bumped into a moving wall.

"Shit. I'm so sorry," I muttered immediately.

Unlike last time, the contents of my bag didn't scatter across the floor.

However, very much like last time, I looked up into familiar dark eyes.

"Shit."

"You said that already." His words rumbled across my skin, mixing with the electric currents his warm hands sent down my arms from where they held me steady. "This seems to happen a lot to you. Running into men. Or is it just me?"

"Hardly." I tried to make my words hard and filled with disdain, but they came out breathy and annoyed at best. More annoyed with my body for the way it reacted to his simple touch and the spicy, woodsy scent of his cologne. I wanted to close my eyes, lean in, and breathe as deep as I could to make the scent part of me.

What the hell was wrong with me?

Pulling my shoulders back, I lifted my chin, ignoring the way his eyes dipped down my body. "Besides, *again*, you bumped into me last time. Probably all the drinking on the job," I added.

"Excuse me," a woman said behind him, wanting to get through. He stepped closer, and I backed up until I hit the wall, the dim lights of the restaurant fading to nothing, his body a dark shadow closing in.

One hand moved to the wall beside my head, and his eyes scanned my face, his jaw ticking under the thick scruff. I tried to stand tall, but all I wanted to do was melt under the heat of his stare.

What was he doing? What was happening here?

I licked at my dry lips, and his growl vibrated in the space between us.

"Nicholas." His name rushed from lips past my panting breaths. My lungs working overtime. Panicked at wanting more. Panicked at getting out.

His lips curled on a silent snarl, and within a blink, it was all gone. He stood back and shoved his hands into his pockets, nothing but a professional who happened to also look down on me and question my morals.

"How do you know Camden Conti?" he asked, his voice hard enough to bring me out of any haze I'd slipped into.

"What?"

Smooth, Verana.

Internally, I rolled my eyes. The question hadn't been expected and hit me like a bucket of cold water, spiking my nerves to life. I couldn't answer truthfully, but I didn't want to lie either.

Instead, I answered as vaguely as possible and hoped social niceties wouldn't have him prying. "He's my father's friend's son. Just an acquaintance."

Who was also my future husband. But I wasn't lying; he really was nothing more than an acquaintance right now.

His jaw worked back and forth, chewing over the information and unsure if he liked how it tasted.

"How do you know him?" I asked before he could push for more.

"The business world isn't as big as you think." He turned to walk away but quickly turned back. "Careful who you go after, Miss Barrone. Some men may not be what they seem."

"I am not—" I started, but he didn't stick around to listen. Before I knew it, I stood alone in the hallway—still needing to go face Camden when all I wanted to do was go home. Only now, I had to do it with the scent of Nicholas on my tongue and a fiery anger close to overflowing.

But fate apparently decided it had dealt me enough bad luck for the evening because when I went back, Camden was just accepting his card back from the waiter.

"I hope you didn't want dessert. I just got a call, and we need to go."

"Oh, no." If he could hear the complete lack of sincerity, he didn't comment on it.

"I can drop you off on my way."

"No, that's okay. I'll take a cab."

"Are you sure?"

So fucking sure. "Yeah. Work is important. I don't want you to be late."

He smiled approvingly like he was proud of me for my new

47

trick. I almost waited for him to pat me on the head when we walked out, telling me how proud he was of his pretty future wife.

"By the way, you'll be attending the gala with me next week," he announced.

I opened my mouth to protest that I had plans with the girls but never got the chance.

"Don't argue and wear something sexy. I want to show off my future wife."

I almost cringed but stopped when I met Nicholas's eyes over Camden's shoulder. Camden leaned in to kiss me goodbye, and I quickly turned my head. His lips still landed against my cheek, and by some miracle, I managed to not jerk away.

"So pure," he whispered against my cheek. A shiver worked its way through my limbs when he pulled back with a smirk and pinched my chin, swiping his thumb across my lips. "Soon."

And with that last eerie promise, he walked away. Without looking around to find Nicholas's reaction, I dove into the waiting car and sent a message to Raelynn to meet me at home.

I needed someone to help me process the night and drink with me until I passed out.

Maybe if I drank enough, I wouldn't dream of Nicholas for just one night.

SEVEN

Vera

"I'm so proud to be your friend right now," Raelynn said, smiling at me like a proud mom as we strolled into the gala. "That dress screams seductive strength and fuck you, *and* you wish you could have this, all in one. The perfect dress for Camden."

I snorted a laugh.

"I mean, the blood-red says I'll kill you and bathe in your blood. But the touch of lace along the back says I'm a lady. But it's the fit, bare back, and flashes of skin that make it so utterly sexy."

I dropped my chin, a blush rising into my cheeks. I didn't usually wear something like this, but when I saw it—after the past month—I had to have it. I liked the way it wrapped around my neck, and the soft silky material cradled my breasts. It wasn't just a deep v down to my belly button; it was like it had been twisted to my hip and threatened to expose my left breast at any moment. I loved it.

"Look who's talking." I gestured to an unashamed Raelynn, throwing in an extra strut in her beige, black, and silver glitter dress. She reminded me of the Black Swan with everything strategically glued in place to cover anything important.

"Yeah, but this is me. I wear shit like this all the time. You, are the muted color cardigan and pearls."

"I don't wear a cardigan and pearls all the time."

"Economics. Sophomore year. You sure did."

"It was cute."

"It was. It fit your personality of goody-two-shoes perfectly."

"I'm not a goody-two-shoes."

"Well, not after all the years with me," she said, delivering a devious wink.

I wasn't. I just always followed the rules. My family was in the public eye, and my mother instilled being a lady. I had fun. I did.

But with my impending marriage to Camden hanging on the horizon, I had to admit, maybe it wasn't as much as I wanted.

"They always go so over the top at these things," Raelynn said.

I looked around the open ballroom of the hotel, the chandeliers dripping with crystals, gold curtains hanging open, pooling decadently on the ground. Waiters wove between patrons almost invisible in their black and white tuxes.

Everyone sipped champagne, lavish fabrics making the most expensive dresses cling to their lithe bodies. Hair styled to perfection, and makeup done expertly even under all their masks.

I adjusted the black lace clouding my vision, making sure it hadn't shifted too much in the car.

"Shots?" Raelynn suggested.

I cringed. The night was still young, and I hadn't even seen my father yet. Maybe shots weren't the best idea. A waiter walked by, and I snagged two flutes of champagne. "How about some champagne first."

Raelynn accepted the glass with a raised brow. "Careful. That stuff will sneak up on you just as bad as tequila."

The bubbles tickled their way down my throat as my mother's words floated through my mind.

Never drink too much at these big events. You don't want to be known as the drunk woman everyone murmurs about. But always have a glass to keep your hands busy. A lady doesn't fidget.

My mother wasn't wrong, either. There was always one or two women who always showed up and got a little too loud. I'd stand back and watch as everyone gawked and whispered behind their manicured hands.

"I'm surprised you came," I said. "I thought you'd still go see Nova."

"Nah. We agreed I should come be here with you. I think Nova is taking the chance to detour to another adventure rather than coming too close to home."

Nova had a small apartment in New York, but each summer she rented a van and traveled around, blogging her adventures. She'd gotten a job with an adventure magazine, and I wasn't sure if she'd ever stop living out of a van now that she got paid to do it. We were supposed to meet up for a girls' weekend outside of the city, but Camden's order squashed that.

"Besides," Raelynn said. "I have an acquaintance hosting another...party here, too."

"An acquaintance?" My brows scrunched, taking in Raelynn's Mona Lisa smile as she scanned the crowd. That smile and the lack of eye contact always raised some red flags with her.

Before she could answer, my dad's booming voice interrupted the quiet bubble we'd created since entering.

"Verana." He leaned in and softly kissed my cheek, reminding me of all the times he'd tucked me in at night as a little girl. I'd been short-tempered with my father since graduation, but I had to have faith that, like Mama said, he would always take care of me—he loved me.

"Father."

"I wish you would have come to the house, so we could arrive as a family."

"My fault, Mr. M," Raelynn cut in.

My father's smile grew tight. He tolerated Raelynn because of her family and their wealth, but he saw her as too wild and a bad influence.

"You look ravishing," Camden said, coming up behind my dad.

I fought my heavy sigh at Camden's compliment. There wasn't anything wrong with it, and from anyone else, I'd smile and say thank you, but annoyance still pricked at the surface from our last meeting.

"Thank you," I managed to ground out.

He stepped close, sliding his arm around my waist, his fingers skimming along the bare skin of my back. My muscles clenched as if trying to pull away from the slight graze.

"And who is this stunning creature?"

Raelynn's lip curled into a smile that resembled a snarl. Camden held out his hand, never unraveling his other arm from my back, and waited for Raelynn to place hers in his. I could tell she wanted to do a lot more violent things with her hand than give it to him, but like me, she'd had too much etiquette drilled into her to ignore his request.

Camden brought her hand to his lips and would have probably kissed it for too long if Raelynn hadn't gently jerked it back.

"This is my friend from college, Raelynn Vos."

"Vos?" Camden studied Raelynn with a little more interest that went beyond lust. "As in Vos Enterprises?"

"The one and only," she said, lifting her champagne in a toast to her family company before taking a long sip.

"Will the Vos family be attending our wedding?" Camden asked me.

"Ummm…" I stuttered. We hadn't even talked about being engaged, let alone the wedding.

"Of course, they will," Raelynn answered for me. "At least I'll be there ready to help her bolt, like the good maid of honor I'll be."

Camden missed the threat and tipped his head back with a loud laugh. "You're a funny one. I look forward to getting to know you better."

"I bet."

"Well, ladies, we should probably mingle and talk business among the men." I blinked to hide my rolling eyes at Camden's condescending arrogance. "Also, I still need to submit the sizable donation the Conti family will be making tonight, of course."

"Of course." Raelynn's smile was small and bland while her eyes narrowed like they were trying to burn him alive.

I covered my laugh with a fake cough, kind of loving her blatant irritation with him. Especially since Camden didn't notice at all. My father noticed, though. His eyes flicked from Raelynn to Camden, and finally, to me, widening as if pleading to get my friend under control. I almost wanted to send one back for him to get his employee under control.

"Cam. I saw Joe Banks by the bar. Let's go introduce you as the newest member of Mariano Shipping."

Camden leaned down and pressed a kiss to the crown of my head, lingering to whisper, "Save a dance for me."

Before he stepped way, his fingertips dragged down my spine, daring to dip below the fabric of my dress, getting dangerously close to the crack of my ass before finally pulling away.

"What a dick," Raelynn announced once they'd walked away. "I can't believe you're going to sleep with that for the rest of your life."

I downed the last of my champagne, setting it on a passing tray and grabbing another. "Ugh. Don't remind me."

"You know...you could still find someone else," she singsonged.

"I don't even want to bother with the effort of it."

"You could try Tinder."

"Ew."

I wasn't a one-night-stand kind of girl. Especially with the creeps I heard about on Tinder.

"What if…"

"What?" I asked when she didn't continue.

She licked her lips and studied me like she was trying to guess my answer to whatever her suggestion would be. "What if I told you another kind of party was happening tonight?"

My gaze narrowed, knowing she wasn't talking about an actual party. The hotel would never be so crass to throw two parties on the same night. Which meant it had to be a Raelynn type of party. Probably illicit and full of bad decisions.

"I'd say that you being so eager to come tonight makes a lot more sense."

She shrugged, unrepentant as usual. "I know someone who works here at the hotel. He runs a little side business for when they host big events like this."

"What kind of side business?"

"A kinky one."

"Oh, boy." I took another fortifying sip of champagne. "Tell me."

"You submit your name and fill out a questionnaire. He will then pair you with someone else."

"Who? And what do you mean pair?"

"Someone to fuck tonight," she stated bluntly. My jaw dropped. Before I could protest, she pushed on. "It's completely anonymous. You won't remove your mask or say any names. Frankly, I've had a few times that I don't even want them to talk. It's like a fishbowl party; you toss your keys into a bowl and never know who you'll get at the end of the night."

"But…what if it's someone I know? Someone old? Someone unattractive? What if it's Camden?"

We both shuddered at the thought.

"It's like an elite Tinder, except he's the only one that sees the profiles. He makes sure not to pair you with anyone too familiar. As for the rest, that's what the questionnaire is for. Hotel room? Random tryst in the garden or on the roof? Spanking? No talking or dirty talking? Anal?" I pulled away with a cringe, and she laughed, holding up her hands. "No judgment. Whatever you're into."

When I didn't immediately say no, she smiled. My heart thundered in my chest, and I twisted my mother's antique ring around my finger.

A lady doesn't fidget, my mother's voice rang in my head.

Sorry, Mom. A lady also doesn't consider letting a stranger fuck her. I finished my champagne and snagged another. "I don't know."

"You don't have to do anything you don't want to. It's just a way to experience someone else outside of Camden without the hassle of actually looking for it."

My eyes darted around the room, taking in all the masked men, wondering if I did this, if one of them would be who I'd be with.

A tall man dressed in black stopped me. As if he could feel my gaze raking across his broad frame, he turned, his dark eyes clashing with mine. I sucked in a breath. His ornate silver mask looked like the top half of a skull. The narrowed eyes created a startling yet beautiful picture. Even across the room, through his mask, I could see his dark eyes sparkling through the thin slits. My body heated under his stare as he made a point to move his head enough to let me know he was looking me up and down.

Something about him, about the way his attention burned me, had a familiar warmth to it like we'd met before.

What if…what if I got paired with him? That had my heart thundering for a whole new reason beyond nerves. A man approached the stranger, pulling his attention away, freeing me from his trance.

I looked over the rest of the room before looking back to Rae when Camden caught my eye and lifted his glass, offering a wink. My cheeks twitched but never quite formed a smile. Could I marry him knowing I'd never really experienced anything? Would I always regret being a perfect lady when I had the chance to not be? Did I want to be celibate until we married? Was *he* being celibate?

A giggle broke free. Probably not.

I remembered the way he called me a good girl before I got in the car after dinner. I remembered the way he called me pure, like I was saving myself for him.

He probably assumed I'd maybe slept with my college boyfriend with the lights out and under the covers. And he wouldn't be completely wrong. My first time had been in college with my long-time boyfriend, and it had been missionary with the lights low. But there'd also been a few others. More than that —just because I'd only had sex like that, didn't mean it was all I wanted. Pure wasn't the word I'd use to describe the fantasies that only came late in the night.

No. I didn't want to save anything for him—especially not my fantasies. I wanted to live those out on my own terms. He could earn my affection later, like my mom said he would. For now, I was ready to deliver a big fuck you to the man who assumed he could boss me around.

Fuck being a goody-two-shoes.

"Let's do it," I said before I could change my mind.

"Yay," Raelynn squealed.

"If anything goes wrong, I'll just blame it on the champagne." I raised my glass, and she tapped hers against it, both of us downing the fizzy bubbles.

I followed her to the lobby and giggled when the alcohol finally reached my bloodstream, making me lightheaded.

She approached a man in a suit behind the concierge desk, and he produced a pen and paper. My eyes widened at all the selections. There was an age block, fetishes, hard limits, and a line for any extra notes. I made sure to write down Camden's name and my father's in the space for requests the match not be, because better safe than sorry. I crossed off the option for a room, wanting to be able to escape whenever. What that meant, I didn't know, but a thrill shot through me thinking about all the places that could replace a room.

Without thinking too much, I slid the paper back to the man and pulled my hand back before changing my mind.

"Instructions will be delivered when a match is made," he said with a curt nod.

Raelynn linked her arm in mine and tugged me back into the ballroom. "You won't regret this. I've never had a bad experience."

"How often do you do this?"

"Why do you think I actually attend these events?"

I thought of all the times she'd gone home to attend a gala with her family over the years. "Damn, Rae."

"Hey, no judgment."

"None at all."

"Come on, brave little toaster. I think one shot is in order."

On our way to the bar, my eyes caught on a familiar silver mask. He stood taller than the others in his circle of conversation, but his attention wasn't on them.

It was on me.

My heart fluttered like a bird trapped in a cage, begging to be set free. A thrill of excitement shot through me, imagining him as the man I got paired with tonight. His head tipped to the side, and I held his stare until a group of people moved between us, breaking the contact.

"Two shots of tequila, please," Raelynn ordered once we reached the bar. With glasses in hand, we lifted them high. "To bad influences."

"To the best influences."

We tapped our glasses and downed the tart liquid, bringing a lime to our lips.

"Hey, I see an acquaintance. Do you mind if I leave your side for a moment?"

"No. Go ahead. I think I'm going to hang out here for a bit." I could use some time in the corner of the bar to gather my bearings.

"Okay. Let me know if you need me."

Surprisingly, only a few minutes after she left, a man approached, sliding a folded card across the bar top, meeting my gaze with a serious one of his own before releasing the card and walking away.

I snatched it up with trembling fingers and swallowed hard, opening it.

Meet me on balcony four.

That was it—nothing else. No time. No instructions or hints about what would happen.

Balcony four was the one on the floor above us. I wasn't even sure if I could get there.

Would I be able to make it to where he wanted me? What if I didn't? Would I miss the opportunity? Did I ask for a redo?

I shook my head. If I let myself, I'd sit there all night, thinking of every scenario, but none of them mattered unless I actually tried. I'd come this far, I needed to go all the way.

Pulling my shoulders back, I gripped the card tight and walked with confidence. If I looked like I belonged, maybe no one would stop me.

I climbed the stairs, and the music slowly faded. The carpeted floor muted the sound of my heels as I approached the closed doors, fully prepared for them to be locked. No one was around when I gripped the handle and tugged, surprised when they opened without a fight. Slipping through the crack I'd created, I looked around to see if anyone noticed, but I was alone. In the dark, I could make out a smaller ballroom with glass doors across the floor, leading to the large balcony.

Twisting my mother's ring again, I took my first step, halting at the loud clip my heels made on the hardwood. Rather than giving in to the tension screaming at me to turn and run, I pushed on. Power and strength surged through me with each step closer to the balcony.

I half expected someone to be waiting for me when I opened the glass doors, but it was merely the dark sky sparkling with the lights of the city. Faint music reached up, and I walked to the railing to find the party right below us. Partygoers mingled on the balcony below, smoking and laughing with friends.

I'd been so focused on everyone else, I hadn't noticed I wasn't alone until two hands with long fingers wrapped around the edge of the stone railing. Arms encased in black caged me in. Heat poured off him, bringing my skin to life before he'd even touched me.

I'd been ready to bolt, to change my mind and demand he set me free when his deep, rich voice ghosted along my cheek.

"Don't turn around."

EIGHT

Nico

"What?"

Her whispered word hit me with a familiarity, just a prick at my conscience before it fell away into the night.

"Don't turn around."

Despite my order, her head jerked to the side, her bold red lips coming into view. As punishment, I leaned down and nipped her ear, soothing it with a lick. Her gasp shifted to a soft oh, her lips forming the perfect circle I wanted to slide my cock into.

"Don't talk." I pressed my chest to her back, grinding against her to let her feel how hard I already was. "Just feel me."

Her chest heaved over her labored breathing, and I ached to tug the fabric aside and bare the hard tips pressing against the thin fabric, but I used restraint, instead focusing on her petal-soft skin as I dragged my fingers up her arms. Goose bumps rippled along her skin, and her head fell forward at the same time she pressed into me.

I'd noticed her as soon as she'd come into the room. Her body wrapped in red, the dress twisted in ways it looked like one wrong move could lead to a peep show. Her dark hair piled on her head had me itching to rip the pins free just so I could watch it cascade down her back.

Half her face was covered by the black lace mask, but the perfect cupid's bow of her full lips reminded me of a woman I couldn't escape.

Verana.

I knew it wasn't her. I'd overheard her at the office, talking of plans with friends this weekend. But in that moment, I wanted it to be her.

So, when I'd made my request, I asked specifically for the woman in red. It wasn't always one-hundred-percent, but the fifty-dollar tip helped. Walking into the upstairs room to find her leaning out against the railing of the balcony, her back bare and begging me closer, I knew I would've paid five-hundred dollars to make sure this woman was the one waiting for me.

For tonight, I'd allow myself this fantasy—just once—to exorcise my demons.

I issued my command to face forward and not speak. I didn't want to take the chance of her mask coming off and breaking the illusion. I didn't want to hear a voice that wasn't Verana's. Maybe tonight would ease the ache—the frustration—and I could put her behind me.

I skated my fingers along the fabric where it stretched across her neck, dropping them to skim the black floral lace that spread along a single shoulder blade like it was reaching for her spine. Her muscles tensed when I dragged a single finger down each vertebra. She gasped when my hands spanned her hips. She was so small, my thumb dug into the ripe flesh of her ass at the same time my fingers pressed into the hollows of her hips. I couldn't wait to hold her here in place as I fucked her hard.

Soon.

First, I wanted her panting and wet. I wanted to know if she tasted as delicious as she looked.

"Hold on to the railing," I said against the hot skin of her neck.

With her fingers pressed to the cement, I jerked her hips back, forcing her to stumble a few steps back. Her back arched and presented her ass perfectly to me.

With the first press of my lips to her back, she arched more, searching to make contact. I worked my lips down as my fingers slowly inched the fitted skirt up. By the time I reached the base of her back, she could barely stand still, rocking side to side to help me move her dress higher while also causing friction between her legs.

"Don't move," I ordered again.

She nodded jerkily, and I dropped to my knees, skimming my hands up her firm legs. Her dress rested just below the cheeks of her ass, and I pushed my fingers under the fabric, shoving it up and over, baring every creamy inch to me.

She tensed, squeezing her thighs in modesty, and I groaned at her sweet scent that hit me.

Only a thin layer of black lace stood in my way, and I considered ripping them off, not wanting to wait a second to bury my tongue inside her, but I liked the tension threatening to snap between us. I wasn't ready to give it up.

I took my time easing the delicate fabric down her legs, directing her to lift her leg to step out of them. Eyeing my prize, I shoved her panties into my suit pocket.

"Spread your legs."

"What?" she gasped.

"I want to eat your pussy. Now let me."

She took two tiny steps out, still hiding what I wanted. With a deep chuckle, I worked my palm back up her leg and gripped her firm ass, holding her steady as I knocked one foot wider. She stumbled in shock, and I slid my hand past her soft cheeks to press her back flat, forcing her to shove her ass in my face.

Finally, the pink wet folds appeared, and every second of drawn out torture had been worth it because she was stunning. My dick throbbed, and I gave a quick squeeze to remind myself I'd be buried there soon.

My hands swallowed her round cheeks, the smooth skin pale under my tan fingers. She thrust back, and I couldn't wait anymore. Using my thumbs, I pulled her apart like the petals of a flower, and without any teasing or warm-up, I swiped my tongue from her clit to her opening, shoving inside.

She cried out and squeezed, her hips pushing forward. She would have pulled away if I hadn't gripped her so tight. With my tongue buried in her wet pussy, I reached around her hips and found the top of her slit, fingering her bundle of nerves.

"So fucking good," I murmured against her skin between fucking her with my tongue.

She pressed down on my hand and rocked back against my mouth, searching each time I pulled away.

I lapped at every inch I could reach, sucking on her folds, licking her wet cum from where it dripped down her thighs.

She panted harder. Her legs shook, and she rocked back, riding my face. It had to be one of the sexiest things I'd ever seen.

Needing to feel the wet heat against my cock, I flicked her clit hard and shoved my tongue as deep as I could. Her hand slammed against her mouth, and her entire body vibrated with each tight squeeze of her pussy pulsing around me. Before she was even done, I worked the buckle of my pants open, desperate to free my cock. The cool breeze did nothing to calm the hot blood pulsing down my length. For once, I was grateful for the extra layer of the condom to help me last inside her. I didn't know who this woman was, but I knew I'd think of her long after the night ended.

She'd be my moment with Verana, and I'd hold it close. I knew it was wrong to be with a woman and imagine someone else, but this whole situation wasn't about respect and caring. It was about fucking a stranger. The illicit excitement of finding someone random and losing yourself inside them with no expectations. It could be anyone, and tonight, I wanted it to be Verana.

With one last swipe of my tongue, I stood tall, teasing between her legs, rubbing the head of my cock up and down her drenched slit.

"Please," she begged. "Do it."

I intended to ease in. I knew she was wet enough, but she was swollen from her orgasm, and I was big. But with her breathy plea, I couldn't hold off. The need drummed inside me like a crazed beat. It was all I could hear—all I could focus on.

One hand gripped her hip and the other her shoulder, I lined myself up and shoved in hard. Her hand slapped back over her mouth just in time to cover her cry.

"Fuck. Shit. Shit," she panted.

Shit. Had I hurt her? I knew the risk, but fuck, I hadn't expected her to be so tight. Her heat clenched like a fist, and when I moved to ease the pressure, she squeezed me like a vice trying to suck me back in.

"I'm sorry. I should have given you more time."

Her hand shot back and gripped my hip, holding me in place. "No. Please. You're just—" she sucked in a breath. "So freaking big. But god, it feels so good. I'll die if you stop."

My ego grew. I knew I had a big dick, but having her stretched out, panting over it stretching her so wide it hurt, but still wanting me to fuck her made me want to beat my chest and rut against her like an animal.

I pulled out slowly until only the tip rested inside and thrust back in, my balls slapping against her. She bit the palm of her hand and pushed back every time I thrust in. Small whimpers escaped but were lost to the night before anyone could hear.

Moving my hand to her neck, I jerked her upright and moved us against the railing, the rough cement digging into her hips. Her head fell back against my shoulder, giving me the perfect view of her ruby lips parted, sucking in air.

"Better be quiet, vixen. Wouldn't want everyone below to know how much you like having your tight pussy fucked by a stranger."

Her jaw clenched tight like that could stop the cries of pleasure she couldn't hold back. Her hand slipped behind us and squeezed my ass, urging me faster.

"You can try to hold back your moans, but nothing can hide the sound of how wet your tight little cunt is."

The wet suction of my length, forcing its way inside her body, echoed around us. I knew no one could hear, but it sank into my blood and heated it further.

"Let them hear."

With those three words, the thin thread on my control snapped. This woman truly was a vixen. I imagined it was Verana, and we were in my office with her pinned against my desk to do what I wanted. I imagined I had control to take my frustration out on her.

I held her like I was trying to meld her to me and pistoned my hips harder and faster. Her nails dug through the material of my suit and stung my flesh, sending lightning bolts of pleasure to my balls.

Her breasts swayed, and I gave in to the need to see them, almost tearing the material in my desperation. Immediately, my hand shot up to cup the heavy weight, pinching the deep pink tip between my thumb and finger. Her other hand held my wrist as if I'd pull away. If possible, she got wetter with each tug and twist. I knew her cum would be on my pants by the end of this, and I may never wash them again, so I could remember the tight squeeze of her body.

"Please. Yes." She whimpered incoherent words of pleasure and begging. When I dipped my hand between her thighs to strum her clit, she dug her teeth into her bottom lip and pressed her palm over it, falling over the edge into her orgasm. Despite her efforts, her cries slipped free, barely masked by the soft music and conversation below.

Her fluttery pulses demanded I orgasm with her, and I was useless to hold back any longer. Not willing to remove my hands from any delicious part of her, I buried my teeth at the base of her neck and groaned as pulse after pulse of cum shot from my body. Coming inside her felt like touching an electrical wire, and my body vibrated and tingled as I slowly came down from the high.

Gently, I brushed my fingers against her clit one last time and around her flushed nipple, loving the shudder that wracked her body. Pulling back, I licked and kissed the bite mark I left in my crazed orgasm. She rested both hands on the railing, her head lolling to the side while she gasped for air. Hating every second, I tugged the material back over her breast, doing my best to rearrange the neck to cover the bite mark. Part of me wanted to demand she leave it uncovered, so when we went back down to make small talk and drink champagne, everyone could see my mark.

We both groaned when I pulled my softening dick free despite her core squeezing like she wanted to keep me there forever. Before releasing her, I issued one last command. "Wait for me to leave before you turn around. Then wait a few minutes to walk out."

She merely nodded, and I struggled to pull back and tuck myself away. She stayed slouched over, leaning against the railing as I fastened up my pants. Her soft skin called to me, begging me to touch it one last time before I left. She may not have actually been Verana, but she had me on edge, barely holding back just like Vera did.

Stepping close, I leaned down and pressed a lingering kiss between her shoulders. "Thank you."

And before I could talk myself out of it, I walked away, refusing to look back.

My plan hadn't worked. I hadn't fucked Verana out of my system. I hadn't fucked Verana at all. If anything, I'd only made myself want her more.

Maybe I needed another round. Maybe I did need to see the woman's face. Lose myself in the stranger. Maybe that was the answer to blotting Verana out. Something about her was off, and I hated that my gut screamed that she was using me while also screaming for me to take her.

I didn't like liars, and the instinct that Verana was lying had me holding back.

With that reminder, I decided to grab a drink and approach my vixen again before the night was over. Surely, I could find a way to convince her to come home with me and help me lose myself.

Before I could even make it down the stairs, my phone rang with a call from my grandfather's caregiver.

At ten o'clock on a Friday night.

Adrenaline flooded my system and had me running down the stairs and toward the door before I'd even answered.

"What is it?"

"Mr. Rush? This is Anthony from Beckett Homes." The aide annoyed me with his pointless introductions.

"What's happening?"

"Oh, sorry for the late call. Your grandfather is very disoriented, and we had a hard time getting him to calm down. Then he began asking to talk to you, getting very upset when we didn't immediately comply, so I figured it couldn't hurt to call."

"Give him the phone." I didn't have time to be polite.

"Yes, sir."

"Nicholas?" My grandfather's frail voice hit me like a ton of bricks, knocking the wind from my sails. I remembered his booming voice when I was younger. His proud laugh. It killed me to hear him so confused and small now.

"Hey, Grandpa. It's me."

"I miss you so much, Nicholas. When will you visit again? I wanted to talk to a manager and figure out where you were. These men kept trying to make me sit down, and I didn't want to. I just wanted to know where I was, dammit."

I climbed into the back of the car, sure my molars would crack at any moment.

"They gave me a medicine, and I said I didn't want it, but

they gave it anyway. My memory, Nicholas, it's not—" He cut off with a frustrated grunt. "I feel like I've lost days somewhere, and I just wish you were here. It's been so long."

It'd been a few days. Not long at all.

"I'll be there. I'm on my way now. Get some sleep, and I'll be waiting for you in the morning."

"Okay. Okay. Does that throw off your plans?"

My mind flashed back to the woman in red.

"I don't want to ruin any plans. Especially if it's with a lady. You need to find a good woman, Nico. Give me some great-grandbabies."

I smiled at the familiar words. He said I was nowhere near as great as I could be unless I found a good woman to stand beside me and raise me to my full potential. I just didn't have time to look for one when I split my time between New York and Charleston.

"No plans, Grandpa. I'm already on my way to you."

His heavy sigh reached through the phone. "All right. Maybe I'll have to set you up. There are some pretty nurses here."

I groaned playfully and relished in his almost familiar laugh.

"I'll see you soon."

"Okay. Love you."

"I love you too," I said.

Enough that I was willing to do whatever it took to build our family business back to its former glory before it was taken from him. Enough that I'd spend another night thinking of Verana—trying to figure out which side of my gut was right—instead of blotting her out with someone else.

NINE

Vera

I DIDN'T MOVE beyond digging my fingers into the cement railing so hard the tips turned white. It took everything in me to not turn around, to not run after him and beg him to do it again. The clip of his shoes on the hardwood floor faded until the soft creak of the door, followed by the snick of it closing, announced I was alone.

My thighs clenched, and my core ached. I'd never ached after sex—never been so thoroughly used that I knew I'd feel him days later.

Who was I?

I'd always had nice sex—romantic sex in a bed with my boyfriend on top of me. We'd done different positions, but it had always been slow and tender. I'd come and enjoyed it, but the memory faded to nothing now that I'd experienced the rough fucking that had just happened.

I had no idea it could be filled with so much passion and desperation between two strangers. I had no idea I'd love it so much—that it would turn me into the vixen he kept calling me. I was careless and brash and bold, uncaring of who heard my pleasure. I wouldn't have cared if everyone below watched and listened as long as he never stopped.

And though I may not have known who he was, my mind conjured an image. I knew his body type. Once I saw the flash of his silver mask out of the corner of my eye, I knew it was the sexy stranger I couldn't stop looking for all night. But when I inhaled his familiar spicy, woodsy cologne, the stranger quickly shifted to Nicholas. My mind had stuttered over the thought, frantically piecing together the glimpses of him I saw, trying to decide if it was actually him. Then I remembered him talking about heading to Charleston this weekend, and I quickly shoved it off.

It didn't stop my imagination from picturing him behind me. It may have been a complete stranger fucking me, but in my mind, it was Nicholas. I both hated and loved it. I didn't want to imagine a man who constantly battled me, but there was no denying our attraction and how much I liked the idea of pleasing him so much. I remembered his moans and grunts of pleasure, the way he latched on to my neck to hide the sounds of his orgasm that he couldn't hold back.

My fingers stroked the tender patch of skin, and I smiled.

Another surprise, I liked how rough he was. I looked forward to going home and finding each mark, reliving the moments he gave them to me.

A loud laugh brought me out of my daze, and I decided I'd waited long enough. Making sure everything was back in the correct place, I turned and headed out, highly aware that I no longer had my panties. It only added to the excitement.

Maybe it gave me a reason to approach him again and demand he give them back. Maybe he'd ask me to earn them.

I knew it was only supposed to be one time, but it'd been too good to not at least try for a repeat. Just enough to get me through my freedom before I was given to Camden.

The chandeliers, candles, and sparkling dresses shined too bright after the shadows of upstairs, and I blinked to adjust. I, of course, looked for my sexy stranger first, but I didn't spot him. Not that I wanted to run to him as soon as we parted. I wanted to be the equally sexy stranger from upstairs. Not a stage five clinger.

No. First, I needed to find Raelynn. She'd know what to do. She'd help me be the vixen and not the good girl. Stepping around a few people, I spotted her across the room, catching her eyes. She was mid-conversation, but when she did a double-take, I knew she could see my flushed cheeks, heated eyes, and faded lipstick from where I chewed it all off. Her eyes widened, and a slow smirk tipped her lips. She made her excuses and walked my way. Before she could reach me, Camden stepped between us, blocking my view.

"There you are."

I blinked, adjusting to the man in front of me. He smiled down, and for once, looked like he saw me, his eyes soft. Immediately, guilt flooded me, and I wondered if I'd made a mistake. The feeling was dashed when I shifted, feeling the tenderness between my thighs. Even with the guilt, I'd never regret what I'd done.

"Hey," I said, trying to give a real smile.

"Dance with me. Please."

He didn't wait for an answer, not that I would have said no. He held my hand and led us to the floor, twirling me once before pulling me into his arms. His fingers splayed along my bare spine, and I tensed, not wanting to replace my sexy stranger's touch with Camden's.

"Have I mentioned how stunning you look? Red suits you."

"Thank you." I tried to keep the confusion from my tone. His comment sounded genuine and not cloaking some pompous meaning.

"So, your father said you went to Wharton."

"I did."

"Is Dr. Mulrooney still there? I always hated his class."

"You went to Wharton?"

"Of course. It's one of the best. I also got my MBA there."

"Yeah." I would have loved to get my MBA, but why bother

when I wouldn't even be using my bachelor's for long. Add in my father's lack of support, and it was a moot point. "And yes, Dr. Mulrooney is still there and still just as difficult."

He let out a low chuckle. "I think I barely passed his class."

"I managed to get out with an A, but it was a close call."

His brows rose. "Wow, smart, and beautiful."

For the first time with Camden, I blushed under his compliment. "Thank you."

He spun me out and tugged me back in. Maybe it was the champagne. Maybe it was my loose muscles from being used so thoroughly. Maybe it was the fact that Camden wasn't being a complete dick, but for the first time since I came home, and my father announced his plans, I didn't hate them. For the first time, I thought maybe my mother was right, and this was the beginning of Camden earning my respect, and maybe our life wouldn't be as hard as I kept imagining. Maybe my father knew what was right after all.

Despite being in my future fiancé's arms and the positive feeling of hope for my future, I couldn't stop looking for the man who'd just fucked me so thoroughly.

"What happened to your neck?"

His question doused me like a bucket of cold water. My hand shot to the tender skin where my stranger bit me, and I tugged the material of my dress back in place to cover it. "Oh." I laughed uncomfortably. "Just this silly dress. It must be rubbing and leaving a mark."

He studied it for a moment longer, like he could see through the material, and I held my breath. But he shrugged and offered a lopsided smile. "Women's fashion always seems so painful."

"Yeah," I said on my relieved exhale.

"Let's walk around and chat," he said when the song ended. "I want to show you off."

This time I didn't hesitate to take his hand, and when I saw Raelynn standing off to the side with confusion marring her perfectly made-up face, I merely shrugged. I couldn't quite explain it myself, so I'd just enjoy it.

By the third group we went to, the positive hope had vanished, and I wanted to go back to the Camden on the dance floor. He certainly bragged about me and my degree. Told everyone how smart and beautiful I was and how he was going to work to win the boss's daughter over. Yet, he never let me speak. Every time someone directed a question my way, he answered for me and went back to treating me like the pretty, little woman he hoped I'd be.

As frustrated as I got, I pushed it down. We were just getting started. We were taking baby steps, and I didn't want to forget the tiny silver lining I saw on the dance floor. Over time, I was sure I'd see more. Surely. I had to keep hoping.

By the end of the night, exhaustion hung around my neck, and I snagged a bottle of champagne on my way out. Not that I needed to because Raelynn greeted me outside with one of her own.

"Damn. Look who it is. My long-lost friend who abandoned me all night. The one who I damn well know has things she needs to tell me but left me hanging before she could. I swear, I almost tackled Camden to get to you. I could see sex written all over your body. And it looked good."

"Rae," I whisper-yelled, looking around for anyone who heard. "Keep it down."

She rolled her eyes. "Ahhh, the good girl is back."

"Shut up."

"Bitch, get in my car and start talking before I start guessing right here."

I widened my eyes, knowing damn well she would, and scrambled into the backseat.

"How'd you escape lover-boy? I thought fo sho he was going to superglue you to his side and kidnap you tonight."

It was my turn to roll my eyes. "I told him I was staying with you tonight since all my stuff was at your house."

She nodded, rolling the privacy window up, and passed me a bottle of champagne. "Drink and talk."

I sipped from the bottle and then sipped from the bottle some more.

"That bad? Because it looked good."

Falling back to the seat, I closed my eyes and sighed. "So fucking good."

"Daaaaamn."

"Yeah. Damn."

"Tell me more."

Heat flushed my cheeks, but then I remembered it was Rae, and she wouldn't judge. Even still, I kept the details to myself, instead opting for the location over what we actually did.

"Again, daaamn. You won the lottery. So, does this mean you'll come to the next party and do it again?"

"No. Once was definitely enough." Unless it was him. I wanted a repeat with him every time. But I believed Raelynn. I think I hit the lottery, and I didn't want to do it again only to have a sub-par experience. I'd hold tonight close and cherish it. If I saw my sexy stranger at another party, maybe I'd forgo the middle-man and approach him myself.

The problem was, would I recognize him without his mask?

No. Once was enough. Wasn't it?

"Well, maybe give yourself a round two tonight," she said, waggling her brows.

"Oh my god," I laughed.

"I'm proud of you." She took a long drink and passed the bottle back to me. "My little, good girl is loosening up a bit."

I chugged the champagne, finishing the bottle, and sat back with a contented smile.

"Maybe I am. A little."

I just didn't know what that meant for me if I let go of the tight control I had over everything. Of the beliefs I was raised on.

But I was excited to find out.

TEN

Nico

"Is it safe to enter?" Ryan called through the crack in the door.

I pried my thumbs from my dry eyes and watched a hand holding a cup of coffee slip through the door.

"I come bearing gifts."

"Come in," I answered gruffly.

He strode through the door with the coffee and a stack of papers tucked under his arm. I barely held back my groan, mentally berating myself for being in this position. Maybe if I'd forgone sleep, I could have been at the meeting this morning and missed this recap I knew was within those papers. The coffee didn't soften what was the uphill battle clutched under his arm.

I'd driven in from Charleston late—or early, depending on how you looked at it. My bed welcomed me at four am after an accident on ninety-five had me sitting in stand-still traffic for almost two hours. When the soft comforter hit my face, nothing was getting me up again for at least three hours. Hence why I missed this morning's meeting.

As much as I hated showing up late, I'd do it all again to see my grandfather light up when I entered the room.

"I researched Troy Shipping," Ryan began, jumping right in. "It's a smaller company with a lot of potential to grow. I can see why you're interested."

Troy Shipping was a good company, but their potential was a minor aspect of my desire to mesh them with Rush Shipping.

"Upon further research, I found you're not the only company interested."

His brows scrunched, and he took a deep breath as if preparing to deliver bad news. Not that it mattered because I knew what he'd say before he said it, and honestly, it was the furthest thing from bad news. It was the carrot making me chase it.

"Continue," I ordered at his hesitation.

"It seems Mariano Shipping has been in contact with them for a while. Almost like they're grooming them for a merge, but I don't think that's what their main goal is. At least not historically. Mariano Shipping is more of a take control rather than let's be partners."

I snorted my disdain.

Of course, merging wasn't their plan. It never was. Even though I was expecting the news, my fists still clenched when he said the name.

Mariano Shipping.

The company that had almost completely dismantled my family's. The company that had taken and taken, leaving my grandfather struggling and overworked at his weakest, breaking him down to the man who faded every day before it was his time.

Mariano Shipping was the reason for my interest in Troy. Obviously, they were a good business decision. I wasn't about to cut off my nose to spite my face. But the joy of snatching a company out from under Mariano filled me with a petty joy. I did it quietly with one of my other companies I'd added to my empire. I did it for me.

That, and there were also rumors that Mariano was hiding a

closet of bad business moves that were slowly bulging out in the open beyond their control. The more I studied them, the more I believed it. To some, it may look like them moving at a faster pace, but when you added the quick purchases all up, it resembled more of a scramble than a strategic plan.

Buying businesses on the edge of a breakout, made quickly, quietly in a manic way. Like a vampire on the edge of death, desperate for any source of blood, even if it was a small, inconsequential animal, unable to stand on its own.

Just recently, they'd hired Camden Conti as their new CFO, and I couldn't help but wonder why. He was let go at his last job for questionable reasons, but he was also heavily connected. It made me assume that what he'd done at his previous company far outweighed his connections. Which made me wonder why Mariano needed those connections over a morally sound CFO.

Mariano looked to be crumbling—quietly and slowly—but doing it on their own. And the pieces fell right into place for me faster than I expected, putting my goal within reach. I had to remember to be patient and not show my hand too soon when I reached out to take it. I needed to continue to wait, just as I had for years.

"Good," I said to Ryan. "Keep looking and notify me if anything changes. What's next?"

"We discussed moving forward with the Sequirus project. They came back to us and listed off three times as much as originally planned within the time limit they originally requested."

"No. We outlined what our process is, and they agreed. I won't compromise our company because they squabbled their time away and decided they wanted more after we'd reached an agreement."

"Would it help to know they offered to double the fee on top of the baseline cost to ship?"

I hesitated, running the numbers in my head. "It still puts us in a position to struggle to meet the demand of other projects."

"About that." Ryan flipped through some papers before

pulling one with scribbled notes to the top. "Ms. Barrone offered an exceptional plan that has a few kinks but could definitely work. She briefly jotted notes of a schedule and organization that is different from what we usually do but has merit. Especially for one created in the moment. With more details and time, she could create a functioning plan." My lip curled at the same time my cock twitched in my pants. "Don't look too excited," Ryan deadpanned.

Even after the weekend—after my tryst with the vixen in red —I couldn't get Verana off my mind. My dreams started with the masked woman in my arms, only for her to turn and tug off her mask to reveal brown eyes that screamed innocence and devilry all at once. I'd hoist her in my arms, and before she could sink onto my cock, she would whisper, "I'm a liar, but I can make it worth it."

Counting to ten, I focused on relaxing my jaw and forcing my cock to focus on the lying part of the dream and not the wet heat.

"Send her in after lunch. She can go over her notes with me, and Angie can take it from there."

Ryan froze, blinking slowly. I liked Ryan as my assistant because he didn't bother hiding his thoughts. I didn't have to worry about him lying because they were always written all over his face moments before they came pouring out of his mouth. It didn't matter that I was his boss; he gave it to me straight.

"Don't." I held up my hand, halting any reprimand about unfairly taking someone else's idea and passing it off. "Angie has more experience, and maybe once we're done with our meetings, she can meet with Ms. Barrone to review everything, and Ms. Barrone can use it as a learning opportunity."

As long as I didn't have to see her every day. The Sequirus project was mine, and I couldn't put myself close to her like that.

Ryan's lips pursed, and despite my logical reasoning, guilt still closed in.

"Anything else?" I asked, brushing it off.

"No. That was the bulk of it. I'll send you the meeting minutes before the end of the day."

"Thank you. Please, send Ms. Barrone in after lunch."

"Yes, sir."

I ignored the irritation coloring his tone and focused on the emails filling my inbox.

I worked through lunch to make up the missed morning, and soon after, a soft knock preambled Verana's lithe form.

"You wanted to see me?" Her tone was cautious but hopeful. Obviously, Ryan hadn't explained my plan. Maybe he had some misguided hope I'd change my mind.

"Come in. Sit. Please," I added as an afterthought.

I watched her glide across the office in her black cropped pants and basic white blouse—pearls lining up perfectly with her sharp collarbone. She sat, and the opening of her shirt shifted. I swear, I almost also moved to see if I could get a glimpse of her cleavage. And that right there was all the reason I needed to stick to my decision to remove her from any possibility of this project.

Her eyes shifted from cautiously hopeful to guarded when they met my cold ones. Her whole demeanor went stiff, ready to defend her secrets.

"I heard you had some ideas at the meeting today."

"I did."

"Do you care to explain?" I asked slowly as if talking to a child. It was immature but added a splash of ice water between us.

"I wouldn't have to if you'd been there. Another wild weekend?" she asked with false sweetness.

I clenched my jaw, wanting to watch her eat her words when I let her know I was with my ailing grandfather. Instead, I didn't play the games I wanted to, cutting right to the chase.

"Fine. Pass on your plan to Ms. Donald, and my team will handle it."

"I'm more than capable of growing this plan."

"I'm sure you are."

Her mouth opened and closed over my condescending smile, too flustered to form a rebuttal. Good.

Her jaw clamped shut, and she pulled her shoulders back. She brushed her hair behind her ear, lifting her chin proudly.

Exposing a deep mark where her neck met her shoulder. Almost like a bite.

Her tongue slicked across her ruby red lips, and as if in Deja vu, my mind flashed to the vixen in my arms doing exactly the same thing. The same shape. The same perfect cupid's bow on top. The same jaw. The same dainty ears.

How the fuck had I missed it? How had I not seen it was her? Had I wanted her so bad that I assumed the similarities were all in my mind?

Was I making it up? Was I imagining it now?

No.

There was too much of the same.

She shifted again, and the mark mocked me—screamed at me that I was a blind fool.

Had she known it was me? Had she planned the whole thing? Was this more of her game?

"Mr. Rush—"

"What the hell are you playing at?" I asked. I didn't stop to think or confirm. My mouth opened, and the need to know poured out.

Her mouth snapped shut, and she jerked back like I'd accused her of secretly being a mermaid. "What?"

"Your neck. The bite I remember giving you quite vividly."

Her hand shot to the mark, and a flicker of heated recognition passed over her eyes, only to be lost to confusion.

I should've stopped. Thought this through more, but the memory of her in my arms pulsed through me, and I had to know if she was fucking with me this whole time. If I could reveal it on my time, then maybe it would dash whatever her plans were.

"Did you plan this whole thing?"

"I don't know what you're talking about."

I laughed, and her confusion shifted to anger. Ready to shove that I knew in her face, I reached inside my briefcase and pulled out her black lace panties I hadn't been able to part with, slapping them on my desk between us.

Her eyes shot wide, and the color drained from her face. Her chest worked overtime, flashing the bite mark on her neck with each deep inhale. She looked around the room as if looking for an excuse to recover that I knew before her eyes slid to mine, wary.

"Where did you get those?"

"I think you know."

Again, her mouth opened and closed as she stuttered over her words, unable to form a single one. Her refusal to admit defeat had my irritation spiking.

"Did you plan on fucking your way to the top?"

"Excuse me?"

"It's too much of a coincidence that you fuck me this weekend and then come in today with a grand plan for one of our biggest projects, you know I'm in charge of. Did you think it would help you get picked for the team if you got my dick wet?"

Blood rushed into her cheeks, her jaw clamped shut, and her eyes alight with fire like she wanted to burn me alive. Playing dumb hadn't worked, so now it looked like she'd use outrage.

She swallowed twice, and I only added fuel to the fire by smirking. Maybe if she got mad enough, she'd slip up and finally admit how she lied.

"I didn't know it was you. If I had, believe me, I would have run as far and as fast as I could in the other direction."

"Please," I scoffed.

"You are rude and cold and—and an asshole."

I leaned back in my chair, feeling victory over her floundering insults. "Big words for a little girl who rode my face and came all over my cock this weekend."

If possible, her cheeks grew redder. She hopped up from her chair and stared down her pert nose at me. "I assure you; I didn't fuck you to get anywhere. I can do it on my own, so don't flatter yourself," she almost growled. Just as quickly, she pulled her shoulders back and pursed her lips like an old, proper, prude. "Now, if you'll excuse me, I have to set up a time to meet Angie. I'll be forgetting any of this happened. I suggest you do the same."

She marched over to my desk and snatched up her panties, stuffing them between her and her notebook, and stormed out.

She didn't slam the door like I'd expected, but nothing about her reaction was as expected. Now that she wasn't right in front of me with the energy of a bomb between us, I thought back to her reactions that looked all too honest to be faked.

But if she hadn't been lying about this weekend, then what was she hiding?

I looked down to where the panties had been.

Damn. I wanted to keep those.

ELEVEN

Vera

I SOMEHOW MANAGED to make it to my cubicle despite my legs shaking like Jell-O. I barely remembered the walk, solely focused on my panties, burning a hole against my chest. I'd bolted from his office as controlled as possible with my chin held high, the world a dull, blurry roar around me.

I fell into my seat and shoved the black lace to the bottom of my bag. Maybe if I shoved deep enough, they'd disappear along with the knowledge that Nicholas was the man who'd fucked me so thoroughly this weekend.

My boss.

My boss, who hated me, had buried his face between my legs and made me come harder than I ever have before.

Maybe I could dive to the bottom of my bag with the sordid panties and get lost in Narnia with them.

Dropping my head to my hands, I managed to bite back my groan. It was one thing to imagine the illicit encounter had been with Nicholas and another thing entirely to actually have been with him. One was a fantasy I didn't have to admit to anyone playing out in my mind. The other was so wrapped up in complicated strings I couldn't see beyond it.

The bruises on my hips from his hard grip throbbed, and I

fought from banging my head against the desk to knock out any memories trying to rear their head.

He'd thought I planned the whole thing. He actually thought I planned having sex with him so he would give me a position on the upcoming project. How could one man make me burn with so much heated desire and raging anger all at the same time?

Oh, how I hated him.

I hated Nicholas Rush.

Part of me wanted to quit now. I didn't need the job. I didn't need the stress of facing him or walking around with a guillotine over my head, waiting for him to find a reason to fire me.

But there was no way I would give him the satisfaction.

It wasn't that I had to face him; it was that he would have to face me and the realization that I would conquer this job on my own. I'd climb the ranks and keep delivering my ideas until he was forced to recognize I succeeded through his company all on my own.

At least until I got married.

My stomach bottomed out, and the bubbling pride simmered to a calm.

I had at least a year, I tried to reason. I'd have time before this marriage took off. We hadn't even announced an engagement. I'd take every second to excel.

My determination came in waves, split up by doubt, and I needed to squash it. Digging in my purse, I clutched my phone, pulling it out and opening my group chat with Rae and Nova.

Me: 911. Who's in town?
Nova: Sorry, babe. I'm in North Carolina.

A picture of her red hair blowing in the wind with the mountains behind her came through.

Raelynn: I'm in London.

Me: What? When did you go there? Why?
Raelynn: When the opportunity strikes, you take it.

Her message was quickly followed by a man's muscular back down to a perfectly firm ass barely covered with sheets in a bed.

Nova: Your pic is way better than mine.
Me: FOCUS!! I need an emergency FaceTime
Raelynn: What's up?
Nova: Are you okay??
Raelynn: Do I need to kill anyone?
Me: I'm fine… physically. I can't dive into it right now. I just need to know you guys are waiting for me when I get off work.
Nova: Always. I was planning on a stop tonight anyway.
Raelynn: You two are my number one. I'm always here. And I'll be up anyway. ;)

Knowing I'd be able to talk to my best friends tonight had my heart rate slowing to a fast gallop over a rushing freight train. Not great, but I'd take it.

I just wasn't sure how the hell I was going to make it through the next few hours. I considered feigning sickness but quickly shot down that idea. That's all I needed, for Nicholas to think I was running. He'd probably assume I was off to plot a new plan to take over his company.

"Hey, guys," Debra, one of the marketing executives, called from the front, pulling me from my woes. "It's that time of the month to do the grunt work. Old projects need to be taken down and filed. Also, the research for new vision boards needs to be organized and put up. I know it's busywork, and we try to rotate, but if someone could volunteer so I don't have to ch—"

"I'll do it," I almost shouted, jumping out of my seat and flinging my hand in the air. I may as well have reenacted the scene from *Hunger Games*; I was so dramatic. I got a lot of wide side-eyes, but the grunt work was done two floors below, and no one went there unless they needed to. It was the perfect escape to get through the day.

"Thank you, Verana," Debra said slowly, probably gathering her wits after I almost threw myself at her.

Before I could follow her out, I remembered Nicholas's demeaning order.

"I just have to talk to Angie, and I'll head down."

I may have to pass my ideas off to someone else, but everyone in that meeting knew who they came from, and I'd keep showing up with more. Nicholas couldn't block me out completely. Eventually, someone would request my presence on a team for what I brought to the table. Consistency always won.

By the time I walked into my house, I could have collapsed. The work hadn't been hard, but the mental battle I'd waged on myself took its toll.

I dropped my bag and trudged to the kitchen, popping open a bottle of wine. I didn't bother to wait for a glass. I lifted it to my lips and let the rich berry flavor explode in my mouth. I took a solid three swallows before I finally grabbed a glass and took both to my living room, where I set up my computer for my much-needed FaceTime.

They picked up immediately. Nova had the mountains behind her through the open doors of her van. Meanwhile, Raelynn sat in an oversized chair, the London Eye shining in the dark through her windows.

They wasted no time with greetings and small talk, instead pushing me to spill what had me calling this emergency meeting. The more I explained, the wider Nova's eyes got, and the bigger Raelynn's smile grew until she was almost bouncing in her seat and laughing.

"Oh. My. Gawd," she practically squealed.

"You did *what?*" Nova screeched.

"Don't worry, Nova. I can hook you up at the next party we're all at," Raelynn joked. Nova's face scrunched up in disgust, and she shuddered.

"You guys," I whined, flopping back on the couch. "What the hell am I supposed to do? I know I still want to work there and show up every day, but hooooow am I supposed to pull it off?"

"Keep going," Raelynn said with a shrug like it was so easy.

I shot up from the couch, grabbing the bottle of wine to top off my glass, looking like a crazy woman with wide-eyed panic. "I can't keep going. Are you kidding me? Hello? Camden?"

"What about Camden?" Rae scoffed.

"You're not even dating yet," Nova added softly.

"He was actually…kind of sweet this weekend. My mom said that she hated my dad when they first met, but they ended up falling madly in love. What if this weekend was the beginning of Camden showing me a more affectionate side? And I ruined it? What if I ruined our future?"

"Oooookay. Deep breath," Raelynn encouraged. "You didn't ruin anything. Especially because you don't owe Camden any explanation about anything."

"He's going to be my husband, and I want this to work. I always knew this was my future and this past weekend showed me a glimpse that my parents were right, and this could work. He's probably a good man under all his bravado. He's probably just set in his ways and needs to adjust to sharing his life with someone."

Nova's lips pursed, and her eyes looked anywhere but at the screen.

"What?" I asked. She sucked at hiding her thoughts.

"Nothing."

"Oh, it's definitely something," Raelynn said. "Probably the same something I'm thinking."

"What?" I asked in exasperation.

"He's…" Nova hesitated, looking around like the right

words were written on her van walls. "I've obviously never met him, but he doesn't seem super great."

I sat up straighter, hating that my friend didn't like him. I got it, but I wanted this all to work out even if I had to force it. I opened my mouth to object when Rae cut in.

"You know we support you no matter what. And maybe he will shift to someone better. But for now, you're not obligated to anyone. If you want to fuck your boss all over the office, all day, every day. You can without having to answer to anyone but you."

I drained my glass in an attempt to coat my dry mouth. Sleeping with Nicholas didn't sound horrible when I remembered our night on the patio. However, remembering our meeting from earlier sounded horrible. My lips twisted at the memory of how rudely he spoke to me.

"It wouldn't matter anyway. He accused me of knowing it was him I was sleeping with to get a position on a new big project he's in charge of.

"What a dick," Nova said.

"Ugh. Men," Rae added at the same time.

"What if…" I started, scared to voice my biggest worry. "What if he finds out why I was really at the party. He was so focused on the fact that it was me, that he didn't even consider to think *why* I was at an expensive charity event among the shipping elite. He'd probably fire me if he knew I lied about my name to get this job."

"Nah," Raelynn said, shrugging it off. "You're still you. You still got the job with your own amazing credentials. You used your grandmother's maiden name. It's not like you created a whole new alias that didn't even graduate high school."

"I don't know."

"You stick to your plan," she said. Nova nodded in the screen next to her, agreeing with Rae. "You push past this, show up every day, conquering that job, and you treat him like he doesn't exist."

"Kill him with kindness," Nova said. "Show him how you kick ass all on your own."

"He doesn't exist, and his cock doesn't exist…even though it was pretty big. How big again?" Rae asked, holding her hands apart like she was guessing the length.

"Raelynn!" Nova scolded.

"Are you sure you have to stop fucking him?" Raelynn asked, only partly joking.

"Oh my god," I said, laughing this time. "Yes. We have to stop."

A knock at the door pulled my attention away from the screen.

"Okay, guys. I have to go. Someone's knocking. Thank you so much for talking me down and helping me through my crisis."

"Anytime," Nova said.

"Keep us updated," Raelynn requested.

We said our goodbyes, and I closed my laptop, heading to the door.

I was a little shocked to find Camden on the other side. I opened it to find him in a Navy suit he probably wore to work that day, sans tie.

"Camden. Hey. What are you doing here?"

He pushed past me and turned right into the living room. "I'm glad you're home."

My brows rose high, and I looked side-to-side like someone else would be looking back with the same shock. I slowly closed the door and met him standing in the middle of my white living room.

"Yeah," I said lamely, not sure where to go with this. "Can I get you something to drink?"

"I'll just have some of this wine. Thank you." He filled the empty glass about half full and drank, scrunching his nose.

"Sorry, it's not a great bottle."

"Yes, well. When we're married, I'll have to take you to a vineyard and teach you about better wine."

I ignored the arrogant tone and instead chose to focus on how he wanted to travel together. "I look forward to it."

He finished the wine in three swallows and set the glass down before digging in his breast pocket. His smile tipped his lips slowly, and the two measured steps closer had my shoulders pulling back. He produced a white envelope, and something about the glint in his eyes warned me that I should just shove it back and say no thanks.

Instead, I tugged the small rectangle from his grip and barely breathed, trying my best to keep my unease hidden.

"Open it."

With a swallow, I slid my thumb under the fold and tugged out the thick cream cardstock.

My brows furrowed as I read our names on the invitation, confused until one word caught my eye. Every ounce of blood dropped down to my feet. A tingling buzz started in my head and spread like ice through my veins.

"What is this?" I breathed the question.

"An invitation to our engagement party, silly."

Engagement party.

Engagement. Party.

Engagement.

No matter how many times I read the words, they didn't change.

"It's in a little over a month."

"I wanted to do it sooner, but planning required more time."

More time? This was not the more time I thought I'd have. I thought I had a year. I thought I had *at least* six months. I thought I had…more.

Irritation simmered in my veins, heating up the ice that had frozen me stiff. "You didn't even talk to me."

"It fits with our schedule. There was no need to discuss it."

"No," I said, dropping the card at my side and pulling my

shoulders back. "It fits with your schedule. You never asked me about mine."

He laughed softly. "You don't have a schedule. You don't work, and I spoke to your father about any charities you may be working on, and there was nothing. Maybe you had a playdate with your little friends, but that can be changed. Your schedule is my schedule."

"I'm not a child," I ground out. "I'm an adult that needs to be consulted on things like this."

His smile shifted, turning mean. With each step he took closer, more warning bells rang. "The only thing you are is my future wife. And as my wife, I expect your attention on me."

He stood less than a foot away. I stood helpless against his hand shooting into my hair and jerking me against his body, holding my face up to his. I gasped at the sharp sting and hated the rush of fear that flooded my body. I'd never been handled so roughly in anger, and the dark glint in his eye terrified me.

"You will be a good wife, right?"

Despite the fear flooding my body, I didn't want to back down. Maybe if I fought softly, he would see. He would understand what kind of marriage we could have. I would set the precedent and pray that he'd follow. "You don't own me," I said softly. "I'll be the best wife to a *good* man. It's a compromise."

He ran his nose along my cheek and squeezed my hair tighter. "Wrong. I will own you."

"You're hurting me."

He loosened his grip marginally and stroked his thumb across my cheekbone. Some of the panic eased, and I hoped it was merely a moment of loss of control. One that wouldn't happen again. When he leaned down for a kiss, I turned my cheek. I couldn't. It was too soon, and he'd scared the hell out of me. We still had so much to discuss and work out. I couldn't kiss him. We needed to talk first.

I opened my mouth to let him know we needed to sit down and talk first when the words died in my throat over a choked gasp. The backs of his fingers skimmed over my breast, turning to pinch my nipple.

"Camden," I cried, trying to pull away.

In turn, he palmed my breast. "So innocent. A virgin, I wonder?"

I couldn't have refuted him if I wanted. Everything inside me retreated to a corner as his hand moved down my body.

"Either way, I'll leave you until our wedding night."

Run. Knee him in the balls and throat punch him and run. Nova and Raelynn's voices rang in my head, but I couldn't move.

His hand slipped between my thighs and roughly gripped me. "But I plan on claiming this tight, young pussy as soon as the ink is dried. As much as I want. However, whenever, wherever I want." He leaned in and bit the soft lobe of my ear. "Whether you want it or not."

With that, he jerked me to him again and pressed his lips to mine like he was trying to mark me. I kept my lips pinned closed and squeezed my eyes shut tight.

He stepped back, and I almost collapsed when he let go. Shifting his cock in his pants, he licked his lips and looked me up and down. "Yeah, you'll be the perfect bride."

I managed to stay upright until the door slammed closed behind him. As soon as he left, I ran to lock the door and fell to my knees, gasping for breath.

What the hell happened? How had I let that happen?

Tears burned the backs of my eyes, and I slammed my fist against the door in frustration.

That wasn't the man my parents said they wanted for my future. That wasn't a man who would change and compromise with a wife.

That was a monster.

He must have been the charming man from the gala to my father. No way my father knew who the real Camden was and would expect me to marry him. He always wanted what was best for me. He and my mother promised.

He couldn't know.

Well, he was going to find out.

Standing on shaky legs, I grabbed my purse and called for a car.

It was time I put an end to this once and for all.

TWELVE

Vera

_____

By the time I reached my father's house, my legs were no less wobbly. But my spine hardened on the drive, adrenaline from the assault mixed with a burning righteousness. I would put an end to this. I'd tell my father about Camden being a monster in sheep's clothing, and he'd end our arrangement.

I stormed inside the foyer, slamming the door so hard, the flowers on the round table shook in the middle of the entryway. A wide-eyed maid came around the corner, but I didn't stop to explain. Instead, stomping down the hall to the office, where my father spent most evenings.

I could have laughed at the way he almost skidded out the door to his office, his glasses perched above shocked eyes, a stack of papers gripped in his fist. I could have if this day hadn't already sapped all humor from me.

"Verana?"

"I can't marry him. I can't."

He blinked a few times at my outburst, looking me up and down. I hadn't checked myself in the mirror before I left, and I could only imagine what I looked like. Tear tracks down my cheeks, my hair tangled, and a mess from where Camden roughly shoved his fist into it. My clothes wrinkled from where I had momentarily collapsed on the floor. My eyes crazed with wild determination.

"What?" he asked once his jaw finally snapped shut, his eyes still concerned. "*Bambina*, what happened?"

Hearing him call me by the pet name my mother always called me, had me almost falling into his arms, begging him to make it all better, like I had when I was a little girl. But disgust over how I got here kept me standing with determination to stop this.

"Camden," I sneered his name, throwing my arms wide. "I can't marry him. I know you and Mama had a good marriage, and I know it can take time. I know you think you chose a good man for me, but Papa, he's not a good man."

I bit my lip to hold back the trembling my outburst caused.

He swallowed and looked me up and down like he was hesitant over his next words. "He will take care of you, Verana," he said, but it lacked conviction.

"No. You're not hearing me," I pleaded. "He *threatened* me."

Papa's jaw clenched and the papers crinkled under his tightening grip. My father loved me—even if he'd struggled to show it after my mother died. He'd never tolerate anyone treating me poorly.

His whole body expanded and grew into the man who saved me from my nightmares. And then it deflated like I'd never seen before. The hurt written all over his face, the sorrow in his familiar dark eyes had me holding my breath. I waited anxiously for him to rage and take my side. I waited for him to angrily state how we were Marianos, and we were not disrespected.

But it never came.

Instead, a shutter came down on any familiar emotion, and he shook his head, waving the papers around like he was trying to shoo an annoying fly. "This is absurd."

Did he not believe me? Something was off, and I wanted to ask him where the worry went, but my emotions ran too high. I had to make him hear me. "It's not. I'm not making it up. H-He threatened me with...*duties* as his wife. Horrible things." I couldn't even bring myself to repeat what Camden promised to do.

My father stood tall and hard—this time missing all the knight in shining armor and leaving a statue I didn't recognize. His face set in a scowl but determined. Alarms blared that it wasn't determination to help me.

"Then be a good wife and do them," he said, his voice rising.

"What?" I stumbled back, his words hitting me like a physical blow. "No. I can't."

"It's not all about you, Verana." Whatever calm he'd held on to snapped, and his lips curled in frustration, his fists tight at his side. "We all must make sacrifices. Now, I—I'm done with this discussion."

My jaw dropped at his outburst, at his complete willingness to let this continue. I was his daughter—his little girl—his *bambina*. What the hell was going on?

I watched him turn and walk away, my vision blurring like it was all a dream. Surely, that had to be what this all was. Surely, the man walking away from me in my time of need wasn't real.

"No," I said, bringing his retreating form back to me. "No, I won't. I won't do it." I shook my head and barely held back from stomping my foot like a child. If he could be someone else, then so could I.

He turned back with narrowed eyes, and he stalked closer like a lion cornering his prey. For the first time ever, I retreated from my father. He'd treated my mother and me like royalty— rarely ever raising his voice, let alone being threatening.

"Don't make me be this man with you, Verana. Don't make me be mean."

"Then don't. Please, Papa," I pleaded, my hands reaching out for the loving father I knew had to be there. "Surely, you can't want this for me. Mama—"

"Isn't here," he cut in, his hand slashing through the air

before digging his finger into his chest. "I am, and I'm ordering you to marry Camden."

His face colored red with anger, and I knew the man I'd come to for help didn't stand before me. My chest heaved over the panic that I didn't recognize him. This was a stranger, and I'd never felt more alone in the realization that he didn't care, that I was stuck. My eyes looked left and right around his angry form, searching for a way out of this. Searching for someone to pop out and tell me it was all a joke—for my father to laugh and pull me into his arms and apologize for scaring me.

But it was just me.

"Why are you doing this?" Something had to be wrong. Something had to be forcing him to be this man with me.

He swallowed but held strong to the shield blocking me out. "Because it's what must be done for the company, and that is your job."

"I can marry someone else. There has to be a balance between what is good for the company and what is good for me. There *has* to be."

"There isn't because Camden is who I've decided is the best fit, and you *will* marry him."

I slid my eyes closed and remembered the scowl on Camden's face as he promised to own me. I remembered the way his fist dug into my hair, the way he touched me without my permission.

I never truly talked back to my father. I never had to beyond a few petty arguments. I was the good girl. The obedient daughter who never complained about the future set out for me, even if it wasn't what I wanted.

But that was because he'd always been in my corner, standing behind me.

Pulling my shoulders back, I stood tall. I couldn't afford to be the good girl who never talked back right now. No one else stood in my corner anymore but me.

"And if I don't?" I asked, my voice strong but quiet.

"Th-then I'll cut you off," he stuttered, flustered a moment with my response.

"Fine. I don't need you, anyway." While he stood shocked with the turn of events, I stood taller—more confident. "I'd rather be poor than forced into a marriage with that monster. I'll leave and never look back."

He collected himself quickly at my challenge. His already dark eyes grew darker, but I saw the indecision that lurked in the depths. I hesitated for a moment, thinking that maybe it hinted that my father was still there, not this stranger.

I was wrong.

"Verana…" he barely said my name and prowled the last two steps until he looked down his nose at me, all signs of a father gone. "There is nowhere you can go that I won't find you and drag you back kicking and screaming. You *will* marry Camden."

I'd heard about this side of him. The shark in the business world. The man who conquered all and rose to the top even when it meant being hard. But never with me.

Why? Why was this happening?

Feeling the loss of his support took more wind out of my sails than anything else. Unable to stop them, tears burned the backs of my eyes and slipped free.

For a moment, Papa softened. He ran a hand through his salt and pepper hair and sighed. "Maybe I can talk to him. Maybe if you make him happy, he'll allow you to work, and you can be a part of the company."

He'd *allow*? Like it was a privilege to work at the company I was qualified to work at? The company that had *my* family name on the building.

This wasn't what was promised. This wasn't what was explained at bedtime. This didn't end with us dancing in the kitchen one day. This was selling myself for anything, and anywhere in the hopes he'd *maybe* allow me some basic decency.

My father finally softened, the dangerous challenger from a

moment ago fading to reveal that one I'd been searching for. But it was too late.

Allow.

Allow.

Allow.

Each time I thought the word, the fire grew inside me. It exploded like a bomb, heating every inch until I was sure I'd combust myself.

"Fuck him," I snarled, leaning in so he could feel the rage pouring off me. "And fuck you too. Mama would be ashamed of you."

I heard the smack before it registered. It rang out in the hallway, the perfect preamble to the burning sting of the back of his hand across my cheek.

The pain didn't only stay on my cheek. It sunk into my chest and squeezed so hard I was sure I'd stop breathing. I covered the hot spot and looked at the man before me. Maybe he was a monster just like Camden, wearing sheep's clothing as well.

His chest worked overtime; his jaw clenched tighter than his hands. But his eyes swirled with their own battle. Rage, regret, sadness, frustration. I saw it all, and none of it mattered. We'd both gone too far.

"Get out," he ordered—pleaded.

Still holding my hot cheek, I stumbled back the way I came, not stopping until I cleared the door.

Tears clouded my vision as I fell into the backseat of the car.

"The liquor store, please," I choked out. I didn't have enough alcohol at my house to go back to. I wasn't sure there was enough alcohol in this city to help with tonight.

I opened my phone and tapped the group message with Raelynn and Nova, but I couldn't begin to find the words to explain the night. So, I locked my phone and slid it in my purse. I'd talk to them eventually, but everything was too raw tonight. I could barely process it myself.

I ran into the liquor store and saw the bottles of champagne.

It hadn't been what I wanted but seeing them reminded me of the last time I felt free, the last time I considered myself in control of my future.

The last time I felt pleasure.

With Nicholas.

Realization hit me like a tidal wave. I wouldn't get my chance to keep working at Rush and prove to him what an asset I was. With my engagement party in a month, the cat would be out of the bag. My name would be revealed when Camden, no doubt, shouted it from the rooftops and got the most publicity he could out of it. I'd have to quit before I could even get started.

Grabbing two bottles of the champagne, I decided to bite the bullet and quit before I was forced out and revealed as the liar Nicholas accused me of being.

At least I could do it without the watchful eyes of the office.

It was late, but my badge should work. If it didn't, then it wasn't meant to be, and I'd march in tomorrow, in front of everyone, and quit, leaving my head hanging low. The image of packing up my desk with everyone's eyes on me made my skin crawl.

Please, let my badge work.

I lifted the first bottle to my lips and clung to the other like it would save me before making my final stance for the night.

Maybe my final stance ever.

"Rush Shipping Industries, please."

THIRTEEN

Nico

FOR EVERY HOUR I was late this morning, I spent two working after.

And yet, I still had a mountain of emails to get through and files to look over. Maybe because all day my mind kept straying to Verana.

Now that I truly knew she was the vixen from the weekend, it took on a whole new meaning. Any thought of finding the woman and hoping she'd wipe Verana from my mind vanished, and all I saw was her. I saw her in my bed. I saw her peel the mask away as she sank to her knees. I saw her in my office, over my desk.

Fuck.

It was one thing to imagine and another thing to know. Now my fantasies came with a feeling that had been etched so deeply in my memory, I knew it would be with me on my dying day. Her heat, her soft skin, her moans vibrating up her neck against my lips, her hands clinging to me.

How the hell was I supposed to make it through day by day knowing all that?

Her parting words that she suggested I forget it like she would, had me both grateful and wanting to prove her wrong.

That night was anything but forgettable, and my male pride reared its head, demanding a repeat.

The trilling of my phone pulled me from my thoughts.

My private lawyer's name, Archer, popped on the screen, and I scrambled to answer it. His sole job was to work on helping me complete my revenge and takedown of Mariano Shipping. The fact that his father had lost his job when Lorenzo dismantled our family company, added to his determination to reach a mutual goal.

"Archer," I answered.

"Nicholas," he responded, and just from my name, I knew he didn't have good news. "The shares went up, but the sale fell through."

"Son of a bitch."

This had been a rare chance at a larger chunk of shares. It'd been an opportunity I hadn't expected, and I'd stupidly got my hopes up that my plans would be achieved sooner than planned. Now the finish line stretched further than before, and after the day, it only added to the exhaustion.

"I'll keep my eye on them to see if anything changes."

"Thank you."

And with that, he hung up, leaving me with my disappointment and defeat. I dug my fingers into my eyes, trying to ease the headache I couldn't seem to shake.

The phone rang again, this time my office line. I considered not answering it, not wanting to deal with another task today, but picked up anyway.

"Hello?"

"Mr. Rush, sorry to disturb you so late," Hank, the front desk security, said.

I looked at the clock, seeing it was after nine. Where the hell had the time gone?

"What is it?"

"Ms. Barrone just came in, and I thought you should know. She uhh…had a bottle of champagne. She tried to hide it but didn't do too well of a job," he explained with a laugh like he found her attempt cute.

"Did you confiscate it? Stop her?"

"Uhhh," he hesitated. "No, sir. She seemed harmless and had a card. But I wanted you to know as it's so late."

"Thank you."

I hung up and shot from my chair, charging for the door, ready to take my frustration out on someone other than myself.

What the hell was she playing at? Was she meeting someone else for a romantic rendezvous? Not in my fucking office. It was time I caught her red-handed in her lies. It was time for her to confess she was just like I thought, trying to woo her way to the top.

Despite knowing I'd finally catch her, I slowed. I realized I didn't want to be right.

Feeling less victorious than I thought, I made my way toward the dim light coming from the cubicles. Soft clatter and shuffling let me know she was there. Was she with someone at her desk?

"What the hell is going on here?" I growled.

She popped up with a gasp, her brown hair swaying with the jerky move. The dim lighting didn't let me see her well, but even from afar, I could see she looked in disarray. Her hair sloppier than ever, her makeup smudged, and her shirt wrinkled with a few extra buttons undone. A hand slapped to her chest like I'd startled her, but she quickly recovered.

"Oh...hi." Her soft greeting was quickly followed by a giggle.

A fucking giggle.

What the hell?

I rounded the corner, ready to find out who she had with her, only to find her alone with a box that held her measly belongings.

My brows furrowed. "Are you...packing up?"

"Yup," she said with a snap of the p, completely unrepentant. She lifted the bottle of champagne, clutched in her other hand, and took a swig, facing back to her desk. Just as quickly, she turned over her shoulder. "I quit. By the way."

As if she hadn't dropped a bomb, she went back to organizing papers in a folder and adding them to the box.

"What? Are you drunk?"

"Sure am. Want some?" She offered me the bottle, and my lip curled in distaste.

Was that…Cooks? I turned my nose up at the bottom shelf champagne. Shaking my head and pushing the bottle away as if it was diseased, I focused on getting some answers. "Ms. Barrone, what the hell is going on here?"

"I quit," she said again. She turned and leaned against the desk, dropping her eyes to her toe sliding around the floor. "Figured I'd clean out without an audience. Not that I have much with all of the two months of freedom."

She scoffed the word freedom like it was a joke to her. Her hair fell over her face, only leaving a view of her lips twisted in derision. What the hell had happened between now and our meeting? She'd handled the knowledge it was me at the party so much better earlier. What had changed?

Seeing her defeated, begrudgingly softened my accusations against her—that and finding her alone. If I absolutely had to admit, maybe she was a good worker. And maybe I didn't want her to quit, especially because of what happened.

"Look, Verana." I sighed, dragging my hand through my hair. "You don't need to quit because of earlier."

Her shoulders shook, and I froze, bracing for tears I hadn't expected. I stood like a dear in headlights until she looked up, and I realized she was laughing.

"Oh, no. It's not because of *you*." She said it like it was the craziest thing I'd said to her ever, and my irritation roared back. "My future husband won't *allow* me to work. So, with my impending engagement—that I had no say in, by the way—I figured I'd quit now."

I had to close my eyes to even try to process the wealth of information she announced. But one word made its way to the forefront of my mind: engagement.

If I thought I was angry before, it didn't come close to the rage at thinking of her with someone else.

"Were you seeing someone when we slept together?"

"No." She shook her head hard, her hair whipping back and forth. But then she shrugged and tipped her head. "Well, not *really*. It's kind of arranged."

"That's barbaric."

"Right? But it is what it is." Her energy fell away, and her humor vanished, her shoulders dropping in defeat. "I thought it would be fine, like my parents' marriage. I thought it would work out. At least until he showed up and was a giant dick."

She pushed her hair back and finally looked directly at me for the first time. Standing so close, I could see a red discoloring on one side of her cheek, and fury ignited inside me. I stepped forward, like I was readying for battle. "Did he hit you?" I asked, dangerously soft.

She touched her cheek before quickly dropping her hand and rolling her eyes. "Not like you'd care."

"I do not condone abusing women."

"Well, it wasn't him." Another shrug like she wanted to pretend it wasn't a big deal when the reality was too much to bear. "My father didn't take it well when I said I wouldn't marry Camden. He took it even worse when I threw my dead mother's disappointment in his face."

Another barrage of information, and I fumbled to process it all. But her struggle to hide her pain pushed all of it aside.

"Verana…"

"My future husband assaulted me, and my father still wants me to marry him. Seems about par for the day."

Finally, the first tear fell, only to be quickly wiped away. Instead of freezing like I had before, a sharp pinch pierced my chest, and I had to force myself to stand still, despite wanting to comfort her.

"What do you mean, assaulted?"

"Nothing." She took another swig of her champagne and plopped it down on the desk with a loud thud, turning back to packing up her belongings. "By the way," she said over her shoulder. "My real last name is Mariano. I used my grand-mother's maiden name to get the job since my father forbade me from working, you know, because of the future engagement and all that. He said he'd blacklist me, so I worked around him."

Thankfully, she had her back to me, missing the information hitting me so hard, I stumbled back a few steps.

Mariano.

Holy. *Fucking.* Shit.

Holy shit.

She was Verana Mariano.

Lorenzo Mariano's daughter.

Under my nose this whole time.

Of everything that came pouring out tonight in this small cubby, this almost brought me to my knees. She'd been hiding something, all right. She'd been lying this whole time. I just hadn't been looking in the right place. No wonder she knew so much about shipping. She'd grown up in it.

My mind whirled with thoughts and ideas like a computer screen with windows opening and closing as I considered and rejected ideas. Missing out the stocks factored into each one, and the hope that vanished earlier slowly seeped back in. One idea piqued my interest, but I needed more information before shut-ting it down.

"So, let me get this straight," I said in the strongest voice I could form around my shock. "Your father wants you to marry Camden Conti, his new CFO. And you don't want to. And you used a fake name—"

"My grandmother's name. Not fake."

"You used a name that isn't legally yours so you could find a job in the shipping industry without Lorenzo blocking you?"

She stopped but didn't turn. "Yup. Sums it up. Lucky me."

"Why here?"

At this, she did turn and gave me the full force of her dark eyes and delicate lips. "K. Rush Shipping is less known. Recently brought to the forefront of the industry and acquiring companies to grow—like Pacman," she said with a giggle—even adding the chomping motions—before sobering to continue. "You're on the cusp of being huge, and I wanted to be a part of it. Also, you had very little interaction with Mariano Shipping, so I assumed you'd be less likely to figure me out."

My chest puffed with pride at her analysis of my company. She had no idea about the full history of the company. She didn't know what the K signified. I'd worked hard to hide it in plain sight. But the future she laid out was all true and all because of me.

I watched her, the giggly, frantic energy from before gone, leaving a tired girl in its place. Defeat clung to her, and she wore it uncomfortably. I didn't blame her. From the small time I'd known her, Verana Bar—Mariano, wore her strength like an armor. She stood tall with her back ramrod straight as if daring anyone to doubt her. Her pearls, cardigans, and sweet smiles presented a kind woman, following the rules, but somehow, with me, I saw the fiery determination beneath. She may follow the rules to a t, but she didn't want to.

The idea from earlier expanded with the added information. It shifted and grew like a snowball down a hill, picking up pace, racing to an answer. It was a risk with zero facts behind it, but most elites distributed shares to members of their family. Surely, Verana had some too.

Before I could think it through and fully weigh the pros and cons, my lips parted, and blurted it out.

"Marry me."

Her head jerked back. "What?"

"Marry me. If you marry me, you can't marry Camden." I practically sneered his name. She seemed to just be discovering what an asshole he was, but I'd always known.

"I—I can't. My father—"

"Can't hurt you under my care," I interrupted, daring to reach out and run my finger along her reddened cheek. Electricity shot down my arm, and I struggled to remain still.

"Nico," she breathed the nickname only my parents called me, and pleasure mixed with the jolt, creating a dangerous concoction I shoved aside. Now wasn't the time. I dropped my hand and shoved both hands into my pockets to keep from repeating the process.

"Listen, Verana. Leave the box. Go home and think on it. Take tomorrow off. Then come to my place tomorrow evening for dinner, and we can discuss it more. It's been a long day, and this isn't a discussion to have after a bottle of champagne."

"Two," she muttered.

My brows shot high. Two bottles in her tiny body? Jesus… would she remember this tomorrow? Ignoring that for now, I pressed on.

"Come on. I know it sounds crazy, but just…think on it and promise we can talk." I struggled to keep my tone neutral and not plead for her to accept the crazy idea.

God, it was so crazy. But it was crazy with a chance of victory—to replenish the opportunity I just lost. And I hadn't gotten as far as I had without seizing every opportunity I had.

"Ummm…" She shook her head, pinching her eyes shut, and I took my chance to push the box to the corner. Not wanting to startle her, I gently rested my hand on her hip and guided her away from the cubby.

She let me lead her to the elevator and stood in silence, waiting for it to come. I glanced her way, watching her study the floor like it had the answer to the question I asked. Her lips pursed, and her brows pinched. I studied her like she did the lines in the hardwood, and I wished I knew what went on in that head of hers.

The doors slid open, and she stepped in. Before they could close, she finally spoke, "But you hate me."

Maybe it was the hope she wouldn't remember from all the alcohol or the raw honesty that had spilled around us tonight, but my tongue loosened, and my admission slipped free. "I don't hate you. Far from it. I might even admire you a little."

In the final moment, before the doors slid closed, her lips tipped in a shy smile.

With her gone, the reality of what I'd just offered roared around me.

My blood pumped harder, adrenaline flooding my veins. I'd asked Verana Mariano to marry me. She hadn't said no. The daughter of my enemy had been under my roof this whole time, like a gift I'd yet to find.

Of all the emotions and doubt swirling around me, excitement hit me the hardest.

I just didn't know if it was because I had an ace up my sleeve to take down my opponent or if it was because my ace was *her*.

FOURTEEN

Vera

Unknown: I'll have a driver pick you up at 6:30.
Me: Who is this?
Unknown: Nicholas Rush
Me: How'd you get my number? Or my address?
Nicholas Rush: It's in your file.
Nicholas Rush: Or did you lie about that too?
Me: No.
Nicholas Rush: Good. See you then.

He didn't ask if I still wanted to come or if I had any plans. He commanded.

Surprisingly, after the last twenty-four hours, I didn't mind.

I'd waffled all day. I'd stumbled home last night and passed out, his offer barely touching the alcohol. However, when I awoke this morning, it slammed back to me like another painful slap to the face.

Along with shame, embarrassment, anger, and a whole hurricane of emotions.

I'd considered calling the office and telling him that there was no way I'd even consider his offer, but I always stopped, knowing it was a lie.

How Camden treated me, left its mark. While I may have drank until my face tingled, I'd checked my locks twice and slid a chair in front of my bedroom door just in case. And my father. I didn't even know where to begin. Something lingered behind it all that I couldn't see but knew was there—like an ominous shadow. Whatever it was, I didn't care to find out. I wanted no part of it. I'd gone to him for help, and he'd hurt me. My own father. My Papa.

There is nowhere you can go that I won't find you and drag you back kicking and screaming.

His words played on a constant loop, stopping me from packing a bag and running. All my doors closed just as I tried to open them.

So, just as fast as I'd dialed the office number, I set it aside and went back to pacing my apartment.

I'd also picked up to call Nova and Raelynn just to toss my phone in a drawer and walk away. They'd have questions I didn't have answers to, and I had enough crowding my mind without others there joining in. I decided to wait.

So, when his order came without question, I'd almost been relieved at having the decision made for me. Besides, I could always walk out.

The driver was professional and cordial on the drive over, nice enough to not comment on my wringing hands and tapping foot.

Knowing Nicholas didn't spend all his time in New York, I was shocked to be pulling up to a fancy building on the edge of Central Park.

I said thank you to the driver and made my way to the glass doors, my heart thudding a million miles a minute. As fast as my heart raced, my legs slowed.

This was stupid. I should hail a cab and run.

He probably just wanted me to come over so he could fire me in private. He wanted to let me know he was sorry, but last night had been a mistake, and he wanted to let me down softly.

Because it *was* a mistake, right?

I shook my head in the middle of the sidewalk, not caring of the looks I got from passersby. This was crazy.

I took one step back when the memory of Camden's cruel words, and my father's harsh slap had me standing still.

Even if the whole thing blew up in my face, and I walked away without a job, still set on a path to marry Camden, I had to at least try. I had to know I'd at least listened to all my options.

With my chin high, I walked through the glass doors into the exquisite lobby. The concierge sent me to the top floor, of course. The doors slid open to a small lobby with one door behind a round table holding flowers. The lobby looked like an illusion to the man I knew resided behind the door. The soothing creams and soft, warm lights hid the cold man who lived here.

Leaving it behind, I knocked on the door and held my breath, waiting.

The door opened to a version of Nicholas I'd never seen. He still wore his pants and shirt from work but stood barefoot on the soft gray wood floors, his tie long gone, and top buttons undone, revealing a smattering of dark hair.

Had I ever found chest hair so sexy?

All of a sudden, my fitted black slacks and starched white shirt screamed overdressed.

"Verana. Welcome," he said when I stood there even after he stepped back.

I swallowed and snapped into action, taking the final steps over the threshold, leaving the illusion behind.

"Vera. You can call me Vera."

"Vera, then. It suits you."

"Thank you."

He took my purse and set it aside on the entryway table before leading me further into the apartment. Surprisingly, while the colors weren't warm, it didn't have the chill I'd expected. The gray couch begged to be slept on with its fluffy pillows and throw blanket. I wanted to slip out of my pumps and dig my toes into the cream area rug designating the living room in the open space.

All of it said comfort, even if it did look impersonal.

To top it all off, the sun going down over Central Park made everything else almost irrelevant.

"This is beautiful."

"Not a bad view. I'd offer to eat outside, but it rained earlier, and humidity is making the summer heat close to unbearable."

"Of course."

"The dining room's view isn't bad, though."

The wall of glass extended the entire length of the open room, encompassing the living room, dining room, and modern kitchen.

I followed him to the long wooden table. "Do you have many guests?"

"No."

"Oh. It's just a big table."

"I didn't pick much of this out. I had a say in the bedroom, office, and living room since I spend most of my time there. Otherwise, I left it to the designer."

"Oh."

So eloquent, I scolded myself, fighting to keep from rolling my eyes.

"Wine?"

My lingering headache almost had me saying no, but my tight shoulders and tingling nerves had me nodding my head.

Dinner melted on my tongue. By far, one of the best risottos I'd ever had.

"This is phenomenal."

"Thank you. My grandmother loved to cook and made sure I knew all her recipes."

"*You* made this?" I almost spit my food out.

"I'm a grown man in his thirties. I know how to feed myself."

"I kind of just assumed you ordered out."

"I do, for the most part, but it's mostly for convenience. I don't have time to cook like I want to."

"Well, thank you for this. It really is amazing. My mother made an amazing risotto, but she never taught me."

"Maybe I can show you one day."

My eyes lifted to his across the table, the first hint of our conversation to come settling between us. His full lips slid across his fork, and his sharp jaw flexed under the thick scruff he wore so well.

With the sunset behind him, his dark eyes held none of the glints of hazel I'd seen before. They looked so deep I could get lost in them if I went too far.

I dropped my gaze back to my plate, trying to ignore the warm rush in my chest. He may have been relaxed, but we met on his turf. I needed to treat this like a business meeting on enemy territory. If the last day taught me anything, it was that I needed to stand on my own. I needed to let go of the fairy tales and hope that it'd all work out.

Conversation died a quick death after his comment. I avoided eye contact, and the longer the meal dragged on, the more worried I became that he really would say he'd made a mistake and fire me. Maybe I read his comment wrong.

From the corner of my eyes, I watched him calmly set his napkin across his plate and lean back in his chair. I didn't have to look up to know his eyes were on me. I felt them, like a burning touch—like a whisper urging me to look up and face the truth.

Shit. He was going to fire me. Why couldn't he have just let me walk out last night?

I held my breath, but when spots danced in front of my eyes, I let it all rush out and sat up, lifting my chin, ready to conquer the situation no matter what it held. "Look, if you're going to fire me, then just do it. I was drunk, and you were shocked. I understand if you changed your mind. You don't need to soften the blow with dinner and wine."

His lips tipped softly as if he found my rant amusing.

When he still didn't say anything, I slapped my napkin down and waited. "Well?"

"I wasn't wining and dining you to soften a blow. I was just hungry and thought we could eat before talking about anything too serious."

"Oh…" Back to being the eloquent graduate from Wharton. Awesome. "So, you still mean what you offered?"

"Yes."

Our eyes locked as if waiting for the other to flinch first. In the end, it was me because one question burned that I couldn't figure out in all of it.

"Why? Obviously, I get out of a marriage to a monster. But, then again…" I hesitated, considering something for the first time. "What if I'm just jumping from the frying pan into the fire, aligning myself with another monster?"

"I assure you, I'm not. Camden is…" The muscle in his jaw ticked as he assessed his words before speaking. "Less than savory in this world."

I scoffed. "Yeah. So, back to my question. What do you get?"

His tongue slid across his lips, and I became dazed with the simple action. "For one, I don't like Camden. I can admit taking you from him has its own appeal." He shrugged, unapologetic. But then he sat taller and ran a hand through his hair like that was the simplest of reasons. Prickling awareness tickled down my spine and whispered that maybe he got more out of this than he was admitting. However, it quickly dashed away when he shrugged again, his shoulders softening. "Also, it's convenient. My grandfather is ill, and my only living family. It could do him good to see me with someone—he's asked for it enough. I want to make him happy."

"I'm sorry to hear that."

"Thank you."

"It still seems like not enough reason to marry someone," I said slowly. I didn't want to talk him out of it, but I couldn't believe someone like Nico would marry a woman out of the kindness of his heart.

He worked his jaw back and forth, taking a deep breath. "There are many events, and having a wife at my side makes me look more stable."

"And there's no other woman you could offer to marry to be by your side?"

He smirked, looking down to where he twisted his wine glass by the base. "I'm sure there are, but having one who understands the business adds a tally in your column."

"Lucky me."

"Also, as you know, this industry can be small, despite being so large. I can admit that having a Mariano as my wife would open K. Rush to a lot more opportunities."

"Fair enough."

The conversation dwindled again, and we entered into another pseudo staring contest. Again, I caved first.

I could have won, but the longer I looked, the more heat flooded my veins, and I didn't want to confront the way he made me feel. He was my boss, the asshole who doubted me at every turn. The one who questioned my morals and work ethic. The one who tried to take my ideas from me.

"So, what's next?"

He got up and walked to the kitchen island, pulling a stack of papers. "I had a contract drawn up. Kind of like a prenup."

"Okay. That's good." Rules were good. It kept us in line. It made it clear where we stood.

"We stay married for at least five years. If it suits us to stay together longer at the end of five years, we can discuss it then. If at any point in the five years you feel unsafe, you may leave."

"Thank you," I said softly.

He nodded and kept going. "In that time, no children will be brought into the situation. When it ends, we will leave with the assets we brought into the marriage. If we acquire anything together in those five years, we will do our best to split it evenly."

"This all seems straight forward."

"One last thing. We will both remain faithful to each other. There will be no affairs, quiet or otherwise."

I scoffed, giving him my most dubious stare when all he did was raise an arrogant brow. Nicholas oozed sex. Not wanting to touch that subject with a ten-foot pole, I returned to scanning other portions of the contract. "What's this? The marriage needs to be consummated?" I shrieked. My eyes shot up, waiting for him to elaborate because surely it didn't mean what I thought.

"I want this marriage to be true in every sense of the word. We may be going into this because of the convenience for both of us, but I want us to be partners. This is five years of our lives with a commitment to one another—a commitment that will only be solidified if we're both…satisfied. You will be my wife."

"You don't own me," I stated, but the words came out weak. Something about him calling me his wife hit me harder than anything else that had been discussed. It brought reality crashing through my thin bubble, masking this with a veneer of business. What stole my breath the most was how much I liked hearing him say it.

"I never said I owned you. Your choices are your own. You're free to work and continue with your life as normal—just with me as your husband."

"I—I'm not sleeping with you. You can't legally put that in a contract." Could he?

Would he be Camden and think he had a right to me however and whenever he wanted?

Nicholas smirked, the look shooting straight to my core, making a liar out of me. "Again, I need to remind you. You seemed to have enjoyed it the last time. Why not do it again? And again."

"I didn't know it was you."

Why wasn't my voice working like I wanted it to? Why was it so breathless?

"Well, have no fear. I won't force you."

He stood. His broad shoulders and hard body towered over me as he walked close, the words a façade for a lion amusing itself with its prey.

By the time he reached my side, my chest worked overtime, heaving from my panting breaths. One arm rested on the table and the other on the back of my chair. He caged me in, leaning into my personal space. Everything stopped when he dragged his nose along my cheekbone to my ear.

"Tell me, Vera. Will you kiss me on our wedding day? Or only offer your cheek?"

I opened my mouth, not knowing what would come out, when he pressed a quick kiss to my cheek and stood back, grabbing the dishes with him.

I glared at his retreating back, hating how much he affected me. His stupid smile left no doubt that he knew it too. I grabbed the other dishes and brought them to the island, sliding them across to the sink, barely managing to set them down softly and not shatter them at his feet.

"I want an actual wedding," he said without looking up from washing dishes.

"Why?"

He paused for only a moment before easily answering, "Appearances."

That made sense. Especially if he hoped marrying a Mariano would garner him more recognition—a big event would only add to that.

"Seeing as we're going against some opposition, we should hurry the process along. I'm thinking in a month or so. I'll contact someone and make it all happen per our timeline. Money isn't an issue."

I fell back against one of the stools at the island. He talked about it all so easily like it was a done deal. He didn't appear to be struggling with any of this, while my body twisted with indecision and heat.

He spoke as if planning a New York wedding in a month was as simple as grabbing a bite to eat.

For the first time, I really considered Nicholas's wealth. Between his apartment and being able to pay whatever it took, maybe his company was more successful than I'd originally thought. Maybe it was more than a company on the brink of success. Looking back at the view of Central Park, I'd say a lot more.

"So? Are you in?"

He rested his hands on the counter, bunching his strong shoulders under his shirt, the opening shifting to give me a better view of his chest.

"I never thought my fairy tale wedding would be discussed over a contract and granite."

"It's marble."

"Of course, it is," I muttered.

"If you wait for a fairy tale, you'll never be happy. I may not be the prince charming you imagined, but I am here offering you what you need."

My eyes shot from where they ogled his chest to meet his, the setting sun bringing out the hints of green.

"What did you just say?" I asked, barely over a whisper.

Blood rushed through my ears, blending with the memory of my mom's favorite thing to say when I watched all the Disney princesses.

If you wait for a fairy tale, mia bambina, then you'll never find happiness. Sometimes Prince Charming is everything you need when you didn't know you needed it."

"I'm just saying that it may not be perfect, but you can make it what you need. At the very least, a stepping stone," he said, shrugging. "So, what will it be, Verana? Will you marry me?"

I didn't believe in signs, but if I ever did, this had to be it.

I grabbed the contract and slapped it on the counter between us, crossing off the part about consummating the marriage. "Yes. I'm in."

He merely smiled at my act of defiance as if he didn't need a contract to make it happen.

"Good. We'll have an engagement party next weekend."

"What?" I gasped.

"Does that not work for you? If you have other obligations, we can reschedule. I just have to redraft the contract with your…corrections, then we'll be good to go."

To my utter horror, fire burned up my throat to my eyes, and I quickly looked away to hide it. He actually meant it. He really wanted my opinion on our engagement. And after what happened with Camden, and my father, and the last few months in general, it was the most valued I'd felt in a while.

Swallowing my emotions back, I lifted my head with a smile. "Yeah, that sounds fine."

"Good. Now, let me show you around the apartment. You can move in once we're married."

"But what about my place?"

"Do you own it?"

"Yes."

"I mean, in your name. Not your father's."

"Oh. No. He bought it."

"I'm assuming he won't be thrilled to have me living there with you. Besides, I'd rather live in a box in an alley than be inside anything owned by Lorenzo. Also, this is close to the office."

The sneer in his tone made me wonder if there was a bigger reason he disliked my father beyond his abuse and associating with Camden, but he turned away, starting the tour before I could think more about it.

"Good point," I muttered, looking around—another blast of reality on how my life would change within the month. The comfy gray couch would be mine. The sunsets over Central Park would be my view every night. The sleek kitchen in the fancy apartment in the expensive neighborhood, would be mine.

"What about your place in Charleston?"

"I'll obviously have to keep it for when I travel to that office. But New York has taken more of my time in the last few years, so it's not a huge change to make it my home base for the next five years. When things settle down, I'll take you to Charleston to show you around."

"I've never been."

"It's a beautiful city."

"Will you be happy here? Full time?"

He looked over his shoulder, slowing his pace. "I think I will."

I couldn't help but think he meant with me. He thought he'd be happy with me. The idea was crazy. We barely knew each other—barely liked each other. Actually, we didn't. I'd say we tolerated each other. But still, the way he looked at me now, I couldn't help but hope our future was the one Mama described.

Of course, he dashed all that by opening his mouth as he turned back to lead the way down the hall. "By the way, don't be late to work tomorrow. Just because I can take care of you, doesn't mean I will."

"Of course," I muttered, giving in to the eye roll.

FIFTEEN

Nico

MEETING AFTER MEETING kept me busy all morning. At least that was the excuse I created. I took on meetings and pushed up others, so I had no reason to leave my office.

Leaning back in my chair, I set the tiny black box on my desk, flipping it open and closed, a pinch of anxiety and doubt hitting my chest with each glint of the two-carat oval diamond. I'd made a special trip to my bank as soon as the ink dried on our contract.

I imagined the rose gold against the tan skin of her finger. I imagined her in nothing else but the ring, a stamp of my ownership, the only thing against her soft flesh.

The box clicked closed a little harder this time.

I needed to shut those feelings down. I hadn't lied when I told Verana that I wanted a true marriage, but it might have been the only thing I'd been truthful about. When she'd asked what I got out of marrying her, I'd created a reason on the fly. Both of which I listed were true, but not the real reason.

In fact, I needed to make a phone call to set one of the reasons in motion.

"Archer," he greeted.

"It's me."

"Is it done?"

"I'm sending the file now." I typed in his email and sent the signed contract.

"If you don't mind me asking, how did you get her to sign it?"

I chuckled. "I added a clause in the contract I knew she wouldn't agree to, leaving me to redraft a copy. When I did that, I added a new clause at the end, buried in jargon, stating she'd sign over her shares to me upon our wedding day. It was a risk, but I banked on her having gone over it with a fine-tooth comb the first time and only glancing for the one change when I brought it to her to sign again."

"Damn. That's ballsy. You're a lucky son-of-a-bitch."

"I'm beginning to think I am."

"And if she finds out and sues your ass for fraud?"

"I guess I'll cross that bridge if it comes up."

He grunted but let it go. "I'll need about two weeks once I have the shares if all goes to plan over the next month—which it should. But she can't interfere. If she were to fight you on this, it could drag it out long enough to give Mariano a fighting chance."

"I'll come up with something. Take her away on a honeymoon."

"Have you heard of phones?" he deadpanned.

"My buddy, Xander, is a tech genius. I'll have him rig something to keep her out of communication. I'll make this work."

"We've worked a long time. I hope it does."

"It will," I said before hanging up.

If I said it with enough conviction, fate would make it happen. Not that I believed in fate. You made your own, and I'd be damned if I didn't lock in the most secure plan for it to all fall in place.

Conversation done, I sat back and wondered what she would do when she discovered the truth—that she played a role in me finally crumbling her family's company under my feet? Not that it mattered. We'd made a deal. She was mine for five years, and I had to constantly remind myself of why when the appeal of having her preceded my thoughts for revenge.

So many factors were in play, and I had to remain focused on the goal—I had to keep a distance.

I had to admit that having her by my side filled a hole I hadn't known was there—an emptiness I never planned to fill, so I never acknowledged its existence. But when I imagined Verana on my arm at events, I thought of my mother and my grandmother and how they'd stood by the men in our family. When I pictured myself, I always stood alone. Now, I had Verana, and it sparked an emotional response I needed to shut down. I planned to keep her physically close enough to not run but use my coldness and previous arrogance to put a barrier around the possibility of falling into a trap of wanting her for more than sex.

No woman had lured me away from my revenge—not even close. She wouldn't either. I'd be the asshole she accused me of, and if I could slowly chip away at her resolve to not fuck me, then even better.

It wasn't just me I was thinking about. I had a company, and my grandfather. One of my meetings this morning was with a caregiver in New York. He wouldn't be thrilled to leave his warm ocean and southern hospitality, but I couldn't have him so far away either.

I'd make it work.

I'd make all of this work.

Starting with making it official.

Snagging the box off the desk, I headed toward her desk.

I walked across the floor with purpose, garnering other employees' attention.

Debra noticed my approach into the main cubicle area and came out of her office. "Mr. Rush. What can I do for you?"

At that, Vera lifted her head and met my eyes. Something

about my face alarmed her, and her eyes widened as she scooted back like she wanted to bolt.

"I'm good, Debra, thank you. I'm just here to speak with Vera."

"Ms. Barrone?"

I laughed softly, like I found her correction to Vera's formal name cute. "Yes, Ms. Barrone. Although, not for long," I muttered, really amping up the show.

If I thought she looked alarmed before, it was nothing compared to the way her body tightened, and her jaw clenched. The soft smile I gave her probably set off even more alarm bells, considering we mostly glared at each other.

I locked the soft look in place, adding adoration in there too as I approached her desk.

"Vera," I started, closing in. She shook her head just the tiniest bit, and I almost laughed at her desperation to make my attention on her in the middle of the office stop.

The whole floor was absorbed into our perceived private moment. The phones placed on mute, keyboards quiet with frozen fingers hovering above the letters, barely even any whispers or breathing, everyone on edge and holding their breath.

"Mr. Rush," she choked out, her hands clutching her armrests.

"Vera," I said again, revealing the black box from my pocket.

"No," she whispered so quietly I barely heard.

Ignoring it, I dropped to one knee, creating an echo of gasps from around the office. "Since you started here, I haven't been able to take my eyes off you. We tried to keep it professional, but the feelings between us couldn't be stopped. You're smart, beautiful, and represent everything I want in my life." Cracking the box open, I congratulated myself on coming up with a mostly truthful proposal. "Verana Ma—" I stumbled over the name and decided to leave it off as to keep with the truth. "Verana, will you marry me?"

Hands flew to mouths like some kind of romcom. All while Vera watched the ring in the box like it'd explode at any minute.

Seconds ticked by, and my hands grew damp with each moment I had to wait to hear her say yes. What if she changed her mind? What if she made a fool of me in front of my own employees? My muscles tightened like a corkscrew waiting for her answer.

Despite knowing what she'd eventually say, I sighed, my muscles releasing like Jell-O when she finally whispered, "Yes."

Applause broke out, and I slipped the ring on her delicate finger. I took advantage of her distraction with the ring and gripped her other hand, pulling her to her feet and right into my arms. Pushing my luck, I leaned in for a kiss, only to catch the corner of her mouth when she turned at the last minute.

"Careful, Vera," I muttered against her ear. "We have to make them believe."

She pulled back, her hand covering her face like a kiss with her fiancé pushed against her modesty. When she looked up, the smiling bride-to-be with fire in her eyes, she gritted out between clenched teeth, "Well, darling, they know you and what a dick you can be and how many women you've fucked. No one would blame me for not wanting to kiss you in fear of getting a disease."

I barked a genuine laugh. I couldn't wait to make her eat those words, along with my cock.

"Mr. Rush, I had no idea. Congratulations," Debra said genuinely. "You too, Vera."

Everyone rushed to give hugs and their own words of cheer. They all called Verana, Vera, and joked with her as friends. I hadn't realized how much she had made herself part of this company until then. I'd been so focused on what her friendly actions secretly meant that I'd missed how real they were.

For the first time, guilt pricked at my conscience, but I shoved it away. It was business, and we each got something from the transaction. She'd proven more than once she could handle herself, and she'd handle this too.

"If you'll excuse me, I'd like to celebrate with my fiancée in private." I delivered the words with an illicit wink, bringing giggles from the women.

"Nico," Vera scolded, only adding to our familiarity. She slipped, using the shortened name more and more, and I liked it.

I shamelessly shrugged and tugged a wooden Vera behind me.

"What was all the cheering about?" Ryan asked.

I held up her hand. "Vera has agreed to be my wife."

Ryan's brows shot high, and his eyes slid closed like the information was too much to process. With a small shake of his head, he finally opened them but looked no less shocked.

Giving him a pointed stare, I gritted out, "I was shocked too. How did I get so lucky?"

Pulling himself together, he offered Vera a smile. "Congratulations, you two."

"Thank you," she said.

"Please, hold my calls. My fiancée and I need to chat."

As soon as the door closed, Vera yanked her hand from mine and crossed her arms, making her breasts plump up under her blouse. "What the hell is wrong with you?"

"I won't hide our marriage, Verana. This is where we both work. How long did you think it would take for them to find out? Besides, you're mine, and I want everyone to know it," I added, rounding my desk, giving a pointed look to the ring.

She scoffed and rolled her eyes at the precious stone. "Where did you get this? A gumball machine on your way to work this morning?"

"It was my mother's, which was her mother's. I got it from the bank the morning after you signed the contract."

All cockiness drained from her face. "Oh."

I sat in my seat and shifted papers around but didn't see any of them. Instead, I focused on her taking soft steps to the chairs across from my desk and gracefully sitting on the edge. Her fire from moments ago gone, lost under her gaffe.

She studied the ring and twisted it this way and that. "It's beautiful. Thank you."

My heart lurched, wondering what my mother would say at seeing it on her. Would she approve?

Shoving the emotions aside, I changed the subject. "Have you told your father yet?"

"No. I haven't seen him since our last encounter."

"And Camden?" I asked, still not looking up but feeling the tension from across the desk.

"No." When I didn't speak, she filled the silence, her nerves palpable in her shaking voice. "I'm a little nervous to face my father again, and it seems too big an announcement over the phone."

"I'll go with you."

"No. That's okay," she laughed unexpectedly, finally pulling my attention up. "No need to place you in the middle of it."

"I'll face it eventually as your husband. We'll face it together."

She sobered, and a softness I barely caught glimpses of entered her gaze. Warmth bubbled uncomfortable through my chest, and I shook it off, looking back down at nothing.

"We'll go after work."

She stiffened again, back to her stubborn, annoyed self. With a nod, she left, taking any warmth with her.

PULLING up to the regal brownstone, I wondered if it was the end of the line for going incognito. Would Lorenzo recognize me? Would he see my father and grandfather he so cruelly almost destroyed in my features and know? Would he see me and raise his guard higher than I could get past? It would be one thing for me to swoop in to take his daughter, but if he knew I had even the slightest desire to do it to his company too, the game could end before I was ready.

I banked on his arrogance and the view of my company being too small to be threatening. Even if he did recognize me, he wouldn't know I was gunning for him.

Coming with Vera was a risk, but the slight tremor she tried to hide behind a ramrod spine had me wanting to be by her side. I couldn't send her to the wolves alone. Especially not after what happened the last time they spoke.

"I never disobey my parents," she admitted quietly, staring out the window. "I push at my boundaries, but never outright disobey."

I let go of the handle and turned to face her.

"You wouldn't have to if they had your best interest at heart."

She turned, laying the full effect of her large doe eyes on me, bringing the warmth back. "I thought they did. In a million years, I never thought I'd be here, ready to stand up against my father—my mother—and the tradition we've had for years. Maybe this is a mistake. Maybe I'm making a mountain out of a molehill."

I grazed my thumb along her cheek, reminding her without words of the abuse her father gave to her. "For one thing, it's not just your father. No one should cave to a man like Camden." She chewed her lip in indecision, dropping her gaze. Lifting her chin high, I tugged the thick flesh from under her bite and dragged my fingers back and forth, soothing the assault. "Secondly, never cower for anyone's approval. Make mountains. Then crush them under your own decisions. Traditions are the past, and the past is never more important than our futures. Own it."

I soothed her panic because it spurred my own. My vision of the future shifted into high-gear when she came into my life—I couldn't have her backing out now. But a part of me also soothed her panic because I just wanted to. I wanted to infuse her with strength and watch her stand on her own. She deserved it.

A soft nod, and then she lifted her chin on her own, no longer needing my support. It was a beautiful sight to watch her tug her armor in place, pull her shoulders back, and slip her cloak of strength around her.

She sat like a queen and waited for me to open the door. Letting me help her from the car and guide her up the steps, like a peasant there for her bidding. It was awesome.

A maid let us in, and when Lorenzo rounded the corner, Verana's composure slipped, but I was there, my hand at her back to remind her of her place.

"Verana, what are you doing here?" His question hinted at his nerves and hope. This wasn't a man used to opposing his daughter, but he was also a man who needed her to obey. Neither of us knew the reason behind it, but whatever it was, it obviously trumped all else.

"Papa, I came by to introduce you to my fiancé."

Lorenzo's eyes jerked to mine and narrowed in suspicion. I waited for the flash of recognition, but it never came. "Your what?" he sputtered. "You're engaged to Camden. Not this-this—"

"Nicholas Rush," I supplied.

Again, I waited for the recognition in case he'd done his research better than I assumed, but again, it never came.

"He asked me to marry him, and I said yes."

Pushing for a politeness the situation didn't have, I reached out my hand, hating even pretending to be polite to the man who destroyed my family. "Nice to meet you, Mr. Mariano."

He looked down at my hand and back up. Then over to his daughter, then back to me, his face growing more and more red.

"Verana Mariano," Lorenzo practically growled, pulling his shoulders back just like his daughter. At least he tried to. It lacked the conviction of Vera's stance. His brow grew damp, and his hands fidgeted at his sides. This was a nervous man on the edge of losing. "Get over here right now."

Vera took a step closer to my side and slid her hand down my arm to link her fingers with mine. Pride swelled, being the man she reached for. I'd be a liar if I didn't admit a part of me feared she'd go to her father.

Using her free hand, she reached in her purse and pulled out an envelope I'd given her on the way. When her father didn't grab it, she set it on the round table, holding a large flower arrangement, and then stepped back to my side.

"I came by to drop off the invitation to the engagement party this weekend. I wanted to give you the same courtesy Camden gave me."

Her father's face reddened at the jab. "Your mother—"

"Isn't here, as you stated the last time we spoke."

Visibly trying to pull himself together, desperation gave way to anger, and he glared at her, taking deep breaths. When his daughter didn't crumble under his ire, he refocused his direction to me. "She's engaged to another man."

"Not anymore," I responded easily. "She's to be my wife. Mr. Conti is welcome to object directly to me but will go nowhere near my fiancée."

Lorenzo dragged a hand through his hair and down across his mouth, pacing away three steps and turning back. "How the hell did this even happen? Did you meet him at college? On the fucking street?"

"She applied at my company a couple of months ago. Of course, we hired her with her impressive resume. Things progressed from there." Vera's head snapped to me at the compliment about her resume, but I refused to pull my attention from her father, instead offering another squeeze to her hand.

"What fucking company?"

"K. Rush Shipping."

Again, I held my breath, but he was too far gone to even bother to put anything together. He narrowed his eyes at his daughter and took a threatening step closer. I hated the way she flinched when he raised his finger to point at her.

"We talked about this, Verana," he growled, his hand shaking with anger. "You have obligations to this family. To our community. You've known your place, and here you are, acting surprised, lashing out at your own flesh and blood. We raised you better."

Vera took her own step forward but didn't let go of my hand. "You've done a lot I don't appreciate."

"Verana Mariano, I swear to god, I—I will take everything from you."

"Have it," she growled. "I don't need anything from you. This visit is a courtesy. Not an opportunity to intervene."

Father and daughter stared off until I gently pulled her back.

"We hope to see you this weekend," I said softly. "For appearances, at the very least."

Lorenzo remained glued to the spot, his jaw stubbornly clamped shut, as we walked out. Somehow, I managed to hold back my smile from winning the first battle of the war. I opened the door for a still-strong Vera.

Victory surged through me, and I took my time rounding the car, letting a small smirk slip free before sliding in beside her. However, it all stopped when I found her struggling to fasten her seatbelt with trembling hands. I gently set her hands aside and let the seatbelt slide back. She sniffed but didn't look up or pull back from my touch as I tugged her across the seat and into my arms.

The car drove off, and we said nothing. She burrowed her head into my neck with my arms around her shoulders. Her soft sniffs ended long before we got to her place, but not once did she move away.

When we pulled up, she carefully extracted herself, acting like the last fifteen minutes never happened.

"Do you need me to walk you up?"

Her hand on the handle, she looked over her shoulder with a soft smile and eyes that showed none of the turmoil she'd been in moments before. Back again was the strong Verana in pearls and a cardigan, made all the more attractive because I got to see all the layers beneath.

"I'm good, thank you. I'll see you tomorrow?"

Despite the lies I swam in, I let another truth slip-free. "I look forward to it."

SIXTEEN

Vera

I GLADLY TOOK the back corner of the elevator behind the crowd, just as eager as me to get home after a long day.

It'd been two days since Nico's grand show, and I was exhausted. There was always some level of scrutiny when you started a job, but now, everyone really watched. I hated it.

Their gazes like the sun through a microscope, a burning reminder to be on my best behavior. God forbid I showed any emotion other than happiness because I was sure it would get the rumor mill going about what happened behind the scenes between the boss and me.

However, when a group of friends piled on at one of the stops, my attempts to stem the rumor mill proved fruitless.

"I still can't believe he's marrying someone within the company," one of the girls whispered.

It was obvious they were trying to keep the conversation private, but when you're crammed into an elevator with seven other people, nothing was private. And with me shoved in the back corner, they obviously didn't recognize my presence.

"If I'd known I had a chance, I'd have pushed for a job on his floor."

The door opened, and a large group piled off, leaving only a

few of us. I still stood unnoticed while the two others had headphones on. The pseudo privacy boosted their honesty, making
me long for a pair of headphones myself.

"I think it's pretty obvious how she got a job on his floor."

"No," one tried to defend. "She's a project organizer. They
all work on his floor. I'm sure that's it."

"There are project organizers everywhere."

I rolled my eyes. They weren't everywhere, and I clamped
my jaw shut so tight my molars ached.

"She probably slept her way there. Can't blame her either. If
I knew it was an option, I'd let him do anything he wanted."

Their giggles raked across my already raw nerves.

Be nice. Be nice. Be nice.

"Honestly, she's not even that pretty. I mean, her boobs are
kind of on the small side, and Mr. Rush seems like a boob
man."

The doors slid open, and I took my chance to escape this
hell. With each step toward freedom, I reminded myself to hold
my head high and be the lady my parents raised me to be. But
then my phone vibrated for the seventh time that day with
another call from my father. I declined the call, but it was too
late. As if the small vibration slid up my arm and loosened my
jaw, I thought *fuck it* and turned. I slapped my hand against the
closing doors and met each woman's eyes, enjoying the way they
widened in shock.

"I assure you, I didn't sleep my way into a job where I work
on a single pie chart on the least important tab of the least
important spreadsheet of the least important project."

Their jaws dropped, and I let my hand fall. Before the
doors could close completely, my lips moved again without
remorse.

"And my tits are awesome."

Once their shocked faces disappeared, so had my energy,
and I slouched forward, breathing through the flood of adrenaline that left me exhausted. Looking up, I saw I'd gotten off on

the fifth floor. Not wanting to risk another elevator encounter, I took the stairs.

As luck would have it, I wasn't safe there either. The door just closed behind me when a deep voice greeted me two flights up.

"Hello, future wife."

Rolling my eyes, I huffed a breath and leveled him with the most annoyed glare I could muster. Raelynn would be proud.

"Don't look so happy to see me."

Still on edge, I shook my head and proceeded to make my way down. If I could get home, I'd be fine. A bottle of wine, a comedy show, a chat with the girls, and maybe a bath could cure this day.

Nico missed my cues and followed behind, pushing my buttons even more.

"You avoid me at work and give short replies to my messages, and now you're ignoring me completely. Will this be our marriage? Do you plan to not talk for five years?"

His questions beat against my back lightly but held the sharp edge of irritation. And I didn't have enough room for his irritation on top of mine.

He almost slammed into my back when I whirled around at the next landing.

One arrogant brow slowly rose at my defiant stance, and he looked like the perfect target.

"Thanks to your spectacle earlier this week, I'm the talk of the office. And not in the way I want to be. I went to freaking Wharton and graduated with a four-point-freaking-oh, but do they say I got a job because of that? Ooooh, no. They say I got the job because of my underwhelming tits." Both brows shot up when I barked that word at him. "God forbid you ever notice how hard I work, and I get an actual project role because no one will believe I got it for my ideas and smarts. Oh, no, they'll assume I fucked my way into that position."

My chest heaved by the end of my tirade, and he took the time to look me up and down, spending extra time at my chest.

"If you get a promotion, it will be because of your work, and I will not be the one to give it to you. That would always come under fire as nepotism. People can gossip all they want, but it's just words. Words I will shut down, nonetheless. I can't have people spreading false rumors about my company."

His calm response in the face of my ire brought me back to earth. I took a deep breath and let it out slowly, feeling more like myself than the banshee from moments before.

"And I assure you, Vera, your tits are more than enough. A perfect handful."

He gave my chest an appreciative glance, and I swallowed, pulling my shoulders back to stand tall. Not at all to make them look more impressive. He was kind enough to merely smirk than call me out on my move.

"Thank you."

"Do you have plans this evening?" he asked as if asking about the weather.

"I have to get my dress for the party this weekend."

"I'll go with you."

"No, thank you. I'm going to grab a cab and head home."

"Take my car."

"A cab is fine."

"Nonsense." He didn't even bother looking at me to argue. He pulled up his phone as he moved down the stairs again, leaving me to follow behind. He held the door open and pointed to the black car waiting out front. "Take a picture of the dress and send it to me."

"No," I scoffed. "And I'm fine with a cab."

My argument fell on deaf ears as he guided me to the car and opened the door.

"I'll take a cab. Now get in."

I considered arguing, but the lush interior called to me, and after the day, the privacy and comfort were too nice to pass up. "Fine. But I'm not sending a picture," I assured, climbing in.

Before he closed the door, he winked and smiled. "Sure. Okay."

I wanted to be irritated at his arrogance, but it was the most playful I'd seen him since the moment we collided in the lobby. I couldn't help but lean back against the cool leather and smile.

Thankfully, I only had to run in to grab the outfit I'd picked out online, and I was home in no time.

My key slid into the lock when I heard the first peel of laughter. Whatever weight I'd carried around for the rest of the afternoon fell away. The plans to be alone in a hot bath faded away as I opened the front door and slammed it hard enough to announce my presence.

"Well, it's about damn time," Rae called from her spot sprawled on my couch.

I expected her. Who I hadn't expected was the red-headed friend sitting cross-legged on the floor in her oversized corduroys and crop top, stating she *liked hiking and like three people*.

"Nova!" I shouted, throwing my hands up. "You're here."

"Yeah. This is an all hands on deck issue," Raelynn said before directing her attention to Nova and pointing her wine glass at me. "This bitch *messages* me that she's engaged to someone *not* named Camden and then says she's '*too busy.*' I don't think so."

Accepting my fate, I collapsed to the couch with my bags and purse still in my arms.

"And enough of this one word shit you keep responding with. It's time to spill."

"How was your trip, Nova?"

She curled her lips inward to hold back her laugh, knowing my avoidance would only spur Rae on more.

"Nuh-uh. I don't think so. Not in *my* house."

"This isn't your house," I reminded her with a laugh.

"We are in the bubble of sister sharing—which is *my* house," she stated with her chin high, daring me to contradict her.

"What's in the bag?" Nova asked around a giggle.

Raelynn glared at Nova. "You know what, I'm going to let that slide because I love that store, and I want to know what you bought. But let it be known, I don't appreciate you two bitches ganging up on me."

We both laughed, and Raelynn gave us a haughty stare that was ruined by her twitching lips.

"It's my outfit for the engagement party."

Raelynn stared for a while, considering her response. She struggled to remain stoic with her arms crossed but eventually failed, throwing her arms up in defeat. "Ugh, fine. You know I love clothes. Try it on for us, and then you can spill."

I dashed up the stairs to my room and quickly changed, excited to get Raelynn's opinion.

When I came down, Rae squealed. "Oh my god. A white jumpsuit. It's perfect. Turn. Let me see it all." I obliged and laughed at her excited clapping. "He's gonna diiieee over that back. All that skin. Yum, girl."

"I have to admit," Nova added softly. "The long sleeves and wide pants set off the bare back and deep v perfectly. It's pretty sexy."

"Yeah?"

"Hell, yes. Nicholas will be drooling."

"He wanted me to send him a picture, and I told him a hell no."

"Dude, send it," Nova said, shocking me.

"What?"

"If Nova says to do it, then you know you have to," Rae stated.

"I'm not sending him a picture."

"Do it. Do it. Do it," they both chanted at the same time. Nova smacked her hands against the table with the beat while Rae grabbed my phone. Me? I stood there, unable to stop it.

"Oh my god. No."

"Pose," Rae commanded.

"No."

"Naughty Nova over here is coming out," Raelynn joked, tilting her head toward Nova. "She wants you to send a pic too. And when Naughty Nova speaks, you listen."

I laughed. Raelynn and I came up with a name for when Nova let loose from her usual, relaxed self. Shrugging, I gave into the losing fight and struck a pose.

"Yas, queen. Be sultry. Be sexy."

After a ten-minute photoshoot, which turned to tackling Nova and a lot of selfies, Rae commanded I go change before ruining my outfit.

When I came down, she informed me she took the liberty to send her favorite to Nico.

"I didn't want to give you a chance to be a chicken-shit and back out."

"Oh my god. Give it to me." My heart stopped, and I scrambled, fumbling for my phone, almost dropping it in my haste to get it unlocked.

She sent one of me laughing over my shoulder, my hand covering part of my face. My bare back stood out against the white since my hair was piled in my hand on top of my head. I'd never have thought to send it to him, but I liked the candid shot. It looked like an Instagram worthy one that people would pose hours to get.

I didn't hate it.

It didn't stop me from tossing it to the side to avoid waiting for his response.

"All right," Raelynn said with a clap. "Enough playtime. Spill. The. Beans."

Grabbing my wine glass, I curled up in the corner of the couch and told it all. From Camden coming by, to my dad losing his cool, and confessing it all to Nico. They gasped, swore, and threatened to murder a few people through it all.

"Damn," Nova said once I'd finished.

Before Rae could make a comment, a knock at the door came.

"That's probably the Chinese I ordered," Rae announced.

"I'll get it," I said.

Grabbing my wallet, without a care in the world about who would see me with my messy bun, striped PJ shorts, and big black T-shirt that said, "Fuck off. I'm sleeping," I swung the door open to *not* the Chinese delivery man, although he did have our food.

"I arrived at the same time as the food, so I took care of it and thought I'd bring it in."

"Fuck," I whispered, looking up and up into deep chocolate eyes.

"Not the reaction I expected."

"I mean—shit."

"Still not the one."

Shaking my head, I gathered my wits, a little blown away by Nico standing at my door while I looked like a hot mess.

"Can I come in?"

"Yeah. Sorry. I wasn't expecting you. It just threw me."

"Obviously," he said, his full lips tipping up into the smirk I loved and hated all at once.

"Stop flirting with the delivery guy and bring me my food. I'm getting hangry!" Rae shouted from around the corner. "I may have to start eating No—"

If I hadn't been so concerned with covering my braless chest and tucking away stray strands of my bun, I would have laughed at Raelynn's dropped jaw.

"Wow," Nova whispered from her spot at Nico's feet.

"Ladies, this is Nico, my fiancé. Nico, these are my best friends, Raelynn and Nova."

"Good evening," he greeted, not missing a beat, totally ignoring the gawking women. "I believe I've seen you before, Raelynn, but not yet had the pleasure of meeting you."

"Please, call me Rae," she said, finally pulling herself together. Her socialite came out, and she stood tall, stepping over Nova to shake Nico's hand.

Nova clambered to her feet and offered her hand too. "Nice to meet you."

"I'm sorry, I didn't realize you had company," he said to me. "I won't keep you long."

"Do you want to stay to eat?" Raelynn offered, completely ignoring my wide eyes, screaming at her to shut up behind Nico's back. "I ordered enough for an army."

"I appreciate the offer, but according to the look Vera is currently making, I shouldn't overstay my welcome."

Nova snorted, and I quickly cleared my face. How the hell did he even see that when I stood behind him?

My confusion must have shown because he turned to me with a knowing smile and explained. "The mirror above your fireplace."

Looking up, I met my makeup-free face underneath a mop of tangled hair and rolled my eyes. "Duh."

"Either way, I have work to do at home, and I just ate. I wanted to come by and drop these off."

He presented a small box from his pocket after setting the food on the coffee table. I gingerly grabbed the item, careful not to brush his skin, and stroked the soft black velvet before prying the top back.

"Oh my," I gasped, my hand shooting to my mouth. In a soft dark cushion laid a pair of stunning earrings. The rose gold stood out against the sparkling diamonds, adding to the intricate design. At first glance, it looked like a mosaic of diamonds thicker on top. Almost like an upside-down, curved teardrop. But when I looked closer, it was actually a flower made from a pear-shaped diamond and leaf-shaped diamonds draping away from it. "Are these your mother's?"

"No. I picked these out myself after work when I found out

you were dress shopping. I hoped it would work, and it matched your mother's ring you always wear."

"Oh," I breathed, fingering the fine band. For a moment, Rae and Nova ceased to exist. My chest warmed, and I wanted to step into his arms and let him know without words what his gesture meant to me. He'd gone out and got something. Just for me.

I swayed on my feet and almost gave in to take a step forward when Nova cleared her throat.

I blinked out of the trance and snapped the box shut. "Thank you so much, Nico. They are stunning and will look perfect this weekend."

"Of course." He ran a hand through his hair as if he was just as uncomfortable as Nova had been with the intimacy. He turned toward the girls and offered a smile. "It was nice to meet you. I hope to see you this weekend."

"Duh," Raelynn answered, making him huff a laugh.

"I look forward to it."

With that, he walked out, and I scrambled to follow.

"I'm sorry for interrupting," he said again.

"It's not a big deal, really. Maybe a little warning next time, though." I gave an embarrassed laugh and gestured at my attire.

He scanned me up and down, and I heated under his scrutiny. Even more so from his easy compliment. "You look good in anything."

Before he stepped through the door, I snatched his hand on impulse and squeezed. "Thank you again for the earrings. They really are beautiful."

Instead of offering any more words, he merely nodded and squeezed back before walking out.

As if they'd been counting to ten once the door clicked, the girls screeched on cue to my entrance.

"Oh my god, he's delicious."

"Let me see the earrings."

"I had no idea he'd be so hot."

"Fuck me, those are perfect. Totally vintage. Nova, you'd even like these."

"Oh shit. Those are totally vintage."

"Can I have him? If you don't want him, can I have him? Just to fuck a time or two?"

I laughed at the barrage of questions. "You guys. Stop. Remember, we don't like him. He was demeaning to me and still kind of is."

Both of them fell back, pouting like I'd taken their favorite toy.

"You could always have hate sex. So hot. Trust me. I've fucked a lot of people I hate."

"Stop," Nova exclaimed, covering her ears.

"Oh, Naughty Nova went back into hiding," Raelynn joked. "But seriously, have you hit that again?"

"No. And I don't want to."

"Okay…" Nova said mockingly.

"I don't."

Raelynn shrugged. "Fine then. If you're not sleeping with him, you won't mind if I do."

"No," I almost shouted.

Her smirk let me know I'd been had, but I refused to let her think it was anything beyond following rules.

"It's in our contract that we aren't going to be with other people."

"Contract? Oooo, like Fifty Shades of Grey?" Nova asked with too much excitement.

"No. It's more like a prenup."

"Well, I suggest you take full advantage of your five years and hop on that every chance you get."

I opened my mouth to deny I wanted to, but it didn't come out. Maybe I could live in denial by myself, but I'd never been very good at lying to my friends.

"Let's eat before Raelynn eats you, Nova," I said, avoiding commenting.

"Hey, maybe Nico can come back and eat Vera." Rae waggled her brows, and we all laughed.

Thankfully, she was too focused on the food to see how much the thought of Nico kneeling at my feet affected me.

It didn't matter, though.

All that mattered was getting out of marrying Camden, making it through five years, and not giving in to a man whore who acted like a prick.

Sometimes.

He acted like a prick sometimes.

More and more, he acted like my future husband, and it kind of scared the shit out of me.

What if I believed in those moments more than the dickish ones, and at the end of five years, wanted more?

SEVENTEEN

Nico

_____

THE PICTURE HADN'T DONE her justice.

She strolled in, the mid-day sun illuminating her in that white outfit. It was like a foreshadowing of what it would be like when she walked down the aisle, and a feeling like no other washed over me.

A mixture of warmth, electricity, and a shudder of desire worked its way down my spine, pulling my skin too tight.

She looked like the perfect bride-to-be, flanked by her two friends. She clutched her small bag, looking around, appearing both shy and excited all at once, and I couldn't help but wonder if it was an act or if maybe part of her was at least a little excited to celebrate becoming my wife.

Another wave of emotion moved through me, more intense and harder than the last, bringing a wave of questions after it. My skin grew even tighter, and I struggled to mentally shake myself back to reality.

I had a goal, and she was a means to an end. It didn't matter if she was excited. It didn't matter if she liked the idea or not. She served a purpose.

Despite my best efforts to push off anything but indifference at her presence, I stood a little taller. My basic caveman instincts roared, making me want to beat my chest, throw her over my shoulder and claim her as mine when she shifted her head too quickly, making the sparkling diamonds against her dainty ear sway.

Mine. Mine. Mine.

Seeing the jewelry I picked out for her filled me with pride. Even more so when she brushed stray strands of hair back from her cheek, and *my* ring shone brightly.

She was mine.

Her father approached, and she stiffened. He nodded to her friends, and with a hand to her elbow, pulled Vera off to the side.

It was time to claim my fiancée.

The conversation appeared calm and pleasant between father and daughter, but as I got closer, I saw the clenched jaw and tight hold he had on her arm.

"Hear me out, Verana. I talked with Camden, and he was extraordinarily remorseful of the way he acted. He had a stressful week and took it out on you. We all did, and it wasn't fair."

My blood ran cold at his cajoling tone. Did she hear how fake it was? Did she believe him? What if she did? I wanted to close the gap between us, stop anymore lies spewing from Lorenzo, but my feet held me glued to the spot, wondering how Vera would react.

"Fair doesn't begin to cover it," she said.

"I know, and that's why I wanted to talk to you. I looked into the position you're holding at Rush, and it's shameful. No Mariano should be working at such an entry-level position. I—I want to offer you a job at Mariano."

"What?" Vera asked, shocked just as much as me at the offer.

"Yes," he went on, excitement over dangling a winning carrot in front of her speeding up his words. "A project manager. You'd be at the family company, just like you wanted."

I held my breath waiting for her answer, more than half expecting her to say yes to what she always wanted.

"And Camden?"

"Verana," he almost pleaded. His jaw ticked, and he dragged a hand over his mouth. "You can have time—time for Camden to prove he's not who he acted like. But our traditions…"

"Are more important than me," she finished for him.

"No, Verana. You're my daughter. You're important."

I could only see her profile, but the sleek lines of her back straightened, flexing when she pulled her shoulders back. "No."

"Wh-What? No? To what?"

"To all of it," she answered coldly.

"But I'm offering what you want," he said. "You're my daughter—my family."

"Exactly. But you're still not hearing me, Papa," she said softly.

"*Mia bambina*, I am hearing you. I'm giving you what you want."

"At a cost." Lorenzo remained silent. "Tell me, who would organize the galas?"

"Well, you," he explained like it was an honor. "You're the project manager. You're skilled enough to handle them."

"And what about when I start a family?"

"Verana," he said with a nervous laugh. "Stop being so stubborn. I don't even recognize you."

"And I don't recognize you either." Her tone rang with strength and underlying hurt. "Maybe this is who we've always been."

"No. We raised you better. We raised a woman who held pride in her family. This needs to stop, Verana." His words lacked control, dripping with desperation. He needed her to give in. But would she?

"Thank you, but no thank you for the offer," she finally answered. "I'm sticking with my position at Rush Shipping.

They have great potential, and I'm excited to expand with them —with Nico. He's a good man who will be a good husband."

A knot I hadn't known had tied itself around my lungs loosened.

She turned him down.

Not only did she turn him down, but she stood up for me in the process. I blinked, trying to process the influx of information —of feelings. It squeezed inside my chest, uncomfortably and foreign.

"Now, if you'll excuse me, I should find my fiancé."

"Vera, it's time you stopped your tantrum and call this charade off," her father softly spoke between a forced smile, the façade fading away.

"I assure you, Mr. Mariano, our engagement is not a charade," I said, finally stepping in.

His smile slipped, but the professional man he was refused to allow him to show his true emotions at such a public event.

I slipped my hand around Vera's hip, extracting her from his grip, and tugged her to my side. Taking full advantage of the situation, I pressed my lips to her soft cheek and grazed my fingertips along her bare back.

She gasped, and a shiver down her spine chased my touch.

"You look breathtaking," I said softly for her, but loud enough her father could hear. "I can only imagine how beautiful you'll look on our wedding day."

Red tinged her cheeks, and I fought against leaning in again to press my lips to the heat.

"Thank you."

"Mr. Rush," her father greeted stiffly.

"I'll be your son-in-law soon. Please, call me Nicholas."

"Well, Nicholas, was there a reason my daughter had to walk in alone? As her fiancé, shouldn't you escort her?"

"Papa," Vera reprimanded.

Lorenzo was fishing in an empty barrel for reasons to find me lacking. "It's okay, Vera. I can see your father thinks you need a man to enter a room, but he doesn't seem to realize that you are strong enough to stand on your own. You don't need me. But I'm lucky you'll have me."

All my compliments were true, despite never having said them before. However, I said them easily with the benefit of annoying Lorenzo and winning Vera over more and more.

His nostrils flared at the slight, and for the first time since she entered the room, she looked to me. With wide, brown eyes, she looked at me like a mirage. As if she'd never had someone tell her she was strong enough all on her own. Curiosity and awe flickered in the depths, along with something more—something deeper I couldn't quite decipher.

Whatever it was, it had me standing taller beside her. She matched my posture, and together, we created a united front against Lorenzo.

Victory surged—a win I hadn't planned on gaining. One I hadn't even considered. I had no doubt that at some point, I would take Mariano Shipping out from under Lorenzo's feet, but to also take his daughter? That was a prize I didn't even think to play for.

A prize that fell into my lap, and I took without thought.

"Verana," Lorenzo growled. "This—"

"Lorenzo," another guest greeted jovially. He approached with his hand out, a warm smile in place, completely oblivious to the tension brewing. "It's good to see you again and at such a happy occasion."

Lorenzo shook his hand, shifting his mood to the winning businessman he was believed to be. "Andrew, it's good to see you. And yes, such a happy event."

"Nicholas," Andrew greeted. "Thank you for the invite. It's always good to get out and see everyone outside of typical business. Laura sends her best but is home with the newborn."

"Of course. I hope she can make it to the wedding."

"Oh, definitely. She let me know I could stay home with the baby if we didn't find a sitter." He laughed and turned to Vera, clear affection in his eyes. "Verana, I can't believe you're getting married. I can still remember you running around at the galas, sneaking cake."

She laughed at the shared memory. "I think I recall you stealing some with me."

"I was a young pup, fresh from college. Cake helped ease the nerves."

Jealousy pierced my chest.

Those should have been my memories. These should have been my acquaintances. I should have grown up among the elite in shipping at charity galas. Instead, it had been snatched from my family before we had the chance.

"I'm happy for you. Nicholas is a good man, but probably not good enough for you," he joked, nudging me with his elbow.

Despite not having grown up with everyone, I'd made a name for myself in the past few years. I'd carved my way back in, and this time, I planned to cut Lorenzo out.

"Definitely not good enough for her."

I wrapped my fingers around her waist, settling on the curve of her hip, pulling her close to my side. With everyone's eyes on us, she couldn't pull back, and I had every intention of touching her every chance I could get.

"I should mingle," Lorenzo muttered. "Andrew, it was good to see you again." He gave Vera and me a curt nod and turned to go, snagging a glass of champagne on his way.

"I guess I should leave you two to greet everyone and follow Lorenzo's cue. Even when it isn't business, it's still business."

"It always is," Vera agreed with a rueful smile.

Andrew hugged Vera and shook my hand with another congratulations, leaving us alone.

However, as soon as he left, her two friends took his place.

"So, how was daddy dearest?" Raelynn asked.

"He was fine," Vera answered.

"You're so full of shit, but I'll allow it."

"Ladies," I greeted.

"Hello, Nicholas," Raelynn greeted. Nova smiled softly.

The three women made a hell of a triad. Raelynn, the bold one who probably got them in the most trouble. Nova, the quiet one who followed along, picking up any messes so they wouldn't get caught. And then Vera, the one somewhere in between. Prim and polite but hiding a side that got set free when Raelynn was around.

"This place is beautiful. I can't believe you're living here," Nova said.

"Lucky bitch," Raelynn added. "It's always so hard to find good real estate around Central Park. And one with event spaces available? A needle in a haystack."

"I haven't moved in yet."

"Why not?" Raelynn asked, looking me up and down with a raised brow. I felt like a piece of meat being sized up for a meal.

Vera laughed uncomfortably but managed to glare at the same time. Nova shoved Raelynn with her elbow, and the three had a silent argument before Raelynn rolled her eyes, deciding to drop the question.

"So, Nicholas. Are you going to take care of our girl?"

Vera and Raelynn turned wide eyes to Nova, who looked like a prudish mother deciding if I was good enough for her precious child.

"As much as she will allow me to."

Nova's lips tightened as if holding back a laugh. "Good."

"But the real question is…"

Vera's eyes widened, swiveling to Raelynn, and I braced myself for whatever would come from the bold woman's mouth.

"Will you fuck her well?"

"Jesus. Stop," Vera whisper-yelled, looking around to see who else might have heard.

I met Raelynn's challenging stare, answering her honestly. All while issuing my own challenge to Vera. "As much as she will allow me to."

Raelynn's slow smile confirmed she knew the truth about

our situation, and no doubt, knew more than I did about Vera's stubbornness keeping her from enjoying all the benefits of our marriage.

"Good."

"Well, now that that is out of the way," Vera said, exasperated with the two of us.

Nova emptied her champagne. "Yes. I don't know about you, but I could use another glass." She linked her arm with a still-smirking Raelynn. "We'll leave you to greet everyone."

Vera pressed her fingers to the center of her forehead. "Sorry about that," she murmured.

"Don't be. I like her."

Questioning eyes snapped to mine, concern marring her features. "Oh, well, most men do."

How she could assume I preferred Raelynn over her, I had no idea, but I shut it down before it could begin. "Not like that. She's entertaining to listen to. But I do like your concern I'd want anyone other than you," I gloated.

"I'm not." She stood taller and tried to brush away her unfiltered reaction.

"Hmm." I slowly backed her to a private corner. "Are you sure?"

"Yes. Why would I care who you like and don't like? It's not like we like each other?"

"You don't like me? I'm hurt."

"Yeah, right," she said with a roll of her eyes.

"You seemed to like me once."

"I didn't know it was you." Her sassy response was ruined by her stumbling when her back hit the wall.

I stepped into her space, resting my hand on her hip, stretching my thumb to graze low on her hipbone. "I could remind you. No masks. Face-to-face. Your legs wrapped around me."

I gave her points for thrusting her chin up and arching an arrogant brow, but her heaving chest and heavy swallow gave her away. Her tongue slicking across her lush lips as her eyes flicked to mine.

"No," she whispered, trying to lie. But desire swirled in the depths of her brown eyes like melted gold.

I shifted my hand to her ribs. "You really do look stunning."

Another swallow. "Thank you."

"It takes all I have not to have you right here in this corner. All this white, all this purity when I know different, I love it. Like our little secret, how dirty you like to be." Leaning down, I grazed my nose to hers, breathing in her quick exhalations. "Or are you only dirty for me?"

Her parted lips begged me to kiss her, to take and take and take. Wanting to prolong the moment, wanting to see if I could hear the plea for more fall from her lips, I held back. Instead, lifting my hand higher to smooth over her breast. My thumb swiped back and forth, bringing the hard tip to life, pinching the tender bud.

"You'll be my wife soon enough. Why not just give in? Sweeten the deal of our bargain."

And just like that, the woman melting in my arms stiffened. A firm hand landed against my chest, shoving me back easily.

"I may be agreeing to marry you, but that's it. I'm not selling my body like a prostitute. Besides, you couldn't afford me. I'm not like all the other women you only had to snap your fingers at to make them jump. Unfortunately for you, I'm more work than that."

She stormed past, even having the audacity to clip me with her shoulder. A single laugh slipped free, a little turned on by her defiance. More than a little turned on with the way she almost caved under my touch. She may not want to admit how much she wanted me, but soon enough, we'd live under the same roof, and she'd have nowhere to run.

I snagged a glass of champagne and left the room, giving my future bride a reprieve. I'd only gone a few feet when voices had me slowing to a stop out of view.

"I've already asked twice."

"Angelo was always a stubborn asshole. Jealous of my company name."

I didn't recognize the first voice right off the bat, but I knew Lorenzo's in my sleep.

"Which is why if we don't marry, my name isn't going on the building. He won't invest as much as he initially agreed if the Conti name isn't right next to Mariano."

Camden.

I couldn't stand having him here, but appearances demanded no one be left out. Especially someone so high ranking in Verana's family company.

"Cazzo! Camila's family haunts me even when they aren't around. That damn amendment in the company contract. Having to be a family member to add their name to the company is archaic and bullshit. It's my company. I should be able to add whoever I want."

Lorenzo forcing Vera to marry Camden made a lot more sense after that angry rant. I knew Mariano Shipping was crumbling, but I never expected Lorenzo to sell off his own daughter to some asshole like Conti to save it.

Although, I should've known better. I knew first-hand how cold and calculated he could be. It made taking Vera away from him all the sweeter and left me with zero regrets about using her in this game. She should be grateful it was me instead of Camden, she was forced to marry for reasons outside of her control.

"Fucking Rush," Camden sneered. "Something new and shiny in front of Vera, and she's off after his dick like a whore."

My fists clenched, and I moved to round the corner when a thud followed by an oomf stopped me.

"That's my fucking daughter you're talking about," Lorenzo growled.

"A daughter you were selling off to me to save your company," Camden shot back, slightly strangled.

"I did it with the interest that you'd take care of her. Not be some selfish prick that chased her off. Don't look at me like I ruined this when your shitty personality pushed her away."

"Whatever. She's a lost cause and missed out. Rush is new money without half the connections we have. He'll never be able to provide the life she's used to."

"This is all a fucking mess."

"But not a lost cause. My father will still invest as I'm working my way to the top. All we need is another investor. I'll play the long game, and whenever Verana leaves that arrogant asshole, I'll be there to sweep in. We'll marry, and the Conti name will be added to Mariano. We just need patience."

"And a silent investor. And hope that Verana doesn't get knocked up in the meantime. Camila's father left only a few shares in her name when he passed away, but any child of Vera's would get more. With the way things are going, losing any more shares is too dangerous. I needed to keep as many as I could under my control."

"*Our* control," Camden corrected.

"Whatever," Lorenzo grumbled. "I'll call my lawyers to ensure I protect what is mine—what I have left of Camila. Not that Rush has enough money to be a threat."

Disgust rolled in my stomach. Part of me wanted to believe he cared for Vera, but not as much as his company. She was a pawn to him.

Fucking over someone else's family was one thing. But to do it to your own was another.

My determination inched higher. I'd take his company, and I'd take his daughter, protecting her from the two monsters on the other side of the wall.

Walking back to my future bride, I did my best to blot out the information that a child would gain extra shares of the company. We'd agreed, no children in the time of our marriage, but I couldn't ignore the allure of making my victory all the more assured with a child.

But no. I was marrying Verana under false pretenses, using her for my own gain she didn't even know about.

Knocking her up would make me no better than the monsters using her like nothing. I couldn't do it.

Could I?

EIGHTEEN

Vera

THE PARTY PROGRESSED IN A BLUR. Other than the small stretch of time I'd stormed away from Nico, he hadn't left my side. His touch remained firmly glued to my hip, only leaving to hold my hand, brush my hair aside, stroke down the bare skin on my back, or any other way he could touch me with the excuse of portraying a loving couple.

My muscles remained stiff the entire time, holding strong as to not fall to a puddle at his feet and beg him to take me like he'd said earlier.

No. I would not give in to Nicholas Rush. Especially when he assumed he had the rights to my body just because I agreed to marry him. We were helping each other. I was not indebted to him, owing him whatever he wanted to take.

Even if I did have dreams about letting him.

Remembering those nights I woke up aching, imagining exactly what he said—my legs around his waist, no masks—had me hesitating when he asked if I wanted to grab a drink at the swanky bar next door. But a nightcap after a long day sounded nice. And eventually, I'd have to find comfort in being around him. In a little over a month, I'd be living with him—surrounded by him.

God, I was screwed.

It didn't help when he held the door open for me into the dimly lit bar. Or when he rested his hand against my back, guiding me to a stool. The rough scrape of his hand against my skin sent tingles up my spine. The utter gentleman he was, waited for me to be seated first before grabbing his own.

"Another glass of champagne?" he asked.

"Just a red wine, please," I asked the bartender.

Nico ordered the same, and we both sighed, the tension easing with our first sip. I closed my eyes, the soft murmur of conversation mixing with the clink of glasses on a table. Friends laughing over the easy jazz filtering through the speakers. All of it working to let the stress of being on for everyone fade away.

"I didn't notice any family there today," I said, breaking the silence.

"I could say the same about you. Our engagement party resembled a shipping convention more than a gathering of friends and family."

"True. But my dad was there—unfortunately—and Rae and Nova. They're like my family."

"I know you mentioned your mother passed, but is there no one else?"

"I never knew much about my father's side of the family. He wasn't close to them and apparently became even more distant when he married my mother. My mother was an only child, and her mother lives in Italy. My grandfather passed away soon after my mom died, and my grandmother moved, not really coming to visit anymore. I think it's hard on her."

I took another fortifying sip of wine, hiding any lingering resentment that my grandma put a wall up between us.

"But you?" I narrowed my eyes and pointed an accusing finger at him. "You can't distract me."

His lips tipped into the tiniest of smiles, knowing I'd caught him doing just that. "I told you. My parents died, and I didn't have any siblings. I have a grandfather in Charleston, and he can't really travel easily for a weekend party."

"Will he be at the wedding?"

"He'd kill me if I got married without him there," he said, affection changing his tone to one I'd never heard before. Warmth slipped through my chest at his endearing smile.

"You're close to him."

"He's the only family I have left, and he taught me everything I know. He built our company from the ground up."

My brows furrowed. "I thought K. Rush Shipping was newer. When I looked into it before applying, I thought it was only ten years old?"

His eyes flicked away from mine. "It is. His company hit a few stumbling blocks before I had a chance to work there."

"What's his company's name? Maybe I remember it."

"It was a small company. You wouldn't recognize it." Nico shook his head and waved the question away, going back to who attended the reception. "And you may not have had much family there, but you knew almost everyone."

"I grew up in this world."

I'd attended galas since I was little. I'd done all the charities and business events that included mingling with other companies. It was its own small world within the world.

"So, why not work for your dad?"

Such a simple question with so many difficult explanations.

"To keep it short—I'm a woman."

"I've noticed."

I sipped my wine to hide the heat bleeding into my cheeks at his blatant perusal of my femininity.

"Well, in my family, that means I have a role to play. I'm to marry someone who would fit into the company and be able to take it over. And my job would be to be a socialite. Sit on charity boards, be a public face for Mariano Shipping. A freaking mascot."

"That doesn't sound like you."

"It isn't. Even if I tried to be. Despite knowing what my future held, I followed my passion. I grew up in this world, and I loved it. I figured maybe I could be more than a mascot. And if nothing came of it, at least I tried. I had to believe in the future they painted. My parents had an arranged marriage, and my mother told me about how they hated each other but fell in love. She told me how I'd marry a good man and to trust them. She'd tuck me in and talk to me like it was our secret that she'd have the final say in who I'd marry, and she'd always promise to pick the most handsome of men for me." Memories pressed heavily on my chest. "Then she died, but I still trusted my father. I trusted in the love I saw between them. Never in a million years did I expect someone like Camden. There was no amount of time that Camden could have grown into a decent husband."

Nico scoffed and wore a grimace to match mine. "There'd never be any room for Camden to love you. He's too in love with himself."

He hit the nail on the head, and I couldn't help but laugh at the accuracy.

"He'd probably take you on a golf trip for your honeymoon."

"What if I like golf?" I asked just to be stubborn.

"Then he'd only talk about himself and forget you were even there. He'd probably drive away on the cart, not even seeing you standing there."

"Oh, and do you plan on whisking me away on a romantic honeymoon and seeing me?" I pretend swooned and batted my eyes.

"Oh, I plan on seeing all of you."

Again, another up and down perusal. This one more intense and filled with the unspoken memory of every illicit thing we'd done on the balcony. My core clenched, in complete opposition with my brain, wanting more—morals be damned.

I remembered being sore days later. I remembered the bruises, the bite mark—the intensity.

Dammit. I was melting again.

"And yes, I have a yacht booked in Italy with various stops for our honeymoon."

"What?" Between the melting and the shock, I almost fell out of my chair. "You booked us a honeymoon?"

"Of course, I did. Why wouldn't I?"

"Because this marriage isn't real."

"I've already explained this, Verana. I want it to be a real marriage. And frankly, a vacation sounds nice."

A vacation did sound nice. A vacation away from reality. Running with my hand in Nico's as my world crumbled behind me. It would be stupid to argue.

"What about work? A trip to Italy sounds like more than a weekend trip."

"I have people to handle everything I need while we're away. And I booked flights for us to stay a little less than two weeks, but we can extend it if we like. You only get one honeymoon."

Maybe not, a small voice whispered. "You can always get married again after five years. Find a woman you truly love—or at least like—and have it all again."

"I like you just fine. So, we better do it right the first time, just in case."

Something about the way he said it held an underlying current—like maybe he didn't believe there would be anything beyond our firsts.

Maybe because the dim lighting brought out the specs of green in his eyes that always held me entranced. Maybe it was the wine. Maybe it was the trip down memory lane and remembering asking my mother for a dark-haired and dark-eyed prince.

But I couldn't help but wonder—would Nico be the man Mama always promised I'd find. Would he be the one I married and ended up falling for?

The only one?

NINETEEN

Nico

"ARE you sure you're happy here?"

"I'm happy with my family, Nicholas."

Grandpa laid his weathered hand on top of mine, and I stared at the frail fingers and wrinkled skin. These were the hands that tossed me into the air as a boy. The same hands that taught me how to shoot and throw a punch. While he'd taught my father everything he knew about the business, he taught me everything he knew about life.

He had so much left to give, and yet stress, a heart attack, and one too many blows from fate left him in a home, his mind slipping away faster than his body.

"Besides, my love is buried here."

"We can visit her this week."

His eyes slid closed, and a warm smile he reserved only for my grandma covered his face. "And as long as you take me to the ocean every once in a while."

"Of course, Grandpa."

"Good. Now, you said work was keeping you here. Tell me about the business. What's going on that has you so busy?"

It'd been a hard decision to move my grandpa up here. We both loved Charleston so much. The ocean, the sun, the

163

southern comfort—the lack of memories of what was taken from us at every turn. But when I'd explained why I wanted to move him, he agreed without hesitation.

But having him here was like looking in a mirror and facing how much had changed in the past few months—facing everything I was doing and the moral lines I toed. I grimaced, thinking about ways to get around the truth.

"Don't give me that face. I know my mind isn't as sharp as it used to be, but I taught you all you know, and you can humor an old man by talking shop. So, what about work has you moving back full time to the place you said you disliked so much?"

Turned out, just like when I was a kid, there was no getting around the truth with Grandpa. Rubbing a hand down my face, I considered the most delicate way to deliver the news without inspiring the third degree. "It's not all about work."

"Ohhhh." He dragged the word out around a smirk, even managing to bounce his brows in insinuation. "A woman."

"Yeah," I said on an exhale.

"It must be serious."

"We're getting married."

Blink. Blink.

Five.

Four.

Three.

Two.

I held my breath, telling myself I'd speak first once I got to one.

One and a half.

One and one quarter.

"Hot, damn, Nicholas," Grandpa yelped. He slapped his leg and laughed, grabbing my hand in his and holding tight.

When Vera asked me what I got out of marrying her, I gave a half-truthful reason of making my grandfather happy, but seeing his joyful elation settled something in my chest I hadn't realized was out of place.

"I didn't even know you were seeing someone," he exclaimed around his brilliant smile. "How long? Do I get to meet her?"

"Not long. It's been a bit of a whirlwind," I answered as honestly as I could, hoping to avoid the second question. In the end, I only prolonged the inevitable of explaining it all. His mind may wander in and out, but he had moments of being sharp as a tack. There would be no getting around explaining who I was making my wife.

It was like walking into a volcano, unable to turn around, knowing you were fucked, but continuing on your path anyway.

"So, will I get to meet her?" he asked again. "Or am I going to meet your bride after you say your vows?"

"Of course, before the wedding. Soon. Promise."

"Don't sound so excited," he joked. "Gosh, I don't even know her name. Tell me, Nico. Tell me the name of the angel who has claimed your heart."

The romantic image he painted made the truth all the harder to admit, but it was better he knew before he met her. My chest pinched, and all the happiness I'd given moments ago slipped away like sand between my fingers.

"Verana Mariano," I choked out.

He sat up tall, his jaw working open and closed as if he wanted to laugh it away as a joke and then tell me I was full of shit or that it was wrong. Each possible reaction had a different emotion flashing across his face until finally, realization and frustration settled in.

"Nicholas Knightly Rush. What the hell are you doing?"

"It's not—"

"What I think?"

I winced, hating that he called me on my bullshit answer because we both knew that deep down, it had to do with my revenge.

"Yes and no, but I didn't seek her out. She just…fell into my lap."

One brow slowly lifted, reminding me of all the times he'd find me with cookie crumbs on my mouth after I'd already gone to bed. Without saying a word, he leaned back with a deep breath, resting his linked hands atop his stomach, and waited.

Time to jump into the volcano.

With my own deep breath, I explained how I became engaged to the daughter of the man who I hated most in this world.

"She's an innocent woman, Nicholas. Don't involve her in your revenge," he said when I finished.

"She's getting more than enough out of this."

"And how will she handle knowing she was the key to the downfall of her family company?"

"She's smart enough to start her own, and after everything her father has put her through, she may want just that." Grandpa shook his head, but I wouldn't let his disappointment sway me. I'd come too far—we'd gone through too much. "I know what I'm doing, and we'll all be better on the other side of it."

"A marriage built on lies is not a marriage at all, Nicholas. Even a fake one. No one is better with that."

"It's a marriage we're both walking into with more honesty than most. This arrangement suits us both."

"Five years is a long time. A lot can grow between two people who live together—a lot of emotion. If I thought I loved your grandma when I married her, it was nothing compared to how much I adored her five years later. Don't hurt her."

"Impossible," I said with a huff of laughter. "We don't… particularly care for each other. All we can hope for is a partnership in this. She's smart. Talented. Beautiful. Brave."

"Don't care for her, eh?" he asked with a smirk.

I scowled, not bothering to defend my choices anymore. The truth was out there, and frankly, his cocky smile irritated me more than the disappointed frown from before.

"Just…do me a favor," he finally asked when I didn't respond to his prod. "Tell her before you do anything drastic."

Feeling the weight of his request every second I tried to avoid answering, I finally caved. "I'll tell her."

At some point.

With that, I left with the promise to be back with Vera and to take him to see Grandma.

I wouldn't say I quite ran to the exit after our conversation, but someone would probably say it was a speed walk.

I needed to get out of there.

Pushing his disapproval to the side on the ride back to work came at a cost, and by the time I reached the office, my mood dipped into dangerous territory. One that allowed for little politeness and courtesy. So, when I saw Vera standing to the side, laughing with coworkers, I didn't care how my actions came off. I needed to talk to her, and I didn't care to wait.

Add in the way just seeing her shot lightning through my chest, making my heart jump an extra beat. Or the way my cock twitched imagining unbuttoning that pressed white blouse one button at a time, revealing her perfect breasts, and the sexual frustration mixed with every other emotion brewing, stealing any semblance of control.

I walked up, slipping my hand around the small curve of her waist, and leaned down, brushing her hair aside to issue my demand against her ear.

"My office. Now."

She looked up with wide eyes to her coworkers before quickly looking away. I didn't bother to check anyone else's reaction or see if she'd comply. If nothing else, I knew she'd follow so she could reprimand me in private at the very least.

"What the hell is wrong with you?" she demanded, almost slamming my office door behind her.

"I needed to talk to you."

"So, send a request like a normal person. Not come whisper in my ear like I'm-I'm—"

I waited, brows raised, for her to find her words, fully enjoying her arms flailing in frustration.

"Some *booty call*," she finally screeched.

"I assure you, you're not a booty call."

"Well, it sure as hell looks like it to everyone else. I already told you, I will not lose the respect of others because they think I'm fucking the boss when I should be working."

"And I already explained that I don't care. You'll be my wife and if they want to think I'm fucking you over this entire office, then so be it. Thankfully, I'm the boss, and their opinions don't matter."

"They matter to me." She glared, but beneath the clenched lips and tight fists, I saw the plea.

Don't hurt her.

My grandpa's words created a wave of irritation. However, the wave was thin, failing to hide the truth behind them. Vera and I may not particularly care for each other, but I wanted respect. I could do the same for her.

"Fine," I answered. It was short and still bubbling over with my frustrations from the day, but it was something. "If I need you, I'll send for you like a normal employee—even though you're not."

She rolled her eyes, apparently being no more mature than I could. "What did you need to talk to me about?"

"I want you to move in before the wedding."

"What? Why?"

I didn't appreciate her reaction like I'd asked her to skydive without a parachute. "Because I said so."

And she—fairly—didn't like my answer. Her brows shot high. "You want to try that again, Nicholas?"

Taking a deep breath, I ground my teeth, unused to having to explain myself to anyone. "It makes sense. We'll be gone right after for the honeymoon, and then we will need to get caught up with work after. I want it done before then."

She studied me, and I struggled to remain silent, letting her process. She took so long, I almost considered sitting down to answer some emails when she finally spoke up.

"When?"

"This weekend."

"I have my bachelorette party."

"You're having a bachelorette party?" My face twisted at the idea. Strip clubs and flirty women came to mind, followed quickly by a pinch of irritation. My future wife better not be going to stick dollar bills in some beefed-up stripper's thong.

"Raelynn doesn't pass up a chance to celebrate."

Awesome.

"Where are you going?"

She narrowed her eyes and hesitated. So help me, if she didn't answer, I'd lock her in this office. Thankfully, it didn't come to that.

"Dinner and maybe a bar."

I nodded. "Fine. Take a day off this week to arrange everything to be moved in before then. You can work from home if need be."

She swallowed. "Okay."

"Good. Also, I'd like you to make time to come with me to visit my grandpa. He wants to meet you before the wedding."

"I can do that."

"Thank you. If only you were so agreeable to everything. We wouldn't waste so much time."

"Well, Nicholas. One is to go meet a man who, I assume, has to be a saint for putting up with you, while the other is so you can bend me to your will because it makes it easier for you to do God knows what."

"Yes, Grandpa is a good man, but who do you think I learned it from?" I said with a wink. If Grandpa had been there, he would have backed away with his hands up, not laying claim to teaching me any of the nefarious things no doubt running through her head.

"Ugh. Is there anything else I can do for you?" she asked, her annoyance on full display.

A million requests rolled through my head.

Get on your knees. Let me actually fuck you in this office. Ease some of this tension burning in my veins every time I see you.

Somehow, I didn't think those would go over well, so I opted to keep my mouth shut and continue with the arrogance. It worked so well. She riled up beautifully.

"That will be all."

"Yes, sir."

Watching her walk out, her tight skirt hugging her plump ass, I promised that at some point, I'd get her to say that to me again. Only naked. And fulfilling at least one—if not all—of my fantasies.

TWENTY

Vera

_____

WHAT THE HELL was I doing?

How well did I know Nico?

What if he was a con-man?

What if who he was at home was completely different than the man I'd come to know?

Any answers I came up with lacked the confidence I usually had when I made decisions.

The questions came comically late since I currently stood in the middle of the large open penthouse, watching movers set box after box wherever I directed them to.

Was I being crazy?

I knew the answer to that one without question. *Yes. Probably certifiably insane.*

"What about these?" one of the men asked. "It says bedroom."

I opened my mouth to tell him the first door on the left. I knew without Nico directly telling me that he'd expect me to share a room to have the *real* marriage he asked for. Instead, the questions hovered, doubt crept in, and I said, "First door on the right."

The guest bedroom.

To say Nico wasn't happy when he came home would be an understatement.

"Vera?" his deep voice reached down the hall from the entryway and stroked up my spine. Just my name, and my skin prickled, partly from nerves, partly from something else I refused to put a name to.

"In here."

I folded another shirt, trying to focus on the task when, in reality, every inch of me zeroed in on each hard step against the hardwood floor getting closer. They stopped a couple feet away, where I could imagine him looking into the master suite with confusion at not finding me or my belongings there before continuing again, closing in.

The steps stopped right outside the open door, his presence looming like a command to look up. I tried to stay focused on the task, to not show my trepidation at him staring at me.

The silence stretched, and my muscles ached with the refusal to look up from my shirt. "How was work?"

My voice cracked, exposing my nerves, and when he still didn't answer, I finally caved, moving my eyes just enough to meet his. His nostrils flared. His jaw ticked. He looked like a bull ready to charge, barely holding on to control. I met his dark eyes for only a moment before going back to folding the same damn shirt.

Finally, with a huff sounding scarily close to a growl, he stormed away, releasing me from the tension tightening every muscle like a screw. I'd just released the breath I'd been holding when the door slamming down the hall reverberated through the apartment, making me jump.

This time, I scowled, jerking my gaze to the door like he'd be able to feel my disapproval through the walls. Seriously? He wanted to slam doors like a child because I wasn't...what? Waiting in his bed like a good woman?

All the apprehension from a moment ago shifted. Irritation, and once again feeling like a toy that didn't perform as expected, washed over me. The need to stomp down the hall and fling open his door just so I could slam it again pulled my muscles tight all over again. The desire to make my own noise became too much, and I refused to stoop to his level.

Giving up, I tossed the damn shirt in a random drawer. It took me digging through three boxes before I found my robe and headed to the bathroom. Hopefully, a hot shower would burn off the anger simmering just beneath the surface.

The steaming water and vanilla body wash did the trick to bring me back to the calm woman my mother raised. By the time I dried off and wrapped myself in my silk robe, I was ready to face Nico again. This time to have a conversation about our living arrangements like two adults.

At least, until I opened the door to find him pulling out handfuls of my clothes I'd just put away and heading for the door.

"What the hell do you think you're doing?" I screeched.

He didn't bother to stop, merely calling over his shoulder, "Moving your shit where it belongs."

"It belongs where I put it."

I stormed to the doorway in time to watch him walk the few feet to the master bedroom and listen to a dresser drawer open and slam closed. As quickly as he disappeared, he came around the doorway, storming toward me like I was the next thing he'd pick up and toss in the room.

I clutched my robe tighter and backed away into the room, chin held high. When he reached past me to grab more clothes, I stepped sideways, blocking him. "No."

"Vera," he growled.

"Isn't the whole point of this arrangement for me to gain freedom and get away from everyone dictating everything for me? So, who cares where I sleep?"

"You are my wife."

I couldn't help my snort of disbelief, apparently pricking at his male pride. He stood taller—bigger—and for every step closer inching into my space, I crept back until my ass hit the edge of the dresser, and his large hands gripped the wood on either side, pinning me in.

"I'm doing you a favor here, Verana," he reminded me in a dangerously low voice. Not that my body took it as the warning it was meant to be. My nipples hardened like they were being invited to a party, and I crossed my arms in indignation and shame. "I'm not making you sleep with me, even though we both know you want to. So, the least you can do is share a room with your husband and stop acting like such a fucking diva."

His eyes dared me to dive into their black abyss, so deep, not even the bedside lamp could touch their depths. They dared me to give in, but I refused. I lifted my chin higher and remained mulishly silent.

"What will people think when they come over and find us in different rooms?"

"I'd be more concerned about why anyone is snooping around our bedrooms."

"And guests? Where would they sleep?" he asked with less and less patience.

"Please," I scoffed. "What guests? I have yet to meet a single friend of yours."

The muscle in his jaw ticked. "And Raelynn? Nova?"

"They can sleep with me. They know the truth." I shrugged, proud of meeting him argument for argument.

"Stop being so stubborn." For the first time, he raised his voice beyond the low demands.

So, I raised mine back. "No."

Another stare-off where the inches of space between us vanished and the heat of his determination clashed with mine.

His lip curled like an animal baring its teeth.

All I had as a final warning was his deep growl. Then those strong arms and large hands gripped my ass as he dipped low and hefted me over his shoulder.

I screeched, my hands both trying to support myself against

the flexing ridges of his back and pulling my robe down to cover my ass that felt entirely too much breeze to be covered.

The world turned, and I watched the safe haven I'd planned on being mine for five years get further and further away. I bounced against Nico's shoulder while he walked me the same way he had my clothes across the hall.

"Dammit, Nicholas fucking Rush. Put. Me. Down." I punctuated each demand with a small fist to his back. In return, I got a hard smack to my ass, the crack meeting my ears a moment before the sting bloomed on my cheek.

The shock rendered me speechless. Shock that I currently sat atop his shoulder while he dragged me around like a piece of furniture. Shock that he'd spanked me. Shock that the sting faded to a burn that warmed my core, and part of me wanted to keep hitting his back in the hopes he'd spank me again.

All that shock faded in a flash when the room moved too quick, and he whipped me back over his shoulder, tossing me on the bed like a rag doll.

He didn't give me a second to escape, instead, following me to the bed. He leaned over me, his clenched fists dipping the mattress at my sides. I flipped my hair out of my face and held his stare, a little less sure of my stance than before. All while I did my best to arrange my robe to cover anything important.

"You are my wife, goddammit."

The cool, calm, dangerous warnings from before vanished. In their place was a heated Nico—a man beyond patience and reasoning. The dark abyss from before blazed with something I couldn't quite place—something that called to me to actually listen—almost something like desperation.

"This is our marriage—*our home*, and I won't sleep in this bed alone while my *wife* is across the hall. Now, stop. Please."

Somewhere in those last three words, something cracked in his façade, and I saw past another domineering man. I saw a piece of the man who worried about his grandfather and genuinely smiled any time they spoke on the phone. I saw a piece of a man who asked about a coworker's wife and child. I saw—just a man. Maybe a lonely one.

For a moment, I looked at Nico as someone other than another person trying to control my life and heard my mother's words.

It won't always be hard, but you must be strong enough to get past the tough exterior these men portray. The truth is, we're stronger than them all, and they just need to know they can be vulnerable with us. That, mia bambina, is when the real marriage replaces the arranged one.

"Fine," I almost whispered.

He blinked like I'd hit him but quickly recovered, patching up any cracks that exposed any weaknesses. He stood tall and nodded, finally giving me room to breathe. "Thank you."

I'd just agreed to share a room—a bed—with him, and he nodded at me like it was a business merger. It ticked me off just enough to slide back to petulance. "But I call the right side."

His nostrils flared. "Ver—"

"Right. Side. Nicholas."

I followed his eyes to where they flicked to a book, watch, and alarm clock on the right nightstand. My lips twitched, barely holding back a smile, knowing he was considering fighting this battle, but knowing he would lose.

His fists clenched, but he eventually caved. "Fine."

"Thank you. It was a pleasure doing business with you."

Not appreciating my gloating, he stomped to the bathroom and slammed the door again. While he showered, I took extreme pleasure in moving my bedside knickknacks to the right side-table.

That night, I clung to the edge of the bed, both hoping and terrified to turn into him. I took a modicum of pleasure, pretending to sleep like a baby as I listened to him toss and turn, grumbling about discomfort and the damn left side.

I was almost completely asleep, relaxing away from the edge, when I heard his muttered, 'fuck it,' and as soft as a parent too scared to wake a sleeping child, he slipped his arm around my waist and tugged me back to meet him in the middle.

My first instinct was to jerk up and demand to know what the fuck he was doing, but curiosity won out. Would I feel him pressing his erection against my back as he tried to take advantage of us in the same bed? Did he want to see if he could catch me off guard in my sleep?

Did I want him to? Did I want to blame being half-awake as the reason I even considered letting him take advantage of me?

But I never got the chance because he didn't do any of that.

Instead, soft lips caressed my shoulder, and for the first time all night, he stopped tossing and turning, falling fast asleep with me in his arms.

The craziest thing was, so did I.

TWENTY-ONE

Vera

"Three more shots of tequila, sir," Raelynn shouted at the bartender.

"Two," Nova called over Rae's shoulder.

"Oh, come on, Nova. You tried to get out of drinking at the last bar," Rae whined.

"One of us has to get us home…hopefully soon."

Rae rolled her eyes. "You know my driver will get us home. Just a little tappy-tap to my phone and poof, he whisks us away in a chariot."

"And when will you be tappy-tapping? Before we're throwing up our lunch from last year or after?"

"Definitely after," Raelynn said with a smile and a wink. "That salad was a waste of time, and I want it purged from this temple."

Nova tried to hold her stare, but her lips pinched, the first sign of her breaking and fighting off a smile. She shook her head and gave in, her lips parting around a soft laugh. "You're crazy."

"One of us has to be."

Grabbing my shot glass from the bar top, I winked at Nova. A camaraderie of sorts between the two non-crazy girls

178

completely in love with a wild one. She rolled her eyes but winked back, and neither of us mentioned how she didn't actually drink the shot, but instead, lifted it in a toast with us and quickly slid it back to the bartender.

With the alcohol burning through my veins, mixing with the other copious amounts of drinks we'd had that night, I decided to ruffle Raelynn's feathers.

Apparently, she noticed Nova's full glass because she quickly snatched it back and glared without heat while she took the shot for Nova. I waited until she'd almost emptied the glass when I struck.

"Besides, Nova. She probably is hoping for an excuse to drunk text Austin, and he'll come to her rescue. That way, she can grind all over him and say it's just because she was drunk and not in love."

Raelynn coughed hard, barely avoiding spraying us with tequila. She slapped the glass down with a thunk that matched the beat of the bass flooding the dark bar and glared over her hand covering her mouth.

Nova and I laughed.

"I. Am. Not. In lo—" she coughed, either from the alcohol still in her lungs or because Raelynn tended to choke over the word when it wasn't with us. "It's not like that between Austin and me."

"Of course not," Nova said, her words dripping with sarcasm.

I snorted because while Nova could look like a deer in headlights when she faced off with Raelynn, she always won with her sarcastic comments. She was a death by a thousand cuts, while Rae was a wrecking ball.

"So, you're saying if Austin came in and offered to let you climb him like the tree he is, you would turn him down?"

She lifted an arrogant brow. "No, because I hope *all* of him is as big as a tree, and I never turn down something that can make me feel that good."

Austin was Raelynn's other best friend—the complete oppo-site of her. They met at a college party her sophomore year and somehow became friends, despite her best effort to sleep with him. I think Raelynn liked—and probably hated a little—that he was the first guy to not want to sleep with her. She was all city, and he came from a farm in upstate New York.

Their friendship was…intriguing, and Nova and I may or may not have a bet on them being married by the time they were forty.

"Besides, he's visiting family and not in town."

"Is he your date for the wedding?" I asked.

"Of course. Friends to weddings are perfect. And I've seen him in a tux once and, damn, that man fills out a suit better than anyone."

"That poor man," Nova laughed. "How he's fended you off, I'll never know."

Raelynn shrugged, unapologetic of her objectification of her friend. "*Three* more shots," she said to the bartender, eying Nova with a challenging stare.

This time she obediently drank, not even wincing. Deep down, we all knew how much Nova liked tequila. My rebel side sat closer to the surface than hers, but she still had one—and Naughty Nova loved tequila.

The lights flashed, and the club enveloped us in one remixed song after another without consuming our words. We stood at the corner of the long bar, swaying to the music, laughing, and talking. We had to shout a little, but not so much we'd be hoarse in the morning.

"Question," I started, holding up my finger like I was preparing a declaration. Both girls laughed when I had to close my eyes and brace my hand on the bar for a moment because the alcohol hit me a little too hard. I shook it off and continued. "Is it really a bachelorette party if it's not a real marriage?"

"Why isn't it a real marriage? It's legal. You live together. You're sharing assets," Raelynn ticked off each argument.

"Because it's not. It's an arrangement. Like a business contract."

"Was that not what it was between you and Camden? Isn't that what your parents planned the whole time?"

I shuddered at the mention of Camden. "This is different."

"How?" Nova asked.

"It just is." My brain struggled to form a coherent argument with all the liquor.

"Would you have fucked Camden?" Raelynn asked.

I fake-gagged.

"That's a yes."

"I don't know. Maybe because I'm choosing this and not anyone else. I figured if I chose my husband, it would be for love."

"Love-shmove." She waved the word away like a fly. "You've just upgraded your arranged marriage package deal. I call it a win."

"Camden was pretty bad," Nova added.

"It just all feels fake," I said, waving my hands around to encompass the room.

"Does the sash not make you feel like a real bride to be?" Raelynn asked with mock seriousness, her hand on my shoulder.

I looked down, stroking the cheap satin and rough, patchy glitter, declaring my status. The stark white material stood out against my black top and black leather pants, making it impossible to miss. Which was why we were so drunk. People loved to buy drinks for a bachelorette party.

"If that doesn't, then the tiara and bouquet of flowers should," Nova said.

"Too much?" Raelynn asked, her face scrunched up with fake concern.

"No," I said.

"A bit," Nova said at the same time.

Raelynn shrugged, striking a pose like a supermodel,

showing off her dark yellow silk top and black leather mini-skirt. "Tough shit. I'm too much, and you bitches love it."

And just like that, we moved on from the edge of my deeper concerns. That was the joy of being drunk. Honesty came pouring out, just to be washed away by a random joke—shoved back down where it needed to stay buried.

"We love you." I wobbled the two steps and wrapped my arms around her.

I opened an arm for Nova to join, and she came in, slapping a kiss against both our cheeks. Her focus shifted behind us, and her lips parted, only to snap closed just as quick, before smiling at Raelynn.

"I love you so much that I want to take you home before you hate yourself."

A chorus of boos from both of us met her declaration.

"Come on. Where's Naughty Nova?" Raelynn asked, searching Nova's face like she'd find Nova's inner party girl hiding in her eyes.

Nova was the stable one. The one that gave in last to Raelynn's antics. But when she did, she gave in full force.

"We fed her tequila. Why won't she come out to play?" Raelynn asked, looking to me with a pout.

"Maybe she wants to dance. We haven't danced enough," I added.

"Naughty Nova does love to dance."

We closed in, and she half-heartedly tried to shove us back, laughing as we danced around her. I turned and leaned my back to her chest, rubbing my hands down my body all the way to my feet. With my legs still straight, I did my best ass-shake to Raelynn's catcalls. A firm slap to my ass had me pulling upright and glaring at Raelynn.

"You liked it."

I flashed back to Nico carrying me into the bedroom against my will and slapping my ass. I remembered the heat that bloomed, and I remembered how much I *had* liked it. The same heat came back with a force, not because of Raelynn, but because every time I thought of him, my body softened like it was preparing to give in.

"Come on, Nova. We have to get this bride-to-be so liquored up she stops being a stubborn bitch and finally bounces on her fiancé like a pogo stick."

I shoved Raelynn and stumbled back in my spiky heels. "Stop it."

"Many more drinks, and she won't be able to stand," Nova laughed, holding me steady.

"You don't need to stand to fuck."

Nova blushed; the dark club unable to hide the heat flooding her freckled cheeks.

"Okay, okay. Serious-time." Raelynn turned to me and held two fingers to her eyes before pointing at me. "Just one question. Please."

"Fine," I said, already knowing I'd regret it.

"The fucking? Was it good? Great? Epic? Bad? What? Hit me with a number? One-to-ten."

I sighed. Part in defeat, part in dreamy remembrance. "The. Fucking. Best. Like a twenty."

"Damn," she breathed. "And you didn't even get undressed. Okay, how big?"

I blamed the alcohol for answering as honestly as I did. "I didn't get to see. He was behind me the whole time. But he felt big and so, so good. Big like you imagine Austin to be."

"Damn," she said again. "I bet your poor vibrator is getting a workout."

Nova choked on her water. Raelynn slapped her on the back but kept going.

"Will you *please* just fuck him. For us. We know you want to."

I curled my lip and was a second away from crossing my arms and stomping my feet. "I don't *want* to want to."

"But you do want to," Raelynn exclaimed, pointing her finger at me victoriously.

"I'm definitely done with this conversation."

"But I'm so interested to know."

I wanted to blame the liquor in my veins for hearing the familiar deep voice. Like my imagination conjured the rough rumble that haunted my dreams. But the words stroked down my bare back, heating my core—too intense to not be real.

That and Raelynn's brows trying to merge with her hairline as she focused over my shoulder let me know this was no figment of my imagination.

TWENTY-TWO

Vera

I whirled around, coming face to face with a perfect row of black buttons I followed up to a strong neck into dark scruff that led to his full, smirking lips. After lingering there for too long, I finally met his eyes, dark pools of even darker promises just waiting to be fulfilled.

"Ho—How long have you been here?"

The real question was how much he had heard.

Actually, the real question was *why* he was here, but my mind stumbled over itself, trying to process the situation.

"Not too long. I'd say I walked in just in time." He scanned me from head to toe, his examination like a finger's touch, leaving fire in its wake. "That was some impressive...what's that word called? Twerking? Nova looked a little uncomfortable, but I'd be happy for you to perform that dance on me any time."

My eyes widened, and my jaw dropped open. The world swayed, the lights flashing in a blur around me, all focusing in on Nico's smirking face.

"Oh my god." The least intelligible words, but all I could manage to mutter in my drunken shock as I tried to imagine what he saw. As I was unable to *not* imagine what he suggested: me dancing for him.

"I taught her all she knows," Raelynn chimed in, pulling me from the image.

"How did you find us?" I asked.

He glanced over my shoulder, and I followed his gaze to a wincing Nova.

"You little tattletale," Raelynn scolded with a tiny shove.

Nova, completely unrepentant, rolled her eyes. "It's for your own good. You sure as shit weren't giving up your driver's phone number, and I know Vera's passcode. It was the only way to stop us all from vomiting in some back alley with a homeless man who would ask us if we wanted to live in his box."

"That was one time," Raelynn defended.

I snorted, vaguely remembering that night. It'd been fun. At least until that moment. I wasn't sure which had been scarier, the homeless man threatening to keep us in his alley forever or Austin storming down the street and taking us home in the chilliest silence ever.

"One of many," Nova said.

"Nova's never going to forgive you for that," I managed to get out through my drunken giggles.

If I remembered correctly, Nova had been his favorite.

"Fine," Raelynn caved. She crossed her arms and lifted her chin like a princess who knew she was wrong but wouldn't admit it. A princess with ample cleavage perfectly displayed in her low V-neck.

I fully expected Nico to be staring at her chest—hell, I was. Instead, I found him looking at me, his smile gone and a look of cautious curiosity, like he was doing a puzzle he couldn't quite figure out but couldn't wait to see it all together.

"Silver lining is that Vera gets to deal with the man picking her up this time, and I kind of like that he overheard her admit she wants to fuck him."

"Raelynn fucking Vos."

Now it was my turn to glare, Nova's turn to laugh, and

Raelynn's turn to shrug unrepentantly. We made a hell of a group.

"I love you, bitches," Nova announced, hopping down off the stool. She wrapped an arm around us both and smacked a kiss to our cheeks. "Now, let's get the hell out of here. Nico can only take his eyes off Vera when he's watching us banter. Seriously, it's like watching a cat watch a tennis game. Hilarious," she announced.

I snorted a laugh and blushed. Had Nico been watching only me? I forced myself to look at the girls, afraid to find a denial if I gave the comment too much attention.

Raelynn smacked Nova's ass and returned the kiss. "You're lucky I love you."

"Sure am." She turned us to face Nico. "Where to, sir?"

He took us in. Two overly drunk girls hanging on a slightly less drunk girl. He lingered on me, and I held my breath, waiting for him to deny Nova's accusation. Instead, he shook his head, huffing a laugh. "I've got my car with the valet, and my driver is around the corner. I figured I'd take Vera home, and you two could go with Xavier."

With a nod, Nova led us past him to the door. More cheek kisses, ass slaps, and hugs commenced before Nova finally managed to pull Raelynn into the backseat, leaving me to collapse into Nico's car.

The buttery soft leather and heated seats cradled my heavy body. I wanted to stay awake. I wanted to see if he'd say anything else about what he overheard. I wanted to watch his profile in the flash of the city lights shining through the windows as we drove past. Instead, the hum of the engine lulled me to sleep.

I jerked awake when two strong arms slipped under my back and thighs and hefted me against an even warmer chest.

"Shit," I slurred. "I can walk."

He didn't bother responding. Especially when, despite my

objections to being carried, I still wrapped my arms around his neck and rested my head on his shoulder.

Everywhere he touched, I burned like fire. It spread from his fingers, digging into my ribs, up my chest, and down to my core. I followed the path of the heat through my limbs, becoming both more relaxed and tense with need all at once.

The world swayed when he stepped from the elevator and walked down the dimly lit hallway to our front door.

Our.

Maybe it was the seven shots of tequila or earlier champagne with dinner, but somewhere through the night, calling his home *our* home settled a broken, floating piece about our upcoming marriage.

"Can you stand?"

"Yup."

He shook his head when I popped my p, but I caught his smile before he turned to unlock the door.

He held the door open, and I stumbled through, heading down the hall to *our* bedroom. He followed behind, picking up my carelessly dropped items. My shoes. My purse. My sash. My tiara.

"Should I expect this sash and tiara at the wedding?" he joked, laying it on the dresser.

"Maybe. I think the hot pink glitter might go well with our cream peonies. Think we could add a new color scheme last minute?"

He snorted, watching me undo my pants.

Shit.

Realizing I was undressing in front of him, I turned to head to the closet. All while still trying to get my pants off.

Halfway there, I focused too much on getting my hands under the waistband of my leather pants and stumbled over nothing.

Rough hands spanned across my ribs, keeping me from face-planting.

"Are you okay?"

My body shook. Laughter started in my chest and slowly worked its way free. He turned me around and pushed my once perfectly curled hair, but now a sweaty, tangled mess, from my face, even taking care to pluck the few strands from my eyelashes.

"Oh, my god. I'm just going to live in these pants now. There's no way I'm getting them off," I claimed through peals of laughter.

"I'd suggest baby powder and lotion, but then it might turn into a paste."

My jaw dropped. "You watch *Friends*," I squealed in excitement.

I realized the pitch I'd reached when his eyes widened before he exaggeratedly winced and rubbed at his ears.

"Oh, shut up," I said, shoving his hard shoulder.

Of course, having much more mass and a better center of gravity than me, he stood still, and I stumbled back. He gripped my waist again, and I went back to laughing.

"How much did you have to drink?"

"A lot. We kind of started at Raelynn's place when we were getting ready."

"At four?"

"We at least waited until five."

"It's two-thirty now."

"Damn. I'm kind of impressed I'm still standing."

"Well, I am holding you up."

"Very true." I tapped his chest and nodded like he'd imparted some epic knowledge.

I sighed, my shoulders dropping as the adrenaline of the night left my body with each passing second. I eyed my leather pants, remembering thinking they were the best idea ever and now wanting to just cut them off.

"Maybe I'll just sleep in these."

"Really?" he deadpanned.

"Well, I'd cut them, but I kind of like them."

"Do you want help?"

"I definitely think it's a two-man job. And since it's just you and me, you're in luck. Strip me," I proclaimed.

The sweat from all the dancing cooled and made the leather stick to my skin like glue, and in that moment, I didn't care if I undressed in front of him. I just wanted the damn things off.

We both bowed our heads and dug our hands into the waist-band, trying to pull them down. I stumbled again and bumped my head to his.

"Shit. Sorry."

"Always bumping into me," he joked.

"Ha-fucking-ha."

His lips tipped, softening the usual scowl or arrogant smirk. "You swear a lot when you drink."

"Like a fucking sailor."

Pulling his hands free, he held mine and guided me to lay on the bed. "This may be easier."

"I bet," I muttered, laying back.

He gripped both sides at my hips and tugged. Some pulls had me sliding down the bed with the pants, and by the time he got them down far enough to roll them off, I had both arms around my waist, clutching my stomach in a fit of laughter.

"Jesus Christ. Why bother wearing them?" he asked, out of breath.

"Because I look hot in them."

"Can't argue with that."

He tossed the pants aside, and I stood, lifting my arms up like a child.

"Need help with your top?"

"It's tight," I whined. "And everything is spinning a wee bit faster. Just…don't look."

I closed my eyes like I was the one not supposed to look.

"Okay."

His hands skimmed the bare skin of my hips, stroking softly

in a way that had nothing to do with helping me take my shirt off, but I just kept my eyes closed and arms up. If I didn't see it, I didn't have to acknowledge it, and it could happen. Right?

Right.

He peeled that black, lacy, stretch material up my ribs, and I held my breath when the cool air reached the underside of my breasts. Seconds stretched into what felt like forever, his breathing picking up pace. The material scraped past my nipples with a rush of cool air, pulling them to aching points. He tugged the top up and off.

I dropped my arms to my sides and forced my eyes open, half expecting to find him staring at my breasts. Instead, I found him staring at me. Our eyes collided, and Raelynn's questions about why I wouldn't just fuck him came roaring back.

His eyes beckoned me like the snake in the garden of Eden.

Give in. I promise I'll make it worth your while.

I knew he would. I remembered. And that was at a party, fully dressed—imagine what he could do naked with an entire bedroom at his disposal.

But like I'd said, I didn't want to want him.

The truth was, that Nico was a choice. It wasn't an arranged marriage like it had been to Camden. I chose to agree to Nico's proposal. And when I was little, in the moments I let myself imagine a future that had me choosing my own husband, it was never one who didn't love me.

I didn't *want* to want him—a man who openly claimed he'd never love me.

But I did.

And maybe—just for tonight—I could repeat the gala. If I woke in the morning with regrets, I'd blame it on the alcohol and swear I'd never do it again.

The tension grew like a living thing between us, wrapping around our bodies, urging us closer. It spread across our backs, like a bubble enveloping us in our basic needs.

Despite standing in front of him in only a tiny scrap of lace, his eyes never wandered.

I rested the tips of my fingers at the bottom of his abdomen, a thrill rushing through me when his hard muscles rippled under my seeking tips. Slowly, I lifted each palm, rising higher past his chest to his shoulders.

Using him for support, I pressed to my toes and leaned in.

Only for him to grip my wrists like shackles and tug them away as he stepped back.

My heart stuttered over the quick, hard beat. Doubt squeezed my chest too tight.

"I don't fuck drunk women," he said.

Embarrassment washed over me like a bucket of cold water, freezing me on my toes, my wrists in his hands, and my jaw hanging open. All in a scrap of lace that felt sexy moments ago and now felt like that last shred of dignity I had left.

The heat burning in his eyes simmered, and part of me wondered if maybe I'd imagined the whole thing. Had it actually never been there?

Fuck.

Fuck.

I swallowed, struggling to pull myself together, grasping for any emotion—unable to feel anything beyond the alcohol sloshing in my stomach.

Oh, my god.

What a fool.

He'd said he'd fuck me anywhere, and here I was throwing myself at him just for him to reject me.

Was that his plan all along? To have me give in just to turn me down?

Shit. What an idiot.

I closed my eyes to focus, and one emotion shined in the dark. The one that was fast becoming my constant companion. The one that got me to this very moment in a room that wasn't mine. In an apartment that wasn't mine. In the arms of a man that technically wasn't mine. With an engagement ring that should have never been mine.

Anger.

I reached out and clutched it tight like a shield.

Opening my eyes, I clenched my jaw and ripped my arms from his grip. I stumbled, and he reached to steady me, but I sidestepped, resting my hand on the nightstand to keep from falling.

"I'd regret it anyway," I spat. "Just like all the other women you've probably fucked and left with regrets."

Apparently, my anger sparked his own because a waterfall of ice covered any lingering heat in his gaze, and instead of the almost-smile from earlier, his lips curled into a cruel smirk. "Trust me, Vera. There's nothing about me being inside your tight little body to regret. What did you say earlier?" He pursed his lips. "The best ever? Like a twenty?"

Embarrassment tried to slam into me again, but I used my shield as a weak defense. "Fuck you."

"Happily. How about in the morning when you can actually participate?"

I choked on a forced laugh. "Yeah, right. You missed your chance. I wouldn't sleep with you if you were the last man on Earth."

"We'll see about that." Confidence dripped from every word, putting a dent in my shield more than embarrassment did.

Unable to form any more arguments as exhaustion crept through my limbs, I held my chin high. Struggling to not cover my chest, I portrayed my own confidence that was all a façade.

I bumped past him, wobbling as I stormed into the closet and clumsily got into a T-shirt and shorts. The shirt was inside out, and the shorts were on backward, but I didn't care. I had about two-percent life left in me, and I was using every ounce to salvage my mangled pride.

I opened the door to find him still standing there, so I bumped him again and climbed into the right side of the bed.

"Goodnight, Nico. I really look forward to the next five years of not fucking you."

With that, I flicked off the bedside lamp and rolled over, smiling at my small victory of having the last word.

At least until his low chuckle crept through the shadows like my darkest fantasy, poking holes in my thin confidence.

"Goodnight, Verana."

TWENTY-THREE

Vera

───────

"Last chance. You want to run?" Raelynn asked. Her ocean eyes met mine through my veil. She looked like a grenade with the pin pulled but not released. I may not be marrying someone I loved, but I had love around me today. "I already prepped Austin to clear us a path and call it all off. Bruce is on speed dial around the corner with the car."

"Raelynn!" Nova reprimanded.

"What?" She looked at Nova like *she* was the crazy one. "We're her maids of honor. We wouldn't be doing our jobs if we didn't ask her to run."

"Fine. Vera, you know I'm always in if you want to run," she said, the perfect supportive friend. Then she focused her pinched brows back at Raelynn. "But still."

Raelynn shrugged and turned back to me, searching my face for any signs I wanted to run. "Are you hesitating? Because I'm serious. We can run. Platonic, all-girl, love island, here we come!"

She added a shimmy, looking stunning in her pale rose dress.

I laughed, wondering if maybe an all-girl island was better than the current situation.

I looked in the mirror. The veil slightly blocking my view of a woman in all white. The lacy top cutting into a deep v that met at the fitted waist of my dress before flowing out into soft, heavy silk. I hadn't been sure about the more revealing top, but Raelynn promised it was classy-sexy.

Meeting the dark eyes of the woman looking back, clutching her all-white peony bouquet, she looked so familiar, yet like I'd never seen her before in my life.

Standing taller, I lifted my chin, portraying the defiant courage stirring in the chocolate depths. I may not recognize every inch of the bride in the mirror, but the strength filled me just the same. I was no longer the docile, obedient woman who waited for her future to be chosen because everyone told her it was the right thing.

No. I was Verana Mariano.

And although she looked like a stranger, she was me. She was just a newer version I hadn't realized had been lying dormant all these years.

"I'm ready."

"Then let's go."

With one last deep breath, I headed to face my future.

To Nicholas Rush.

With each step closer, I thought over the last week after I'd embarrassingly thrown myself at him.

I'd expected to find him gloating the next morning. Instead, I'd woken up to a water bottle and ibuprofen on the nightstand. In fact, we never spoke of it beyond a glare across the kitchen island—he'd sat greasy bacon in front of me when I'd finally found the courage to leave the bedroom, and it pissed me off that he was making it so hard to be mad at him.

Work consumed our days, leaving no room for alone time to face the consequences of my drunk actions. At least, until we both crawled into bed at night. I'd get ready in the guest bathroom to avoid running into him showering. That had happened once, and I'd immediately closed my eyes, running in the other direction like a prude, his laugh following behind.

I considered trying to hide in the guest room, but the petty joy of taking his side of the bed always brought me back to the master bedroom, where I crawled in bed and clung to the edge.

Each night, I'd turn the lights out and feign sleep, but he knew better. He'd repeat the same arrogant chuckle and ask me if I wanted to offer myself up on a silver platter.

"I'd gladly eat you up, Verana. I remember how sweet you tasted on my tongue."

"Well, hold tight to that memory because it will never happen again."

"Oh, I do. I hold it tight in my fist every morning—usually in the shower. You could have seen if you'd stayed."

I'd swallowed my moan, reminding myself that he was a disrespecting man whore. Yet, despite my best efforts, there were times I still woke up in the middle of the night in his arms. Despite hating him and refusing him, I never pulled away, instead, staying put, only to wake up alone in the morning.

Nico got up early to hit the gym before holing up in his office for meetings to prepare for the two-week honeymoon he'd planned.

He'd been so busy that he'd actually given me a job beyond the usual menial tasks. *Gasp.* I'd gloated when I'd crushed the job, and the client said my ideas were unique and had the potential to reach new heights. It'd forced him to acknowledge my awesomeness. I'd met his dark glare across the conference table with a winning smile. But then his lips twitched to a semblance of a smile, something like pride flashing across his face before he quickly moved the meeting on.

Remembering that moment made me smile all over again, even picking up the pace to get into position.

He may be a dick, but something brewed beneath the surface that intrigued me to go further. No, I didn't need to run away. Even better—I didn't want to.

I was ready.

"What the hell, Nico?" Raelynn screeched, stiff-arming me

from walking around the corner. Nova scrambled to keep my dress from tripping me up before joining Raelynn to create a bridesmaid barrier—arms out and all. "You can't see her before the wedding."

"I just wanted to talk to her a moment."

A slither of dread coiled its way around my chest and squeezed. Did he want to call it off? Did he have someone asking him if he wanted to run? A friend I hadn't met? An old lover?

Ohmygod. Ohmygod.

The thoughts brought waves of adrenaline. My limbs shook so hard I almost dropped my bouquet. My vision darkened on the edges as scenario after scenario ran through my head.

I'd have to marry Camden.

I'd be stuck forever.

I glanced at Raelynn's hand, picturing grabbing it and running.

"You better not be ditching her," Nova said in the coldest voice I'd ever heard from her gentle soul. Even Raelynn's head snapped her way in shock.

"I'm not. I just wanted to have a few words—privately—before we said our I dos."

Relief almost took my knees out, and a giggle broke free because all I could think was that if I was going to pass out, at least I was surrounded by a heavy mass of silk and tulle. It'd be the softest landing ever.

Nova looked to me for permission, and I nodded, pulling myself together.

"Fine."

"But stay around the corner. No peeking, or I'll poke your eyes out with my stilettos," Raelynn threatened.

"Jesus," Nico muttered, pulling another giggle from me.

"It's her wedding day. Real or not, it's special."

"I assure you, it's very real."

"Mmhmm." Raelynn turned to me. "You okay with this?"

"Yeah. I'll stay around the corner. Thanks, bodyguards," I joked.

"Anytime. We'll wait for you at the stairs."

Both girls kissed my cheeks and headed out. Nova faced Nico and held two fingers to her glaring eyes before pointing them at him. I kind of wished I could see his face, but despite all this feeling like a hoax, I wanted it to be as real as possible. I always liked the silly traditions, so I stayed around the corner.

"What's going on, Nico?"

I heard the fabric of his suit rub together, and I imagined him leaning his broad shoulders against the wall to get comfortable. Maybe he had his hands stuffed into his pockets, pulling the material tight across his bulge.

"I'm going to kiss you today, Verana."

Of all the things I considered him saying, that hadn't even crossed my mind. It took a moment to process, the rough words rounding the corner to sink into my chest like a promise. Crazily, in all this time, we hadn't kissed. I knew how roughly his hands palmed my breasts, how hard they gripped my hips. I knew what his tongue flicked like between my thighs, how his cock stretched me to the max. I knew all of this, but I didn't know how his lips moved on mine.

It was the last line we'd cross, and it felt more intimate than sex.

"Are you sure?" he asked so softly I almost missed it. It lacked the usual confidence he oozed without trying.

"About the kiss or the marriage?" I asked, just as softly.

"Both."

Was I sure I wanted him to kiss me? Was I sure I wanted to follow through with the wedding?

I hesitated, considering running.

But I remembered the ten seconds of dread that swallowed me whole when I thought he was coming to cancel it all. And if I had to be honest, maybe I looked forward to finally kissing him. Maybe I'd wanted to for longer than I'd admit and doing it to lock in our arrangement sounded like the perfect excuse.

Still, I couldn't give up all control. "I guess," I answered playfully.

"About the kiss or the marriage?"

"Both."

He chuckled. I closed my eyes, imagining his chest moving with the deep rumble, his full lips twitching into a begrudging smile.

"Does this mean you'll let me fuck you properly on our wedding night?"

I swallowed down the *yes*, sitting on the tip of my tongue. "In your dreams."

"We'll see," he promised.

I rolled my eyes, hearing all the confidence that had been missing before.

"I can't wait to see you."

With those parting words that rang with sincerity and something I hadn't expected to hear from anyone beyond an actual groom who loved his bride, he left.

A moment later, the rustling of dresses announced Raelynn and Nova's return.

"What did he say?"

"Did he look?"

"Are you okay?"

"You look pale. Do I need to stab him?"

They hit me with a barrage of questions too fast for me to keep up. I held up my hands and laughed. "I'm fine. I think it was just to make sure I actually showed."

Appeased with my answer, they relaxed. "Okay. Well, let's get this party started."

They helped me up the old steps to the narthex, where my father waited, pacing the tiled floor.

I swallowed down the nerves and smiled at Nova when she gave my hand a reassuring squeeze.

Part of me hadn't wanted my father to walk me down the aisle, our relationship torn into fractured pieces I didn't recognize. But there he stood, mostly there for appearances—and for Mama. She would have risen from the dead to yell at us both if he wasn't there for me today.

He stopped when he saw me. His jaw dropped as he looked me up and down.

For a moment, it was the moment I'd imagined as a little girl. He'd look at me with pride, his eyes filling with tears, and pull me into his arms, telling me I was the most beautiful bride he'd ever seen.

I waited, holding my breath.

His wrinkles deepened with this frown like the weight of all we lost sat too heavy for him to bear. My nose burned when I forced myself to hold back from running into his arms. I wanted the man who'd threatened my prom date. I wanted the man who took me to a One Direction concert and even danced with me. I wanted the man who held me when I cried over losing Mama.

He looked like that man, but I knew he wasn't, and I ached with the truth.

"You look beautiful, Verana."

"Thank you," I squeezed out past the lump choking me.

"You don't have to do this," he said, taking a step forward, almost pleading.

"I want to."

And there it was, the reminder of all we'd lost. His eyes slid closed, hiding the adoring love he may have had for me. When they opened, all that was left was the void of all that was missing.

A barrier to slide in place like it did in business meetings. His jaw snapped closed, and he swallowed, adjusting the sleeves on his jacket as he stood tall.

"Then let's go," he said.

Raelynn grumbled, but thankfully, stayed silent, getting in line.

My father linked his arm through mine, and I shut down all I'd lost, focusing on slow deep breaths, waiting for the bridal march.

"Maybe I can talk to your groom after the wedding. Business stuff."

My eyes slid closed, controlling the flood of disappointment as the dream I'd had faded further away.

"Sure, Dad."

The song started, and the doors parted, revealing the long nave lined with flowers and guests. The tall arched ceilings stretched above, making everything look so small. Each click of my heels against the tile vibrated up my body to my chest, making my heart skip a beat. The organ music filled the massive church and pressed in on my chest.

I began to shake but kept walking.

I was doing this.

It was happening.

If I turned and ran, would Raelynn follow? Would Austin hold everyone back? Would I make it to the car before Nico made it to me?

Nico.

I looked to the end of the aisle, and there he stood, stunning in a black tux. His hair styled to perfection, his beard trimmed shorter, framing his full lips perfectly.

I'm going to kiss you, Verana.

My heart stuttered for a whole new reason.

I met his dark eyes and took my first deep breath.

We were in this together. It may not be the marriage I dreamed of, but it was a partnership—one that I got to choose. One that I was safe in.

Sometimes Prince Charming is everything you need when you didn't know you needed it.

Mama's words wrapped around me, reminding me that just

because she wasn't here physically, didn't mean she wasn't with me always.

I didn't look away from Nico the rest of the walk. He met us at the altar wall, and as soon as my hand slipped into his, I stood taller.

Before I knew it, my lips promised to be his, and his promised to be mine.

Before I knew it, the priest said, "You may kiss the bride."

My heart thudded so hard, I wondered if Nico could see.

He lifted my veil, giving me the first clear view of flowers and candles. But I couldn't look anywhere but him.

He leaned in, and I held my breath.

I'm going to kiss you, Verana.

"Are you sure?" he whispered inches from my lips.

I breathed a laugh, the question catching me so off guard. Meeting his eyes, I slicked my tongue across my bottom lip, loving the way he followed the movement and did the same to his own, and shrugged. "I guess."

With a growl at my playful answer, he closed the gap and crashed his lips to mine. His long fingers spanned my waist, stretching up my back, getting tangled in my veil. He pulled me in, touching every part of our bodies together.

Our first kiss was on our wedding day, and it was just as indecent and passionate as our first night together.

It didn't matter that there were over a hundred guests watching. It didn't matter that we stood on one of the oldest altars in all of New York. It didn't matter that a priest stood five feet away.

Nothing mattered except the feel of his lips moving on mine.

Nothing mattered except the fireworks shooting off throughout my body, bringing every inch to life.

Nothing mattered except how I didn't want it to end.

I wrapped my arms around his shoulders, burrowing my fingers into his hair, holding him just as tight as he held me.

His tongue flicked playfully against my lips, and I parted just enough for a taste.

Roaring applause crept past our bubble, and we slowed the kiss, both of us panting like we'd run a marathon—both of us looking a little shocked by the intensity that consumed us.

"I present to you, Mr. and Mrs. Rush."

He linked his fingers with mine and smiled a smile full of victory and promise.

I smiled a challenge back and shook my head, letting him lead me down the aisle to the awaiting limo.

He helped me in and poured me a glass of champagne. With eyes scanning every inch of me, I took my first sip, the bubbles tickling my tongue.

"You look fucking beautiful, and you're all mine," he almost growled.

Heat bled into my cheeks. Surprisingly, I didn't mind being called his. Surprisingly, I liked his coarse compliment.

Maybe it was the moment—the champagne, the kiss, the cheers, the limo, the dress and tux, or flowers. I didn't know, and I didn't care. Euphoria and boldness had me scooting closer, looking him over before meeting his heavy-lidded stare.

"Am I?" I challenged softly. "Am I all yours?"

The pads of his fingers teased up my bare arm, playing with the lace strap against my shoulder before tracing the line down into my cleavage.

I didn't stop him.

I sat still, breathing hard.

Want burned me from the inside out.

He set his glass aside, grabbing mine to do the same. His fingers traced the edge of my cheek, down my neck, and slid behind my head, holding me in place as he leaned in.

"Yes," he answered, his hot breath against my lips. "You. Are. Mine."

"Nico," I said, a hollow effort to stop.

"Just…one more."

This time, *I* closed the gap, feasting on his lips. This time there was no one around to stop us. There was no church to keep us in line. Only my stubborn pride and a dress entirely too large to straddle his lap like I wanted without it engulfing us both in the process.

Instead, we kissed. Our hands holding each other in place so we could taste every inch we'd only imagined for the last few months.

His tongue dueled with mine, and he gave as good as he got. Surprisingly, never once did his hands stray below my neck. It was like he wanted to indulge what I'd denied him for so long.

Part of me demanded I stop—to not give in.

And I would.

But not yet.

"Just for the limo ride," I panted between drugging kisses.

He smiled, his look doubtful, but I didn't care because he went right back to kissing me, and I wanted to take as much as I could before I forced myself to hold true to that promise.

However, my promise was useless when we got to the reception. Everyone tapped their silverware against their glass, huge smiles waiting for the newlyweds to kiss. And each time I tried for a peck, Nico held me in place to devour me. And each time, I gave in.

As soon as we finished eating, he linked his hand with mine. "I want you to meet someone. My grandpa," he explained.

"Of course."

I followed him to a broad man with white hair and the same mouth as Nico. I couldn't help but wonder if this was what Nico would look like when he grew older—and if I'd get to see it.

"Grandpa, I'd like you to meet my wife, Verana. Verana, this is Charles."

"Charlie, please." He stood and took my hand, pressing a soft kiss to my knuckles. "Welcome to the family, my dear. Although, Nico was supposed to bring you sooner," he said with a glare at Nico.

Despite the look having no heat behind it, Nico still rubbed a hand along the back of his neck and looked away. I could imagine him as a little boy, getting in trouble and kicking at the dirt.

"I felt terrible to miss meeting you beforehand. Work has been fairly busy. Especially since we have such a long honeymoon planned."

"Well, if he ever works too much, you can come visit me. I'm much better company, anyway," he said with a wink.

"I'll definitely make sure to do that. Do you like cards?"

"I may have been a bit of a shark in my day. I taught Nico everything he knows. Don't let him swindle you into a game of poker. He's better than he'll pretend to be."

"I may be a bit of a shark myself."

"A woman after my own heart. Beautiful, smart, hardworking, and can put you in your place, Nicholas."

"We'll see about that," Nico muttered, giving me a challenging stare. I gave one of my own, making a mental note to pick up a deck of cards for our honeymoon.

"Your grandma would have loved to be here," he said to Nico. "Now, there was a shark. The prettiest, strongest woman I'd ever met. She held me up when I was weak and made our life what it was."

"She would have loved Vera. Telling me she was smarter than I deserved," Nico added.

Nico's hand slipped around my waist and held me close, and I had to remind myself that this was what he got out of the marriage. A happy picture to portray to his ailing grandpa. He'd been attentive all day, but I had to remember that it wasn't real.

"I can see how much you care for each other."

I looked away, unsure of lying to an old man I'd grown to like in the short time we'd been chatting.

"Be kind to your hearts through it all. Love is a dangerous game with many rewards. So, when you have it, fight hard to keep it." He looked down at the ring decorating my finger, probably remembering it on his wife's finger. "It's precious."

His love filled the room and warmed me from the inside out. His was the love a girl dreamed about.

How a man like Nico—marrying a woman for convenience, full of arrogance, and missing a good dose of empathy—came from a man like Charles, I could never guess.

"We'll do our best," Nico promised.

"If not, you come to me, and I'll knock him into shape," Charlie promised with another wink.

"I look forward to it," I said, smiling at Nico.

"Thanks, Grandpa. Aren't you supposed to be on my side?"

"Nah, I raised you to be a good man, and I know you can take care of yourself."

Nico stood a little taller, and for a bit, despite his towering frame, I saw a little boy, putting every ounce of pride in his spine, rising up under his grandpa's praise. Charlie was a man Nico respected and loved, and it was a side I'd yet to see from him.

This wasn't the arrogant businessman or the devious flirt—this was just a man—a good one. If I had a camera, I would have taken a picture and tucked it away to pull out when I wanted to imagine Nico as my prince charming. Instead, I tucked it away mentally, wanting to remember this softer side of him.

"Besides, I'm looking for any reason for this beautiful young woman to come visit me, so I can share all the ways to beat you at cards—I can tell you all his secrets."

Nico stiffened, and Charlie laughed, softly smacking his hand against Nico's chest. "Loosen up, Nicholas. You're nervous like a girl bringing home her first boyfriend."

Nico's cheeks turned a ruddy color and leveled Charlie with a disapproving glare, but Charlie met him with one of his own. The duel stretched until it became abundantly clear another conversation took place without words.

Finally, Charlie broke the staring contest with a huff. "I won't spill *all* your secrets." Nico's jaw twitched, and my eyes flicked back and forth like watching a tennis match. When the tension became almost too much to bear, Charlie winked at me and turned back into the flirt. "Not yet, at least. Although, I'm not sure how much longer I can hold back telling Vera about the year you refused to wear pants."

Nico groaned, and I laughed—the tension fading. But I pocketed away the staring contest next to all the other tidbits I'd learned about Nico, unable to ignore that maybe Charlie was hinting at secrets Nico didn't want me to know. Part of me wanted to prod more and roll the information around to study it at all angles, but the ambiance around us had me saving it for another time.

That, and Charlie telling me more stories of Nico as a boy that had him reaching for a tumbler and trying to hide his blushing cheeks. I found it terribly adorable and promised Nico I'd never let him live the embarrassing stories down.

Soon after, Charlie left, and the night moved in a blur, people dancing and eating and laughing. Deals were made at the open bar as can only happen at a wedding with mostly business associates. Raelynn managed to drag Austin out on the floor and danced around him in a way that made him blush. I laughed when Austin danced with Nova, and Raelynn glared when she thought no one was watching.

By the end of the night, everyone was laughing and having fun. Nico—a surprisingly good dancer—twirled me around, pulling me right back into his arms.

Another round of clinking glasses at the end of the night had his lips on mine again. Only this time, when he pulled away, he hefted me in his arms. I yelped, holding on tight around his neck.

"It's time to go, wife," he whispered.

He made his way to the exit, nodding his farewell to everyone we passed.

"Nico. This is rude, and oh my god, what are they going to think?"

"That I'm taking my brand-new bride to our suite, so I can tear you out of this dress and fuck you as your husband."

His words shot straight to my core, and I squirmed in his arms. His deep laugh rumbled like a promise of dirty things to come.

But I'd made a promise of my own to not sleep with him. I just hoped I could hold on to it.

All of a sudden, five years looked like an eternity.

TWENTY-FOUR

Nico

NEED PULSED with each step closer to our suite. I didn't know if I'd make it to our room. Her light puffs of air against my neck. Her small hands holding tight to my shoulders. The soft weight of her body cradled in my arms.

I wanted to get to our room so I could have all of this, minus her dress, with her legs wrapped around my waist. Hard. Against a wall.

At least the first time.

The memory of her heat crowded my brain day and night. Especially having her curled up in bed beside me. And now she was my wife. I had a lifetime—or at least five years—to fuck her every way I wanted to.

I just had to make her admit she wanted it too. After all the drugging kisses from lips I'd imagined tasting from night one, I knew she was just as ready as I was.

I almost ordered the attendant to get the hell out of the elevator so I could tease her more, but Vera smiled and laughed with giddy wonder when he handed us each a glass of champagne and pushed the button for our floor.

"A good night?" the attendant asked.

"Yeah, it was," Vera answered.

Her smile grew into something soft, and she looked down, biting her lip, like she could barely contain her genuine happiness.

A flicker of emotion that sparked in my chest when I'd caught my first glimpse of her walking down the aisle flared again. Small and unidentifiable.

Uncomfortable with the odd warmth, I focused on my pride —on the victory flooding my veins. Watching Lorenzo's barely contained scowl as he escorted Vera to me had been icing on a cake I never imagined having. Even better because he didn't even know he was handing his daughter over to his enemy. Yet.

Fortunately, he missed Grandpa at the ceremony, and Grandpa hadn't been well enough to stay long at the reception. Not that Lorenzo had stayed long after I shot down his attempt to talk business. Obviously, because his plan with Camden fell through, he looked at his next best cash horse. Part of me wanted to play him like he played my grandpa. But I didn't want to play games. I wanted to hide in the shadows and slowly pick him apart until I could step forward with the direct blow.

Just like you're being direct with Vera?

I shoved any guilt down and almost dragged her out of the elevator.

She said she wouldn't sleep with me, but she also said she wouldn't kiss me, and she'd had her lips on mine all night.

I held the door to the suite open, a round table in the middle of a small foyer with two doors on each side. A bottle of chilled champagne sat next to a bundle of red roses and candles.

"Wow," she breathed.

Soft music played from the open doors on the left. Her dress rustled loudly, almost drowning out her gasp when she took in the room beyond. Red rose petals and candles covered every surface. With her hands to her chest, she spun, emitting a high-pitched sound of joy, making my lips twitch.

In her white dress—standing out among the deep red petals —the dim flicker of candles, and the New York City skyline

211

twinkling through the corner of the windows behind her, she looked like a fairy tale.

"Oh my gosh. Nico."

She said my name with wonder and joy—like she'd never said it before—and that flicker of warmth roared back. I looked around and stuffed my hands in my pockets, feigning a lack of interest as I took it in. "The hotel really goes all out for honeymoon suites."

Of course, they went all out because I asked them to with very specific instructions to use buttercream scented candles and the deepest of red like the dress she wore to the masquerade party.

"Oh…" she said softly, her excitement fading.

The flare in my chest grew uncomfortably large with the way she looked at me, and I wanted it gone, so I let her think it wasn't me, but the disappointment bothered me even more. And a disappointed Vera wouldn't sleep with her husband. At least, that was my excuse, and the only reason I could understand why I uttered, "Dance with me."

"What?"

"Dance with me," I said again, holding out my hand, walking to meet her in the middle of the room.

Some of the disappointment faded, and curiosity took its place. She studied me, and I tried to hold still, wondering if my small fib had ruined our night, and she'd turn me down. Instead, one side of her mouth tipped, and she closed the gap, slipping her hand in mine.

I pulled her close, wrapping my arms around her waist, my fingers playing with the exposed curve of her spine, and started swaying.

"Where did you learn to dance?"

I huffed a laughed. "My mom taught me some basics when I was little. She claimed a good man could win any woman over with smooth moves; at least that was her excuse for falling for my dad."

"They sound like they were happy."

"Very. When she died, I took a few classes to keep part of her close to me." I pulled back enough to meet her eyes and smirked. "And to win over the ladies."

She rolled her eyes but smiled before tucking her head back against my chest.

"My mom loved Billie Holiday. She loved all the oldies."

I knew that. She'd mentioned it in passing when I caught her in the kitchen with Dean Martin on. It was why I requested they play them in the suite.

Billie Holiday shifted to Frank Sinatra to Ben E. King, and with each song, I worked us closer to the bedroom across the foyer. By the time we reached the foot of the bed, my body ached to feel her lips on mine—to peel her wedding dress from her body and bury myself inside her all night long.

I drifted my hand up her back and into her hair, softly tugging her head back, so I could lean in for a taste. Her glossy lips parted, and I was inches from heaven when she pulled away.

Wide, nervous eyes met mine. But behind the nerves sat the resolve I'd been trying to break through all night, and my brows lowered before she even spoke.

"We're not in the limo anymore, Nico. And no one is clinking their glasses."

My teeth clenched, and I inhaled through my nose, searching to hold my irritation back.

"I said I wasn't sleeping with you."

"Vera," I growled.

"Nico," she said, standing taller. Her resolve locked in place, and I knew there would be no getting past it.

Frustration had me wanting to storm out. To slam the door behind me. We both knew she wanted to sleep with me and that it was sheer stubbornness that stopped her. My blood pumped for release, and my muscles ached from holding back for so long.

But it was my wedding night, and I wouldn't run from my own wife. If I was frustrated, then she could damn well deal with it, even if I was a bear for the rest of the night. She could deny me, and I'd always respect her, but it didn't mean I couldn't be pissed about it. It didn't mean I couldn't still get what I wanted in another way.

With a growl, I turned her around to face the bed and started working the tiny buttons on the back of her dress.

"What are you doing?" she gasped.

"Helping you out of this contraption. I'm assuming someone helped you in, and unless you want to sleep in it forever, you'll need me. Or should I call someone to come up?"

"No. But Nico, I said I'm not sl—"

"So I heard."

Working the last button free, the heavy skirt parted, and I groaned.

"Like a fucking present I can't even open."

I stared at the small satin bow adorning the top of the strings holding mostly transparent lace over her ripe ass. She shivered when I dragged my fingers up her back and brushed the straps of her dress off her shoulders. The material fell down to pile against the full skirt. Holding one of her hands for support, I used the other to push the skirt down.

"Step."

She did as she was told, revealing lace garters I wanted to rip off her. I pushed the dress aside, not caring about anything but making this inferno inside me ease. My cock throbbed from the constant teasing all night long, from knowing that this woman was *mine—my wife.* A word I never knew would make me as hard as stone.

My desperation made me rough when I gripped her hips and jerked her around to face me before lifting her enough to toss her back on the bed. Her bare breasts bounced, adding fuel to the fire, the rosy tips hardening to stiff points. Without wasting time, I put one knee on the bed and then the other, shedding my jacket and bow tie before working on the buttons of my shirt.

"Wha—what are you doing?" She scooted back to the pillows, worry and excitement, coloring her beautiful face.

I could have her, I realized with each inch I moved closer. I could have her, but I wanted her to come willingly. I didn't want her giving in because I'd seduced her into caving. I wanted her to give in because she wanted it and knew she'd want it again every day after. If I had her tonight, she'd make excuses tomorrow.

But I took note of her excitement as I prowled closer, liking that she liked me being rough. I took note and stored it away next to the soft moan I'd heard when I'd spanked her weeks ago.

"Nico?" she asked, her words breathy and unsure.

"It's my wedding night," I explained, stripping my shirt before working on my pants. "At the very least, I'd like to come. Now, stay put while I jack off."

Her eyes widened, tracking down my body, almost panting by the time I pulled my pants down far enough to free my length. I moaned, and her eyes snapped back up to mine. I raised a brow, half expecting her to tell me to fuck off and bolt —ready to pack it all back up if she really wanted me to. Instead, she rose to the occasion and clenched her jaw, lifting her stubborn chin like a dare. She leaned back on her elbows, pushing her pert breasts out, and I craved to fall over and suck on them until they were rosy and so tender that the softest brush of air would set her off.

I moaned again, giving myself another rough stroke. Unable to help herself, she watched. And I watched her.

I squeezed up my shaft and around the head, using my thumb to smear the precum leaking from the tip. "You can still have this inside you," I offered one last time. "I can remind you how good it felt."

She swallowed but held strong. "No." Her denial, weak and needy.

"Fine."

With one hand rolling my balls, I stroked myself faster and

harder, taking in her sleek skin. She squirmed and panted, her hard nipples begging for attention. Every once in a while, she'd part her thighs just enough to give me a glimpse of her smooth folds under the sheer fabric, the scent of her arousal hitting me like an aphrodisiac.

"Just because I'm not fucking you, doesn't mean you can't get off. Feel free to play with your pretty pussy."

Her tongue slicked across her supple lips, and I held my breath, praying for her to say yes. Instead, she snapped her jaw shut and shook her head, continuing to pant and writhe on the bed.

"I've had to do this more since I've met you than when I was a teenager. Every morning, I go to the shower and remember your soft wet pussy on my tongue. I remember the way you bent over and let me feast on you. The way you rubbed your cunt on my face as you came. I remember how tight you were. How I had to wedge my fat cock between your swollen lips and ease in. I remember the way your cum slid down my cock and coated my balls as I played with your tits."

"Nico," she moaned.

The desperation in just my name raced down my spine, and I knew I was about to come.

"I remember the way you cried out as you pulsed around me, milking the cum from my cock."

With that memory and watching her strong thighs rubbing together for friction, I came. Cupping the head, I worked my hand faster, jerking every last drop of pleasure from my body. Goose bumps spread across my skin, pulling it too tight as wave after wave hit me. With a few more slow swipes, I calmed, focusing on Vera. She laid back, breathing just as hard as me, a flush working its way down her neck.

Good.

"I'm going to clean up. Feel free to join me."

A swirl of need and anger raged behind her caramel eyes, and I added fuel to the fire by smirking before disappearing into the bathroom. I imagined the anger was directed as much at her own stubborn pride as it was at me.

Not surprisingly, she didn't join me in the shower. I wrapped the towel around my body and walked out to find her lounging in a small silk and lace nightgown.

"Did you wear that just for me?" I taunted.

She didn't bother to look up from the magazine she flipped through. "Hardly. Raelynn packed it for me."

"Did she pack all your lingerie?" I asked, both hopeful and worried at the same time. If she had a nightgown like the one currently riding up her thigh and doing nothing to hide the hard points underneath, then I was going to die a slow death over the next two weeks of our honeymoon.

"I guess you'll have to wait and see," she taunted.

She never looked up directly, but I felt the way she tracked me around the edge of the bed. She wanted to torture me. Well, two could play that game.

Standing by the bed, watching for her reaction, I dropped the towel.

"What the hell?" she practically screeched.

Pleased that she couldn't take her eyes off my cock as I climbed in bed beside her, I smirked. "I'm your husband now, so the kid-gloves are off, and I sleep in the nude. Feel free to join me."

With effort, she dragged her eyes away and glared. "You wish."

I sure fucking did.

TWENTY-FIVE

Vera

———

ROLLING OVER in the clouds of blankets and pillows, I squinted at the long rays of the sun reaching through the window across the cream carpet to wake me up. I stretched after a sleep just as luxurious at this bed until a glint from my left hand reminded me of the day before.

I married Nicholas Rush.

I was no longer Verana Mariano, but Verana Rush—Mrs. Rush.

Turning softly, I rolled to my side, facing Nico. His bronze skin stood stark against the white sheets that barely clung to his naked hips. I studied each dip and groove of his body. I'd seen him without his shirt a few times, but never had I allowed myself the luxury of memorizing each ridge and valley. One arm stretched behind his head, and the other rested on his stomach—his own wedding band impossible to miss.

Just like it had been hard to miss last night when he'd jacked off in front of me.

Heat spread through my body all over again like a fire to tinder. I closed my eyes, and like a movie on fast forward, images of him flashed behind my lids. The veins along his arms straining with the effort to stroke his thick length as he reached for his peak. His firm chest rising and falling with his panting breaths. His flushed cheeks and sweat-dampened hair. His full lips slicked by his tongue, teasing with the filthiest words. His broad head leaking pearly liquid until his palm came up to swipe it away. His heavy balls cradled in his hand, his brand-new wedding band shining—a bright reminder that this was my husband. That if I wanted him, he would, could be mine.

I almost gave in. I almost said fuck it and demanded he fuck me. Every second of watching him was like an hour in the most intense game imaginable. My body hot, tense, aching.

I knew I should have run. I should have shoved him away and slept in one of the other rooms.

But the way he looked at me as I laid back in my white, lacy wedding lingerie, filled me with an intense power. His heavy-lidded eyes took me in like he'd never seen anything like me. The way he'd stared in awe and couldn't look away had me glued to the bed. Here stood a man who respected me enough to listen to my words—even though part of me wanted him to push, so I could give in and blame him in the morning—but still wanted me any way he could have me.

Power.

It had flooded my veins and held me in place. It was amazing what feeling like you're being heard—being seen—can do to you. As soon as he'd gone to shower, my hand flew between my legs, and I'd clamped my bottom lip under my teeth to hold back my moans as I came within seconds.

I'd wanted to give in.

But I didn't. I wouldn't be someone's booty call for five years.

I wouldn't be ordered to be a body purely for pleasure just because I was his wife.

I hadn't escaped Camden just to do it with Nico.

Camden's promise of having me whenever and however he'd wanted me haunted me more than I thought. I'd shoved it aside, focused on my plans with Nico, unaware that it lingered, touching every decision I made. Like a scar, it wasn't very visible, but always there.

I'd almost forgotten it after the magical day and night, but when he'd started undoing the buttons on my dress and tossed me on the bed, I was sure he would take, especially when I just sat there panting with need.

But he hadn't. He'd been arrogant and demanding but still respectful.

I focused back on the man in front of me, his chest a dusting of dark hair rising and falling over his deep, even breathing. His face calm in sleep without his usual look of annoyance or placidity.

We left for our two-week honeymoon today, and I couldn't help but wonder if every night would be like last night.

Would I be able to be as strong as last night with my body on fire? How long could I burn when he offered to put out the fire? Was I strong enough?

I had to be. I would be.

At the very least, I wanted a friendship—a partner like my mother had described. Even if it never turned to love, five years was a long time to be with someone you disliked. I couldn't sleep with someone who saw me as an inferior woman, there to service their needs, and Nico had made his thoughts clear about how he saw me with each menial task he gave me at work. Part of the reason I'd gone through with this was because I could still work—I could prove how valuable I was.

I needed Nico to see that value beyond being a plaything before I ever considered sleeping with him.

So, even if every night for the next five years was a repeat of last night—even if I was nothing but a pile of ash in the end, I would hold strong.

At the very least, I would enjoy the vacation and seeing the world.

I was in control. Me. Not him. Not anyone else.

"Good morning."

Nico's morning voice always hit me differently. The deep rasp sounded like sex—hard, rough, intense. It slipped in my ears and climbed down my body to my core. Dammit.

"Morning."

Tension pulled tight like a rubber band. There weren't many mornings we woke up together since he woke up first to exercise most mornings.

His eyes roamed my face, and I strived to hide the mixture of heat and nerves flooding me. His lips ticked up on one side, and without my permission, my eyes dropped like a homing beacon, remembering every second that they'd been on mine.

The blankets shifted, and I tensed, holding my breath, trying to mentally prepare for him to strut around the room naked, like an unashamed Greek god.

Don't look. Don't look.

Ooooor, don't let him catch you looking.

Seriously, how did that fit inside me?

Jesus, Vera. Don't look.

I was so lost in my thoughts, I didn't have time to pull back when he leaned in, placing a quick peck to my cheek, grazing the corner of my mouth. I blinked, shocked by the move, staring off at the perfect spot that when he flung the covers back and stood, his firm, hard ass lined up perfectly with my shocked gaze.

His ass was the definition of the saying, you could bounce a quarter off it.

Too quickly and not quickly enough all at once, a pair of sweatpants covered his perfect butt, and he turned, leaving me to stare at the bulge pressing against the material.

Is this how he felt when he came out to find me in my lingerie? Because men in sweatpants was like lingerie for women.

"We leave in a few hours. I figured that gave us enough time for breakfast."

I blinked away, finally looking up his sculpted chest to meet his humored gaze.

"I'll order breakfast then shower. Care to join me?" he asked with a smirk.

I swallowed and shook my head, striving for an annoyance but failing when I couldn't even open my mouth in fear that I'd end up begging him to let me join him.

"Fair enough." He picked up the phone and dialed to order. "Banana pancakes and bacon, extra crispy, right?"

I nodded, surprised he remembered how I like my breakfast. I might have mentioned it in passing. He had meals delivered, and I'd cringed at the blueberry pancakes one morning, briefly mentioning banana pancakes were the only way to go.

And he remembered. He listened. I hadn't even thought he heard me.

"H-how did you know?"

He rolled his eyes but smirked. "Banana pancakes are my second favorite pancake, and the smell of burnt bacon has lingered in the apartment for almost a week. It's hard to forget."

I didn't know why him noticing hit me so hard, but I zoned out, remembering that my father didn't even remember I only liked banana pancakes. A drop of heat, unlike the heat that spread like wildfire at seeing him naked, spread like a drop of food coloring in an ocean. It barely changed the color—barely noticeable—but it *did* change things.

Uncomfortable with the feeling, I shook my head, carefully edging my way out of bed to grab my robe. Last night, I'd wanted to torture him in my nightgown, but with the sun lighting up the entire room, I may as well have been naked.

"Feel free to join me," he offered darkly, walking past.

This time, I managed to work up a weak glare. One side of his lips kicked up as he stretched his arms above his head. Watching Nico stretch in the morning should have been its own specific fetish tab on Pornhub.

A thin scar caught my eye above his Adonis belt on his left

side. Before I could ask, he turned to go, and I shrugged into a thick robe and nabbed my phone, heading to the dining room.

Raelynn: Did you fuck him? Tell me you fucked him all over that suite.
Nova: How was your night? Did you survive?
Raelynn: Yeah. Did you survive? Or did you have death by orgasms? Please say death by orgasms.
Nova: Jesus, Raelynn.
Raelynn: Don't act like you're not curious.
Nova: I mean, I am, but we can be a little less direct.
Raelynn: Nah. Not my style.
Raelynn: Sooo…
Nova: …
Raelynn: Okay, okay. It's still pretty early. I'll wait and hope you're having epic morning sex.
Nova: Just message us to let us know you're alive.
Raelynn: Also, message us so I can tell you about how Nova went Instagram live with PARKER FREAKING CALLAN from her fav band.
Nova: I hate you so much.
Raelynn: Naughty Nova came out to dance after too many Vodka Gimlets last night, and he was doing an Instagram Live, inviting fans to join him and talk. I maaaaaay have requested to join under her name, and he maaaaaay have accepted, and I maaaaaay have shown her shaking her ass while she rapped out Missy Elliot.
Nova: Seriously…the worst friend ever.
Raelynn: You're spelling best friend wrong.

I laughed, looking over their exchange this morning, wanting to FaceTime them and hear all about what happened.
"What's so funny?"
Nico walked in, sweatpants back in place, his hair damp and pushed back carelessly, somehow still looking perfect.

"Just the girls."

"Tell them I said hi."

"Umm…okay?"

"What?" he asked.

"Why?"

"Well, they're your friends. You're my wife. Your friends are important to you, so it's in my best interest to be friendly with them."

"Oh…well, thank you."

He nodded and almost sat down when a knock at the door announced our food.

They rolled the carts in, placing the silver domes on the long table so quickly and quietly, it was like they weren't even there.

Again, I found myself wondering about the kind of money Nico had. My family did well, but we didn't stay in penthouse suites of one of the top hotels in New York. We didn't have silent butlers deliver our food in a way only an obscene amount of money could buy. I'd done research on his company, and it had barely dipped their toe into international shipping, but his wealth screamed worldwide success.

He poured himself a cup of coffee—no cream or sugar—and sat down, pushing a plate of pancakes and bacon my way.

"So, do you have any friends I should be friendly with?"

He chewed his bacon and watched me, thinking over his answer. I was having a moment on our first day of marriage, realizing that I still knew so little about him.

Not that it mattered. Our agreement was for a purpose, and that purpose wasn't to know every little detail about each other. This was business.

"I have Ryan."

"Your assistant?"

"Yeah, who else?"

"A Ryan you don't pay?" He looked perplexed, and I wanted to laugh that he was so thrown by me asking him about friends.

"Do you have any friends you get drinks with? Hang out with? Went to school with?"

"I have acquaintances I get drinks with."

"Jesus, Nico. Do you talk to anyone outside of work?" I asked, laughing.

"I have a friend from college, Xander. But he works just as much as I do and does most of his business overseas. Which was why he couldn't attend the wedding."

"Oh. Maybe I could meet him sometime."

"Sure. The next time he's in town. I think he's just as intrigued to meet you."

"Oh, yeah?"

"He wants to know the woman who could make me settle down."

"Did you not plan on ever marrying?"

He took another bite, his brows dropping. "I didn't think about it. I was so focused on work and building my business, I never considered anything beyond that. And then my grandpa's health declined, and he pushed his desire to see me with a family on me, and then...you came crashing in."

"I'd hardly call it crashing."

"You did bump into me," he joked.

"Oh, my god. I *did not.*"

"Is this going to be like Ross and Rachel and the whole break thing, where we argue about who was right and wrong for years to come?"

"One—I'm right. You were drunk and looking at your phone. Two—I still can't get over that you watched *Friends.*"

"I had the flu last winter and happened to start it on Netflix and ended up watching it the whole way through."

"It happens," I said, nodding in understanding. "So, what are we doing with all our stuff?"

"We'll leave it at the front desk. I have someone picking it up to take it to the house."

"What airline are we flying with?"

"It's a private jet Xander and I share and rent out on occasion."

"You have your own plane?" I asked, my brows shooting high.

"It's not like it's a seven-forty-seven."

"Still. I've never been on a private plane before."

Giddiness flooded through me, and I couldn't help but smile. The more I imagined driving right up to the plane and walking up the steps to the soft buttery leather, a flight attendant bringing me champagne and strawberries, the happier I got. A giggle slipped free, and I bit my lip to hold back any more.

He watched me like he saw something he'd never seen before, and I heated under his inspection.

"I'm glad I'll get to be your first."

He finished the innuendo with a wink, and between the night before, the pancakes, the happiness, and playfulness, something clicked in place. Something that lay with the other shards of my life in my chest snapped together with another one and eased some of the pressure.

It's slow, bambino. A marriage born from a merger isn't scary. It may not be the princesses you love to watch, but it has its own magic. Kind of like Beauty and the Beast. *She did it for more than herself—for her family. Our business and our traditions are our family. We must respect them. This marriage may start off with resentment and a begrudging respect, but with time and patience, it grows. One sharp piece at a time, the marriage comes together, and before you realize it even happened, you love each other and can't imagine ever not.*

My mother's words stole my breath a moment.

Were these the pieces she told me about? Did I want them to be?

Was I falling in love with my husband one small piece at a time?

For the first time, I wondered if maybe Nico was the man my mother told me about.

For the first time, the thought of Nico being my first—of being many firsts didn't sound so bad.

Maybe this honeymoon would lock more in place.

Maybe he had the shards too, and we'd both create something by the end of all this.

Maybe I could be some of his firsts too.

TWENTY-SIX

Nico

LORENZO MUST HAVE BEEN HURTING FINANCIALLY LONGER than I thought because Vera's wonder at every extravagance was better than the last.

Of course, the private plane was over the top even with the wealthiest of people, but when I asked if she flew first class, she let me know that she really didn't travel at all. Her father went alone or not at all. She'd only been to Italy once when she was little before her mother passed.

For a family rooted so deeply in tradition, they didn't do much together. The last time she'd seen her grandparents was a month after her mother's funeral.

"This is where we're staying?" she gasped, looking out the window of our hired car.

She looked like a kid outside of a candy shop, almost pressing her nose to the glass to get a closer look. She whipped her head around with wide-eyed wonder, her smile growing bigger by the second. She'd been doing it the entire drive, trying to take in every inch of history she could. But now that we'd stopped in front of the double doors of the hotel, she unbuckled and closed the gap between us, pressing every inch of her leg to mine.

The sun hadn't even begun to rise yet, but the streetlights illuminated the Spanish Steps stretched down below. Her excitement blinded her to how tightly she pressed against me while she tried to look out my window. However, not even the pope with hundred-dollar bills raining from the sky could pull my attention away from her soft breasts pressed against my arm— the heat of her thigh warming mine. I ached to brush the hair back behind her ear to bare her smooth neck and rain kisses down until she became lost in the pleasure.

"Signora?" A member of the hotel staff held her door open.

She looked back at the open door and quickly flicked her eyes to me before scooting back.

"Sorry," she muttered.

"Don't be. Your excitement is quite endearing."

She exhaled a soft laugh and smiled. Tucking the strand of hair I so desperately wanted to touch behind her ear, she scooted back, thanking the attendant as he helped her out.

By the time we checked in, the sun had just begun to crest the edges of Rome.

"I can't believe this is our room," she said, twirling to take it all in. She stopped and faced me, her lips stretching into a devious smirk. "I mean, it's only the second to top floor, but I guess it will do."

My lips twitched at her sarcasm. "Ha. Ha. We would have been at the top, but I think someone famous already nabbed it."

Her eyes widened further. "I wonder who it is?"

"Probably no one special." For a moment, I struggled to hold back the words rolling through my head. I forced myself to stop before I added no one as special as you. The warmth from our wedding came back, bigger than before, and I struggled to push it back like I had before, but I refused to focus on it, the truth of what it may be too much to handle at six in the morning.

"If Raelynn was here, she'd make us stake out the room to figure it out."

"You mean, she'd stalk them."

She scrunched her nose but then shrugged and laughed. "Yeah, I guess."

Silence fell, filling the room. Opulence surrounded every inch around us, and we stood like two strangers who knew what the other was thinking, but neither would admit it.

At least, she thought she knew what I was thinking. She probably assumed I was looking for a way to seduce her, but instead, I grew frantic with a way to make this soft heat growing in my chest go away.

She looked stunning in black leggings, tennis shoes, and an oversized cardigan. Her hair flowed around her face, and her eyes shined with excitement. The longer they took me in, the more they softened and warmed. She may not know what I was thinking, but I knew she thought about our wedding night and how she wanted more. I also knew her stubbornness would hold her back. Then she blinked, and a new look softened her face. She smiled, looking almost embarrassed as she dropped her eyes to the floor. When she lifted her eyes to mine, something I'd never seen before—from any woman—hit me hard. A look I couldn't identify but felt like kerosene to the warmth in my chest.

"It's early," I said, almost choking on the words, desperate to escape. "Why don't you clean up while I unpack and get us settled."

She blinked again, and the look disappeared. I told myself I was grateful, but a part of me missed it already.

"Okay. I'll just take a quick shower. Maybe I can take a nap before we head out for the day."

"Sounds good."

She grabbed a few items and disappeared into the bathroom with one last look over her shoulder, like she was looking at me for the first time.

I quickly unpacked a few items and stowed our suitcases

away, wishing I could shove this feeling into the drawer with our clothes. Hearing the shower running, a plan hit me. The most surefire way to make Vera look at me with annoyance again, and hopefully, take this feeling away was to press her.

I grabbed a pair of pants and headed into the bathroom. Her long limbs and slick skin had me hardening instantly. I tracked the water, sliding down her body, across her pert nipples, and between her legs. God, I wanted to storm in there, pick her up and shove inside her, putting us both out of our misery. Her body was a work of art, and I wanted to study every inch—with my tongue.

I stripped and waited for her to notice me, but she closed her eyes and rinsed her hair, letting out a yelp when I announced my presence.

"What the fuck, Nico?" she screeched and struggled to cover her body.

Infusing arrogance into action, I slowly cocked a brow and looked her up and down. "I've seen it all before, Verana. Why hide?"

Instead of answering, she lifted her chin and glowered, doing her best not to look me up and down as well.

"I was ready to shower now, so why wait?"

"Because I'm in here."

"So? You're my wife."

I hit a button with that comment, and she dropped her arms, stepping close. "So? It doesn't mean you get me whenever you want."

I stepped into her too, groaning when the head of my cock brushed her stomach. She gasped but didn't pull away. "Are you sure about that, Verana?" I asked, brushing her slick hair back from her forehead. "Would you like me to jack off for you again?"

She scoffed but didn't say no.

"Don't think I couldn't hear your little pants of need. Hell, I could smell your sweet arousal. It reminded me of how delicious your pussy is." She swallowed, and my lips quirked up, and I leaned closer. "I could drop to my knees right now, lift your thigh over my shoulder, and eat your sweet cunt. I'd love nothing more than to bury my tongue inside you and flick your clit. Best fucking breakfast ever."

I ran my nose along her cheek, moving to nip at her ear.

"Five years is a long time, Verana. Just give in."

And that snapped her out of it. She stepped back, and I watched her struggle to harden against the desire flooding her body.

"No." With that, she quickly rinsed off and left, snagging a towel on her way.

"You can run, Verana, but we both know you want it as much as I do."

She glared over her shoulder. "Fuck you, Nicholas."

I laughed at her frustration, feeling a little lighter, with most of the warmth gone. But worried because some still lingered, digging in deep to places I never knew existed.

When I got out of the shower, I found Vera curled up on the edge of the bed, already passed out. I even whispered her name to make sure she wasn't feigning sleep. But when I removed her phone from her nightstand, she still didn't move a muscle.

I quickly guessed her password for her phone and connected it to the USB Xander gave me. The program would keep her phone looking like it was working but block any news and calls from her father and their company. Two weeks was what I needed to complete the takeover, and if she knew what was going on while we were gone, she'd turn us around before I could hit go.

I sat the phone back down and plugged it in just as it was. Slowly shutting the door, I watched for any movement from her and hit Archer's number.

"The shares just went through," he greeted, not bothering with niceties. We'd worked together so long, there was no need.

"Good. Has anyone been alerted?"

"Not that I can tell. I had to do some digging in the records, but the clause states that once she is married, they are hers, free of anyone else's control."

I'd been acquiring shares of Mariano Shipping for years. Small bits here and there through various shell companies as I didn't want to raise any red flags, but it had never been enough. At least it hadn't until Verana fell into my lap with just enough to her name to put me over the edge. With her portion now mine, and Mariano Shipping scrambling silently with finances, I had everything I needed to put it in motion.

"We're here for three days and then onto a yacht. Xander gave me a program that makes her phone lose service, and she'll be none the wiser."

"Good. I'll push these papers through and wait for your signal."

"Good."

"I can't believe it's finally happening."

"Yeah," I muttered.

"Don't sound so excited," Archer deadpanned.

I rubbed at the growing warmth in my chest, flashing back to Vera's giggles when we received champagne upon entering the private jet.

Then I remembered my grandfather's cries when he realized he was losing his wife's family's company—the only thing he had left of her.

Like ice water to a fire, I hardened my heart. With an ounce less of confidence than before, I answered. "I am happy this is happening."

"Good. Keep it that way."

We hung up, and the long day of travel hit me. I went into the room and found Vera now sprawled, her lithe body taking up every inch of space on her side of the bed, her hand reaching out to my side like she unintentionally searched for me.

I lay down and dragged my fingers down her open palm, unprepared for when she latched on and curled closer to me.

No doubts. I reminded myself.

I'd worked for too long and too hard to let this woman hold me back.

I refused to let this heat she created in me burn my goals to the ground.

TWENTY-SEVEN

Vera

"Okay, I have to ask. What are you doing?"

My face scrunched while I watched him bend down for the third time that day to pick up a rock and shove it in his pocket.

"Oh, just a tradition we did with my family," he explained.

He looked away and huffed a laugh. I watched him, intrigued by the soft curve of his lips as he thought over whatever this family tradition was. The Italian sun slowly dropped in the sky as the day turned to night and the reds, purples, oranges, and pinks glowed like the perfect backdrop behind his broad chest encased in a snowy white shirt. His dark complexion made him look more Italian than me, and yet, he still stood out as unique among the straggling tourists around the Trevi Fountain.

"My father started it. He would collect rocks at special locations everywhere we went, and my grandfather continued it for me after my parents passed."

"I love that." My family was based around traditions, but none that made me smile quite as much as Nico's. "I had no idea. I've never seen it displayed anywhere at home."

I didn't even struggle in the slightest at calling Nico's apartment home. If anything, I usually had to stop in shock at how easily it rolled off my tongue.

"Because I don't have one. We've always just kept them in plastic bags.

"Were you close with them?"

"Very," he said, his gaze dropping. When he looked back, he had a small tilt to his lips but tinged with sadness. "We always traveled together. My dad said that just because work pulled him away from home, it didn't have to pull him away from his family. He was a good man."

"He sounds like it."

"When I was too young to travel too much, he'd bring the rocks back to us until we could start collecting them together. Mom complained about them being shoved in a bag in a drawer but eventually rolled her eyes when my dad would tell her there were more important things than decoration. She'd argue because she really did love to decorate, but he'd swoop in and let her know he'd rather dance."

"My mama and papa would dance around the kitchen all the time. I loved watching them."

"Did they have an arranged marriage?"

"Yes, and Mama hated Papa when she first married him," I explained, laughing.

"Then why did she marry him?"

"The arranged marriage. My family was built around traditions. My great-grandparents came to the US from Italy and set up Mariano Shipping with the archaic tradition they brought with them from a strict family in Italy. It just stuck."

"Until you."

"Until me," I agreed. "I always wanted a marriage like theirs. I never saw when they struggled. Of course, I saw them fight. My mother was a passionate Italian woman, which she said was how she earned Papa's respect. She said after that, they slipped into love without her even knowing. They worshipped each other, and it destroyed the core of my father when she died. I guess I just never realized how much until now. He hasn't been the man I remember raising me."

A veil slid over Nico's eyes like it usually did when I mentioned my father. I assumed it happened because of how we ended up in this situation, but a part of me wondered if there was more.

An awkward silence stretched, and I struggled to fill the void. The day had been nice. We'd talked about the history; he'd explained his favorite parts of Rome, and we ate entirely too much food. We'd been typical tourists, and he'd been kind enough to take pictures of me whenever I asked. He'd even humored me when I asked him to take selfies with me.

It had been…almost easy.

And I didn't want it to end, so I moved to a safer topic.

"Do you miss work?" I asked.

We sat on the stone edge of the fountain, the splash of water at our backs, and the soft conversation of tourists surrounding us. He considered my question, looking over the fiery sky.

"Yes and no."

"That clears it up," I joked.

He breathed a laugh and shook his head. "It's kind of nice. I thought it would be harder to not be at the office, but I've worked my whole life. I studied the business as a teen, taking internships where I could get them. Once I graduated, I worked overtime to build my business and continue my education. I haven't really stopped."

"I can't believe I'm going to ask this, but how old are you?"

He turned to me and smiled. God, his lips were so full. It should have been feminine, but the dark scruff and sharp edges of his face sculpted them into anything but feminine. Nico was all man, and right then, my mind flooded with all the times his lips had been on mine. An ache started low in my stomach to feel them pressed to mine again, and I fought to push it away.

"I guess we skipped some of the getting to know you parts."

"A little."

"I'm thirty-five."

"Oh, my gosh. You're a cradle robber," I mock-gasped with my hand to my chest.

He rolled his eyes. "Hardly. You're twenty-three and plenty adult—all woman."

His eyes dropped to my chest, and I applauded my choice to wear the padded bra over the lacy bralette. Otherwise, there would have been no hiding how the way he looked at me hardened my nipples to desperate peaks.

"And no vacations in your thirty-five years?"

"A few. Some with Grandpa."

"Maybe a few trips with all the women you've been with?" I asked, trying to make myself believe that Nico probably swooped women away to seduce them, only to leave them. Maybe I'd crave him less if I actually thought he truly was the man who greeted me at the office every day like I was trying to sleep my way to the top.

Instead of a fond smile of his travels like I expected, he snorted. "Hardly."

"What? Can't entice any woman away?"

"Oh, no, Verana. I could have had anyone with me," he said, confidence dripping from his words.

"So, why not take them?"

The arrogant smirk faded, and he studied me again, this time like he was curious and not like he could see through my clothes. My heart thudded at the change, and I held my breath.

"I guess I never found anyone worth traveling with."

The words stole the breath I'd been clinging to, and my head swam with his words. Did he mean *I* was worth traveling with? We didn't have to go on a honeymoon. We could have said our I dos and gone right back to work like normal.

His eyes reached mine, and my body swayed like it had a mind of its own, desperate to taste his lips again.

"A picture?" a heavily accented voice asked.

I blinked, jerking back and looking to the short man, holding up his hands like he would a camera.

"Can you take our picture?" He gestured to the stunning woman behind him. "A few, please," he clarified.

"Um, sure."

Nico and I stood up, and the couple took our place. She wrapped her arms around him and looked up into his eyes. I snapped a picture, wanting to capture the moment. Their love so palpable, my heart beat quicker for them. Then he leaned down, and she met him halfway, their lips crashing with passion. He pulled her close and unsure if they wanted such a moment documented, but needing to do so anyway, I continued to click the red button. They glowed in front of the white stone, and blue water illuminated among the darkness. Their love was beautiful, and I hoped they cherished the photos forever.

"Thank you," he said when they pulled back. "This is my wife. Fifteen years."

My smile grew, hearing the pride in his voice, and I gestured to Nico. "My husband. Only a couple of days, though."

"Newlyweds," the man almost shouted with joy. "I take your picture."

"You don't—" Nico tried to say.

"Nonsense," the man interjected. "Go. Hold your bride by the fountain."

Nico slipped his arms around my waist, brushing the patch of skin bared between my crop-top sweater and high-waisted flowing skirt. My fingers crept around his body, secretly loving every ridge and dip I encountered on their way to his side. He held me close, and we smiled.

Before we could step away, the man held up his hand. "No. You must kiss. My wife—we kissed here when we marry, and we happy still."

"Oh, I don't—" I tried to say, terrified that if I started kissing Nico now, I wouldn't stop.

This time, it was Nico who interjected. "Of course." He turned to me, his smile brimming with promise. "Maybe we can make a tradition of our own."

His words were light and teasing, but they hit me like a train. Despite the archaic traditions, I loved them. We had many that were passed down, and I'd had faith in what my parents had, hoping I'd have the same happiness they found. Even if it didn't happen like I imagined, the traditions still had meaning to me, and him saying we'd make our own meant more than the joke he'd intended.

"Bene!"

I turned in Nico's arms, closing the smallest gap, and gently pressed my fingers to his chest. His long fingers spanned my waist and held me close. His dark eyes shone like an abyss I wanted to get lost in.

He leaned down but stopped, all promise and joking gone from his serious face. "Are you sure?"

"About what?"

"A kiss. I may push you and taunt you because I know how much you want me, even if you won't admit it, but I won't corner you into it."

Flutters spread like a million butterflies in my chest, and I swallowed past the lump in my throat. I wanted to ask what was so different now than our wedding day, but I didn't care. The fact that he hadn't whisked me in his arms and took advantage of the moment sparked something in me that quickly spread like wildfire, and there was no chance of me saying no.

"I'm sure."

As soon as the words passed my lips, his didn't hesitate. He lifted me to meet him halfway, and we both groaned when our mouths collided. It started off slow, but hard, but quickly my hands scraped up his chest, over his shoulders, and into his hair, holding him to me. I flicked my tongue against the lips that had taunted me all day, and his fingers dug hard into my back. With a moan of surrender, he parted his lips, touching his tongue to mine for only a moment before taking control. I pressed to my toes, pushing my hips against his, whimpering at the hardness I encountered.

Laughter brought us out of our bubble and back to the reality that we were in public with a man taking our picture. I wondered if when I looked at them, they'd find the same passion I saw in them.

Nico pulled back, and I quickly leaned in to nip at his lush bottom lip, sucking it between my own before finally settling back on my heels.

"Careful, Verana," he growled.

Unable to meet his eyes after my boldness, I merely bit my lip, slicking my tongue to catch every last taste of him, and turned back to the other couple.

"Tante passione e amore," the man said, handing my phone back to me. "I'm sure you will have a long, happy marriage. Bene."

In that moment, I wanted to believe him. I wanted to ignore the contract we signed for five years and believe our marriage was real.

I wanted to be brave enough to admit that I was falling in love with my husband and believe it wasn't going to break me in the end.

TWENTY-EIGHT

Nico

ON DAY THREE, Vera's enthusiasm hadn't waned in the slightest.

"This whole thing is ours? I mean, do we—you—own it?"

A flare ignited in my chest in her mix-up of calling my things our things. "No. *We* don't own it. But it is ours for the week."

She looked to the luxury yacht, then back to me, then to the yacht, and again back to me, her jaw dropping a little further with each volley. "Nico. It has two whole floors. On a boat."

"Actually, three. You can't see the bottom floor from this angle."

"THREE?"

I playfully rubbed at my ears and winced, her exuberance reaching a new pitch.

"That's insane."

"Champagne for the newlyweds?" a butler asked as we stepped aboard. He earned his full tip for not wincing at Vera's squeal of excitement. She grabbed the glass and ran off, poking her head in each door.

Something had changed after the fountain. We didn't kiss again, but she looked at me differently when she didn't think I noticed and sometimes even when she did notice, almost like a schoolgirl smile, full of secrets and blushes. Hell, this morning I'd woken to her pressed to my back, and I'd been too scared to move. She'd woken soon after, thinking I was asleep. I expected her to pull away, but instead, she'd stayed close, and if I hadn't been mistaken, even leaned in to graze her nose along my shoulder.

I'd stayed still the entire time, not wanting her to pull away. Instead, I'd soaked in her warmth, letting it bleed into the heat that bloomed like a constant companion in my chest.

"This is insane," she said, coming back.

"So you said."

"I love it."

I inhaled, soaking her words in, filling my chest with pride. "Good. I figured we'd unload and sunbathe on our way to Naples and then dock for dinner and a night out."

Her straight teeth latched on to her wide smile, and she nodded, clapping her hands.

"You're ridiculous."

"I don't even care. I'm so damn excited."

I shook my head and led her to our rooms. Despite the boat having almost ten rooms, she didn't argue when I placed our items in the same room. We shared a room at home, but part of me half expected her to argue every step of the way.

Instead, she grabbed her bathing suit and twirled away to the bathroom.

Before I changed, I dug through her purse and grabbed her phone, listening carefully for her coming out. I checked to make sure everything was still blocked, and when I was satisfied, I plugged in the USB and uploaded the second program.

I'd planned this honeymoon specifically to keep her out of the loop. By this point, her friends may have caught wind of what was going on, and I needed to keep her as far away from any information. I planned the yacht because it would be more believable that we lost service out on the water.

Just as I was tucking her phone away, mine vibrated with an incoming text message.

Archer: See if she knows any information on the sale of the company when it transferred to L. Need more to proceed without error.
Me: Get it to you soon.

Guilt pricked, and my grandpa's wisdom about honesty in a marriage hit me.

But like Verana reminded me, this wasn't a real marriage. This wasn't born from love like he had with my grandma. This was business. And for me, it was revenge. Guilt had no place here.

No matter how much her reminders that this was all a ruse created a growing ache in my chest.

It was business.

Maybe if I said it enough, I'd push any doubt away.

I'd barely got my swim trunks on when she came out. When I looked up, I found her eyes glued to where my dick had been hanging out moments before and smiled a victory at her hard swallow.

However, it was short-lived. When we made it to the pool up top, she removed her swim-cover to bare a skimpy black bathing suit, and I was the one left gawking. Her bottoms were more of a thong than anything and the top covered her cleavage, but a strip bared the underside of her breasts. I clenched my fists at my side, fighting the urge to crawl over her and suck and bite at the pale curves.

More champagne was brought, but she asked for water, occasionally humming to the music playing through the hidden speakers on deck. I tensed each time she picked up her phone, but she would merely huff and set it aside.

"Everything okay?" I finally asked.

"Yeah. My phone is just acting up. I've restarted and everything, but I have no service."

"If it makes you feel better, mine isn't getting service either."

Her lips pursed, and she looked at the glittering water stretched along the horizon. "It's just bad timing. Nova is heading on a trip, and it's secluded with an intense hike. I was hoping to FaceTime her before she left since she'll be gone when we get back."

The guilt rushed back, and I opened my mouth before I could let the risks talk me out of it. "I'll call the company and see what we can do. Maybe we can at least call her from the yacht phone."

"Okay. Thank you."

She still studied the water, occasionally picking up her phone. Each time she'd huff, and I hated the pressure it placed on my chest, squeezing tighter and tighter.

Needing to distract us both, I turned to my side, propping up on my elbow and resting my head on my hand. The dock had half a dozen loungers, but she sat on the double one with me, and I counted it as a win.

"You know, sunbathing topless is completely normal in Italy."

I infused heat and innuendo into my suggestion, and some of the pressure eased when she sat her phone aside and barked a laugh.

"You wish."

"Hell, yes, I do." She turned her head, and I took my time scanning her entire body, spending extra time on her chest. "You have perfect tits. I remember them in my hand, your hard nipples scraping my palm and begging for my fingers."

I tracked the way her chest rose a little harder and faster, looking up her neck to watch it work over a heavy swallow, and to her cheeks, turning redder than the sun could make them. She pursed her lips, and I enjoyed watching her struggle to regain her composure.

"You just want me for my body."

"Not true."

"Yeah, right."

I wanted her for her connections. I wanted her for revenge. Her body was a bonus—or at least, I had hoped it would be. However, despite not having her body, I found her smiles to be the bonus—her laughter. Not that I'd admit it. Hell, it sat in my chest like a square peg in a round hole; there was no way I could admit it to her when I couldn't even admit it to myself.

Instead, I settled on the safety of work.

"You've helped my company with your ideas more than once."

Her face softened. "Really?"

"Yes. Your suggestion to Domenic on the latest project shaved off almost a hundred thousand. I was impressed."

"Wow. An actual compliment coming from the man who accused me of sleeping my way into a job."

I shrugged, wincing over my harsh treatment of her at the office. "I may have judged too soon."

She flipped to her side, matching my position, her breasts bouncing, dangerously close to falling out. But I didn't know where to look, the alluring flesh taunting me with a peek, or her radiant smile and perfect dimples.

In the end, the smile won out, and I tried not to think about why too hard.

"Does this mean different tasks at work?"

"Maybe…"

"I'll take it."

"Your very smart, Verana. Your resume speaks for itself—as well as your actions. Your father was a fool to not utilize your talents."

Her smile faded, and she swallowed again, barely choking out, "Thank you, Nicholas."

"It's just honesty. I won't easily hand over the tasks because you're my wife," I said too harshly. She winced. I hated it and immediately backtracked. "But I have no doubt you'll earn it."

She studied me, emotions swirling in the depths of her eyes. It had me feeling like a swinging pendulum with her. I wanted to keep her at a distance but hated when she got too far, so I brought her back. But then she came back and looked at me like I'd given her the most precious gift, making that warmth come roaring back, and I struggled with the way it bled further and further through my body each time. So, I pushed her away again. On repeat.

I knew I was on borrowed time and knew at some point the swinging would stop; I just wasn't sure where it would, with her close or far.

I wasn't sure where I wanted it to stop.

But with her smile back in place and the soft heat fading less and less each time I shoved away, I had a feeling I knew where I wanted it to land.

I just wasn't ready to admit that I may be falling for my wife.

TWENTY-NINE

Vera

THE HEEL of my suede ankle boots caught on the edge of the cobblestone, and I stumbled, latching on to Nico's arm. He looked back to find me giggling, enjoying the feel of his hard arm under my fingers.

"You okay?" he asked, smiling with me.

"Maybe I should have skipped the last glass of champagne."

"Nah. It's our honeymoon. How could you turn down a bottle from the chef?"

"You're right. I made the right choice."

He huffed a laugh and shook his head, not saying anything as I stepped close and kept my hand latched to his arm while we walked.

That had been our night.

After the day sunbathing, we got ready and had the most delicious dinner. But better than dinner had been the walls that slowly disappeared throughout the day. The best part was the laughing and subtle flirting. The best part was the ease that sprouted somewhere between Rome and Naples.

He'd even interrupted my shower again, and instead of a heated argument, I'd merely thrown my loofah at him and stormed off, smiling, kind of loving his taunting laugh behind me.

Nico's laugh…It should be one of the wonders of the world. It rose from deep in his chest and poured from his full lips. The smile disarmed you, and then the gruff rumble of humor struck while your guard was down. It was sensual, deep—rough.

Just like the way he fucked me against the railing at the gala.

All through the night, women looked, desire, and want in their eyes, probably the same way it was in mine. They looked, but the silver wedding band shined brighter on his finger, letting them know he was taken.

Mine.

Possession flooded my body each time I caught a glint of it.

I clung tighter to him, and I wondered if this was what cavemen felt like. This desperate urge to claim him, to mark him as mine so everyone knew he was taken. I wanted to bare my teeth like an animal to ward off anyone who said otherwise.

I wanted him and blamed nothing but my need. No champagne, no living in the moment, no rash decisions. There was nothing to blame but his words weaving their way around the cracks in my wall and the emotions they planted there. They grew like a flower in a desert, rare, and unlike anything I'd ever felt before. The vines wove through my stubborn barrier, creating crevices where the emotions slipped through until it broke free and poured over me. It was all-consuming, washing away any stubbornness I still clung to.

I…cared.

I almost laughed at the simple word. I more than cared, and damn-well knew it.

Maybe it'd been there the whole time, growing in the shadow of my defiance and persistence. But his words shined a light like a ray of sun, illuminating that it'd been there all along.

We walked down the narrow street, people sitting outside, laughing and living, enjoying the warmer night. When we rounded a corner to an opening, we found musicians playing music to a small crowd of dancers. Couples laughed under the string lights, twirling out only to be brought back into their partner's arms. I picked up a few Italian words in the song about getting lost in the night with your lover, and it sounded like the best idea I'd ever heard.

"Dance with me."

"What?" he asked.

I tugged him over to the fringes of the group. "Like our parents did." It was a memory we shared of our parents dancing together. Each time I'd encountered my parents laughing and holding each other tight in the kitchen, it was all I could fantasize about for my own future. "Like a tradition."

His face softened, probably remembering his own parents, and slipped his arms around my waist. "We can make it our own tradition."

His words stole my breath. It was the first time we'd both talked about our marriage like it was real—like it was the beginning foundations of a long future and not just a business transaction.

He pulled me close, and I wrapped my arms around his neck, inhaling his spicy scent. I loved the way he smelled. I had since the very beginning. Not that I'd admit it, but if he ever interrupted my shower at the right time, he may have found me sneaking a smell of his body wash.

The guitar played softly, and the singer crooned. I was too lost in Nico's arms to try to translate the lyrics. Instead, I listened to the beat and let him guide me, focusing on the feel of his thighs brushing mine, on the wind caressing my thighs where my dress rode up. I focused on holding back my whimper when his tongue slicked across his lips, and I held back from tracing it with my own.

The music turned sensual, and Nico's grip tightened, moving up and down my back, sometimes stopping to grip my hips and move me how he wanted. I dug my fingers into the soft hair at the base of his neck and held on. The warm air, the soft music, the twinkling lights, the passion of Italy itself wove around us.

The dance turned sensual, and we clung to each other like we were both barely hanging on to our control. We moved, forming our tradition of foreplay.

When the song ended, he leaned down to my ear. "Ready to go back?"

I nodded, tipping my head to the side in hopes his lips would travel down my neck. They didn't, but he dragged his nose along my cheek, inhaling my scent like I did his. I pulled back to look up at him, but his eyes were focused on something over my shoulder.

"Stay right here."

"What?" That wasn't what I'd expected.

He looked down, a smile tipping his lips. "I want to get you something."

Giddy excitement quickly replaced my confusion. "What is it?"

"It's a surprise."

"Come on. Tell me. I want to make sure it's worth it."

I wanted to make sure it was worth not rushing back to the yacht and continuing where the dance ended. He bopped me on the nose, and I laughed at the playful gesture.

"So impatient."

"Only child syndrome."

"Well, too bad. Stay put and I'll be right back."

"Fine," I whined.

He walked away, laughing at my dramatics, and I stood there in awe, another smile making my cheeks ache. I'd smiled more today than I had in months, and I never wanted it to end. I watched his broad shoulders disappear behind a few people as he perused the street vendor's shop.

I tried to see what he grabbed, but the crowd blocked my view. When he finally made his way back to me, he laughed at the way I couldn't help but bounce on the balls of my feet.

I opened and closed my hands, wanting whatever was in the brown bag.

"Verana Rush," he mock reprimanded. Hearing my name attached to his only amped up my excitement, and I giggled. "I should make you wait until we get back."

"Don't you dare."

He shook his head and gave me the bag. I tore open the paper to find an ornate footed shot glass with the word *amore* etched along the front.

"What is this?" I asked slowly. Surely, he couldn't know what this meant to me.

"I'm assuming you don't have a shot glass from Italy?"

"No…Why?"

"I saw your collection in one of the boxes marked as your mother's things," he answered simply. "I forgot to give it to you, but I also got one from Rome. I figured we could find a way to display them at home when we got back."

"Oh…" I didn't know what else to say. "This is…thank you. My mother had a collection and I've added to it over the years."

"I guess we both collect things to hold on to the people we lost too soon."

"I guess we do."

Tonight, I wanted to hold on to him before I lost him. I wanted to collect memories that I could hold tight at the end of our agreement. No more stubbornness to hold me back. No more denial to keep me from admitting what I knew. I trusted him, and that realization only watered the flower, making it grow into something I knew I was running out of time avoiding.

"Come on. Let's head back."

He wrapped his arm around my shoulders and held me close the short walk back to the yacht. Each step solidified my decision. Need beat through me with each thud of my heels against the pavement. By the time we stepped onto the yacht, every muscle pulled tight with need, ready to snap.

"Nico." My hand held him still, and he turned back to see

why I stopped. I swallowed, and his brows furrowed. "Do you respect me?"

I knew he did. I just wanted to hear it. "Of course, I do."

"Then that's enough."

First must come respect. Then the love can grow.

My mom's words rang in my head, and I had no doubt that love had already begun to grow.

I jerked his hand, pulling him close, so I could wrap my arms around his neck and pull him down to me. "I'm done fighting," I confessed so close to his face, my lips brushed his.

He stood frozen, and to make my declaration clear, I flicked my tongue against his lips and pressed my core against him.

With a growl, his hands dropped to grip my ass and lifted me. I wrapped my legs around his waist and moaned when he turned to press us against a wall.

We inhaled each other like we'd been in a cage starving, staring at a feast just outside. I'd unlocked the door, and neither of us was holding back. He held me so tight I was sure I'd have bruises in the morning, and I looked forward to each one.

He pulled back, and I kissed down his neck, my world turning when he shifted and walked to where we lounged earlier. Cool air caressed the curve of my ass where my dress rode up, and a chill worked its way up my spine when he sat me on the cold surface of one of the tables.

An attendant appeared, and without taking his eyes off me, Nico ordered him to leave.

"Get the fuck out of here, and no one appears until I call for them."

"Yes, sir," the attendant responded, like a grumbling man and half-naked woman on a table were nothing new.

As soon as we were alone again, we collided.

His hands were everywhere, up and down my sides, squeezing my ass to push his groin into mine. Gripping my thighs to pull them tight around his waist, holding on like I'd slip away any moment. On my breasts, grazing my nipples on taunting passes and hard pinches.

My hands moved just as frantically, desperate to feel him. He'd walked around every hotel room naked, his golden body hard like Adonis, and my hands shook with the need to touch him. I fumbled with the buttons, eventually giving up and tugging the shirt open, baring the hair on his sculpted chest, not stopping until I could see each ripple of his abs.

He tugged at the neck of my dress, biting my collarbone, growling like an animal when he couldn't reach far enough down my dress, repaying the favor and ripping the soft sweater material straight down the front.

I didn't even flinch; instead, I arched my chest up, my body begging him to take me. His hand wrapped around my back and hoisted me high, latching onto my nipple through the thin bra. My cry of pain and pleasure echoed in the night sky, uncaring if anyone could hear. I held him to me, mussing up his hair, whimpering, and doing my best to grind my core against the hard length tenting his pants.

His free hand played at my thighs, tugging my panties aside to gently graze through my slick folds.

"Fuck me. I missed this pussy."

Another pass, and my frustration grew. We'd waited long enough, and I wanted now, now, now.

Shoving him back, I slid from the table, tearing at his pants to free his cock.

"Verana…"

"You've tasted me, now let me taste you."

He groaned as his length slipped free into my waiting palm. Looking up, I slicked my tongue along the underside, placing gentle kisses against the slit. Holding his girth in my hand, I stared at it, the length and thickness intimidating. His fingers snaked into my hair and yanked me back to look up. With the glittering lights from the deck, the only illumination, he stared down at me like the devil, and I gladly knelt at his feet.

"Suck it."

"It's big," I said, wanting to fight him because it was all we'd ever done.

He smirked. "I know. Now open those pouty lips and suck my dick like a good girl."

My pussy flooded at his words, and I blushed at being so turned on by his graphic dirty talk. But I did as told, wanting to make him as desperate as me. Opening my mouth as wide as I could and still holding his stare, I sank down his length. He stretched my jaw and prodded at the back of my throat. I swirled my tongue on the underside and sucked my way back up, flicking at the slit again.

"Fuck, yeah. That's it."

I continued to bob up and down, losing myself in the motion, enjoying the ache in my jaw, the sting of tears when he pushed too far.

"Do you know how many times I've jacked off to the thought of filling your mouth? How many times I've come to the thought of you choking on my cum as it spills from your pink lips?"

I struggled to shake my head.

"Almost every morning. I alternate between all the ways I want to watch you take my cum. Over and over again. I'm going to mark you, Verana. I'll fill you with all I have, come where I want on you. I'll make you mine."

I should have been offended. The words were exactly what had me pushing back so hard before, making me feel like I didn't have a choice. But I did. He'd proven it time and time again, and now that I'd made my choice to be with him, I wanted him to make all the rest. I wanted him to mark me and claim me. I wanted him to sneak off to dark corners to fuck me. I wanted him to take me wherever he wanted.

I'd already made my choice.

I wanted to be his.

I hummed, rolling his balls in my hand, and he jerked me back.

"But we'll save that for later. For now. I want to be inside you again."

With that, he yanked me up and tore my panties from me, shoving off the remnants of my dress while I did the same to his clothes. I leaned back on my hands, the table like ice on my heated skin. He parted my legs and rubbed both thumbs along my folds, parting them like he wanted to see every inch, dragging his fingers through the wetness.

"So pretty and pink. So hot." Sliding a finger inside me and rolling his thumb along my clit, he met my eyes. "Can I cum inside you?"

I felt less nervous when he'd suggested we get married. I'd never let a man fuck me without a condom. I was on the pill, and we were both clean, but it was new and personal.

And I wanted it more than anything. The thought of feeling him raw inside me, skin against skin, of having his cum spill inside my pussy only to watch it leak out had a shiver chasing its way through my body.

"Please," I begged.

He swiped his palm through my folds and coated his cock, lifting the head to play at my folds before pushing in roughly. I watched his fat head force its way inside me, loving the sting of being stretched so quickly, and all I could think was that I wanted more.

"More," I pleaded. "Harder."

His eyes glinted, and he leaned in against my lips. "Dirty girl."

I opened my lips for a smart remark, but it vanished on a gasp when he shoved in all the way. Holding me tight, my nipples abrading against his chest, he fucked me. For a moment, I wondered if the night sky carried our animalistic noises across the water to other boats, and I hoped it did.

I hoped everyone knew that he was mine, and I was his.

"Goddamn. I thought I remembered how tight your little pussy is, but I was wrong. So much tighter. You squeeze my cock perfectly."

"You're so big," I whimpered. It sounded cliché, but it was true. "So good."

"So fucking hot. I'm never going in this cunt again with a condom. I can't go back. I never knew it could be so hot."

"You've never…?"

He slowed his pace and slid his hand along my cheek, making sure I could read his sincerity. "Only you."

I pressed a kiss to his palm. "Only you, too."

A moment stretched where he stilled, and we eyed each other. The weight of the words almost heavier than the I do's we said at our wedding. As if a band holding us back snapped, we crashed together at the same time, our mouths and tongues dueling. He fucked me harder and harder, racing to our finish.

I cried out when he pulled out, but before I could object, he flipped me around, my hips digging into the table as he shoved back inside me from behind. His hand dove into my hair and held me upright.

"Look at you. Look at you fucking taking me."

Our reflection in the dark glass doors of the yacht shined back at us. My back arched, my breasts pressed out and bouncing each time he thrust hard inside me. He looked like a dark, dominating shadow behind me, his teeth bared like an animal rutting against its mate.

His hand slid down between my thighs and focused on my clit.

"Fucking mine," he growled against my ear.

"Yours," I whimpered back.

He pinched my clit and pushed hard, sending me over the edge. If it wasn't for his hand between my legs and the table at my hips, I'd have collapsed in a heap. My legs shook, and the world vanished beyond the supernova, exploding like a million fireworks through every inch of me.

His hands tightened, and he buried his head against my neck, his teeth digging into my shoulder like they had the first time we'd been together, and he came.

His moans of release sent shock waves down to my nipples and straight to my pussy, still pulsing around his twitching cock.

I watched our reflection, exhausted and satisfied. I almost didn't recognize the woman staring back, her hair a mess and sweating, her body panting and glued to the man behind her. I didn't recognize her, but I wanted to.

Nico eased out, and a rush of wetness dripped down my thigh, bringing its own mini spasms of excitement. He stumbled back and took me with him, catching me when we fell to the lounger. Kissing me softly, he slipped his fingers between my legs, collecting our cum, only to bring it to my nipple and tweak it.

The move was simple and beyond erotic. I wanted to be covered by him, and I liked to know he wanted the same.

"Why did I fight this?"

"I don't know, but you better stop. This was not a one-time thing, Verana."

I cocked a brow but was too tired to even pretend to be stubborn. "It sure as hell wasn't," I agreed, stroking his softening cock, loving the way our cum covered him too. "I want more."

"Then more I shall give you."

With an energy I didn't know how he had, he stood, scooping me up, laughing at my yelp of surprise.

"Let's try something new."

"Oooo, sounds kinky," I joked.

"How about a bed?"

In a bed, with his big body over mine, sounded like everything I'd hoped for.

"Perfect."

THIRTY

Vera

THE NEXT DAY looked similar to the last, except when Nico climbed into the shower with me and offered to eat me out, I gladly accepted and returned the favor. By the time we finished, the water ran cold, and he said he had to take me back to bed to warm me up.

Now, we lay on the loungers, the yacht skipping along to our next destination, and this time, I took him up on his suggestion, sunbathing topless. He ordered all staff to stay away from the front deck and muttered about ripping eyeballs out if anyone saw his wife's breasts.

I loved it.

I loved—

I cut the thought off and shook it away. If my phone worked, I'd call Raelynn, and she'd promptly squeal, demand details, and then reprimand me for being dick-drunk if I even considered thinking those words.

A warm mouth surrounded my nipple, his rough tongue flicking back and forth. "I love these tits."

"Where are we going today?" I asked, keeping my eyes closed, basking in his adoration of my body.

"Just out to sea for a while and then coming back to the coast a little south."

"Sounds perfect."

His fingers grazed up and down my stomach, circling my belly button. Never touching anywhere important, just moving like he wanted to memorize every inch. I'd stared at his body every second I got and probably knew more than every inch. It made me want to know what lay beyond.

"How'd you get to K. Rush Shipping?"

His finger froze a moment before continuing its path. "What do you mean?"

Finally caving, I turned my head and squinted an eye open to watch him. His hair stretched in all directions from the salty sea and yacht breeze. He looked young and carefree. "You're young and successful beyond what I can imagine. How did you get here? Was it what you always wanted?"

"Yes."

Rolling my eyes at his short answer, I shoved his shoulder. "Tell me more."

"My grandfather owned his own company, and my father worked with him. I learned everything I know from them. Internships over the summer, running mail and coffee before I even reached high school. It's in my blood. Kind of like how it's in yours."

"You had time for work between all those girls you probably dated."

"I worked hard to play hard."

"Is that your life motto?"

"Hardly."

"I bet you were the prom king," I said, rolling my eyes.

"No, I never made it to the actual dance. Got distracted in the limo," he said with arrogance.

"Gross."

He laughed at my fake gagging noises. "But I was captain of the baseball team."

"Ooooo, I bet you looked good in those tight pants."

"I looked good in everything."

I gave him my most deadpan stare while he waggled his brows.

"What about you? Prom queen?"

"Hardly. But I was in control of the committee and set it all up."

"That doesn't surprise me at all."

"You're not the only one who likes to be in charge."

"I noticed how much you enjoyed riding me last night. Controlling the pace and how deep I slid inside you."

I did. I loved sitting astride his large body while he struggled to find his own control. I'd been powerful—seen.

Between our banter and his words, heat pooled low in my belly, and I squirmed on the soft cushion of the lounger. But I didn't want to stop. Each answer revealed a new layer to the image I'd created of Nico. He'd gone from a flat frowning drawing to a 3D image with a heart and soul, and I wanted more.

"So why start Rush instead of continuing to work with your grandpa? I mean, I can hardly imagine you not being the boss," I teased. "You like being in control."

His lips plucked at my nipple but quickly pulled back—just a taunting peck. "I do. And you love it."

"Maybe," I said, shrugging. "So, tell me."

"Like you said, I like being the boss. I like the ins and outs of owning a company and doing it my way. And my family company wasn't quite what it used to be."

"Were any women involved in the company?"

"Not directly. Mom was the trophy wife your father wanted you to be, except she wanted to be. She loved it, and my father loved that she loved it. Grandma loved art and volunteered at museums to satisfy that need."

"Was she an artist? Is that how you learned to draw?"

"Why do you think I can draw?"

"I've seen your doodles when you're thinking. They're quite good."

He grunted a non-answer to my compliment. "No, she wasn't an artist. More of a collector and appreciator. She performed her role of hosting events and charities, but she was whip-smart. She was Grandpa's sounding board. She was hard when he couldn't be and soft when he didn't know how."

"She sounds amazing."

"She was. Both of them were."

I grazed my fingers atop his long roaming ones, offering the slightest comfort, and decided not to dig for more in fear he'd shut down. Talking about those you'd lost rarely set anyone in a good mood. Instead, I moved back to the company. "What happened to your grandpa's company?"

Again, his finger froze, and I realized this topic may not be better than the last.

"Things got hard, and the company dwindled."

"I'm sorry, Nico. I couldn't imagine losing my family company."

This time his fingers pulled away completely, and I immediately missed them. Empathy had me wanting to turn and pull him into my arms, but before I could, his fingers returned—this time turning naughty and dipping beyond the edge of my bottoms.

"What about you, Vera? What made you want to do this?"

I struggled to focus when he slipped his fingers between my folds, past my clit, and shoved two deep inside.

"Ungh. I—shit."

"That's not an answer."

"Fuck you," I breathed without any heat. I spread my legs and closed my eyes, trying to focus. "Like you said, it's in my blood. I wanted to do more than charity functions. I wanted to be useful and part of this company that had dictated so much of our lives. It was my mother's family company, and I wanted to be more involved, holding on to that piece of her."

"It was in their family for generations, correct? How did your father get it?"

"He bought it from them. After Mom—" my words cut off when he pinched my clit. "After her, my grandfather passed, and my grandmother didn't want anything to do with it, so she sold it to him."

"But didn't that go against their traditions?"

His words barely registered. I rattled off answers about how there were specific conditions in the contract, struggling to think beyond his lips grazing my nipple when he spoke.

He could have asked me to sign over my soul in that moment and I probably would have done it without hesitation. Anything to keep him going. I whimpered in need when he shifted, climbing over me and kissing his way down my body. His broad shoulders pushed my thighs wide, and he settled in, pressing his tongue against my clit before sliding down and fucking me with it. I lifted my hips, impatient to come.

"You want control again? You want to ride my face?"

"I want you, Nico."

He bared his teeth like an animal and flipped us, settling my thighs on either side of his head. "Give me your cunt," he ordered.

Even with him beneath me and at my mercy, he controlled it with his large hands on my ass. I gripped the back of the chair and slid back and forth across his lips, loving his scruff abrading my sensitive skin. Part of me worried I'd move the wrong way or do it wrong, but when he sucked my bundle of nerves hard, I didn't care. The water sparkled like diamonds reflecting the sun, and it matched the spots blurring in my eyes.

The orgasm crashed over me, and I held my breath, chasing the pulsing pleasure to the point of almost blacking out. Soft flicks and sucking kisses brought me back to earth—back to Nico. Always back to Nico.

I collapsed to the side, and he pulled me in his arms, his face wet with my cum. "Do you want me to grab my towel?"

"Fuck, no. I want to wear you all day."

I blushed, imagining my cum on his lips for everyone to see.

"Don't be embarrassed, Verana. Your pussy is delicious. Have you ever tasted yourself?"

"No," I whispered, holding my breath again, waiting for what he'd do next.

"That's a shame. Let's fix it."

He leaned down and pressed his wet lips to mine, and I didn't hesitate to open my mouth and let his tongue brush inside. A sweet tang burst on my tongue, and I think I was more addicted to the taste of myself on him than just me. I sucked his lips, nibbling them between my teeth.

"Now do you know why I offered to eat you out every day?"

"I figured it was just to torture me."

"That too."

I shoved him, and he laughed, pulling me back into his arms against his heated chest.

As if he hadn't just made me see stars, he moved back to the conversation from earlier. "There's a project with a newer company that Rush Shipping just acquired. I'd like you to take the lead under the guidance of Domenic."

"What?" I pressed up against his chest, blinking down at him in shock.

"I'm not giving this to you because you suck cock like a pro."

"Fuck you, Nico," I laughed.

He winked. "We do this with lower levels of employees so they can see what it's like and learn from the managers. I've found it encourages them to strive for more. Your resume is beyond what you're doing at Rush, and you deserve more. I want to give you a chance to prove it."

"Nico," I whispered, his words validating everything I'd worked for. A lump formed in my throat, and I forced myself to swallow it down. All those years of hard work, hoping my father would see me—see I'm capable of more than just a trophy wife, and he never had. But Nico saw it. Nico saw me.

"It's not your mother's company, but it's still in the shipping world, and maybe that can be a piece you hold on to of her."

Tears blurred my vision, and another lump worked its way up. Staring down at this man who came out of nowhere and gave me something I'd always wanted, I knew.

I loved him.

Each day he challenged me, and I called it hate, but it also pushed me harder and forced me to grow. He did that for me like no one else had, and I loved him.

The words begged to be set free, but I couldn't.

This marriage wasn't born out of love, and just because I loved him, it didn't mean anything had changed for him.

I shoved the words back down. "Thank you," I choked out. "You deserve it."

And that right there was it. I didn't want it given to me. I wanted to prove myself and have him see I was capable—and he did.

Worried my lips would open and spew words I wasn't ready to say, I decided to put my mouth to work in other ways.

With nothing but the sun and the splash of the waves against the side of the boat, I returned the favor, using my tongue and lips, sucking his cock like a pro.

And when he filled my mouth with his cum, I swallowed and climbed up his body to let him taste himself on my tongue.

Anything to hold back the words that I worried would grow too big to hold back.

I just hoped when they finally broke free, Nico cared enough to let me love him.

Maybe even more than the five years we agreed on.

Maybe more like forever.

THIRTY-ONE

Nico

ARCHER'S NAME flashed on my screen, and I stepped out of the bedroom to answer it away from Vera.

"Is it done?" I asked. Vera and I flew home tomorrow, and this takeover was cutting it close.

"The information you gave me helped, but the hiccup set us back."

I cringed, remembering how I'd gotten the information from her. She'd been so lost in pleasure, she'd barely known all the details she'd admitted. But why would she care? I was her husband, and as far as she knew, had everything I could want. Why would she hold back?

She trusted me.

I cringed again and took the anger I had for myself out on Archer. "What the fuck does that mean?" I asked through clenched teeth.

"We need another week."

"A week?" I took a deep breath, remembering Vera on the other side of the door. "I have a goddamn company to run, and I'm paying you to get this done on time. I can't stay gone forever while you pull your head out of your ass."

"We didn't plan on this happening any time in the next five

years, so we're making it work. It's finally happening, Nicholas. What's one more week if we get what we want?" When I didn't answer right away, he faltered. "You do want this, right?"

I stared at the door like I could see through it and watch Vera getting ready. Guilt closed in on me, and that more than anything was why I wanted this done. Any other time Archer asked me how much I wanted this, I answered without hesitation. Now, I paused and looked for my wife. Now, rather than excitement and thrill rushing through me at the thought of crushing Lorenzo, guilt and second thoughts mixed in with everything else.

"I-I don't——"

"Nicholas," he cut me off, his tone tipping toward panic. "There's no going back. We're on a train going full speed. The only difference is we either crash and burn or pull this off. No matter what you want, when you come back, she will know about your revenge on her father's company. The only option we have left is we go through it with the company in our hands—or not. But everything is already too late to change."

Archer was right, and I cringed at the too-late realization. My heart thudded at the panic of how she would react when she found out. But there was nothing I could do about that now. Like he said, we were moving full force ahead. The least I could come out of this with is the revenge that had been my companion for over a decade. It didn't ease the guilt or panic or that damn emotion pulsing a fire in my heart, but it was something.

"I'll make it happen," I finally answered. "But one more week. No more."

"One more week."

I hung up and dug my hands through my hair, tugging at the strands like I could pull the increasing pressure away from my body. Taking a deep breath, I shook out my limbs, attempting to loosen my muscles. I didn't want to go in there tense and have

Vera asking questions. She'd become oddly good at reading my moods.

Music slipped through the cracked door of the bathroom, and I followed, pushing the door open to find Vera leaning toward the mirror, applying mascara while she sang along with Pressure by Muse. Her ass swayed side to side, her skirt brushing her calves. I didn't know where to look first, her juicy bottom, the soft skin of her bare back, or her breasts barely contained in a lacy bra that did nothing to hide her pert nipples.

"Damn," I muttered.

She looked up in the mirror, meeting my eyes and smiling, not missing a beat when the song changed to WTF by Missy Elliot.

I'd never known who most of these people were as I listened to older alternative and rock music, but her playlists ranged widely in all kinds of music.

I leaned against the doorjamb and crossed my arms, enjoying just watching her. She put the mascara down and turned to face me, rapping the words and putting her whole body into dancing. She snapped her fingers and moved her arms, puckering her lips with attitude as she moved closer. By the time she stood in front of me, I was half hard and smiling along with her. She grabbed my hands and moved me around until I broke and stood up, giving in to dancing with her.

"I never took you for a rap kind of girl."

"I'm an everything kind of gal. I got moves you've never seen."

"Oh yeah?"

She nodded, and I pulled her close, dancing with her. I twirled her out, the soft tendrils escaping the mass of hair piled on top of her head, brushing her cheeks. When I did my own puckered lip face to mimic hers, she burst out laughing, holding her hands to her chest.

The sun shined through the window and illuminated her freckles and deep dimples. Fuck, she was stunning.

The warmth that had come and gone when we first started all this was nothing compared to the fiery inferno that pushed the limits of my control. It wanted free, and I didn't know how much longer I could deny its existence.

The song changed again, this time a slow Nora Jones. I pulled her back in my arms and swayed us back and forth. "We'll be docking soon for dinner. I planned somewhere special for our last night."

Her head tipped forward, thudding her forehead to my chest. "How is it already the end of two weeks?" she groaned.

One more week.

She set me up for the perfect opening, and I didn't even need to concoct a reason. The guilt pressed in a little harder, but I breathed past it. It wasn't a lie.

"How about we don't go home just yet?" Her head jerked up, wide eyes meeting mine. "We could check out France. Maybe try some wine in the countryside?"

I watched the idea sink in and saw sparks of hope. "What about work?" she asked hesitantly.

"Work is more than fine," I reassured her. I needed her to agree to this because if she fought me, I'm not sure my guilt would allow me to make it happen. I pressed harder, pulling her close to brush my nose along hers. "I want another week in paradise with you."

I said it to convince her, but the words were true. Part of me didn't want to go back and face the challenges in front of us.

She studied me, and I tried to convey the truth over the lies. Emotions swirled in her eyes, and a slow smile pulled at her lips. She looked at me like I hung the moon just for her. I got my first taste of it when I offered her a chance with the new project, and seeing it again made me realize I wanted her to look at me like that forever. It was the same way my mother looked at my father, and I never thought I'd find anything near what they had.

But with her in my arms, her gaze adding the final drop of

fuel to the blaze burning through my resistance, I knew I had found it.

I loved her.

Somehow, despite how we began, I loved her.

The truth of it finally broke free and bled through my veins, filling every inch of me. The guilt pressed in harder, almost too much to bear.

"Okay. Yes. Take me away," she said, happiness making her giddy.

Fuck the guilt. Fuck the revenge. I'd come up with a better solution—hell, I could just give her the company. I'd figure it out.

If she'd let me. If she didn't hate me in the end.

THIRTY-TWO

Vera

"Are you all of a sudden scared of flying?" I asked, laughing a little.

Immediately, Nico's leg stopped shaking, and he splayed his palm over it like he could hold it still.

"No. Why?"

"You're just jittery." I'd been watching him the last two hours of our flight home, and he'd been showing nervous habits I hadn't thought he was capable of.

He shrugged it off. "Just too many cups of coffee. Thinking about work and what we have to do when we get back."

We. I loved hearing it. I was part of his life—his business, and after being shut out all my life, I couldn't get enough of it from him. Visions of working my way up the ladder at his company until it was ours filled my mind, making me giddy at the thought. At times, when I really let my mind wonder and hope, I imagined children. I imagined creating our own company and passing it on to our kids, no matter their gender.

Just like with dancing, I wanted to start new traditions with Nico.

As soon as the conversation stopped, his leg started

bouncing up and down again. This time he rested his elbow on the armrest and chewed his nail while he stared off.

Watching Nico act nervous was…unsettling, and I wanted to soothe him for whatever it was.

"How about I give you something else to think about?" I suggested softly, sliding to my knees.

I inched over and pressed his legs wide enough to fit between. His hand left his mouth and gripped the armrest like he was on a rollercoaster without a seatbelt.

He hissed when I dragged my nails up his thighs. "Vixen."

I smiled and continued my task of unfastening his belt. He lifted up to allow me room to tug his pants down enough to free his cock and balls. His length stood tall and proud, thick with veins stretching root to tip. His heavy balls resting above his briefs. He liked when I played with them. I learned that, not with words, but by listening to his groans when I rolled them in my palm. Feeling him jerk in the back of my throat when I tugged and sometimes slipped my finger behind them to play.

Holding his stare, I leaned forward and pulled first one and then the other in my mouth.

"Fuck, Verana."

"Do you like watching me suck your balls between my lips?" We both knew he did, but I liked teasing him with words as much as he did me. "Do you like knowing my pussy is getting wetter by the second because I like it too?"

"Verana," he growled in warning.

"How about when I kiss my way up the back and flick my tongue through your slit? Or is your favorite when you force your fat dick past my lips and push so hard tears slip free?"

"Fuck, yeah." His hand snapped out and gripped my hair, holding me in place. "I want to fuck that tiny throat. I wonder if it's tighter than your little cunt."

My cheeks heated. He'd pushed against my gag reflex, but never too far, and I didn't know what I wanted.

Actually, I did. I wanted him to take control and take what he wanted from me. When I stayed silent, he figured it out, and his grip tightened. One of the things we discovered with each other was how much I liked it when he was rough with me. I'd had gentle and sweet—all the typical college encounters a good girl has.

The way he shoved my face against this crotch was anything but what a good girl would do.

"Suck my balls."

I obliged. Not that I had much choice with my face buried against them.

Once he was satisfied, he leaned close, looking right in my eyes, so I couldn't miss the promise of his words. His finger slid across my already swollen lips. "I'm going to slide my cock all the way down that throat until your nose is pressed to my stomach. And I'm going to stay there until I'm satisfied. Then, I'm going to pull back and do it again. I'll control your breath. I'll control it all. And when you think you can't take any more, I'll fuck your face. You won't be able to stop me because your hands will be busy with your tits, pinching and pulling until they're rosier than your flushed pussy. If you try to stop me, I'll start all over again. Understood?"

Desire infused every inch of my body. I sat beneath him panting, so desperate I almost spread my legs around his shoe and rubbed my clit against it until I came.

Swallowing hard and reminding myself that I was safe with Nico, I nodded.

"Good girl."

He pressed a sweet, tender kiss to my lips, savoring the moments before we were anything but sweet or tender. When he pulled back, his eyes flashed with an emotion I couldn't place. I tried to place it, but he jerked me back and stood.

"Show me your tits. Show me how hard your nipples already are."

The cool air conditioning caressed my chest, pulling my

nipples even tighter. I went to pinch them like he ordered, but his voice stopped me.

"Not yet. Keep your hands at your side until you need to tap my thighs. No other reason."

My hands dropped to my side and fisted, doing all they could to not grip the tender buds until I came.

He hefted the weight of his cock in his palm and held it to my lips. "Open." As soon as they parted a little, he pushed past, groaning the further he slipped inside. "All the way. Tip back and breathe through your nose. That's it, baby."

He hadn't even gone all the way, and already he sounded breathless. His head pushed against the tight opening of my throat, and I immediately gagged. Instead of pulling back like he usually did, he waited for my throat to relax between gags and pushed further.

"Shit. Yeah. There it is. Fuck, that's good."

Oh my god, his length pushed further, and tears burned my eyes, sliding down my cheeks. All of a sudden, my nose was pressed to his groin, and he held me there tightly. With his cock in my throat, he tipped my head back and forced me to look at him. He didn't pull back but instead stayed still like he wanted to live there forever, smearing my tears across my cheek before bringing his thumb to his lips.

"You're fucking beautiful. Every time you fight my fat dick inside your throat, you squeeze me tighter. All I want to do is stay here until I flood you with my cum."

Unable to help myself, I whimpered. Both from the throbbing between my pussy and my nipples and from the discomfort of his length down my throat for so long.

He finally slid from my lips and let me gasp for air, but only for a moment because as soon as he left, he pushed right back in. Again, he held himself there and told me how beautiful I looked. He told me about how he would do this again, but he'd lay me out, so he could watch his cock push against my throat.

He told me he'd take pictures, so I could see how stunning I looked.

Each time was just as hard as the last, and by the time he pulled out for the last time, I couldn't tell if I was crying from want or from gagging. All my makeup had been wiped off, and I could only imagine what a mess I looked like. At least to anyone else. Nico praised how messy I looked, let me know how perfect I looked.

"Now, Verana. That was slow. This will be fast and rough. You're mine to use, and I want to use you up. You keep that mouth open and your hands on your nipples."

My trembling hands un-fisted from my sides. He said it was for him only, but I sat on the precipice of coming and knew it was for me too.

As soon as I put the slightest pressure on my buds, pleasure shot through me so intense, I gasped. He took the opening, gripped my hair back out of my face so he could watch, and shoved in hard. Unlike last time when he stayed, he jerked back out and pushed back in again. He used me like he promised, uncaring of my gag reflex. He didn't wait for my throat to relax, he pushed past it, fucking deep into my throat like he did my pussy.

I rolled my nipples and squirmed side to side; the slightest friction between my thighs almost too much. His thrusts got erratic, and his other hand joined the first, gripping either side of my head, forcing me down when he pushed forward. His moans filled the plane, and I pulled hard on my nipples, afraid that if I didn't hold tight, I'd drop my hand between my thighs and finger myself.

"Fuck, Verana. I'm gonna come. Yes."

He pushed all the way back, his cum shooting straight down my throat to where I barely tasted a thing. But then he pulled back, sending his next spurt of cum all over my tongue. He pulled back again when the final drops of his orgasm merely painted my lips. I tried to lick it all up, but it dripped down my chin.

He panted above me but quickly dropped back in his seat, hunching over to push me back on my heels and kicking my legs wide. His fingers swiped at the cum from my chin before shoving me back to rest on my hands. The position pulled at my hips, but the most discomfort was how it took away my ability to rub my thighs together. I pulsed with need, and my legs were spread wide, my skirt riding up. He shoved it the rest of the way up and pushed his cum-covered fingers under my panties and rubbed hard circles over my clit.

I cried out, my arms almost giving out. My eyes squeezed shut, and I gritted my teeth, the direct contact almost too much for my swollen bud.

I tried to lift my hips against his hand, but I had nowhere to move. Finally, I peeled my eyes open to find his glued to my face, panting just as hard as me. His arm moved furiously. "Nico. I can't."

"You can."

"It's too big. Fuck. Please."

"Nothing's bigger than me. Now come."

He pinched my clit between his middle finger and thumb, tapping it with his pointer finger, and I exploded.

I was surprised no one came running at the cries I let out. I sounded like I was dying, screaming like I never had before. My whole body vibrated, the prolonged torture too much to take. More tears leaked free, and I screamed until my voice broke. The orgasm moved to another and another, one tiny orgasm after the next until Nico finally took mercy on me and slowed his fingers, letting me come back from the suspended explosion. When he finally sat back, I was crying, unable to catch my breath. He pulled me onto his lap and held me close, letting me cry out whatever he set free.

I didn't even know what had me crying, but the emotions

drowned me, and all I wanted to do was confess my love and climb inside him forever.

"You did amazing. So perfectly beautiful. I can't wait to get you home and make love to you on every surface we can. We can mark it as our own—make it our home."

My body wanted to react to the way he said "make-love" instead of fucking, but I was too exhausted to think, let alone move my mouth and ask him. I tucked it away for later and curled tighter.

And that's how we spent the rest of the flight. Me in his lap as he whispered sweet nothings in my ear. At one point, he shifted me astride his lap, slipping inside and moving my hips slowly, not taking his eyes from mine once. When we finished, he slipped free and continued to hold me close, not bothering to wipe away the cum slipping down my thighs.

I didn't bother to wipe it away even when we deboarded and climbed inside the back of the car.

While I relaxed the closer we got to home, Nico's nervous bounce and nail-biting came roaring back.

"How about we order in and open the red you liked so much? The one we got in Sicily," he suggested.

"Okay. That sounds nice."

While I smiled, Nico nodded, his smile there, but forced.

"After we unpack, we can eat, and then…then maybe we can talk. I-I have something I want to tell you."

The hesitant, stuttering words gave me pause. The way he sounded like he was choking them out sent off alarm bells. But I didn't want alarm bells. I wanted my husband. I wanted to start our future together. Maybe tonight was the night.

"Okay. I have something I want to tell you too."

My heart skipped a beat in my chest, knowing I was setting myself up in a way I couldn't get out of, but I didn't want to.

New York welcomed us back with the first cold weather front, and maybe a fire and red wine—naked—would be the perfect time to let him know I loved him. If he tried to run, I'd sway him with my body and convince him of the benefits of staying.

He gave me a firm nod, squeezing my hand tight.

I took extra care to get out of the car as my torn panties were stuffed in Nico's pants pocket. Hours later, and I could still feel the stickiness between my thighs. I bit my lip, blushing at the secret no-one else knew but him.

He took my hand in his and led me in. We'd just cleared the glass doors to the lobby when a haggard-looking version of my father shot up from a chair and stormed over. He didn't have a tie; his shirt was wrinkled, and his hair strayed in all directions. He stomped closer, his face growing more and more red, his eyes glued to Nico.

Until he got only a few feet away, he acted like he didn't even see me. But then his ire redirected to me, and I took a step back, never having felt such anger directed at me.

"What the fuck did you do?"

THIRTY-THREE

Nico

"Fuck," I whispered to myself. Vera's hand gripped mine tighter, and I snapped into action, moving to stand between her and her father.

"To your own fucking family, Verana. Your mother would be ashamed of you."

"I-I don't—what?"

Her tiny, stuttering voice stabbed at my back, and it was like an out of body experience. I stood to the side, watching the bomb slowly drop on us all, knowing there wasn't anything I could do.

"Verana, let's just—" I tried to get her upstairs, but her father was having none of that.

"You spoiled little fucking brat."

"Papa. I—"

"Just because I wouldn't give you a fucking job, because it's not your role in this family—something you've known and accepted since you were little. You lash out and marry this fucking snake and give him your shares. Is that what it was about? You married him so you could work with him to take *my* company out from under me. You wanted to steal it like a fucking thief? Your mother raised you better. How dare you."

Verana stepped out from behind me, the shock of the moment wearing off, and standing on her own again. She took an aggressive stance matching her father's and lost the mousy voice from moments ago.

She was fierce and passionate and beautiful and fire.

I loved her.

And I stood there, unable to stop that I'd lose her.

"I don't know what you're talking about. I didn't give him my shares. And it's not *your* company. It was Mama's."

"Exactly. The last damn thing I had left of her," he said, his voice almost breaking over the words. "And now, it's not even hers. This fucking prick stole it from her—from *me*."

Vera's brow furrowed, struggling to process his accusations.

"Lorenzo, this is not the place to have this discussion," I interjected, trying to diffuse the situation. I needed a second to gather myself, formulate a new plan beyond where I took Vera upstairs, told her I loved her and that I was giving her the company. I just needed a second.

"Fuck you," he spat. "The time would have been in a board-room where you face me like a man. Not some coward letting his lawyer do his dirty work while he gallivants around Europe fucking my daughter."

"Papa," Vera gasped.

"Don't act all good now, Verana. You go against our family and plot with our enemy. He has taken everything, and it's all because you couldn't follow the goddamn rules."

"Nico isn't our enemy. I don't know what you're talking about."

I watched her chest rise, her nerves cracking her façade of strength. Her eyes flicked side to side to see if anyone was watching, but it was just us—just me, waiting for the impending doom.

"Lorenzo," I tried again.

"Don't." He turned his ire to me. "Don't think I don't know who you are. I may not have at first, but your lawyer made sure to say thanks for the company on behalf of K. Rush Shipping —*Knightly*-Rush Shipping."

Every time I imagined facing Lorenzo Mariano after I stole his company, I imagined the victory. I'd close my eyes and picture the shock and ire on his face when he realized who I was. I imagined smiling the same way he had when my grandfather begged him to not dismantle the majority of the company.

I tried to find that rush of adrenaline I'd had hints of each time. I tried to find the words he used. *It's just business.* But they were nowhere to be found. Incinerated by the fire, Vera started inside me months ago. My love for her burned through my revenge and left me with a panic I'd lose her right as I was finally getting her.

"What are you talking about?" Vera asked. She dug her hands into her hair and pinched her eyes closed, shaking her head like she could knock something loose and make sense of it all. "I married Nico so I wouldn't have to marry Camden. I married Nico because I wanted to make my own choices and because I wanted to be valued beyond what I could provide to some man."

Lorenzo barked an unhinged laugh. "They always say to sleep with the devil you know, Verana. And this is why. This is why we followed those traditions and arranged a marriage. We did it to protect our company. And you ruined it by breaking the rules and fucking it all up."

They stared at each other. Him waiting for her to admit what she'd done and her waiting for it to make sense. When she stayed silent, realization dawned on Lorenzo, and he laughed.

"You dumb girl."

"That's enough," I growled.

But it was like he didn't even hear me. His laugh turned to a manic cackle echoing off the tile floors and glass walls. "You don't know. You don't even know that you're being used. Looks like I'm not the only one he stole the company from."

"Goddammit," Vera growled. "Will someone tell me what the fuck is going on."

"Verana, if we can go upstairs, I can explain."

"What?" Lorenzo asked. "More lies? I don't think so."

"You have no idea what you're talking about. And I will not stand here and allow you to talk to my wife like that."

"Your wife? Or the pawn you acquired to win?"

"She is not a pawn," I growled, reaching my own limits of control. Vera was a queen, and I was about to lose her.

He smirked when he saw the panic flash across my face before I could mask it. As if in slow motion, he turned to Vera, and I opened my mouth to stop it, but nothing came out. Part of me wanted to toss her over my shoulder and run, but I knew I was only fighting the inevitable. My grandpa's words came back.

A marriage built on lies is no marriage at all.

"You married Nicholas Knightly Rush. Grandson to the owner of Knightly Shipping—or what used to be." I grit my teeth at his dig. "Until his grandfather made a poor business choice—"

"He did not," I growled.

"—and I stepped in to help. And when he couldn't repay, I sold off what was owed to me."

"You took advantage of a suffering man, you arrogant prick," I said through a clenched jaw.

"It was just business," he threw back.

The words unveiled every ounce of anger that brought me to this moment, and I snapped. I forgot every plan I'd made over the past week to tell Vera the truth over a candlelit dinner at home—preferably naked and tied to the chair so she couldn't run. I forgot everything beyond Lorenzo's shitty barb. "Yeah, well, me buying up Mariano Shipping was just business, and I hope you enjoy watching me take it all away from you."

"You fucking shit." Lorenzo lost his own patience and stepped closer. He tried to get in my face but was too short to come close to being as threatening as he wanted to appear. "What? You couldn't find enough shares for your pitiful revenge, so you took my daughter? That's not business—it's cowardly."

"You practically shoved her in my face with the way you pushed her away. Don't blame me for losing your daughter."

He opened his mouth, but her soft voice cut through all the macho anger spilling around us.

"Revenge?"

I snapped my gaze to her, her brown eyes wide and filled with surprise and hurt. The look punched me in the gut, stealing all the air from my lungs—from my need to win against Lorenzo.

"Vera—"

"He'd been buying shares to Mariano Shipping for years, using shell companies to hide his identity. And you, my spoiled, ungrateful daughter, gave him the final few he needed," Lorenzo supplied.

"That's not—"

"Did you know who I was?" Vera asked, cutting me off. "Is that why you hired me? Because you knew my last name the whole time? Did you know it was me under the mask while you fucked me?" Her questions got louder. "Did you plan this all along?"

"No, Vera. I never planned—" I tried to explain again only to be cut off by Lorenzo raging against Vera.

"Maybe if you hadn't spent an extra week spreading your legs for the enemy, we might have fought this," Lorenzo interjected. "We had one chance, and instead of answering your damn phone, you extend your vacation by another week, giving him just enough time to seal the deal."

She blinked, her brows pulling tight as she put the pieces together. "France?"

"Oh, is that where you went? Was that before or after you gave him the inside details to our company? He knew just where to hit us, Verana. He knew exactly how to get around the clauses your grandma put into that stupid contract. Did you spill the secrets willingly, or did he steal that too?"

She stumbled back like her father's words physically hit her.

"Verana." I reached for her, but she held a hand up, warring me off.

"Was any of it true?"

She clutched her stomach and shook, on the verge of shattering right there, and I wanted to pull her in my arms and hold her together.

"I was going to tell you everything. Explain it all. I was going to give—"

"Would you do it while you seduced more information out of me? Would you use the way I care about you to get what you want?" she snarled.

Sucking in air through her nose, she pinched her eyes shut like she couldn't bear to look at me.

"Verana, I never meant to hurt you."

"Shut up," she snapped, her eyes opening like a blazing fire. The hurt still lingered, but it was quickly being swallowed up by anger. "God, I trusted you."

"You ca—"

"No. I cared for you. I thought you actually saw me—respected me—but it was all a lie. You're just like everyone else. Only seeing what you can use me for. A liar. A user. I actually believed you when you praised my work."

Lorenzo scoffed, and I wanted to punch him but fought the urge and kept my eyes on Vera.

"You know I see how smart you are."

"I don't know anything, Nicholas."

"Please, come upstairs so we can talk about this without your father. You have to listen to me."

I reached for her hands again, desperate to be connected to her any way I could, but she swiped her hand wide, slapping mine away.

"Fuck you," she snarled. Her lip curled like an injured animal fighting off an attacker.

"Don't worry, Verana. We'll get this annulled. We can fix this." Lorenzo tried to step close and reach his daughter, but she turned her feral attack on him next.

"Fuck you, too. Fuck both of you."

She fumbled with her bag, almost dropping it with her shaking hands. I wanted to see her face, memorize it like I hadn't when I thought I had at least five more years to wake up to her smile, her dimples, her fresh-faced freckles. The fear that I'd never get to lay eyes on her again flooded my veins, almost taking my legs out from under me.

"Verana. Please, listen," I choked. I wanted to explain it all right there, shout it out and force her to listen, but Lorenzo lingered like a virus, and the words remained locked in my throat.

I clenched my fists to stop from going to her and brushing her hair back.

She kept her head down until she finally got her bag over her shoulder and her suitcase handle up.

Then she gave me my wish. She brushed her hair back and leveled me with one last gut-wrenching stare. Our eyes met for only a moment before she stormed past, but it would haunt me forever.

The anger still swirled in the brown depths, but it bathed in the sheen of hurt she struggled to hold back. Her nose red from struggling to hold back tears. Not a single dimple in sight.

Before we got out of the car, I imagined curling up with her and telling her the truth. I imagined telling her I loved her, and I'd do whatever she wanted with the company as long as she stayed. I imagined her naked body glowing by the fire while I promised her with my mouth and hands that she was more important.

Instead, I was left with the reality that my revenge had got me exactly what I set out to get.

I won the company—crushed Lorenzo. And I was just as alone as when I started.

"You son of a bitch," Lorenzo growled once Vera disappeared back into the car.

But I didn't care. The victory echoed like a shout in an empty tomb. Hollow with no one to hear.

Exhaustion pulled at my muscles, and I just wanted to lose myself in a bottle of alcohol until I couldn't remember the look on her face anymore.

He followed behind me, raging obscenities and challenges, promising to fight back. But it hit against my numb back as I went to the elevator. He stood in front of the open doors, his face red with anger, but all I saw was Vera's back disappearing beyond the doors.

I should have been happy watching Lorenzo crumble before me.

Instead, I stood like an empty shell. Wishing to go back and do it differently.

Vera's laugh flashed in my mind. The way we danced in the bathroom as she rapped Missy Elliot. The way she fit against my body when we danced in the streets of Italy. Her smile when I praised her work.

No. I couldn't lose her.

Committed to wallowing in my misery tonight, I grabbed the bottle once I reached the empty apartment and fell to the couch in the dark. I took a long pull from the bottle, staring at the dark screen of the TV.

While I did my best to wipe out the night, I also began concocting a plan to get her back. She just needed time. She had to hear me out. She was my wife.

And I wasn't ready to let go of that now.

If ever.

THIRTY-FOUR

Vera

—————

"WELL, look who's alive. I thought you—"

Raelynn's words cut off when she fully opened the door to my splotchy face and suitcase.

"What the fuck?" she murmured.

She grabbed my arm and jerked me inside, looking side to side like someone would pop out from around the corner. But by the time she shut the door and faced me, I'd already started crumbling.

"Oh, shit," she said before tugging me in her arms.

In the comfort of my best friend's arms, the cracks fissured too big to hold together anymore, and I toppled inch by inch. My shoulders shook with my silent sobs. Then my chest as my quiet sobs became loud cries of pain ripping from deep in my stomach. She held me tight, holding me up when my legs shook.

"Who do I have to kill? I'll fucking rip them apart piece by fucking piece. Fucking mutilate them." Her words were meant to be dark and scary, but the way her voice cracked stole her thunder.

She shifted us to the couch, and by the time we sat, she was crying right along with me.

"Vera, baby," she soothed, rubbing her hands up and down

my back. "What happened? God, I can't stand this. I don't even know what happened, but god, your pain—I can feel it, and it hurts."

"I'm so-sorry."

"Don't you dare. Give it to me. Let me help you carry this— whatever this is."

"N-N-Nico," I choked out. Even thinking his name hurt, but saying it tore another rip in my tattered heart.

She froze but didn't let go of me. "Did he hurt you?" Her question held more threat than any of her promises to mutilate before. Raelynn's mother had been abused by her father, and it was a hard line that changed Raelynn from playful to serious in the blink of an eye.

"Not ph-physically."

Her body expanded in my arms with her deep inhale of relief, and her hand resumed its motion up and down my back.

She let me cry, taking shuddering breaths with me. She rocked us back and forth and shhh'd me like a baby. It made me miss my mom but also filled me with gratitude for such an amazing friend. She was part of our tripod, and right now, she took on more weight when I couldn't.

When my cries softened, she finally spoke. "Was the sex that bad?"

I choked out a laugh, tears still leaking down my cheeks. God love Raelynn. Only she could ease this ache when we were both crying with a joke.

"Was all the excitement gone because you weren't at a crowded party, and he wasn't a stranger?" She mock gasped. "Does he only do missionary with the lights out and under the covers?"

"Oh my god," I groaned, laughing harder. I pulled back and swiped at my cheeks.

"Say it ain't so," she said in a fake southern accent, her hand to her forehead.

"Jesus, Rae."

She smiled and brushed back the strand of hair clinging to my cheeks. "Let me get us some wine, and then we can talk. What do you think? No glass? Bottle each?"

"Sounds perfect."

With a smile, she stood up and turned to walk away but came to a screeching halt when the doorknob jiggled frantically, and hard pounding reverberated against the door.

"What the fuck?" she whispered, turning wide eyes to me.

"Does he know where you live?"

"How the fuck should I know?"

We whispered back and forth, not moving a muscle, like maybe if we didn't move, the person wouldn't know we were there.

"Open this goddamn door right now or I'll fucking kick it down. I don't know how because I'm pretty small, but I'll do it. I'll find a way. You bitches let me in."

Raelynn snapped into action, whipping the door open. "Nova?"

She stormed past, her long red hair flowing behind her like a fiery waterfall. "Yes, fucking Nova. Who did you expect?"

She stood in the open space, looking between mine and Raelynn's red eyes and splotchy faces.

"What happened?" Sweet Nova stood tall, looking more imposing than Raelynn ever had.

"Damn, Xena the warrior princess," Raelynn said, looking Nova up and down. "How the hell did you get here so fast? I thought you were out of town. And why are you so dressed up? Are those...heels?"

Nova rolled her eyes and heaved a sigh at Raelynn's joking, only relaxing the slightest bit from her attack position. "Yes, and I just ran up seven flights of stairs because your elevator is stupid slow. I had a late meeting—"

"A date?" Raelynn asked, gasping in excitement. Nova didn't really date, and Raelynn constantly harassed her for it.

"*A meeting* with a publisher from a magazine. I got in this morning, and when I got your message, I bolted, barely giving an excuse before tossing cash at him like a fucking stripper."

"What the hell did you send her?" I asked.

Nova pulled up her phone and handed it to me.

Raelynn: OMG OMG OMG! 911!!! EMERGENCY!! Face-Time immediately. Need you. 911!! Something's wrong with V. Call. Now. 911!!!

"Wow," I said, handing her phone back.

"So, just tell me. Rip it off like a Band-Aid. Are you dying? Sick? God, I don't think I can lose you."

I sniffed, more tears building, and Nova stormed around the couch, pulling me into a fierce hug.

"What the hell is going on?" she pleaded.

"Something with Nico," Raelynn answered for me. "I was about to grab some wine so we could talk. Want a bottle?"

"A whole bottle?"

"When your girl shows up at your door sobbing for the first time in all the years of your friendship, you each get a bottle."

"Ummm…sure."

"Atta girl."

Raelynn disappeared in the kitchen, and Nova pulled back, framing my face with both hands. "Are you okay?"

My face scrunched at the question, my lips pinched to hold back more tears, and I shook my head. My body ached like it'd gone ten rounds with a heavyweight. The sharp pain in my chest stung like a knife through my heart, making it hard to breathe.

"I'm so sorry, Vera," she whispered. "We'll get through this. You're not alone."

More tears leaked free, and I fell into her arms again. Raelynn always made me laugh, and Nova always soothed my soul. Despite the crushing weight of my pain, I knew I'd make it through this with these two by my side.

"Dammit, Nova, I just got her to stop crying."

I laughed again. Raelynn sounded like a pissed off parent mad at her spouse for waking the baby.

I sat back and wiped my eyes. "Sorry, guys."

"Stop apologizing," Raelynn reprimanded.

She sat a bottle in front of each of us, chips and dip, M&Ms, and a charcuterie tray.

"Damn," I whispered.

"I keep a stash, and my cook made one earlier today for me to munch on. I'm skilled, but not good enough to whip up cheese and meat artfully decorated like that."

"Do you want me to grab glasses," Nova asked.

Raelynn sat in the chair catty-corner to the couch, giving Nova a bless-your-heart kind of smile. "Oh, sweetheart, no. We're drinking straight from the bottle."

"Oh. Okay. This went so well last time."

We snickered, mine quickly followed by an unladylike sniff.

"That was a bottle of tequila and nothing goes well when you drink tequila straight from the bottle. Now," Raelynn faced me, looking like a prim and proper politician's daughter, perched on the edge of the couch. All except for the way she clutched her bottle of wine. "Talk."

Snatching my own bottle from the table, I brought it to my lips, taking long pulls. The spicy, berry wine took the taste of Nico away, and I drank more, wanting to do all I could to wash him from every part of me while also wanting to keep every part of him close.

I sat the bottle down with a thud and started from when we walked into the lobby to find my father. By the time I was done, both women looked like they were ready to burn the world down for me.

"What an asshole," Nova said.

"That mother fucking liar," Raelynn added.

"The worst part," I said, huffing a laugh without humor. "I love him. I love him so much."

I tried to swallow down the tears, but they slipped free, and Nova grabbed my hand for support.

"Do you think he cares for you, too?" she asked.

"I guess a part of me hoped he did. Our honeymoon had been amazing. We got to know each other. We laughed and bonded and the sex—god, the sex. He just…saw me."

"It sounds like he cares," Nova said.

"I don't know because now everything is colored with this lie. Every business conversation, every question he asked, every time he got to know me, now makes me see it as a way for him to get information to steal my family's company. The trip to France when I thought he just wanted more time alone together? Now I see it for what it was, just a ploy to keep me away. All of it was a lie, and I was the stupid fool who started to believe it."

"You are not stupid," Raelynn vehemently scolded. "You reacted to the information you were given, and there were no clues to make you think otherwise."

"You said Nicholas did it for revenge, but why?" Nova asked.

I ran through the evening, trying to remember everything that was said but also trying to make it all go away at the same time. "I-I'm not sure. Something about his family's company. I think my father did something."

"What a dick," Raelynn said. "That's a mess between two men fighting with their dicks. Why the hell did he have to pull you in?"

"I-I don't know." My voice wobbled over more tears. I'd asked myself that same question on the ride over. Why couldn't he have just left me alone? None of this pain would have happened if he'd just have left me alone.

Yeah, then you would be married to Camden and never know what love was.

I hated the stupid voice in my head. If this was love, then it could fuck off.

"God," I groaned. "Maybe I should have just married Camden."

"Ew, no," Nova said, cringing. "If nothing else, the silver lining from all of this is that you aren't married to Camden."

"Hear, hear," Raelynn said, raising her bottle.

We clinked bottles, and all took a drink.

"So, what are you going to do?"

I huffed a laugh. "I don't know. I have no house, no job—because I'm sure as hell not going back to work for him. I have nothing."

"Bullshit," Raelynn said. "You have us. And me? I have more than everything. We'll figure it out, and you can stay here while you do it. If all else fails, we can move forward with the platonic love island."

"Now there's the real mistake. Fuck, thinking you should have just married Camden. We really should have just run away when Rae offered it."

We all laughed at Nova's statement.

Raelynn gave Nova and me a change of clothes, and we curled up on the couch, a second bottle of wine each. But no matter how much I tried to lose myself in my friends—to focus on how much love I had for them—my heart refused to forget how much I loved Nico.

And it hurt over and over again when I reminded the stupid organ that he was a liar and didn't love us back.

How could he?

THIRTY-FIVE

Nico

I MUTED THE TELEVISION, not wanting to listen to the newscaster report on the hostile takeover of Mariano Shipping. My biggest dream for over a decade scrolled across the bottom of one of the biggest business channels, and I sat sprawled on my couch, missing my wife.

I called my grandpa to check in on him, but he was having a bad day, and I used that as an excuse to not visit. But four days had passed, and I knew I needed to go. The problem was that I knew he would make me look at myself in the mirror. He'd make me face what I'd done. He always had. When I used to imagine going to tell him I finally won for us, I imagined his reprimanding glare for holding on to revenge, but also the glint of pride in his eyes at knowing a debt had been paid.

Now, I knew any glint of pride would be dashed with I told you so.

"How is he today?" I asked James, the orderly who worked with my grandpa the most.

"Better." His answer was quickly followed by a wince that had me wincing with him, imagining what had happened. "Two days ago, not so much."

"What happened?"

"I had family matters to attend to, and it was Asher's day off," he explained, referring to the other orderly who helped out. "So, Jane worked with him."

"Shit," I groaned, wiping my hand down my face.

"He uh…it wasn't the best day to have her with him."

He rubbed the back of his neck like the memory alone brought back the tension. I could relate.

"What did he do?"

"You know it's not him. His brain…it just…it's different now." I appreciated James's attempt to avoid answering and trying to smooth over any wrongdoings.

"I know. It doesn't make it easier."

"It never does for anyone. Watching someone's mind fade is hard—watching them become a completely different person in the process is impossible. If you ever need to talk…"

He left it hanging like he always did, waiting for me to take him up on his offer. Like always, I shook my head. "What did he do?"

"He flashed her. Like all of himself."

"Jesus."

"And tried to chase her when she ran from the room."

"Oh, fuck."

"Yeah. She's fine, and Charlie's apologized at least a million times. Ordered flowers and chocolates and drops his head like a kicked dog whenever she comes around."

I closed my eyes, waiting for the anger to surface like it did every time I got updates on how his dementia affected him that week. Instead, I just hurt.

I had no more revenge to cling to. I had no wife to hold on to.

No, I was left with what I already had and with nothing to do but face it, and it just plain, flat-out hurt. Now, I was left with knowing what it could feel like when I had it all. I knew taking Lorenzo's company from him wouldn't fix my grandpa, but I'd hoped it would—I don't know. Ease any of this weight pressing in on me. Maybe it would have made it easier to manage—to understand and accept. Instead, I still wanted to rage and make it all go away. I was still pissed he was fading from me, slipping through my fingers like sand.

Maybe that was the theme of my life. I had people long enough just to make me love them, and then they slipped away.

"Thanks, James," I said, pushing the melancholy aside. My grandpa had already beaten himself up enough; he didn't need me going in with disappointed stares.

"Hey Grandpa," I said, walking into the room.

"Hey…Um…Dammit."

"Ni—"

"Nicholas. There it is. Always on the tip of my tongue."

"I do the same thing all the time," I said, but we both knew I rarely struggled with recalling names. My mind was sharp—just like his used to be.

He laughed awkwardly before taking me in. His head tipped to the side, and his white brows pinched together. "What's wrong, Nicholas?"

Plopping down in the chair across from his couch, I blew out a long breath, sagging back like a deflating balloon. "I bought Mariano Shipping last week."

Just as I predicted, a spark of pride flashed before his lips flattened, and he shook his head. He opened his mouth to speak, but before he could, I admitted it all—ripping the Band-Aid off.

"And Vera found out the night we got back—from her father confronting us in the lobby. She hasn't spoken to me since she stormed out."

His eyes slid closed, and he shook his head slowly. It reminded me of the night I crashed the car when I'd only been fifteen. I'd wanted to be yelled at. I wanted anything other than his disappointment. Just like then, I hung my head and stared at my closed palms and twirling thumbs.

"Have you tried to talk to her?"

My eyes flicked up and down, wincing, thinking about the

single message I sent asking to talk—the one she didn't respond to. "No."

He laughed softly, and I winced again. Silence stretched, and I cowardly kept my head down. Nicholas Knightly Rush, CEO of K. Rush Shipping, alpha male who dominated the shipping industry, no longer sat on the couch. No, Nico, the rebellious teenager, sat there feeling ashamed.

"You know your grandma played a bigger role in the company than anyone realized. She may not have actually worked there, but she was my own board of directors. I went to her with almost everything, and she knew the ins and outs just from being my wife and picking up things as she grew up in the world. But it wasn't always that way."

I couldn't imagine it not being that way. That woman had worn pearls and stood tall, her confidence in herself like an aura that followed her everywhere, making people take notice. She'd raised my mother to have the same attributes. My father had been an equally strong man, but I'd emulated my strength from the two women who raised me.

"Man," he started, laughing. "I made a business decision that she'd advised against. The deal had been too good to not take, even if it screwed some people in the process. That was business. But, Diana? Whew, boy. She told me not to do it, but I did it anyway. I told myself that I knew better—that she didn't need to know. Except then she asked me directly, and I couldn't say any of those things to her face, so I lied. Nicholas, when your grandmother found out, she didn't even fight. We'd been married barely a year, and she calmly let me know, a marriage of lies was no marriage at all, packed her bags, and left."

"She left you?" My brows shot to my hairline. I'd witnessed my grandparents bicker more than enough—I'd also witnessed them forgiving each other, but I'd never seen my grandma truly mad. I'd never seen anything but love between them.

"Yup. My macho pride held me back from chasing her for three whole days, but it was all a façade for how scared I was she'd never come back. Times were different then, and I reasoned that if she wanted me, she'd come to me. Then I reasoned that if she wasn't coming to me, then she must have been too mad to talk, and she'd come around. On day three, my façade crumbled, and I went to her. She'd opened the door with her chin high like a regal queen. I'd apologized, and she asked for what. Let me tell you, that was not the response I expected. She sure didn't throw herself in my arms like I'd hoped."

I laughed and couldn't help but imagine Vera looking the same way—chin high and proud.

"What did she do?"

"Well, when I told her I was sorry for lying, she said it wasn't enough. She couldn't be with a criminal and crook. Business may have been business, but she needed to be married to someone who also had some humanity and compassion. Slammed the door and didn't answer it again for another week."

"What did you do to make her talk?" I sat up on the edge of the couch, eager for answers. Maybe he could tell me what to do. Maybe he had the answers to avoid losing Vera.

"First, I got mad and drunk all over again. Then, I thought about what she'd said. Not just when I went to her, but before when she'd advised me against the deal. I'd begrudgingly admitted that she'd been right. And if I didn't believe that, then I wouldn't have had to lie to her about it. The deal had been a shit move—the kind of move I didn't want for our company, and I was avoiding having her make me face that truth—make me look in the mirror to find the kind of man who swindled back door deals for extra money. So, I'd lied to her, compounding the issue. Once I faced that truth, I set about fixing it."

"How?" I almost begged.

"I undid it. I set aside my greed and need to win and chose my wife. She didn't want to be married to a man who lied to win, and I loved her enough to not want it for her either. I sure as hell wasn't going to let her go to find someone else, so I changed me. I went back and pulled out of the deal, giving it back to the company I stole it from, and the next time I went to your grandma, I went with humility and the contract to prove I'd be the man she wanted. I swore to never lie again, and only then did she finally forgive me."

"I can't give the company back to Lorenzo," I stated. "He was running it into the ground, and frankly, the way he treated Vera makes me even less inclined to undo it. I was going to give *her* the company, but I never got a chance to tell her."

"Sometimes, chances aren't given to us—we have to take them."

"What if she still leaves me. What if she can't forgive me, takes the company and runs."

"Ahh, Nicholas," he sighed. "Doing the right thing doesn't come with a guarantee, but you do it because you want it more for her than you want it for yourself."

Dropping my head, I rubbed a hand along the back of my neck, not pleased with my options. Of course, I wanted her to be happy. I just wanted to be happy with her. I wanted to enjoy a life of making her happy every day—one where I go to wake up to her fresh-faced freckles and dimples.

"Do you love her?"

Not bothering to look up, I nodded.

"What happened to barely liking each other?"

This time I did look up with a deadpanned stare. I heard the *I told you so* in his voice. "You want me to tell you that you were right?"

"It never hurts to hear."

I groaned, and he leaned forward to pat my shoulder.

"I saw it the moment you told me about her. I saw it in you both when I watched you say your vows, but you two were a stubborn match, and I knew it would be a hard trip. I just hoped you brought your own humility and maybe realized you loved her more than your revenge before it was too late."

"Obviously, you have too much faith in me."

"Do I? I think you'll figure it out."

"How?"

"Oh, Nicholas," he said, laughing. "Thirty-five years old and still coming to me for answers—even with a half-assed brain."

"You're still the smartest man I know."

Pain stopped his smile from reaching his eyes, knowing each day he lost more and more. "Either way, there are some things we need to answer ourselves. That's how we truly learn and don't make the same mistake again."

"Grandpa…"

"*You're* the smartest man *I* know. You'll figure it out."

I wanted to press more, but James came and let me know time was up. My grandpa had therapy and dinner.

"Stop thinking about you, Nicholas. Put yourself in her shoes and figure out what you can do for her in spite of yourself. Put your pride aside and be vulnerable enough to let her hurt you. Otherwise, you'll never know."

His final words followed me the whole way home. I thought about it all night, another bottle of bourbon for company. For the hell of it, I even grabbed my phone and sent the message I'd typed and deleted a thousand times.

Me: I'm sorry.

I typed at least ten more.

I miss you.

I fucked up.

Call me.

Can I call you?

I miss your body.

Stop being so stubborn.

I love you.

All of them deleted. Especially the last one. If Vera ever let me speak to her again, I'd be sure to say it to her face, make sure she heard me. I even considered calling my driver, going to her right then, and telling her, but I did as my grandpa suggested and put myself in her shoes.

She'd assume I was lying again, and I couldn't blame her.

But it didn't mean I couldn't start a plan to make it better. Unfortunately, I had to admit that I didn't know my wife as well as I wanted to, and maybe some outside assistance would help.

Knowing she'd probably threaten my manhood, I braced myself and hit send.

Me: I need to talk to her. But I need her to hear me.
Raelynn: Fuck off.
Me: Please.
Raelynn: I may be listening but no guarantees. Maybe if you beg more.
Me: I fucked up—with her. Not you. I'll happily beg for her.
Raelynn: Girl code states if you fuck up with her, you fuck up with the friends. Honestly, I'd be more scared of Nova than me right now.
Me: I'll make it up to you all, but I can't if she won't even listen to me.
Raelynn: Oh, you mean she didn't respond to the most curt message demanding a time to talk. Wow. I'm shooketh.
Me: Jesus.
Me: Like I said, I fucked up. I won't explain to you because it's between us, but I want to make it better for her. Even if it's not better for me.
Me: But I can't do that if she won't talk to me.
Raelynn: Do you love her?
Me: That's between Vera and me.
Raelynn: …
Raelynn: Fine. Maybe I can help orchestrate a time to talk.
Raelynn: But if you make it worse. I'll rip your eyes out.
Me: Noted.

One of the four-hundred bands squeezing my chest snapped

loose. It still hurt to breathe without her, but I'd take the iota of release reaching out to Rae gave me. She laid out when I could come over the weekend and said she would help keep Vera there to hear me out.

It didn't guarantee me anything, but at least it was a start.

I went to work the next day, barely focusing on the new project that Vera should have been heading under Domenic, hunting through every bit of knowledge I had to come up with what I would say this weekend. When Ryan delivered the thick file holding the official contract for Mariano Shipping Inc for me to sign, I couldn't even bring myself to open it.

I took it home and finally opened it up for review when the twinkling stars of the night were my only company shining through the large windows Vera had loved so much.

Mariano Shipping had been hurting for longer than I'd assumed. Lorenzo had run the company to the brink of destruction all on his own. The clauses in the contract outlining their traditional views had been the only thing that had almost saved him. But it'd only been a matter of time before he lost it all on his own.

Maybe if Vera saw this, she'd be more understanding. She'd see her father had ruined it all before I stole it.

Yeah, show her how her family company was on the brink of destruction—the thing she'd worked so hard for and loved, if only for the connection to her mother. That'd go awesome.

I shook my head and growled at nothing.

A vision of Vera lounging topless on the deck, smiling as she told me about her mom and how much she'd loved the company but loved the traditions more. She'd admitted she wanted them both to feel the connection to her mom and hated that her father cut her out without even trying.

And I'd stolen it—the last part of her mom—and never made a bigger effort to let her know she could have it. She'd probably spent the week mourning the last piece of her mom she had left—and I'd let her because of my pride.

"Fuck," I whispered.

My phone rang, pulling me from the mess in front of me.

"Archer," I greeted.

"Nicholas. I just saw the papers."

"Yeah, I got them today," I said, looking down at the stacks strewn across my dining room table.

"So, does this mean we're keeping Mariano Shipping for ourselves?"

I flipped through the pages, looking for the added notes about selling the company in relation to Vera. When I saw they were still there, my brows scrunched in confusion. "What? The clauses about the sale are still here. Why would you assume it wasn't going to Vera?"

"Because she filed for divorce. You said you got the papers."

Like a needle to a balloon, it started small, the air seeping out as realization hit. Then it hit like a knife, popping my hope like a gunshot to the chest.

Divorce.

Divorce.

She didn't even talk to me.

She didn't even give me a chance.

Did she even care to know why? Did she even care at all? Her laughing. Her moaning. Her scowling. Her gloating. All of it like snapshots firing in my brain. All of it vanishing.

She didn't even give me a chance.

How dare she make this decision without even giving me. A. Chance.

I clenched the phone tight, the edges digging into my palm.

I realized then that the thought that I'd be okay with her walking away was a lie. I'd had hope that once she heard me out, she'd understand—she'd forgive me, and we'd figure it out together. And if she hadn't, then I would have fought tooth and nail to win her back because I knew she cared—I'd hoped she'd cared as much as I did for her. I'd hoped my love was enough.

But with divorce, I lost that. I lost the ability to fight to keep her. She would already walk away.

"You there?" Archer asked, sounding far off.

"I meant the contract," I ground out through clenched teeth.

"Ohh," he said slowly. "I thought you knew."

"I assure you, I didn't. And nothing changes."

I hung up and looked down at the splayed papers.

Oh, no. She could file for whatever she wanted, but she'd listen first.

A warning whispered in the back of my mind as I grabbed my keys and stormed out, slamming the door behind me. Maybe going to her now, with the rioting flood of emotions raging through me, wasn't the best idea, but I was a hurricane—an unstoppable force.

Fuck Raelynn's plan. Fuck her timeline.

I was done with waiting.

It was time I went to visit my wife.

THIRTY-SIX

Vera

_____

"Should I be buying stock in Talenti? I mean, it has to be going up with how much you're plowing through it this week."

I rolled my eyes at Raelynn, looking down at my slouched position on the couch. "Don't act like you don't have a spoon in your back pocket, ready to join me."

She cocked her hip but quickly dropped the fake attitude. "You're right," she sighed, grabbing her spoon and falling down next to me. "Gimme."

I obliged, holding the container out.

"Oh, god," she moaned after the first bite. "Salted caramel. My favorite. Do you think I could get them to sponsor me on Instagram? I'm not an influencer, but I could become one for free ice cream."

"It's worth a shot."

We both dug in, watching the episode of _Friends_ playing quietly in the background. I held my breath, waiting for her to bring up the day.

"Soooo…how'd it go?"

I shrugged and stuffed another bite in.

"It's a cute outfit. Looking like a badass bitch has to help."

"It definitely doesn't."

I'd thought wearing a black power suit would help me feel stronger than I was. I'd wanted to meet with the lawyer in sweatpants and no bra, unshowered, and slouching. Instead, I'd put on my red-soled shoes and cigarette pants. I'd walked in with my head held high—but trembling.

My heart and brain warred for dominance. My brain pushing my limbs forward to sever myself from the man who stole from me—from my family—and used me in the process. My heart tried to hold me back, screaming that this was a mistake.

In the end, I'd signed the papers. Then I'd gone back out to my car and burst into tears, barely making it home.

That was five hours ago, and I hadn't moved since except to get the ice cream. As a cruel twist, *Friends* popped up on TV, bringing forth the image of a sick Nico in bed, getting caught up on the show.

Everything in me ached. I just couldn't tell if it was from being so mad at him I wanted to shove as far away as I could or fighting off this need to go to him every second of the day.

"Did you message him back?"

"No." Nico's message came right before I fell asleep, and it had followed me into my dreams, reminding me of each precious moment of our honeymoon. The fear that they'd all been set up and fake held me back from going to him. "What would I say?"

"That you miss him?"

I scoffed. "What? Are you actually *wanting* me to talk to him?"

"Listen, I may not want a relationship for myself, but I can see you're hurting, and I hate it."

"I hate it too, but it doesn't change what he did."

"Do you know why he did it? Have you talked to him?"

"No," I answered, pouting because I knew I was being a coward.

"You know I will make that man's balls into my own

personal earrings for you, but Verana, maybe you should at least talk to him."

"Maybe he should have tried," I snapped.

"He's a man. He will forever be waiting for you to tell him what to do, standing around with his dick in his hand until then, looking like a damn fool."

I choked on my bite of ice cream, laughing at her description, but quickly sobered. "It's too late. I've already filed."

"So? Call him and tell him you want to talk first? Marry him again if you want to. Or just be together. Marriage is such a noose anyway. Just because you love someone doesn't mean you have to get all dolled up and get the government involved."

"I don't know."

"Well, thankfully, I do."

I dropped my head back to the couch with a groan, not convinced.

Both of us jumped, letting out the girliest shrieks when a hard knock shook the front door.

Another loud knock made Raelynn jump up, facing the door like a prized fighter. "What the hell are you doing?" I whispered.

"I don't know. They sound pretty serious about getting through the door, and this place isn't big enough to hide for long, so I figure I'll at least look intimidating."

I blinked slowly, my eyebrows lifting with doubt as I looked her up and down in her red stilettos, ripped jeans, and cropped sweater.

"Oh, shut up," she scolded quietly. "It's better than sitting there. What are you going to do? Throw your spoon at them?"

"Maybe."

Another pounding knock.

"Maybe it's Nova again," I suggested hopefully.

Raelynn gave serious side-eye and crept closer to the door. Just as she was about to look out the peephole, a deep voice replaced the knocking.

"Verana, I know you're in there."

Our heads whipped to each other, and I knew my eyes were just as wide as hers.

"What the fuck?" she mouthed, hands out for support.

I just shook my head. To what? I didn't know.

To not knowing what to do.

To not wanting to let him in.

To not wanting to turn him away.

To shake loose the rambling orchestra of chaotic thoughts fighting for dominance in my head.

"Please." He sounded like the Beast from *Beauty and the Beast*. Barely restrained anger and unused to the word—but trying because he cared.

No. Nicholas *Knightly* Rush didn't care about anyone but himself. It'd been a week and not a word beyond a request to talk until I finally made a decision.

"I'm letting him in," she mouthed, looking like a bull ready for a fight.

I looked frantically around, maybe hoping for a hole to open up in the floor I could dive away into, never facing him again.

My chest curled in on itself, squeezing too tight. My muscles seized in a battle to stand and face him or bolt the other way. Was there a fire escape here?

But before I could make my decision, the door was open, and my husband's dark, commanding presence, that had caught my eye from across a crowded restaurant and even from behind a mask, swallowed the room whole—sucking every bit of oxygen into himself.

I jerked to my feet and had to clench my hands at my sides to hide their trembling.

He scanned the room until he landed on me, his eyes darkening like the blackest obsidian. His scruff had grown to a full beard, but still, his lips were too full to be hidden, and I was able to watch the way they curled up like a feral growl.

In my best imaginations, he begged and pleaded, told me he loved me, and he'd made a mistake. When I forced myself to face reality, I imagined indifference and maybe—*maybe*—a hint of regret. But never had I thought about his anger.

Because what the hell did he have to be angry about?

He got what he wanted. He won. He lied. I lost. *I* should be the one mad. Instead, I trembled like a leaf fighting off the urge to run into his arms.

"What the fuck do you think you're doing?" he growled, taking a threatening step closer.

"Hey, now," Raelynn tried to cut in. She rested her palm on his arm, but he shook her off like she didn't even register.

His eyes locked on me and didn't move an inch the closer he got. "We had a deal, Verana. Five fucking years. No backing out."

"What?" I screeched, my head jerking back like his words crossed the space and slapped me.

"Did you think I would just sign the papers? You signed a contract."

"Are you fucking kidding me right now?" I looked to Raelynn for support, but she moved to the kitchen island and studied her nails. Her eyes flicked to mine but just as quickly jerked away. "Seriously, Raelynn?"

She held up her hands, and if she had a white flag, she'd have waved it with pride.

"Do I look like I'm kidding?" His voice went dangerously low, and he closed the space down to only a foot between us. "Because I'm dead fucking serious."

"How dare you, Nicholas *mother-fucking Knightly* Rush." Shock at the entire situation and the flood of emotions I'd done my best to block out all week rendered me damn near speechless. I could hold my own in an argument, and there I stood, throwing his name at him like it was the best weapon I had. I might as well have thrown the spoon.

"Yeah. Nicholas mother-fucking Knightly Rush. Also known as your goddamn husband, *Mrs. Rush.*"

"You can't hold me to that."

"I can, and I will."

His arrogance and the sheer certainty in his eyes had my steel walls sliding shut, blocking everything else out, making me stand taller behind my shield of armor.

I pulled my shoulders back and lifted my chin, each move done with the clang of me locking down the hatches, prepared for battle. I leaned forward and curled my lip to match his. "No."

His only reaction to my calmly spoken word was a blink—a single blink, but it was enough to know I'd landed a blow. Unfortunately, I'd held too much confidence in my defenses and celebrated too soon. No amount of steel, no lock, no stubborn denial could keep Nico Rush out.

"I'm done with this shit. You're coming home." With that declaration, he squatted low enough to wrap his arms around the back of my legs and tossed me over his shoulder.

I let out a feral screech and pounded against his hard back. "Goddamnit, Nico. Put me the fuck down."

"No," he answered calmly, throwing my word back in my face.

"Raelynn," I shouted, trying to support myself enough to look around for my friend.

She stormed over, and I had faith that even in her red stiletto's, she'd stop this man from taking me. She shoved a matching red nail into his chest.

"We said this weekend."

"You never told me about a fucking divorce. It kind of moved things up."

"What the fuck are you talking about?" I screeched.

Raelynn flicked her eyes to mine before returning her glare to Nico. "If you hurt her, I'll fucking kill you. And not in a funny —ha-ha—way. I will legit utilize every crime show I've watched, and I'll get away with it too."

"I would never hurt her," he promised.

He sounded so sincere, and it had rage burning its way

through my chest. "You're hurting me now," I shouted, choking on the words. Seeing him—having his hands on me—for the first time was too much, and no matter how much I tried to escape him, I couldn't.

What if I never could—even when he wasn't there.

"I want messages every few hours," Raelynn stated.

Then, she went to the door and did the last thing I ever expected. She held the door open for him.

"Raelynn, please," I begged. "Please don't let him take me. I ca—I can't do this. Please."

Her face crumbled under my pain and fear of being alone with him. Not because he'd hurt me physically but because of what he'd do to my heart. I barely survived without facing him —how could I do it with him right in front of me. I was so scared I'd forgive all his lies and turn a blind eye when he did it again. I was scared of everything when it came to this man.

"You're one of the strongest women I know. And I'm not doing this for him. I'm doing it for you," she said, her voice cracking over the last words. My body shook against his broad shoulder when he took the first step down. Raelynn's eyes never left mine, even when she spoke to Nico.

"Remember, Nico. I'll kill you."

"Noted."

THIRTY-SEVEN

Nico
_____

VERA SCOWLED out the window the entire ride home. Everything about her body turned away, arms crossed, and clenched
jaw screamed that she didn't want to be here.

But I still caught the quick glances my way like she was just
as desperate to look at me as I was to look at her. We'd barely
been together, yet I took my first full deep breath when I saw her
standing there wide-eyed in the middle of the living room.

It'd been a breath full of fire, but a breath that stretched my
lungs past the crippling pressure that'd weighed on them since
the lobby.

"Will you walk upstairs, or am I carrying you?" I asked once
we parked.

"Fuck you, Nicholas."

I watched her fumble with the door handle before stumbling
out in her high-heeled boots. Her words should have added fuel
to the fire, but I was too happy to hear her say my name again
that I didn't care.

Besides, I deserved her ire. I deserved it all.

If she was going to leave me, it was damn well going to be
after she heard me out.

We walked up to our top floor apartment, and she slammed

the door in my face, shaking the frame. I expected to hear the lock next, but the doorknob turned when I tried it. I pushed open the door in time to watch her brown hair fly behind her as she rounded the corner.

Watching her run from me in our own home had me slamming the door, similar to how she did. Two could play this game of petulance.

"Verana Rush," I bellowed. "Get back here right now."

She appeared around the corner like a bull ready to charge. "I am *not* a child for you to order around."

"Then stop acting like one."

"And don't call me that."

"Why?" I asked, stalking toward her into the living room. "It's your name. Because you're my wife."

"I am *not* your wife."

"Oh, I have the license *and* a contract that says otherwise. For five more years. A legally binding one at that."

Her ire grew, and I waited for the smoke to start pouring out of her ears.

Her nostrils flared over her heavy breaths, jaw clenched just as tight as her fists, and her eyes doing their best to incinerate me.

"I hate you," she hissed.

I flinched, the words a slap to the face. A reminder of all I'd done to deserve her anger and hitting right on the nerves of fear that I'd never get her back to the woman who promised me dinner by the fire in our home.

"How can you file for divorce without even talking to me?"

I shoved my hurt to the side and got to the heart of why I brought her here.

"How can you use me—marry me—to steal my family's company—my mother's company?"

Apparently, she was getting to the heart of her issues too. Neither of us held back punches. My anger had been directed at her filing for divorce without even giving me a fighting chance. I hated to lose—but I refused to lose a race I never got a chance to run.

But now that I stood there, ready to get answers to my questions, I realized I had to answer hers too. I knew I always would, but I stood there like a kid who stared at a test he never studied for. I had the answers, but they were jumbled and raw. They floated through my head without structure and came with more honest pain than I'd ever shared with anyone.

The discomfort of them had me pulling back—avoiding until I could control the direction.

"Verana…"

"No. No," she said, crossing her arms and straightening her back. "Don't you dare stand there like *I'm* the one who's in the wrong. You dragged me here. You put me in this position. *You* did this, Nicholas, so don't you dare act like me filing for divorce is the issue."

"It is when you haven't even talked to me. There are two sides to every story."

"So, you mean to tell me there is a side that makes this all okay?" she asked, sarcasm and mock-hope dripped from her words. "There's a side that makes it okay that you *used* me, lied to me, stole from me? God, Nicholas." She threw her hands up, laughing without humor. "You made me your accomplice in stealing from me. You conned me into helping you."

"I never meant for it to go like this. I never sought you out. You just…just appeared like an opportunity I couldn't turn away from."

"An opportunity?" she screeched. "I'm a real person. Not some pawn."

"I know that. But Verana, I never expected you. You asked me why I never settled down, and I told you the truth. I gave every ounce of myself to my work because building my company was my revenge. For over a decade, all I did was focus on getting retribution for my family."

"So, you took my legacy to avenge yours?"

"Lorenzo was running your legacy into the ground," I shouted, losing my patience. Yes, I had planned to dismantle Mariano Shipping, but it wasn't like it wasn't already going down. "A company that had been running for generations shouldn't have taken only a few years to take over. If you hadn't come along, I would have still succeeded within the next five years. All because Mariano Shipping was a sinking ship."

"No." She exhaled the word like the truth knocked the wind from her. "No. That's not true."

"Why do you think your father was pushing you onto Camden? Because he needed his father's money to keep the company going. And the contract your grandparents wrote stated that the company needed to be passed down to a man carrying the Mariano name. That's why your father changed his name when he married your mother. He promised Camden's father that if he bought into the company, Camden could marry you, and they'd hyphenate the name."

She shook her head, her beautiful lips pulling down. I wanted to pull her into my arms and soothe her. I hated that she hurt.

"I may have taken the opportunity you gave me, but at least I had something to offer in return. With your father, you would have been trapped with a foul man like Camden. I would have given you freedom."

"This is not freedom. I'm just another pawn stolen for someone else's side."

"Are you saying you would have rather stayed with Camden?"

"I'm saying I would have rather made my own choices."

"You did make your own choices."

"Yeah, at what cost? Five years of my life earning it?" She tipped her head to the side and narrowed her eyes. "Tell me, Nico. Why five when you only needed a month? Did you want to keep me as a trophy until you were done with me? One up my father's bad deed by rubbing me in his face?"

315

"No one forced you to sign," I growled. I wanted to cover her mouth and tell her she was anything but a simple trophy.

"I signed based on lies. *You* lied to get what you wanted. Just like my father."

"*Don't* compare me to him," I warned.

"Why? You used me to get what you wanted. You stole a company from my family because he took yours."

"He took everything from me," I bellowed.

She jerked back, and I immediately regretted my loss of control. Taking a deep breath, I shoved past the flare of anger of being compared to Lorenzo. "He didn't just take my company. He took all my grandpa had left of his family—of his wife. And he did it because he's a lying, greedy snake. He did it because he played dirty and enjoyed winning for no other reason than he could."

"And why did you?"

"Because he didn't deserve Mariano Shipping," I said without remorse. "I hate that I lied to you, but I have no regrets about taking Mariano Shipping from *him.*"

"It's not just that you lied to me, Nicholas. You used me. You *used* me to take *my* legacy—to take *my* last connection to my mother. You knew how much I cherished that, and you stole it." Her voice cracked, and she looked on the verge of collapsing— the anger fading and leaving her pain behind. Watching her try to look strong, when I knew how much she hurt, gutted me. "Even worse, you made me feel different. For the first time, I thought someone saw me for more than a way to get what they wanted—who saw me for all I had to offer. And I guess you did," she said with a laugh. "Just not what I was offering will- ingly. You made me think you wanted me for me. You made me lo—" She cut her words off like if she didn't say it, she could make it not true.

"This didn't go how I planned, Verana. I do see you. I... care about you. I didn't plan on it, but you made me lo—"

"Don't." Her eyes slid shut, and she shook her head. "No

more lies. I can't handle any more." With a swallow, she opened her eyes and leveled me with a blank stare. "What's done is done. The damage is done, and I'm too tired of fighting it. You won, and I lost. At least have the decency to let me go. I don't want to stand by your side for five more years only to watch you take apart my company. I can't."

My jaw clenched tight, holding me back from telling her I'd do the right thing. I wanted to grab her shoulders and make her listen, but she wouldn't hear me. My body fought against letting her go when I knew it had to be done.

She heaved a sigh, her shoulders falling forward like she couldn't fight another moment. "I'm going to bed in the guest room. It's too late to bother going back to Raelynn's. Tomorrow morning, I'll grab a few things and leave. Please, let me go."

Again, I stood like a statue, stoically silent, unable to say yes. We stared each other down in the dark apartment, the lights from the kitchen, casting her sharp cheeks with a luminous glow. But it also highlighted the dark shadows under her eyes, her downturned mouth I wanted to kiss into a smile. I missed her dimples, and I knew if I kept her here, I'd never see them again.

Day in and day out, I'd be faced with her disappointment and hurt. There'd be no honeymoon I could seduce her on. Verana wasn't a woman who was fooled easily and definitely never more than once.

So, I remained silent, forcing myself to let the regret, and my own hurt bleed through. I couldn't say the words, but I could let her in. I owed her so much more, but it was all I could make myself give now. Unfortunately, it only made her hurt show more, and tears welled.

But she blinked them back. "Goodnight, Nico," she whispered, walking past me.

I let her go, just like I knew I would in the morning.

The click of her door mimicked the click in my mind, unleashing the torrent of words I wanted to say. She'd come at me swinging like I deserved, and it was like my body went into fight mode, locking down any weaknesses. Now that she was gone, they flooded out.

I'm not dismantling the company.

I made it for five years because I wanted you—for you.

I see you.

I care for you.

Please, don't leave.

You're more important than any revenge.

I love you.

My muscles twitched, wanting to go to her and say them.

But the reality was that she was right. What was done was done. And If I cared for her, I'd give her the true freedom she deserved.

But first, I had phone calls to make.

I had to dig into the back of my liquor cabinet, but I found the unopened bottle I was looking for, knowing it was going to be a long night.

My actions got me here, and my lips remained clamped around all the words I wanted to say, but I could show her.

Sitting down at the table, I skipped the glass and got to work.

THIRTY-EIGHT

Vera

LORENZO WAS RUNNING your legacy into the ground.

I do see you.

I...care about you.

The words had struggled to escape, and I'd wondered if he'd ever said it to anyone before. But then I realized it hadn't mattered because it was most likely another ploy to get me to stay. He most likely just needed something from me. Why else would anyone want me around unless I proved useful to their needs? As long as I stayed quiet and played by their rules.

Our argument wreaked chaos through the night, generating one thought after the other until my head throbbed under the weight of it all. As soon as I'd closed the door to the guest room, the first sob broke free, and I'd rushed to the shower, turning the water scalding hot to wash it all away. The anger, the hurt, the want, the need...the love. I wanted it all gone because it grew too big to bear. I'd stepped from the shower and swiped the steam from the mirror, looking at the shell of a woman looking back—not recognizing her.

The last time I hadn't recognized my reflection had been on the yacht, with Nico behind me, making me his. I'd wanted to be that woman. I'd wanted to be his.

319

I didn't want to be this version of myself, but I didn't see a future where I looked in the mirror and saw anything other than what I lost.

Do you have to lose him?

My biggest fear at seeing Nico again, reared its head. I'd avoided him because—despite the lies and pain—I loved him. I wanted to be the woman he'd set free, and I didn't want to face what I would sacrifice of myself to make it happen. I didn't want to face the chance that I'd be a woman to turn a blind eye to lying because of love. I wanted to love myself more than to be in that kind of relationship.

By the time the sun rose the next morning, I'd maybe had only a few hours of sleep.

I squinted my puffy eyes against the bright rays of light creeping across the floor. Rolling to my back, I dug my hands into my hair to relieve some of the pounding pressure from a night of crying.

Staring up at the fan, I replayed our conversation one more time.

Empathy for what he'd gone through mixed with anger from being used. I swayed like a pendulum from one side to the next, struggling to keep up and process it all. I understood his anger —I was angry for him. I understood his need for revenge.

I just didn't understand why he had to make me fall in love with him to make it happen.

Taking a deep breath, I flung the covers back and sat up. I checked the time and found about a hundred messages from Raelynn and a few from Nova. I'd messaged Rae to let her know I was physically still alive but going to bed and muted my notification.

Raelynn: I'm so sorry. It's my fault I made you go. I should have nut-punched him. I just…I just thought any decision you made would feel better once you heard him out.
Raelynn: I love you.

Raelynn: Do you want me to come get you?
Raelynn: Did I mention I was sorry?

Nova: Raelynn called me. She says not to hate her.
Nova: I won't pretend to know what you're going through, but I will suggest not making any decisions until your emotions calm down. I'd probably feel a little violent if someone carried me out, too. But give yourself permission to take in his words without your anger questioning it all. Yes, he lied, and we should make him suffer for it...but maybe give him a chance to explain.
Nova: Don't let your anger make his explanation fall on deaf ears. Don't let your anger make all the choices. It's okay to listen and take time to process it. It's okay to believe that not everything was a lie. Give yourself permission to think on it. Speaking from experience, but sometimes once a decision is made—especially in anger—it can't be undone. So be 100% sure it's the right one.
Me: But how do I know if it wasn't all a lie?

I didn't know if Nova, wherever she was, even had service in her camper van, but I needed her calm rationale more than ever.

What if everything wasn't a lie?

That was the million-dollar question—the one I wanted to believe, but the one I was scared to hope for. The one I was terrified would have me compromising myself to believe. When the dots started bouncing on my screen, I leaned forward and held my breath, thanking the phone gods for giving Nova service.

Nova: You have to listen and make the best decision.
Me: But what if I make a decision because I love him, and I sacrifice respect just to be with him.
Nova: You'd never do that. I know you. You wouldn't even sacrifice them for the traditions your mother left you and marry

Camden. You're good, Verana, and you want to follow the rules that people set out for you, but you have a line. Have confidence in that line.

Nova: If it helps, I don't think it was all a lie. I saw the way he looked at you, walking down the aisle.

Tears sprang to my eyes. My wedding day. It had been the first day Nico and I had kissed. The first day we'd begun to let our walls down.

Had it all been an act?

But why would he start letting his walls down then after we were married? He'd already gotten what he wanted. Why would he have been more respectful and open on our honeymoon when he hadn't needed to?

He seduced information out of you. He made you believe he wanted a long vacation because he wanted to be with you.

The reminder punched me in the chest, and I wanted to storm out all over again.

But Nova's message to not let emotions make my decision held me rooted to the bed. Taking another deep breath, I closed my eyes and pushed past the fog of hurt to remember it all. I remembered all the moments in between. I remembered the easy laughter. I remembered playing cards one night with no talk of business or family—we just laughed and talked about music.

I remembered how he planned on giving me an opportunity to prove myself at his company. Had he done it from guilt? Or had he really thought I could do it?

That question I could answer with certainty. Nico talked about all he'd done to build his business, and he wouldn't let guilt put him in a position to where he could look bad in front of a client. If he hadn't thought I was capable of performing well, he wouldn't let me.

The nugget of truth blossomed, and I wondered if I set

down the bag of emotions I'd clung so tightly to, then maybe I'd find more.

My mind spun round and round.

Did he, or didn't he? Truth or lie? Really care, or all an act?

Fisting the sheets, I pinched my eyes shut and shook my head, making it all come to a screeching halt. I could do this all day with only a minimal conversation heard in anger.

Maybe I took the first hesitant step and listened.

My phone dinged with another message.

Nova: It's okay to give him a second chance. If he lies again, we all know Raelynn will beat the shit out of him.
Nova: And I will too.

I laughed, the feeling euphoric and foreign. A few weak laughs had escaped while I'd stayed with Raelynn, but they all felt forced and weighed down. This one was soft but slid through my limbs, infusing a tingle of hope that maybe I'd come out on the other side okay. I just didn't know what that other side looked like and if Nico was there with me.

And I never would, sitting on this bed.

With the reminder that I could leave at any time, that listening to him didn't mean I had to forgive him, I stood. I pulled on a sundress I'd stowed away in the extra closet and headed out.

I rounded the corner to the living room to find him at the kitchen table with his computer and a stack of papers.

When he finally noticed my presence, I was halfway across the living room, and he watched silently. Setting his glasses aside, he closed his laptop and never once looked away, drinking me in like he'd never get a chance to see me again.

Was that the look of a man who only saw me for a revenge he'd already gotten?

"There's coffee if you want some," he finally said once I reached the kitchen.

His voice sounded as rough as he looked—not the sexy morning voice that had been my favorite part of waking up. No, this roughened voice sounded exhausted to its bones. This voice sounded heavy, scraping across his vocal cords like an overweight box against concrete.

"When we got back, I made sure to order the pumpkin spice creamer you liked in Italy. In case you came back," he added hesitantly.

So simple, yet so sweet. Those were the ways that Nico broke me down on our honeymoon. It hadn't been the sexual seduction. It had been the simple and sweet gestures that he did because he knew I liked them. Not from me telling him I liked them, but because he saw me. He didn't have to buy me shot glasses because he knew I collected them to get his revenge. He didn't have to make my bacon extra crispy even though he liked it soft. He didn't have to get pumpkin creamer special delivered when I'd given no indication I would come back.

Why would he care if he already had what he wanted?

Forcing myself to move, despite wanting to stare at him all morning, I went to get a cup of coffee. I swiped at the pools of moisture building in my eyes when I grabbed the creamer.

So sweet and so simple, yet so impactful.

When I sat down, he slid two stacks of papers face down across the table, keeping his longer fingers sprawled on top of them. I took in his tan skin against the stark paper and wondered if I would ever feel them again. I clutched the warm mug to hold back from stealing another feel just in case I never got to.

"My parents died in a car accident when I was ten. They were hit by a drunk driver who got off without even a warning. He was a senator's son, and my grandpa was furious. He spent money on top of money to have it looked into. Add in the fact that the senator didn't appreciate it, he bad-mouthed the business, and my grandpa struggled to recover."

"Nico, I'm so sorry." Losing my mother crushed me. I couldn't imagine what losing two at the same time would be like.

"Then when I was twelve, my grandma was diagnosed with cancer," he continued without acknowledging that I spoke, staring down at his hand pressed to the papers. "We were devastated, but my grandpa refused to admit defeat. He loved her, and he's not the kind of man who gave up without a fight. So, he paid for any treatment he thought could give her more time. He took time off work to be with her every step of the way. In the middle of her illness, the company suffered more than ever before. He was on the verge of losing it all, and the last thing he wanted was for his wife to watch *her* legacy be sold while she was still alive. Knightly Shipping was her family's company, and she and her brother hadn't wanted anything to do with it, but she had wanted to be with the man who worked in the mailroom at the time."

He smiled as if remembering their story, and I imagined him as a little boy, sitting around listening to his grandparents talk about how they met and fell in love. But just as soon as it came, the smile faded.

"When Lorenzo Mariano came to him with an offer to help, he took it, despite the outrageous interest and clauses. He was desperate. Desperate men in love take risks."

He lifted dark eyes to mine and pinned me in place, his words pressing on my chest.

"My grandma died a year later, and my grandpa struggled to keep going. He struggled to keep up with Lorenzo's loan and worked himself into the ground, fighting a losing battle. He took riskier jobs and traveled more. He wore himself down and ended up contracting a virus that he struggled to fight off. He eventually did, but it damaged parts of his brain. Maybe it wouldn't have if he hadn't struggled for so long—maybe his immune system would have been stronger if he hadn't used all his energy to pay Lorenzo. Maybe he wouldn't be in a nursing home with growing dementia if it wasn't for Lorenzo."

His jaw clenched, and I knew that no matter my decision, Nico would forever hate my father, and after the past few months, I think I hated him too. He'd shown me his true colors —coming out from behind the façade of a caring father. Maybe it hadn't been a façade before, but once my mother passed away, whatever had been real left.

"Lorenzo ended up taking the company, breaking it apart for money, leaving us with the international side of the business as a gift, as he said," he sneered. "I promised myself to make it right, and when I went to college, I knew exactly how I wanted to do it. I didn't care how long it took; I was determined to make it happen. Then you came along."

I swallowed, remembering that first day we actually met in the lobby. I'd been so happy about the interview and instantly attracted. Lust had almost swallowed us whole right then and there.

"Verana," he said my name like a plea. I looked from his hand to his eyes, wanting to dive into the dark depths and never come out. I wanted to believe the earnest need behind them. "I never planned on you. Not in my revenge or in my life. I had my eyes so focused on taking his company, I never even looked into his family. But when you told me your name with that mark on your cheek, I went with it. My gut urged me to jump. So, I did. I never planned on you."

He repeated the words like they held more meaning than just business.

"It doesn't make it right that I lied, and I'm sorry. I should have been patient and continued with my plan, but I justified it all because we both got something out of it."

"We did both get something," I agreed. However, my anger still lingered, making me add a snappy reminder. But now, there wasn't nearly as much heat behind it as before. "I was just the only one to lose something."

"Trust me, Verana. I'm losing something I never thought I'd want."

My heart skipped a beat—hope and mistrust warring.

Does he mean me? No, he only used you. Nothing more.

But the doubt grew more and more quiet. His eyes softened, the sunlight streaming in to bring out the deep greens that hid in the depths of dark brown. He sat before me, letting me in to see for myself that he could be honest.

I wanted so much to believe that everything I felt had been built on truth. How we got there may have been a lie, but I wanted the respect and friendship—the love—to be real. I was just scared that I'd make it real to have him even if it wasn't true.

"I don't want you to lose anything in this. I got my revenge, but I realized late that what I'd lose wasn't worth it."

I wanted to pick apart his words and delve into their meaning, but he finally flipped over the stacks of papers. He pointed to one but continued to watch me. My eyes flicked up and down, not wanting to lose his eyes, but also curious about the papers.

"This one," he said, his finger atop one, "is signing Mariano Shipping over to you."

"What?" I gasped, finally giving the paper my full attention.

"My plan had been to break it apart, so he could suffer like he made my grandpa. But it's not mine to do with as I please. It's *your* legacy, and you're more than smart enough to run it. Definitely better than Lorenzo was. I'll help you build it back up to its peak, and then it's all yours. I'd had these drawn up while we were in France. I planned on telling you when we got home. I should have told you all of it then, but I hadn't wanted to spoil our extra week. Possibly my last week with you."

Tears burned up my throat, and I struggled to swallow past the growing lump, leaving me speechless. Before I could gather any words, he moved his finger to the other stack of papers.

"Verana," he said, waiting for me to look up to continue. "I've never loved anything more than my revenge. But then I've never met a woman like you. Strong, proud, smart—probably smarter than me," he said with a soft laugh. "You're beautiful and funny. You're…everything I never even considered. I've never loved anything more than my revenge," he said again.

I sucked in a breath, holding it tight in my lungs, holding on to hope that I wasn't imagining the wrong thing. Holding on to hope that it was true. Too scared to breathe in case this passed, and I lost it.

"Yet, here you are, proving me wrong."

"Nicholas…" I pleaded on the smallest amount of air I'd let out.

"I love you, Verana Rush."

My heart beat against my chest, forcing all the air out on a whimper. Doubt tried to rear its head, but why would he say it? What would he gain? Any ideas I could concoct fell away when he explained the second document.

"These are the signed divorce papers, re-done to break our five-year contract—to set you free."

My hand flew to my mouth, and I looked down at both papers, the tears finally falling. Pinching my lips tight, I shook my head, not knowing what the hell to do with this. Was it only less than twenty-four hours ago that I sat across from my lawyer to file for divorce?

Now I had what I thought I wanted, and it had never looked more wrong.

"You really think I can do this?" I asked, tapping the paper giving me my company.

"I know you can."

And that was all I needed to know.

Nicholas may have used my emotions against me, but he would never use business. He'd worked too hard.

Without saying a word, I stacked both contracts on top of each other and stood, holding them to my chest.

"Vera, I—"

His voice broke, and I looked down in time to watch his

throat bob over a swallow, and I wondered if his emotions were just as extreme as mine.

I shook my head and turned my back, heading to the kitchen.

I looked across the island. His hand thudded to the table, and his head hung as he muttered, "Fuck."

When he heard the click of the gas stove turning on, his head snapped up. Holding his gaze, I held the divorce papers over the flame until it caught fire. His jaw dropped, and he shot up from his seat, and we both watched the flame lick at the paper over the sink. Once it reached my fingers, I dropped the remnants of the so-called freedom he gave me and that I didn't want, running the water to wash away any evidence it existed.

Looking up, I sat the other contract between us. "I'm keeping this one. But I want you to help me. I want to learn. I want to be a team because Nicholas Knightly Rush, I love you too."

"What?" he asked like maybe he imagined me saying it and needed to hear it again to be sure.

"I. Love. You. You saw me when no one else did. You appreciated me beyond what you could get from me. It took me a while to see it—for you to show it, but when you did, I never felt stronger—more sure. And I've never had that from anyone." He rounded the island, closing in on me. "Nico, I love you, and I don't want those stupid divorce papers. I don't wa—"

I never got to finish. He pulled me into his arms and slammed his mouth down on mine. I didn't hesitate. I sunk into his hard body, relaxing in his arms like I was coming home. I lost myself to the soft give of his lips, swearing to never go so long without kissing him again.

"Are you sure?" he asked between kisses.

I nodded, not wanting to pull my mouth away, but not given a choice when he pulled back to frame my face and meet my eyes.

"I love you, and I never meant to hurt you. I'm so sorry for everything, Vera. I may have started all this for revenge, but you have to know that how much I love you is true. Everything that brought us here—all the moments, the tiny traditions we created of our own—that was all real. *We* are real, and I will take every day you let me to prove it to you. And if you let me, I'll do it forever and not just five years."

"Fuck five years. I want to burn that contract, too. I want it all, Nico. I want you."

"You have me. I'm yours."

"Prove it," I challenged.

With a growl, he gripped my ass and hoisted me up. I wrapped my legs around his waist and went back to kissing him.

We bumped into furniture, and I didn't even bother coming up for air around our laughs as he carried me to our bedroom, where he spent hours proving how much he was mine, and I was his.

By the time night fell, we finally got our night in front of the fire, celebrating our love the same way it all began.

With a bottle of champagne.

Epilogue

NICO

"I STILL DO, and I always will."

Tears welled in her eyes, and the dimples I loved so much made an appearance with them. The sun reflecting off the water like tiny diamonds illuminated her face, bringing out the pale freckles I could stare at forever.

"I still do, and I always will," she said.

The officiator spoke words on the importance of keeping our promise to each other now and forever, but all I could focus on was her smiling face and soft lips. It'd been almost twenty-four hours since I'd kissed my wife, and a second longer stretched like an eternity.

"Nico," she whispered, laughing.

"What?"

"Kiss your bride," she ordered.

I'd been so lost in her, I'd missed my cue, but I didn't have to be told twice.

Wrapping my arms around her waist, I locked my lips on hers and hoisted her against my chest. Her arms wrapped around my neck, her smiling mouth pressed to mine, locking me in the most secure embrace I feared I'd never have again.

Soft applause mixed with the crashing of the waves, so

different from the roaring applause of strangers at our first wedding.

"I love you, Nicholas Knightly Rush," she said softly against my lips.

I'd never tire of hearing it or saying it in return. "I love you too, Verana Camila Rush."

A loud catcall pulled us from our bubble, and I didn't even have to look to know Raelynn was the culprit.

Linking my hand with hers, I turned us to walk down the short aisle, past the four benches of guests. I looked to my grandpa first and stood a little taller when he winked before wiping a stray tear. Rae cheered the loudest, earning an eye roll from the mountain of a man I'd come to know as Austin. Nova elbowed Rae but laughed, softening the blow. Xander and his wife stood next to Ryan and a few other close associates from the Charleston office.

This was the wedding we were always meant to have.

The night after we burned our contract and divorce papers, I asked her to marry me all over again. I got down on one knee in front of the fire, and damn-near begged her to marry me again. Making me luckier than I deserved, she agreed, tackling me to the blankets for another round of celebration.

"Ready for cake?" I asked.

"I'm always ready for cake."

"Do I get to shove it in your face this time?"

"You can try," she challenged.

We all made our way over to the small tent set up close by, where music played, and champagne was already being served.

Similar to our other wedding, we threw this one together within a month, knowing that trying to pick Mariano Shipping back up to where it needed to be would take all our time and effort.

In that month, Vera decided to get her MBA and further her education. She claimed she wanted to run her family's company, but only when she was the best she could be.

My wife never ceased to amaze me.

"A toast," Grandpa Charlie said, holding up his glass of champagne. Everyone dutifully followed suit. "To my grandson and my beautiful new granddaughter. I don't know what I did to deserve you both, but I'm glad Nicholas could pull his head out of his ass long enough to win you over for the both of us."

"Yeah, yeah," I grumbled.

"Your grandmother would be so proud of you—as well as your parents. You two make a beautiful couple, and I could see the strength of your love even when you couldn't. I have no doubt you both will support each other when you're weak and love each other through it all. Always remember to be honest, be humble, and love even when it's hard." He raised his glass higher. "To Nicholas and Verana."

I swallowed down the lump of emotions working their way up my throat along with the chilled bubbly liquid.

Before I could finish, silverware clinked against glasses, signaling us to kiss.

Not wasting any chance I got, I pulled her back in my arms and glued my mouth to hers, nibbling her soft lips. When she did the same to mine, flicking her tongue along the sting, I set my glass aside and used both arms to dip her back and deepen the kiss.

"Get a room," Xander shouted.

I stood us upright and turned a devious smile his way. "Oh, I plan on it."

Vera slapped my chest but laughed, the lightest blush coloring her cheeks.

"How long do we have to stay?" I asked her.

"Hmm…" she pretended to ponder, pinching her lips. "I'm thinking all night. We may party until dawn. I mean, Rae is already asking the bartender for tequila."

"I don't think so. They can do all they want, but I'm thinking two hours at most."

"Wow, impressive."

"What?" I asked.

"I was thinking I'd be lucky to make it an hour."

"God, I love you."

"I love you too."

"Now, we just need a good reason to vanish."

"It's okay. We can say we're not feeling well. We can blame it on the champagne."

I clinked my glass to hers. "Sounds perfect. Just like you."

***

NOVA

VERA AND NICO left two hours ago, but a few of us had moved the party to the bar.

"Come on," Raelynn whined. "I want to play with Naughty Nova."

I gave her a deadpanned stare as she waved the shot of tequila in my face. She knew it was my weakness, and after the stressful week of meeting deadlines for my new job, I could use a night to let off steam.

"Maybe we can try and Instagram Patrick," she said in her seductive voice, following it up with kissing noises.

Just hearing his name brought forth a slew of emotions tied to a million memories.

"You're horrible," Austin grumbled next to Rae.

"I'm the best, and you love me," she said, smacking a kiss on his cheek.

"Someone has to." He rolled his eyes but continued to watch her even when she turned away. Rae tortured him, and he always turned her down, but it was so obvious to everyone but her why he never took her up on a one-night stand. He wanted so much more.

"Come on, you were laughing right along with me," she said to him.

The last wedding we'd had for Nico and Vera had started with a ton of tequila and ended with me twerking on the dance floor while Raelynn scrolled through Instagram, stealing pics I swore to kill her over if she ever posted.

No, she never posted.

But she had seen Patrick start an Instagram live video that he notoriously invited fans to join. Lucky Raelynn requested to join under my handle and magically got picked. She'd greeted him, announcing she only knew of his band because her friend was half in love with him. At that point, unbeknownst to me, she turned the camera on me mid-ass shake. I had no idea any of it was going on and shimmied toward her, rapping along to Missy Elliot.

Yeah, I didn't want to repeat that performance. But just the memory of it had me wanting to drink the embarrassment away.

"Give Austin your phone," I ordered.

"Oh, come on."

"Do it," I said again, taking the shot.

"Fine." She gave him her phone, and he shoved it into his pants pocket. "I can't wait to hunt for that later," she said with a wink.

"Jesus," he murmured.

She laughed before leaning her ample cleavage on the bar to get the bartender's attention. "Three more shots, please."

We did our shots, and my phone vibrated just as another was handed to me. I dug in my pocket and downed the drink.

"Come dance," Rae pleaded.

I looked down at the screen.

TEXT MESSAGE FROM ROCKSTAR.

"Take Austin. I'll be right out," I said distractedly.

"Thanks for throwing me under the bus," Austin grumbled as Rae tugged him past me.

"Oh, we both know you like it," I shouted.

That had him shutting up.

Just like every time his name popped up my heart picked up pace like an unstoppable freight train. A picture of a carved pumpkin and strong, long fingers holding it in place accompanied a text message.

Rockstar: Remember when your mom made us all carve pumpkins?
Me: Ha. Yeah, like we were the Brady Bunch. That was the first year after our parents married.
Rockstar: A good year, if I remember correctly.

It'd been a great year, but I couldn't bring myself to send that. When I didn't respond, another message came through.

Rockstar: I wish you were here.
Rockstar: When are you going to let me see you again?

When the thought didn't fill me with panic. When I felt like I could meet him and have full control of my emotions, unlike when I was a traumatized teen full of angst.

He'd been asking to meet me since he saw me on that Instagram live video.

See, I'd always been aware of him, even when he lost track of me.

Raelynn and Vera knew I loved his band—they just didn't know I used to love him.

They didn't know he used to be my stepbrother.

About the Author

Fiona Cole is a military wife and a stay at home mom with degrees in biology and chemistry. As much as she loved science, she decided to postpone her career to stay at home with her two little girls, and immersed herself in the world of books until finally deciding to write her own.

Fiona loves hearing from her readers, so be sure to follow her on social media.

Email: authorfionacole@gmail.com
Newsletter
Reader Group: Fiona Cole's Lovers

www.authorfionacole.com

Also by Fiona Cole

The King's Bar Series

Where You Can Find Me

Deny Me

Imagine Me

Shame Me Not Series

Shame

Make It to the Altar (Shame Me Not 1.5)

The Voyeur Series

Voyeur

Lovers (Cards of Love)

Surrender (A Lovers Novella)

Savior

Another

Watch With Me (A Free Liar Prequel)

Liar

Teacher

Blame it on the Alcohol

Blame it on the Champagne

Blame it on the Alcohol (Book 2) Coming Spring/Summer 2021

Made in United States
North Haven, CT
01 July 2022

20830979R00207